STALKER

Also by Lars Kepler

The Hypnotist

The Nightmare

The Fire Witness

The Sandman

STALKER

LARS KEPLER

Translated from the Swedish by Neil Smith

HarperCollins*Publishers*

HarperCollins*Publishers*
1 London Bridge Street
London SE1 9GF

Published by HarperCollins*Publishers* 2016

2

Originally published in 2014 by Albert Bonniers Förlag, Sweden, as *Stalker*

Lars Kepler asserts the moral right to be identified as the author of this work

A catalogue record for this book is available from the British Library

ISBN: 978-0-00-746782-2

Typeset in Electra LT Std by Palimpsest Book Production Limited, Falkirk, Stirlingshire

Printed and bound in Great Britain by Clays Ltd, St Ives plc

It wasn't until the first body was found that anyone took the film seriously. A link to a video clip on YouTube had been sent to the public email address of the National Criminal Investigation Department. The email contained no message, and the sender was impossible to trace. The police administration secretary did her job, followed the link, watched the film, and assumed it was a rather baffling joke, but nonetheless entered it in the records.

Two days later three experienced detectives gathered in a small room on the eighth floor of National Crime headquarters in Stockholm, as a result of that very film. The oldest of the three men was sitting on a creaking office chair while the other two stood behind him.

The clip they were watching on the wide computer monitor was only fifty-two seconds long.

The shaky footage, filmed in secret on a handheld camera through her bedroom window, showed a woman in her thirties putting on a pair of black tights.

The three men at National Crime watched the woman's peculiar movements in embarrassed silence.

To get the tights to sit comfortably she took long strides over imaginary obstacles and did several squats with her legs wide apart.

On Monday morning the woman had been found in the kitchen of a terraced house on the island of Lidingö, on the outskirts of Stockholm. She was sitting on the floor with her mouth grotesquely split open. Blood had splattered the window and the white orchid in its pot. She was wearing nothing but a pair of tights and a bra.

The forensic post-mortem later that week concluded that she bled to death as a result of the multiple lacerations and stab-wounds that were concentrated, in a display of extraordinary brutality, around her throat and face.

The word stalker *has existed since the early 1700s. In those days it meant a tracker or poacher.*

In 1921 the French psychiatrist de Clérambault published a study of a patient suffering from erotomania. This case is widely regarded as the first modern analysis of a stalker. Today a stalker is someone who suffers from obsessive fixation disorder, an unhealthy obsession with monitoring another individual's activities.

Almost 10 per cent of the population will be subjected to some form of stalking in the course of their lifetime.

The most common form is when the stalker has or used to have a relationship with the victim, but in a striking number of cases when the fixation is focused on strangers or people in the public eye, coincidence is a key factor.

Even though the vast majority of cases never require intervention, the police treat the phenomenon seriously because the pathological obsessiveness of a stalker brings with it a self-generating potential for danger. Just as rolling clouds between areas of high and low pressure during stormy weather can suddenly change and turn into a tornado, a stalker's emotional lurches between worship and hatred can suddenly become extremely violent.

1

It's quarter to nine on Friday, 22 August. After the magical sunsets and light nights of high summer, darkness is encroaching with surprising speed. It's already dark outside the glass atrium of the National Police Authority.

Margot Silverman gets out of the lift and walks towards the security doors in the foyer. She's wearing a black wrap cardigan, a white blouse that fits tightly at the chest, and high-waisted black trousers that stretch across her expanding stomach.

She makes her way without hurrying towards the revolving doors in the glass wall. The guard sits behind the wooden counter with his eyes on a screen. Surveillance cameras monitor every section of the large complex round the clock.

Margot's hair is the colour of pale, polished birchwood, and is pulled into a thick plait down her back. She is thirty-six years old and pregnant for the third time, glowing, with moist eyes and rosy cheeks.

She's heading home after a long working week. She's worked overtime every day, and has received two warnings for pushing herself too hard.

She is the National Police Authority's new expert on serial killers, spree killers and stalkers. The murder of Maria Carlsson is the first case she's been in charge of since her appointment as detective superintendent.

There are no witnesses and no suspects. The victim was single, had no children, worked as a product advisor for Ikea, and had taken on her parents' unmortgaged terraced house after her father died and her mother went into care.

Maria usually travelled to work with a colleague of a morning. Since she wasn't waiting down on Kyrkvägen, her colleague drove to her house and rang the doorbell, looked through the windows, then walked round the back and saw her. She was sitting on the floor, her face covered in knife-wounds, her neck almost sliced right through, her head lolling to one side and her mouth grotesquely open.

According to the preliminary report from the forensic post-mortem, there was evidence to suggest that her mouth had been arranged after death, even if it was theoretically possible that it had settled into that position of its own accord.

Rigor mortis starts in the heart and diaphragm, but is evident in the neck and jaw after two hours.

This late on a Friday evening the large foyer is almost deserted, aside from two police officers in dark-blue sweaters who are standing talking, and a tired-looking prosecutor emerging from one of the rooms dedicated to custody negotiations.

When Margot was appointed head of the preliminary investigation she was conscious of the pitfalls of being overambitious; she knew she had a tendency to be too eager, too willing to think on a grand scale.

Her colleagues would have laughed at her if she'd told them at the outset she was absolutely convinced they were dealing with a serial killer.

Over the course of the week Margot Silverman has watched the video of Maria Carlsson putting her tights on more than two hundred times. All the evidence suggests that she was murdered shortly after the recording was uploaded to YouTube.

Margot has tried to interpret the short film, but can't see anything special about it. It's not unusual for people to have a fetish about tights, but nothing about the murder indicates any inclination of that nature.

The film is simply a brief excerpt from an ordinary woman's life. She's single, has a good job, and has almost completed a course of evening classes on drawing cartoons.

There's no way of knowing why the perpetrator was in her garden, whether it was pure chance or the result of a carefully planned operation, but in the minutes before the murder he captured her on film, so there has to be a reason for this.

Given that he's sent the link to the police, he must want to show them something.

The perpetrator wants to highlight something about this particular woman, or a certain type of woman. Perhaps it's about all women, the whole of society.

But to Margot's eyes there's nothing unusual about the woman's behaviour or appearance. She's simply concentrating on getting her tights to sit properly, frowning and pursing her lips.

Margot has visited the house on Bredablicksvägen twice, but she's spent most of her time examining the forensic video of the crime scene before it was contaminated.

The perpetrator's film almost looks like a lovingly created work of art in comparison to the police's. The forensics team's minutely detailed recording of the evidence of the bestial attack is relentless. The dead woman is filmed from various angles as she sits with her legs stretched out on the floor, surrounded by dark blood. Her bra is in shreds, dangling from one shoulder, and one white breast is hanging down towards the bulge of her stomach. There's almost nothing left of her face, just a gaping mouth and red pulp.

Margot stops as if by chance beside the fruit bowl on the table by the sofas, looks over at the guard, who is talking on the phone, then turns her back on him. For a few seconds she watches the guard's reflection in the glass wall facing the large inner courtyard, before taking six apples from the bowl and putting them in her bag.

Six is too many, she knows that, but she can't stop herself taking them all. It's occurred to her that Jenny might like to make an apple pie that evening, with lots of butter, cinnamon and sugar to caramelise them.

Her thoughts are interrupted when her phone rings. She looks at the screen and sees a picture of Adam Youssef, a member of the investigating team.

'Are you still in the building?' Adam asks. 'Please tell me you're still here, because we've—'

'I'm sitting in the car on Klarastrandsvägen,' Margot lies. 'What did you want to tell me?'

'He's uploaded a new film.'

She feels her stomach clench, and puts one hand under the heavy bulge.

'A new film,' she repeats.

'Are you coming back?'

'I'll stop and turn round,' she says, and begins to retrace her steps. 'Make sure we get a decent copy of the recording.'

Margot could have carried on out through the doors and gone home, leaving the case in Adam's hands. It would only take one phone call to arrange a full year of paid maternity leave. Perhaps that's what she would have done if she'd known how violent her first case would turn out to be.

The future lies in shadow, but the planets are approaching dangerous alignments. Right now her fate is floating like a razor blade on still waters.

The light in the lift makes her face look older. The thick dark line of kohl round her eyes is almost gone. As she leans her head back she understands what her colleagues mean when they say she looks like her father, former District Commissioner Ernest Silverman.

The lift stops at the eighth floor and she walks along the empty corridor as fast as her bulging stomach will allow. She and Adam moved into Joona Linna's old room the same week the police held a memorial service for him. Margot never knew Joona personally, and had no problem taking over his office.

'You've got a fast car,' Adam says as she walks in, then smiles, showing his sharp teeth.

'Pretty fast,' Margot replies.

Adam Youssef is twenty-eight years old, but his face is round like a teenager's. His hair is long and his short-sleeved shirt is hanging outside his trousers. He comes from an Assyrian family, grew up in Södertälje and used to play football in the first division north.

'How long has the film been up on YouTube?' she asks.

'Three minutes,' Adam says. 'He's there now. Standing outside the window and—'

'We don't know that, but—'

'I think he is,' he interrupts. 'I think he is, he almost has to be.'

Margot puts her heavy bag on the floor, sits down on her chair and calls Forensics.

'Hi, Margot here. Have you downloaded a copy?' she asks, sounding stressed. 'Listen, I need a location or a name – try to identify either the location or the woman . . . All the resources you've got, you can have five minutes, do whatever the hell you like, just give me something and I promise I'll let you go so you can enjoy your Friday evening.'

She puts the phone down and opens the lid of the pizza box on Adam's desk.

'Are you done with this?' she asks.

There's a ping as an email arrives and Margot quickly stuffs a piece of pizza crust in her mouth. An impatient worry line deepens on her forehead. She clicks on the video file and maximises the image on screen, pushes her plait over her shoulder, hits play and rolls her chair back so Adam can see.

The first shot is an illuminated window wavering in the darkness. The camera moves slowly closer, leaves brushing the lens.

Margot feels the hairs on her arms stand up.

A woman is standing in the well-lit room in front of a television, eating ice cream from the tub. She's tugged her jogging pants down and is balancing on one foot to pull her sock off.

She glances at the television and smiles at something, then licks the spoon.

The only sound in the room in Police Headquarters comes from the fan in the computer.

Just give me one detail to go on, Margot thinks as she looks at the woman's face, the fine features of her eyes, cheeks and the curve of her head. Her body seems to be steaming with residual heat. She's just been for a run. The elastic of her underwear is loose after too many washes, and her bra is clearly visible through her sweat-stained vest.

Margot leans closer to the screen, her stomach pressing against her thighs, and her heavy plait falls forward over her shoulder again.

'One minute to go,' Adam says.

The woman puts the tub of ice cream on the coffee table and leaves the room, her jogging pants still dangling from one foot.

The camera follows her, moves sideways past a narrow terrace door until it reaches the bedroom window, where the light goes on and the woman comes into view. She tramples the jogging pants off and kicks them towards an armchair with a red cushion. The trousers fly through the air, hit the wall behind the chair and fall to the floor.

2

The camera glides slowly through the last of the dark garden and stops right outside the window, swaying slightly as if it were floating on water.

'She'd see him if she just looked up,' Margot whispers, feeling her heart beat faster in her chest.

The light from the room reaches beyond the leaves of a rosebush, casting a slight flare across the top of the lens.

Adam is sitting with his hand over his mouth.

The woman pulls her vest off, tosses it onto the chair, then stands for a moment in her washed-out underwear and stained bra, looking over at the mobile phone charging on the bedside table beside a glass of water. Her thighs are tense and pumped with blood after her run, and the top of the jogging pants has left a red line across her stomach.

There are no tattoos or visible scars on her body, just faint white stretch-marks from a pregnancy.

The room looks like millions of other bedrooms. There's nothing worth even trying to trace.

The camera trembles, then pulls back.

The woman takes the glass of water from the bedside table and puts it to her mouth, then the film ends abruptly.

'Bloody hell, bloody hell,' Margot repeats irritably. 'Nothing, not a sodding thing.'

'Let's watch it again,' Adam says quickly.

'We can watch it a thousand times,' Margot says, rolling her chair further back. 'Go on, what the hell, go ahead, but it's not going to give us a fucking thing.'

'I can see a lot of things, I can see—'

'You can see a detached house, twentieth-century, some fruit trees, roses, triple-glazed windows, a forty-two-inch television, Ben & Jerry's ice cream,' she says, gesturing towards the computer.

It hasn't struck her before, the way we're so similar to each other. Seen through a window, a broad spectrum of Swedes conform to the same pattern, to the point of being interchangeable. From the outside we appear to live exactly the same way, we look the same, do the same things, own the same objects.

'This is totally fucked up,' Adam says angrily. 'Why is he posting these films? What the hell does he want?'

Margot glances out of the small window, where the black treetops of Kronoberg Park are silhouetted against the hazy glow of the city.

'There's no doubt that this is a serial killer,' she says. 'All we can do is put together a preliminary profile, so we can—'

'How does that help her?' Adam interrupts, running one hand through his hair. 'He's standing outside her window and you're talking about offender profiling!'

'It might help the next one.'

'What the fuck?' Adam says. 'We've got to—'

'Just shut up for a minute,' Margot interrupts, and picks up her phone.

'Shut up yourself,' Adam says, raising his voice. 'I've got every right to say what I think. Haven't I? I think we should get the papers to publish this woman's picture on their websites.'

'Adam, listen . . . much as we'd like to be able to identify her, we've got nothing to go on,' Margot says. 'I'll talk to Forensics, but I doubt they're going to find anything more than they did last time.'

'But if we circulate her picture to—'

'I haven't got time for your nonsense now,' she snaps. 'Think for a minute . . . Everything suggests he's uploaded the clip directly from her garden, so of course there's a theoretical chance of saving her.'

'That's exactly what I'm saying!'

'But five minutes have already passed, and that's a long time to be standing outside a window.'

Adam leans forward and stares at her. His tired eyes are bloodshot and his hair is on end.

'Are we just going to give up, then?'

'This is a matter of urgency, but we have to think clearly,' she replies.

'Good,' he says, still sounding annoyed.

'The perpetrator is brimming with confidence, he knows he's way ahead of us,' Margot explains quickly as she picks up the last slice of pizza. 'But the better we get to know him . . .'

'Get to know him? Fine, but that's not really what I'm thinking right now,' Adam says, wiping sweat from under his nose. 'We couldn't trace the previous film, we didn't find anything at the scene, and we won't be able to trace this film either.'

'We're unlikely to get any forensic evidence, but we can try to pin him down by analysing the films and the brutality of his MO,' Margot replies, as she feels the baby move inside her. 'What have we really seen so far, what has he shown us, and what's he seeing?'

'A woman who's been for a run, and is now eating ice cream and watching television,' Adam says tentatively.

'What does that tell us about the murderer?'

'That he likes women who eat ice cream . . . I don't know,' Adam sighs, and hides his face in his hands.

'Come on, now.'

'Sorry, but—'

'I'm thinking about the fact that the murderer uploads a film showing the period leading up to the murder,' Margot says. 'He takes his time, enjoys the moment, and . . . he wants to show us the women alive, wants to preserve them alive on film. Maybe it's the living he's interested in.'

'A voyeur,' Adam says, feeling his arms prick with discomfort.

'A stalker,' she whispers.

'Tell me how to filter the list of creeps who've been let out of prison or psychiatric care,' Adam says, as he logs into the intranet.

'A rapist, violent rape, someone with obsessive fixation disorder.'

He types quickly, clicks the mouse, types some more.

'Too many results,' he says. 'Time's running out.'

'Try the first victim's name.'

'No results,' he sighs, tearing his hair.

'A serial rapist who's been treated, possibly chemically castrated,' Margot says, thinking out loud.

'We need to check the databases against each other, but that will take too long,' he says, getting up from his chair. 'This isn't working. What the hell are we going to do?'

'She's dead,' Margot sighs, then leans back. 'She might have a few minutes left, but . . .'

'I don't know if I can handle this,' Adam says. 'We can see her, we can see her face, her home . . . Christ, we can see right into her life, but we can't find out who she is until she's dead and someone finds her body.'

3

Susanna Kern can feel her thighs tingling from her run as she pulls her sweaty jogging pants down and kicks them towards the chair.

Since she turned thirty she has run five kilometres three evenings each week. After her Friday run she usually eats ice cream and watches television, seeing as Björn doesn't get home until ten o'clock.

When Björn landed the job in London she thought it would feel lonely, but fairly quickly she came to appreciate the hours she had to herself in the weeks when Morgan was with his dad.

She needs this downtime more than ever since she embarked upon a demanding course in advanced neurology at the Karolinska Institute.

She undoes her sweaty sports bra, thinking that she can use it again on Sunday before she has to wash it.

She can't remember a summer as hot as this before.

A scratching sound makes her turn towards the window.

The back garden is so dark that all she can see is the reflection of the bedroom. It looks like a theatre set, a television studio.

She has just made her entrance, and is standing under the floodlights.

Only I've forgotten to put any clothes on, she thinks wryly to herself.

She stands for a moment, looking at her naked body. The lighting is dramatic, and makes her reflection look thinner than she actually is.

The scraping noise is repeated, as if someone were running their nails across the windowsill. It's too dark to see if there's a bird sitting out there.

Susanna stares at the window and walks cautiously towards it, trying to see through the reflections, and grabs the dark blue bedspread and holds it up to cover herself. She shivers.

Fighting an instinctive reluctance she goes over to the window, moves her face closer to the glass and the garden becomes visible, like a dark grey world, like the underworld in a Gustav Doré engraving.

The black grass, tall shrubs, Morgan's swing moving in the wind, and the panes of glass behind the playhouse for the garden room that they never got round to building.

Her breath mists the window as she straightens up and pulls the curtains. She lets the thick bedspread fall to the floor and walks naked towards the door. A shiver runs down her spine and she turns back towards the window again. A strip of black glass is shimmering in the gap between the dark-pink curtains.

She picks up her phone from the bedside table and calls Björn, and as she listens to the call being put through she can't help staring at the window.

'Hello, darling,' he answers, far too loudly.

'Are you at the airport?'

'What?'

'Are you at . . .'

'I'm at the airport, I'm just having a burger at O'Learys, and—'

His voice vanishes as a group of male voices in the background shout and cheer.

'Liverpool just scored again,' he explains.

'Hooray,' she says, without enthusiasm.

'Your mum called me to ask what you want for your birthday.'

'That's sweet,' she says.

'I said you'd like some see-through underwear,' he jokes.

'Perfect.'

She stares at the shimmering glass between the curtains as the phone-line crackles.

'Is everything OK at home?' Björn's voice says in her ear.

'I was just feeling a bit scared of the dark.'

'Isn't Ben there?'

'In front of the television,' she replies.

'And Jerry?'

'They're both waiting for me,' she smiles.

'I miss you,' he says.

'Make sure you don't miss the plane,' she whispers.

They talk some more, then say goodbye and blow kisses to each other, then the line goes dead and she finds herself thinking about a patient who was brought in the previous night. A young man who had crashed his motorbike when he wasn't wearing a helmet, resulting in severe head injuries. His father had come straight to the hospital from his nightshift. He was still wearing his dirty overalls, and had a breathing mask dangling round his neck.

Holding her pink kimono in front of her, she walks back to the living room and closes the heavy curtains.

The room feels suddenly blind, as if a silence had settled on it.

The curtains sway in front of the windows, and she shudders as she turns away from them.

She tries the ice cream. It's much softer now, just right. A dense taste of chocolate fills her mouth.

Susanna puts the tub down and walks to the bathroom, locks the door, turns the shower on, loosens her ponytail and puts the scrunchie on the edge of the basin.

She lets out a sigh as the hot water washes over her head and neck and envelops her whole body. Her ears are roaring as her shoulders relax and her muscles soften. She soaps herself and runs her hand between her legs, noticing that the hair has already started to grow again since the last time she waxed.

Susanna wipes the steam from the glass door with her hand so she can see the handle and lock of the bathroom door.

She suddenly remembers what she thought she had seen in the bedroom window just as she was pulling the bedspread towards her to cover herself.

She dismissed it as a trick of her imagination. It's silly to let yourself get scared like that. She had thrust her anxieties aside, and told herself that she couldn't even see through the glass.

The room was too bright and the garden too dark.

But in the reflection of the dark bedspread she had thought she could see a face staring back at her.

The next moment it was gone, and she realised she must have been mistaken, but now she can't help thinking it might have been real.

It wasn't a child, but possibly a neighbour out looking for their cat, who then stopped to look at her.

Susanna turns the water off and her heart is beating so hard that it's pounding at the top of her chest as she realises that the kitchen door leading out to the garden is open. How could she have forgotten that? She's had it open all summer to let in the cool evening air, but usually shuts and locks it before taking a shower.

She wipes the steam from the glass door and looks at the lock on the bathroom door again. Nothing has changed. She reaches for the towel and thinks to herself that she'll phone Björn and ask him to stay on the line as she looks through the house.

4

Susanna can hear applause on the television as she leaves the bathroom. The thin silk of the kimono sticks to her damp skin.

There's a cold draught along the floor.

Her feet leave wet footprints on the worn parquet tiles.

There's a dark shimmer from the windows at the far side of the dining room. Black glass sparkling behind the ferns in their hanging pots. Susanna feels like she's being watched, but forces herself not to look out, scared of frightening herself even more.

Nonetheless, she keeps her distance from the closed door to the basement as she approaches the kitchen.

Her wet hair is soaking through the back of the kimono. It's so wet that it's dripping inside the fabric, trickling between her buttocks.

The floor gets colder the closer she gets to the kitchen.

Her heart is pounding hard in her chest.

She suddenly finds herself thinking of the young man with serious head injuries again. He was sedated with Ketalar. His whole face was crushed, squashed up towards his temples. His father kept repeating quietly that there was nothing wrong with his son. He could have done with someone to talk to, but Susanna hadn't had time.

Now she is imagining that the heavily built father has found her, that he holds her to blame, and is standing outside the kitchen door in his dirty overalls.

A different song on the television now.

There's a breeze blowing straight through the kitchen. The door to the garden is wide open. The thin curtain of plastic strips is fluttering into the room. She walks slowly forward. It's hard to see anything behind the dancing curtain. There could be someone standing just outside.

She holds her hand out, pushes the swirling plastic strips aside, slips past them and reaches for the door handle.

The floor is chill from the night air flowing into the kitchen.

Her kimono slips open.

She has time to notice that the gloomy garden is deserted. The bushes are moving in the wind, the swing swaying rhythmically.

She quickly closes the door, not bothered about catching part of the curtain in it, and hurriedly locks it, then pulls the key out and backs away.

She puts the key in the bowl of loose change and adjusts the kimono.

At least it's locked now, she thinks, as she hears a creak behind her back.

She spins round and then smiles at her own reaction. It was just the window in the living room shifting on its hinges when the flow of air stopped.

The audience is booing and whistling at the judges' decision.

Susanna thinks about getting her phone from the bedroom and calling Björn. He ought to be waiting at the gate by now. She wants to hear his voice as she searches the house before settling down in front of the television. She's wound herself up too much to relax otherwise. The only problem is that there's no reception at all in the basement. Maybe she could put it on speaker and leave it halfway down the stairs.

She tells herself that she doesn't have to creep about in her own home, but can't help moving quietly.

She passes the closed door to the basement, sees the dark windows in the dining room from the corner of her eye, and carries on towards the living room.

She knows she locked the front door after her run, but still wants to go and check. It would be just as well – then she won't have to think about it again.

There's a whistling sound from the open window in the living room and the curtain is being sucked back towards the narrow opening.

She starts to walk towards the dining room and notices that the wild flowers in the vase on the heavy oak table have run out of water, before coming to an abrupt halt.

It feels as though her whole body is covered by a thin layer of ice. In an instant adrenalin is coursing through her blood.

The three windows of the dining room act as large mirrors. The table and eight chairs are lit up by the light from the ceiling lamp, and behind them stands a figure.

Susanna stares at the reflection of the room, her heart pounding so hard it almost deafens her.

In the doorway to the hall someone is standing with a kitchen knife in their hand.

He's inside, he's inside the house, Susanna thinks.

She's shut and locked the kitchen door when she should have escaped into the garden.

She moves slowly backwards.

The intruder is standing completely still with his back to the dining room, staring at the corridor to the kitchen.

The large knife is hanging from his right hand, twitching impatiently.

Susanna backs away, her eyes fixed on the figure in the hall. Her right foot slides across the floor and the parquet creaks slightly as she shifts her weight.

She has to get out, but if she tries to get to the kitchen she'll be visible along the passageway. Maybe she'd have time to get the key from the bowl, but it's by no means certain.

She continues backing away cautiously, now seeing the intruder in the last window.

The floor creaks beneath her left foot and she stops and watches as the figure turns round to face the dining room, then looks up and catches sight of her in the dark windows.

Susanna takes another slow step back. The intruder starts to walk towards her. Whimpering with fear, she turns and runs into the living room.

She slips on the carpet, loses her balance and hits her knee on the floor, putting her hand out to break her fall and gasping with pain.

The sound of a chair hitting the dining table.

She brings the standard lamp down as she gets up. It hits the wall before clattering to the floor.

She can hear rapid footsteps behind her.

Without looking round she rushes into the bathroom again and locks the door behind her. The air in there is still warm and damp.

This can't be happening, she thinks in panic.

She hurries past the basin and toilet and pulls the curtain back from the little window. Her hands are shaking as she tries to undo one of the catches. It's stuck. She tugs at it and tries to force herself to calm down. She fiddles with it and tugs it sideways, and manages to get the first catch open as she hears a scraping sound from the lock on the bathroom door. She rushes back and grabs hold of the lock just as it starts to turn. She clings on to it with both hands, and feels her heart racing in terror.

5

The intruder has slipped a screwdriver, or possibly the back of the knife blade, into the little slot on the other side of the lock. Susanna is holding on to the handle of the lock, but is shaking so badly that she's scared she might lose her grip.

'God, this can't be happening,' she whispers to herself. 'This isn't happening, it can't be happening . . .'

She glances quickly towards the window. It's far too small for her to be able to throw herself through it. The only hope of escape is to run to the window, undo the second catch, push it open and then climb up, but she daren't let go of the lock.

She's never been so terrified in her life. This is a bottomless, mortal dread, beyond all control.

The lock now feels hot and slippery under her tensed fingers. There's a metallic scraping sound from the other side.

'Hello?' she says towards the door.

The intruder tries to open the door with a quick twist, but Susanna is prepared and manages to resist.

'What do you want?' she says, in as composed a voice as she can muster. 'Do you need money? If you do, I can understand that. It's not a problem.'

She gets no answer, but she can hear the scrape of metal against metal, and feel the vibration through the lock.

'You're welcome to look, but there's nothing especially valuable in the house . . . the television's fairly new, but . . .'

She falls silent, because she's shaking so much it's hard to understand what she's saying. She whispers to herself that she must stay calm, as she clutches the lock tight and thinks that her fear is dangerous, that it might make the intruder think bad thoughts.

'My bag's hanging in the hall,' she says, then swallows hard. 'A black bag. Inside it there's a purse containing some cash and a Visa card. I've just been paid, and I can tell you the code if you want.'

The intruder stops trying to turn the lock.

'OK, listen, the code is 3945,' she says to the door. 'I haven't seen your face, you can take the money and I'll wait until tomorrow before I report the card missing.'

Still holding the lock tightly, Susanna puts her ear to the door, and imagines she can hear footsteps moving away across the floor before an advert break on television drowns out all other sounds.

She doesn't know if it was stupid to give him her real code, but she just wants this to end, and she's more worried about her jewellery, her mother's engagement ring and the necklace with the big emeralds she was given after Morgan was born.

Susanna waits behind the door and keeps telling herself that this isn't over yet, that she mustn't lose her concentration for a moment.

Carefully she changes hands on the lock, without letting go of it. Her right thumb and forefinger have gone numb. She shakes her hand and puts her ear to the door, thinking that it's now been more than half an hour since she told him the code to her card.

It was probably just a junkie who saw an open kitchen door and came inside to look for valuables.

The last part of the programme is over. More adverts, and after them the news. She changes hands again and waits.

After another ten minutes she lies down on the floor and peers under the door. There's no one standing outside.

She can see a large stretch of the parquet floor, she can see under the sofa, and the glow of the television reflected on the varnish.

Everything's quiet.

Burglars aren't violent, they just want money as quickly and simply as possible.

Trembling, she gets up, takes hold of the lock again, then stands still with her ear to the door, listening to the news and weather forecast.

Grabbing the shower scraper from the floor as a rudimentary weapon, she steels herself and cautiously unlocks the door.

The door swings open without a sound.

She can see almost the whole of the living room through the passageway. There's no sign of the intruder. It's as if he had never been there.

She leaves the bathroom, her legs shaking with fear. Every sense is heightened as she approaches the living room.

She hears a dog bark in the distance.

Carefully she moves forwards, and sees the light from the television play on the closed curtains, the upholstered suite and the glass coffee table with the tub of ice cream on top of it.

She's planning to go into the bedroom, get her phone, then lock herself in the bathroom again and call the police.

To her left she catches a glimpse of the glass-fronted cabinet containing the collection of Dresden china that Björn inherited. Her heart starts to beat faster. She's almost at the end of the passageway, and only then will she be able to see all the way to the hall.

She takes a step into the living room, looks round and notes that the dining room is empty, before realising that the intruder is right next to her. Just one step away. The thin figure is standing there waiting for her by the wall at the end of the passage.

The stab of the knife is so fast that she doesn't have time to react. The sharp blade goes straight into her chest.

Her muscles tense around the metal deep inside her body.

Her heart has never beaten as hard as it does now. Time stands still as she thinks that this can't be real.

The knife is pulled out, leaving behind a burning easing of tension. She presses her hand to the wound and feels warm blood pumping out between her fingers. The shower scraper clatters to the floor. She reels to one side, her head feels heavy and she can see her blood splattered across the shiny material of the raincoats. The light seems to be flickering and she tries to say something, that this must be some sort of misunderstanding, but she has no voice.

Susanna turns round and walks towards the kitchen, feels quick jabs to her back and knows that she is being stabbed repeatedly.

She stumbles sideways, fumbling for support, and knocks the display cabinet against the wall, making all the porcelain figures topple over with a clattering, tinkling sound.

Her heart is racing as blood streams down inside the kimono. Her chest is hurting terribly.

Her field of vision shrinks to a tunnel.

Her ears are roaring and she is aware that the intruder is shouting something excitedly, but the words are unintelligible.

Her chin flies up as she is grabbed by the hair. She tries to hold on to an armchair, but loses her grip.

Her legs give way and she hits the floor.

She can feel a burning sensation of liquid in one lung, and coughs weakly.

Her head lolls sideways and she can see that there's some old popcorn among the dust under the sofa.

Through the roaring sound inside her she can hear peculiar screams, and feels rapid stabs to her stomach and chest.

She tries to kick free, thinking to herself that she has to get back to the bathroom. The floor beneath her is slippery, and she has no energy left.

She tries to roll over on to her side, but the intruder grabs her by the chin and suddenly jabs the knife into her face. It no longer hurts. But a sense of unreality is spinning in her head. Shock and an abstract sense of dislocation blur with the precise and intimate feeling of being cut in the face.

The blade enters her neck and chest and face again. Her lips and cheeks fill with warmth and pain.

Susanna realises that she's not going to make it. Ice-cold anguish opens up like a chasm as she stops fighting for her life.

6

Psychiatrist Erik Maria Bark is leaning back in his pale grey sheepskin armchair. He has a large study in his home, with a varnished oak floor and built-in bookcases. The dark brick villa is in the oldest part of Gamla Enskede, just to the south of Stockholm.

It's the middle of the day, but he was on call last night and could do with a few hours' sleep.

He shuts his eyes and thinks about when Benjamin was small and used to like to hear how Mummy and Daddy met. Erik would sit down on the edge of his bed and explain how Cupid, the god of love, really did exist.

He lived up amongst the clouds and looked like a chubby little boy with a bow and arrow in his hands.

'One summer's evening Cupid gazed down at Sweden and caught sight of me,' Erik explained to his son. 'I was at a university party, pushing my way through the crowd on the roof terrace when Cupid crept to the edge of his cloud and fired an arrow down towards the Earth.

'I was wandering about at the party, talking to friends, eating peanuts and exchanging a few words with the head of department.

'And at the exact moment that a woman with strawberry-blonde hair and a champagne glass in her hand looked in my direction, Cupid's arrow hit me in the heart.'

After almost twenty years of marriage Erik and Simone had agreed to separate, but she was probably the one who agreed the most.

As Erik leans forward to switch his reading-lamp off, he catches a glimpse of his tired face in the narrow mirror by the bookcase. The lines on his forehead and the furrows in his cheeks are deeper than ever. His dark-brown hair is flecked with grey. He ought to get a haircut. A few loose strands are hanging in front of his eyes and he flicks them away with a jerk of his head.

When Simone told him that she had met John, Erik realised it was over. Benjamin was pretty relaxed about the whole thing, and used to tease him by saying it would be cool to have two dads.

Benjamin is eighteen years old now, and lives in the big house in Stockholm with Simone and her new man, his stepbrothers and sisters, and the dogs.

On Erik's old smoking table is the latest edition of the *American Journal of Psychiatry* and a copy of Ovid's *Metamorphoses*, with a half-empty blister-pack of pills as a bookmark.

Outside the leaded windows the rain is falling on the drenched vegetation of the garden.

Erik pulls the tablets from the book and pops one sleeping-pill into his hand, trying to work out how long it would take his body to absorb the active substance, but he has to start again, then gives up. Just to be sure, he breaks the tablet in half along the little groove, blows the loose powder off to get rid of the bitter taste, then swallows one half.

The rain streams down the windows as the muted tones of John Coltrane's 'Dear Old Stockholm' flow from the speakers.

The tablet's chemical warmth spreads through his muscles. He shuts his eyes and enjoys the music.

Erik Maria Bark is a trained doctor, psychiatrist and psychotherapist, specialising in psychological trauma and disaster counselling, and worked for the Red Cross in Uganda for five years.

He spent four years leading a ground-breaking research project into group therapy involving deep hypnosis at the Karolinska Institute. He is a member of the European Society of Hypnosis, and is regarded as a leading international authority on clinical hypnotherapy.

At the moment Erik is part of a small team specialising in acutely traumatised and post-traumatic patients. They are regularly called in to help the police and public prosecutors with complex interviews of crime victims.

He often uses hypnosis to help witnesses relax, so that they can get to grips with their memories of traumatic situations.

He's got three hours before he needs to be at a meeting at the Karolinska Institute, and he's hoping to spend most of that time asleep.

But he's not allowed to.

He's dragged straight into deep sleep, and starts dreaming that he's carrying an old, bearded man through a very small house.

Simone is shouting at him from behind a closed door when the phone rings. Erik jumps, and fumbles for the smoking-table. His heart is beating hard from the sudden anxiety of being yanked out of a state of deep relaxation.

'Simone,' he answers groggily.

'Hello, Simone . . . I'm not sure, but maybe you should try to give up those French cigarettes?' Nelly jokes in her laconic way. 'Sorry to have to say this, but you almost sound like a man.'

'Almost.' Erik smiles, feeling the heaviness of the sleeping pill in his head.

Nelly laughs, a fresh, tinkling laugh.

Nelly Brandt is a psychologist, Erik's closest colleague in the specialist team at the Karolinska Hospital. She's extremely competent, works very hard, but is also very funny, often in a rather earthy way.

'The police are here, they're really agitated,' she says, and only now does he hear how stressed she sounds.

He rubs his eyes to get them to focus, and tries to listen to what Nelly is telling him about the police rushing in with an acutely shocked patient.

Erik squints towards the window facing the street, as water streams down the glass.

'We're checking his somatic status and running the routine tests,' she says. 'Blood and urine . . . liver status, kidney and thyroid function . . .'

'Good.'

'Erik, the superintendent has asked for you specifically . . . It's my fault, I happened to let slip that you were the best.'

'Flattery doesn't work on me,' he says, getting to his feet somewhat unsteadily. He rubs his face with his hand, then grabs hold of the furniture as he makes his way towards the desk.

'You're standing up,' she says cheerily.

'Yes, but I . . .'

'Then I'll tell the police that you're on your way.'

Beneath the desk are a pair of black socks with dusty soles, a long, thin taxi receipt and a mobile phone charger. As he bends over to grab the socks the floor comes rushing up to meet him, and he would have fallen if he hadn't put his hand out to stop himself.

The objects on the desk merge and spread out in double vision. The silver pens in their holder radiate harsh reflexions.

He reaches for a half-empty glass of water, takes a small sip and tells himself to get his act together.

7

The Karolinska University Hospital is one of the largest in Europe, with more than fifteen thousand members of staff. The Psychology Clinic is located slightly apart from the vast hospital precinct. From above, the building looks like a Viking ship from an ancient burial site, but when approached through the park it doesn't look out of place among the other buildings. The nicotine-yellow stucco of the façade is still damp from the rain, with rust-coloured water running down the drainpipes. The front wheel of a bicycle is dangling from a chain in the bike-rack.

The car tyres crunch softly as Erik turns into the car park.

Nelly is standing on the steps waiting for him with two mugs of coffee. Erik can't help smiling when he sees her happy grin and the consciously disinterested look in her eyes.

Nelly is fairly tall, thin, and her bleached hair is always perfect, her make-up tasteful.

Erik often sees her and her husband Martin socially. There's no real need for Nelly to work, seeing as her husband is the main share-holder of Datametrix Nordic.

As she watches Erik's BMW pull into the car park she walks over to him, blowing on one of the mugs and taking a cautious sip before putting it on the roof of the car and opening the back door.

'I don't know what this is about, but we've got a superintendent who seems pretty wound up,' she says, passing him one of the mugs between the seats.

'Thanks.'

'I explained that we always have the best interest of our patients at heart,' Nelly says as she gets in and closes the car door behind her. 'Shit! God, sorry . . . have you got any tissues? I've spilled some coffee on the seat.'

'Don't worry.'

'Are you cross? You're cross,' she says.

The smell of coffee spreads through the car and Erik closes his eyes for a moment.

'Nelly, just tell me what they said.'

'I don't seem to be getting on very well with that fucking . . . I mean, that lovely policewoman.'

'Is there anything I ought to know before I go inside?' he asks, opening the door.

'I told her she could wait in your office and go through your drawers.'

'Thanks for the coffee . . . both mugs,' he says, as they get out of the car.

Erik locks up, puts the keys in his pocket, runs a hand through his hair and starts to walk towards the clinic.

'I didn't actually say that bit about the drawers,' she calls after him.

Erik walks up the steps, turns right and runs his passcard through the reader, taps in his code, then carries on along the next corridor to his room. He still feels groggy, and it occurs to him that he really must get the tablets under control soon. They make him sleep too deeply. It's almost like drowning. His drugged dreams have started to feel claustrophobic. Yesterday he had a nightmare about two dogs that had grown into each other, and last week he fell asleep here at the clinic and had a sexual dream about Nelly. He can't really remember it, but she was on her knees in front of him handing him a cold, glass ball.

His thoughts dissipate when he sees the superintendent sitting on his office chair with her feet resting on the edge of the waste-paper bin. She's holding her huge stomach with one hand and a can of Coke in the other. Her brow is furrowed, her chin has fallen open and she's breathing through her half-open mouth.

Her ID badge is lying on his desk, and she gestures wearily towards it as she introduces herself.

'Margot Silverman . . . National Crime.'

'Erik Maria Bark,' he says, shaking her hand.

'Thanks for coming in at such short notice,' she says, moistening her lips. 'We've got a traumatised witness . . . Everyone tells me I should have you in the room with me. We've already tried to question him four times . . .'

'I have to point out that there are five of us here in our specialist unit, and that I never usually sit in on interviews of perpetrators or suspected perpetrators myself.'

The light from the ceiling lamp reflects off her pale eyes. Her curly hair is trying to escape from her thick plait.

'OK, but Björn Kern isn't a suspect. He works in London, and was on a plane home when someone murdered his wife,' she replies, squeezing the Coke-can and making the thin metal creak.

'OK, then,' Erik says.

'He got a taxi from Arlanda, and found her dead,' the superintendent goes on. 'We don't know exactly what he did after that, but he was certainly busy. We're not sure where she was lying to start with, we found her tucked up in bed in the bedroom . . . He cleaned up as well, wiped away the blood . . . he doesn't remember anything, he says, but the furniture had been moved, and the blood-soaked rug was already in the washing machine . . . he was found more than a kilometre away from the house, a neighbour almost ran him over on the road, he was still wearing his blood-soaked suit, no shoes.'

'I'll certainly see him,' Erik says. 'But I must say at the outset that it would be wrong to try to force information from him.'

'He has to talk,' she says stubbornly, squeezing the can tighter.

'I understand your frustration, but he could enter a psychosis if you push too hard . . . Give him time, he'll tell you what you need.'

'You've helped the police before, haven't you?'

'Many times.'

'But this time . . . this is the second murder in what looks like a series,' she says.

'A series,' Erik repeats.

Margot's face has turned grey and the thin lines round her eyes are emphasised by the light from the lamp.

'We're hunting a serial killer.'

'OK, I get that, but the patient needs—'

'This murderer has entered an active phase, and isn't going to stop of his own accord,' she interrupts. 'And Björn Kern is a disaster from my point of view. First he goes round and rearranges everything at the crime scene before the police get there . . . and now we can't get him to tell us what it looked like when he arrived.'

She drops her feet to the floor, whispers to herself that they need to get going, then sits there stiff-backed, panting for breath.

'If we put pressure on him now, he may clam up for good,' Erik says, unlocking his birchwood cabinet and removing the fake-leather case containing his camera.

She gets to her feet, puts the can down on the desk at last, picks up her badge and walks heavily towards the door.

'Obviously I realise that this is seriously bloody awful for him, given what's happened, but he's going to have to pull himself together and—'

'Yes, but it's a lot more than awful . . . it might actually be impossible for him to think about it at the moment,' Erik replies. 'Because what you've described sounds like a critical stress response, and—'

'Those are just words,' she interrupts, her cheeks flushing with irritation.

'A mental trauma can be followed by an acute blockage—'

'Why? I don't believe that,' she says.

'As you may know, our spatial and temporal memories are organised by the hippocampus . . . and that information is then conveyed to the prefrontal cortex,' Erik replies patiently, pointing to his forehead. 'But that all changes at times of extreme arousal, and in cases of shock . . . When the amygdala identifies a threat, both the autonomous nervous system and what's known as the cortisol axis are activated, and—'

'OK, what the hell, I get it. Loads of stuff happens in the brain.'

'The important thing is that this degree of stress means that memories aren't stored as they usually are, but at an effective distance . . . they're frozen, like ice-cubes, separately . . . closed off.'

'I get it, you're saying he's doing his best,' Margot says, putting her hand on her stomach. 'But Björn may have seen something that can help us stop this serial killer. You have to get him to calm down, so he starts talking.'

'I will, but I can't tell you how long that's going to take,' he replies. 'I've worked in Uganda with people who've suffered the trauma of war . . . people whose lives have been completely shattered. You have to move slowly, using security, sleep, conversation, exercise, medication—'

'Not hypnosis?' she asks, with an involuntary smile.

'Sure, as long as no one has exaggerated expectations about the result . . . Sometimes gentle hypnosis can help a patient to restructure their memories so that they can actually be accessed.'

'Right now I'd give the go-ahead for a horse to kick him in the head if that would help.'

'OK, but that's a different department,' Erik says drily.

'Sorry, I get a bit impatient when I'm pregnant,' she says, and he can hear how hard she's trying to sound reasonable. 'But I have to identify any parallels with the first murder, I need a pattern if I'm going to be able to track down this murderer, and right now I haven't got a thing.'

They've reached the patient's room. Two uniformed police officers are standing outside the door.

'This is important to you,' Erik says. 'But bear in mind that he's just found his wife murdered.'

8

Erik follows Margot into the room. It has been furnished with two armchairs and a sofa, a low white table, two chairs, a water dispenser with plastic cups, and a wastepaper bin.

On the floor under the windowsill is a broken pot, the linoleum floor strewn with soil.

The air is thick with stress and sweat. The man is standing in the far corner, as if he were trying to get as far away as possible.

When he sees Erik and Margot he slides towards the sofa with his back against the wall. He's extremely pale, with a hunted look in his bloodshot eyes. His pale blue shirt has sweat rings under the arms, and is hanging outside his trousers.

'Hello, Björn,' Margot says. 'This is Erik, he's a doctor here.'

The man looks anxiously at Erik, then moves back into the corner.

'Hello,' Erik says.

'I'm not ill.'

'No, but what you've been through means that you have the right to treatment,' Erik replies matter-of-factly.

'You don't know what I've been through,' the man says, then whispers something to himself.

'I know you haven't been given any tranquillisers,' Erik says calmly. 'But I'd like you to know that the option is there, if—'

'What the fuck do I want a load of pills for?' he butts in. 'Will pills help? Will they make everything all right?'

'No, but—'

'Will they let me see Sanna again?' he shouts. 'That's not going to happen – is it?'

'Nothing can change what's happened,' Erik says seriously. 'But your relationship to what has happened will change, regardless of whether you—'

'I don't even understand what you're saying.'

'I'm just trying to find a good way to explain that the way you're feeling is part of a process, and that you can accept my help with that process if you want to.'

Björn glances at him briefly, then slips further away along the wall.

Margot puts her little recording device on the table, babbles the date and time, and the names of those present in the room.

'This is the fifth interview with Björn Kern,' she concludes, then turns towards him as he stands picking at the back-rest of the sofa. 'Björn, can you tell me in your own words —'

'About what?' he asks quickly. 'About what?'

'About when you got home,' Margot replies.

'What for?' he whispers.

'Because I want to know what happened, and what you saw,' she says curtly.

'What do you mean? I just got home, isn't that allowed?'

He puts his hands over his ears and stands there panting. Erik notes that the knuckles of both his hands are bleeding.

'What did you see?' Margot asks wearily.

'Why are you asking me that? I don't know why you're asking me. Fucking hell . . .'

Björn shakes his head and rubs his mouth and eyes hard.

'I want you to feel safe here, in this room,' Erik says. 'You don't think you're allowed to relax, you might not think it's possible, but it is.'

The man picks at the edge of a piece of wallpaper with his finger-nails, then tears off a little strip.

'This is what I'm thinking,' he says, without looking at them. 'I'm thinking I've got to do it all again, but do it right this time . . . I've got to go home and go in through the door, and then it will be right.'

'How do you mean, *right*?' Erik asks, managing to catch his eye.

'I know how it sounds, but what if it's true, you can't know,' he says, making a despairing gesture to keep them quiet. 'I can go in, through the door, and call Sanna's name . . . She knows I've got something for her, I always have, something from duty-free . . . and I take my shoes off and go inside . . .'

He looks utterly distraught.

'There's soil on the floor,' he whispers.

'Was there soil on the floor?' Margot asks.

'Shut up!' Björn yells, his voice cracking.

He walks over the soil-strewn floor, picks up the other pot-plant and throws it at the wall. The plastic pot shatters and soil rains down behind the sofa.

'Fucking HELL!' he gasps.

He leans both hands against the wall, his head hanging, and a string of saliva drops to the floor.

'Björn?'

'Fuck it, this is hopeless,' he says, with a sob in his voice.

'Björn,' Erik says slowly. 'Margot is here to find out more about what happened. That's her job. My job is to help you. I'm here for your sake . . . I'm used to seeing people who are having trouble, people who have suffered a terrible loss, who've experienced terrible things . . . things no one should have to go through, but which unfortunately are part of life for some of us.'

The man doesn't respond. He just sobs quietly. His eyes are dark, bloodshot and glassy.

'Do you want to stand over there?' Erik asks gently. 'You wouldn't rather sit in the armchair?'

'I don't care.'

'Nor do I . . .'

'Good,' Björn whispers, turning towards him.

'I've already mentioned it, and I know what you said, but it's my job to offer you all the help that's available . . . I can give you a sedative. It won't get rid of the terrible thing that's happened, but it will help to calm the panic you're feeling inside.'

'Can you help me?' the man whispers after a pause.

'I can help you take the first steps towards . . . towards getting through the worst of it,' Erik explains quietly.

'I start to shake when I think about the front door at home . . . because I must have gone through a different door, the wrong door.'

'I can understand why you'd feel that.'

Björn moves his lips cautiously, as though they were hurting him.

'Do you want me to sit down?' he asks, glancing cautiously at Erik.

'If it would make you feel more comfortable,' Erik replies.

Björn sits down for the first time, and Erik notices Margot looking at him, but doesn't return the look.

'What happens when you walk through the wrong door?'

'I don't want to think about it,' he replies.

'But you do remember?'

'Can you . . . can you get rid of the panic?' the man whispers to Erik.

'That's your decision,' Erik says. 'But I'm happy to sit here and talk to you with Margot . . . or you and I could talk on our own . . . and we could also try hypnosis – that might help you through the worst of it.'

'Hypnosis?'

'Some people find it works well,' Erik replies simply.

'No.' Björn smiles.

'Hypnosis is just a combination of relaxation and concentration.'

Björn laughs silently with his hand over his mouth, then stands up and walks along the wall again until he reaches the corner and turns to look at Erik.

'I think maybe the drugs you mentioned might be a good idea . . .'

'OK.' Erik nods. 'I can give you Stesolid – have you heard of that before? It will make you feel warm and tired, but also a lot calmer.'

'OK, good.'

Björn slaps the wall several times with one palm, then walks over to the water dispenser.

'I'll ask a nurse to bring you the pill,' Erik says.

He leaves the room, confident that Björn Kern will request hypnosis fairly soon.

9

The building at 4 Lill-Jans plan differs from those around it, with its dark façade and Gothic design, ornamental brickwork, oriels, pilasters and arches.

The curtains on the ground floor are closed, otherwise it would be possible to see in through the windows.

Erik looks at the address on the piece of paper, hesitates for a moment, then goes in through the large doorway. He hasn't told anyone about this.

His stomach flutters as he approaches the door. He can hear gentle piano music in the stairwell. He looks at the time, sees that he's slightly early, and returns to the front door to wait.

Back in the spring he found a flyer advertising piano lessons in his letterbox, and rather rashly booked an intensive course for his son Benjamin, who would be turning eighteen at the start of the summer.

It's never too late to learn to play an instrument, he thought. He himself had always dreamed of playing the piano, sitting down alone to play a melancholic nocturne by Chopin.

But the day before Benjamin's birthday Nelly pointed out that you didn't have to be a psychologist to see that he was projecting his own dream on to his son.

Erik quickly booked a series of driving lessons instead. Benjamin was happy, and Simone thought it a very generous gift.

He was sure he had cancelled the piano lessons. But that morning he had received an email reminding him not to miss the first lesson.

Erik feels ridiculously embarrassed, nevertheless he's decided to attend the first lesson himself, to give it a chance.

The idea of walking off and sending a text to say that he had already cancelled the lessons is whirling round his head as he returns to the door, raises his finger and rings the bell.

The piano music doesn't stop, but he hears someone run lightly across the floor.

A small child opens the door, a girl of about seven, with big, pale eyes and tousled hair. She's wearing a polka-dot dress and is holding a toy hedgehog in her hand.

'Mummy's got a pupil,' she says in a low voice.

The beautiful music streams through the flat.

'I've got an appointment at seven o'clock . . . I'm here for a piano lesson,' he explains.

'Mummy says you have to start when you're little,' the girl says.

'If you want to get good, but I'm not going to do that,' he smiles. 'I'll be happy if the piano doesn't block its ears or throw up.'

The girl can't help smiling.

'Can I take your coat?' she remembers to ask.

'Can you manage to carry it?'

He puts his heavy coat in her thin arms and watches her disappear towards the tall cupboards further inside the hall.

A woman in her mid-thirties comes towards him along the corridor. She seems deep in thought, but perhaps she's just listening to the music.

Her hair is black, and cut in a short, boyish style, and her eyes are hidden behind small round sunglasses. Her lips are pale pink, and her face appears to be completely free of make-up, yet she still looks like a French film star.

He realises that she must be Jackie Federer, the piano teacher.

She's wearing a black, loose-knit sweater and a suede skirt, and has flat ballet-pumps on her feet.

'Benjamin?' she asks.

'My name is Erik Maria Bark, I booked the lessons for my son, Benjamin . . . they were a birthday present, but I never told him about the gift . . . I've come instead, because I'm actually the one who wants to learn how to play.'

'You want to learn to play the piano?'

'Unless I'm too old,' he hurries to say.

'Come in, I'm just at the end of a lesson,' the woman says.

He follows her back through the corridor, and sees her trace the fingers of one hand along the wall as she walks.

'I got Benjamin another present, obviously,' Erik explains to her back.

She opens a door and the music gets louder.

'Have a seat,' the woman says, and sits down on the edge of the sofa.

Light is streaming into the room from high windows looking out on to a leafy inner courtyard.

A sixteen-year-old girl is sitting with her back straight at a black piano. She is playing an advanced piece, her body rocking gently. She turns a page of the score, then her fingers run across the keys and her feet press deftly at the pedals.

'Stay in time,' Jackie says, her chin jutting.

The girl blushes but goes on playing. It sounds wonderful, but Erik can see that Jackie isn't happy.

He wonders if she used to be a star, a famous concert pianist whose name he ought to know; Jackie Federer, a diva who wears dark glasses indoors.

The piece comes to an end, its notes lingering in the air until they ebb away. They've almost vanished when the girl takes her foot off the right pedal and the damper muffles the strings.

'Good, that sounded much better today,' Jackie says.

'Thank you,' the girl says, picking up her score and hurrying out.

Silence descends on the room. The large tree in the courtyard is casting swaying green shadows across the pale wooden floor.

'So you want to learn to play the piano,' Jackie says, getting up from the sofa.

'I've always dreamed of learning, but I've never got round to it . . . Naturally, I've got absolutely no talent at all,' Erik explains quickly. 'I'm completely unmusical.'

'That's a shame,' she says in a quiet voice.

'Yes.'

'Well, we might as well have a go,' she says, and puts her hand out to the wall.

'Mummy, I've mixed some juice,' the little girl says, and comes into the room with a tray containing glasses of juice.

'Ask our guest if he's thirsty.'

'Are you thirsty?'

'Thank you, that's very kind of you,' Erik says, and takes a sip. 'Do you play the piano as well?'

'I'm better than Mummy was at my age,' the girl replies, as if that's a phrase she's heard many times.

Jackie smiles and strokes her daughter's hair and neck rather clumsily, before turning back towards him.

'You've paid for twenty lessons,' she says.

'I have a tendency to go over the top,' Erik admits.

'So what do you want to get out of the course?'

'If I'm honest, I fantasise about being able to play a sonata . . . one of Chopin's nocturnes,' Erik says, and feels himself blush. 'But I'm aware I'm going to have to start with "Baa, Baa, Black Sheep".'

'We can work with Chopin, but perhaps an étude instead.'

'If there's a short one.'

'Madeleine, can you get me Chopin . . . opus 25, the first étude.'

The girl searches the shelf next to Jackie, pulls out a folder and removes the score. Only when she puts it in her mother's hand does Erik realise that the teacher is blind.

10

Erik can't help smiling to himself as he sits in front of the highly polished black piano with the name C. *Bechstein, Berlin* picked out in small gold lettering.

'He needs to lower the stool,' the girl says.

Erik stands up and lowers the seat by spinning it a few times.

'We'll start with your right hand, but we'll pick out some notes with your left.'

He looks at her fair face, with its straight nose and half-open mouth.

'Don't look at me, look at the notes and the keyboard,' she says, reaching over his shoulder and putting her little finger gently on one of the black keys. A high note echoes inside the piano.

'This is E flat . . . We'll start with the first formation, which consists of six notes, six sixteenths,' she says, and plays the notes.

'OK,' Erik mutters.

'Where did I start?'

He presses the key, producing a hard note.

'Use your little finger.'

'How did you know . . .'

'Because it's natural – now, play,' she says.

He struggles through the lesson, concentrating on her instructions, stressing the first note of the six, but loses his way when he has to add a few notes with his left hand. A couple of times she touches his hand again and tells him to relax his fingers.

'OK, you're tired, let's stop there,' Jackie says in a neutral voice. 'You've done some good work.'

She gives him notes for the next lesson, then asks the girl to show him to the door. They pass a closed door with 'No entry!' scrawled in childish writing on a large sign.

'Is that your room?' Erik asks.

'Only Mummy's allowed in there,' the child says.

'When I was little I wouldn't even let my mummy come into my room.'

'Really?'

'I drew a big skull and hung that on the door, but I think she went in anyway, because sometimes there were clean sheets on the bed.'

The evening air is fresh when he steps outside. It feels like he's hardly been breathing during the course of the lesson. His back is so tense that it hurts, and he still feels strangely embarrassed.

When he gets home he has a long, hot shower, then he calls the piano teacher.

'Yes, this is Jackie.'

'Hello, Erik Maria Bark here. Your new pupil, you know . . .'

'Hello,' she says, curious.

'I'm calling to . . . to apologise. I wasted your whole evening and . . . well, I can see it's hopeless, it's too late for me to . . .'

'You did some good work, like I said,' Jackie says. 'Do the exercises I gave you and I'll see you again soon.'

He doesn't know what to say.

'Goodnight,' she says, and ends the call.

Before he goes to bed he puts on Chopin's opus 25, to hear what he's aiming at. When he hears the pianist Maurizio Pollini's bubbling notes, he can't help laughing.

11

The sun is high above the trees, and the blue-and-white plastic tape is fluttering in the breeze. A transparent shadow of the tape dances on the tarmac.

The police officers posted at the cordon let through a black Lincoln Towncar, and it rolls slowly along Stenhammarsvägen as a reflection of the green gardens runs across the black paint like a forest at night.

Margot Silverman pulls over to the kerb and glides smoothly to a halt behind the command vehicle, and sits there for a while with her hand on the handbrake.

She's thinking about how hard they worked to try to identify Susanna Kern before time ran out, then, once an hour had passed and they realised it was too late, carried on anyway.

Margot and Adam had gone down to see their exhausted IT experts, and had just been told that it wasn't possible to trace the video clip when the call came in.

Shortly after two o'clock in the morning the forensics team were at the scene, and the entire area between Bromma kyrkväg and Lillängsgatan had been cordoned off.

Throughout the day the arduous task of examining the crime scene continued as further attempts were made to question the victim's husband, with the help of psychiatrist Erik Maria Bark.

The police have carried out door-to-door inquiries in the neighbourhood, they've checked recordings from nearby traffic-surveillance cameras, and Margot has booked a meeting for herself and Adam to see a forensics expert called Erixon.

She takes a deep breath, picks up her McDonald's bag, and gets out of the car.

Outside the cordon blocking off Stenhammarsvägen is a growing pile of flowers, and there are now three candles burning. A few shocked neighbours have gathered in the parish hall, but most of them have stuck to their plans for the weekend.

They have no suspects.

Susanna's ex-husband was playing football at Kristineberg sports club with their son when the police caught up with him. They already knew that he had an alibi for the time of the murder, but took him to one side to tell him.

Margot has been told that after he was informed, he went back in goal and saved penalty after penalty from the boy.

This morning Margot drew up a plan for the initial stages of the investigation in the absence of any witnesses or forensic results.

Paying particular attention to people convicted of sex crimes who have either been released or given parole recently, they're planning to track down anyone who's been institutionalised or attended a clinic for obsessive disorder therapy in the past couple of years, and then work closely with the criminal profiling unit.

Margot crumples the paper bag in her hand while she's still chewing, then hands it to a uniformed officer.

'I'm eating for five,' she says.

Wearily she lifts the crime-scene tape over her head, then walks heavily towards Adam, who is waiting outside the gate.

'Just so you know, there's no serial killer,' she says sullenly.

'So I heard,' he replies, and lets her go through the gate ahead of him.

'Bosses,' she sighs. 'What the hell are they thinking? The evening tabloids are going to speculate, it doesn't matter what we say; the police are fair game to them, but we have to follow the rules. It's like shooting a fucking barrel.'

'Fish in a barrel,' Adam corrects her.

'We don't know what effect the media are likely to have on the perpetrator,' she goes on. 'He might feel exposed and become more cautious, withdraw for a while . . . or all the attention could feed his vanity and make him overconfident.'

Bright floodlights are shining through the windows of the house, as if it were a film location or the setting for a fashion shoot.

Erixon the forensics expert opens a can of Coca-Cola and hurries to drink it, as though there were some magic power in the first bubbles. His face is shiny with sweat, his mask is tucked below his chin, and his protective white overalls are straining at the seams to accommodate his huge stomach.

'I'm looking for Erixon,' Margot says.

'Try looking for a massive meringue that cries if you so much as mention the numbers 5 and 2,' Erixon replies, holding out his hand.

While Margot and Adam pull on their thin protective overalls, Erixon tells them he's managed to get a print of a rubber-soled boot, size 43, from the outside steps, but all the evidence inside the house has been ruined or contaminated thanks to the efforts of the victim's husband to clean up.

'Everything's taking five times as long,' he says, wiping the sweat from his cheeks with a white handkerchief. 'We can't attempt the usual reconstruction, but I've had a few ideas about the course of events that we can talk through.'

'And the body?'

'We'll take a look at Susanna, but she's been moved, and . . . well, you know.'

'Put to bed,' Margot says.

Erixon helps her with the zip of her overalls, as Adam rolls up the sleeves of his.

'We could start a kids' programme about three meringues,' Margot says, placing both hands on her stomach.

They sign their names on the list of visitors to the crime scene, then follow Erixon to the front door.

'Ready?' Erixon asks with sudden solemnity. 'An ordinary home, an ordinary woman, all those good years – then a visitor from hell for a few short minutes.'

They go inside, the protective plastic rustles, the door closes behind them, the hinges squealing like a trapped hare. The daylight vanishes, and the sudden shift from a late summer's day to the gloom of the hallway is blinding.

They stand still as their eyes adjust.

The air is warm and there are bloody handprints on the door frame and around the lock and handle, fumbling in horror.

A vacuum cleaner with no nozzle is standing on a plastic sheet on the floor. There's a trickle of dark blood from the hose.

Adam's mask moves rapidly in front of his mouth and beads of sweat break out on his forehead.

They follow Erixon across the protective boards on the floor towards the kitchen. There are bloody footprints on the linoleum. They've been clumsily wiped, and then trodden in again. One side of the sink is blocked with wet kitchen roll, and a shower-scraper is visible in the murky water.

'We've found prints from Björn's feet,' Erixon says. 'First he went round in his blood-soaked socks, then barefoot . . . we found his socks in the rubbish bin in the kitchen.'

He falls silent and they carry on into the passageway that connects the kitchen with the dining and living rooms.

A crime scene changes over time, and is gradually destroyed as the investigation proceeds. So as not to miss any evidence, forensics officers start by securing rubbish bins and vehicles parked in the area, and make a note of specific smells and other transitory elements.

Apart from that, they conduct a general examination of the crime scene from the outside in, and approach the body and the actual murder scene with caution.

The living room is bathed in bright light. The cloying smell of blood is inescapable. The chaos is oddly invisible because the furniture has been wiped and put back in position.

Yesterday evening Margot saw the video of Susanna as she stood in this room eating ice cream with a spoon, straight from the tub.

A plane comes in to land at Bromma Airport with a thunderous roar, making the glass-fronted cabinet rattle. Margot notes that all the porcelain figures are lying down, as if they were asleep.

Flies are buzzing around a bloody mop that's been left behind the sofa. The water in the bucket is dark red, the floor streaked. It's possible to see the trail of the mop by the damp marks left on the skirting boards and furniture.

'First he tried to hoover up the blood,' Erixon says. 'I don't really know, but he seems to have mopped the floor, then wiped it with a dishcloth and kitchen roll.'

'He doesn't remember anything,' Margot says.

'Almost all the original blood patterns have been destroyed, but he missed some here,' Erixon says, pointing to a thin spatter on one strip of wallpaper.

He's used the old technique and has stretched eight threads from the outermost marks on the wall to find the point where they converge – the point where the blood originated.

'This is one precise point . . . the knife goes in at an angle from above, fairly deep,' Erixon says breathlessly. 'And of course this is one of the first blows.'

'Because she's on her feet,' Margot says quietly.

'Because she's still on her feet,' he confirms.

Margot looks at the cabinet containing the prone porcelain figures, and thinks that Susanna must have stumbled and hit it when she was trying to escape.

'This wall has been cleaned,' Erixon shows them. 'So I'm having to guess a bit now, but she was probably leaning with her back against it, and slid down . . . She may have rolled over once, and may have kicked her legs . . . either way, she certainly lay here for a while with a punctured lung.'

Margot bends over and sees the blood that has been exhaled across the back of the sofa, from below, possibly during a cough.

'But the blood carries on over there, doesn't it? It looks like it,' she says, pointing. 'Susanna struggled like a wild animal . . .'

'And we don't even know where Björn found her?' Adam asks.

'No, but we do have a large concentration of blood over there,' Erixon says, and points.

'And there,' Margot says, gesturing towards the window.

'Yes, she was there, but she was dragged there . . . she was in various different places after she died, she lay on the sofa, and . . . in the bathroom, as well as . . .'

'So now she's in the bedroom,' Margot says.

12

The white light of the floodlamps fills the bedroom, forming blinding suns in the glass of the window. Everything is illuminated, every thread, every swirling mote of dust. A trail of blood runs across the pale grey carpet to the bed, like tiny black pearls.

Margot stops inside the door, but hears the others carry on towards the bed, then the rustling of their overalls stops.

'God,' Adam gasps in a muffled voice.

Once again Margot thinks of the video, of Susanna walking about with her trousers dangling from one foot as she kicked to get rid of them.

She lowers her eyes and sees that her clothes have been turned the right way and are now piled neatly on the chair.

'Margot? Are you OK?'

She meets Adam's gaze, sees his dilated pupils, hears the dull buzz of flies, and forces herself to look at the victim.

The covers have been pulled up under her chin.

Her face is nothing but a dark-red, deformed pulp. He's hacked, cut, stabbed and carved away at it.

She goes closer and sees a single eye staring crookedly up at the ceiling.

Erixon folds the covers back. They're stiff with dried blood; skin and fabric have stuck together. There's a faint crunching sound as the dried blood comes loose, and little crumbs rain down.

Adam raises one hand to his mouth.

The inhuman brutality was concentrated around her face, neck and chest. The dead woman is naked and smeared in blood, with more stab-wounds and further bleeding beneath her skin.

Erixon photographs the body, and Margot points at a mottled green patch to the right of her stomach.

'That's normal,' Erixon says.

Her pubic hair has started to regrow around the reddish blonde tuft on her pudenda. There are no visible marks or injuries to the insides of the thighs.

Erixon takes several hundred pictures of the body, from the head resting on the pillow all the way down to the tips of her toes.

'I'm going to have to touch you now, Susanna,' he whispers, and lifts her left arm.

He turns it over and looks at the defensive wounds, cuts which indicate that she tried to fend off the attack.

With practised gestures he scrapes under her fingernails, the most common place to find a perpetrator's DNA. He uses a new tube for each nail, attaches a label and makes a note on the computer on the bedside table.

Her fingers are limp, because rigor mortis has loosened its grip now.

When he's done with her nails he carefully pulls a plastic bag over her hand and fastens it with tape, ahead of the post-mortem.

'I pay house visits to ordinary people every week,' Erixon says quietly. 'They've all got broken glass, overturned furniture and blood on the floor.'

He walks round the bed and carries on with the nails of the other hand. Just as he's about to pick it up he stops.

'There's something in her hand,' he says, and reaches for his camera. 'Do you see?'

Margot leans forward and looks. She can make out a dark object between the dead woman's fingers. She must have been clutching it tightly because of rigor mortis, but now it's visible as her hand relaxes.

Erixon picks up the woman's hand and carefully lifts the object. It's as if she still wants to hold on to it, but is too tired to struggle.

His bulky frame blocks Margot's view, but then she sees what the victim was clutching in her hand.

A tiny, broken-off porcelain deer's head.

The head is shiny, chestnut-brown, the broken surface at the bottom white as sugar.

Did the perpetrator or her husband put it in her hand?

Margot thinks of the glass-fronted cabinet, she's almost certain that all the porcelain figures were intact, even if they had fallen over.

She steps back to get an overview of the bedroom. Beside the dead woman Erixon stands, hunch-backed, photographing the little brown head. Adam is sitting slumped on a pouffe in front of the wardrobe. It looks like he's still trying not to throw up.

Margot walks back out to the glass-fronted cabinet again, and stands for a while in front of the toppled figurines. They're all lying as if they were dead, but none of them is broken, none is missing its head.

Why is the victim holding a small deer's head in her hand?

She looks over towards the bright light of the bedroom and thinks that she ought to go and take one last look at the body before it's moved to the pathology department in Solna.

13

It's morning, and Erik Maria Bark is standing at the till in the cafeteria of the Psychology Clinic, buying a cup of coffee. As he takes his wallet out to pay, he feels the ache in his shoulders from his piano lesson.

'It's already been paid for,' the cashier says.

'Already paid for?'

'Your friend has paid for your coffee all the way up to Christmas.'

'Did he say what his name was?'

'Nestor,' she replies.

Erik smiles and nods, thinking that he really must talk to Nestor about his over-effusive gratitude. It's Erik's job to help people, Nestor doesn't owe him anything.

He's still thinking of his former patient's friendly, cautious manner when he hears muted footsteps behind him and turns round. The pregnant superintendent is rolling towards him, waving a shrink-wrapped sandwich in his direction.

'Björn's fallen asleep, and seems to be feeling a bit better,' she says breathlessly. 'He wants to help us, and is willing to try hypnosis.'

'I've got an hour, if we can start now,' Erik says, quickly drinking his coffee.

'Do you think it's going to work on him?' she asks as they head in the direction of the treatment room.

'Hypnosis is just a way of getting his brain to relax, so that he can begin to sort his memories in a less chaotic way.'

'But the prosecutor's unlikely to be able to use statements made under hypnosis,' she says.

'No,' Erik smiles. 'But it might mean that Björn will be in a fit state to testify later on . . . and it could definitely help move the investigation forward.'

When they enter the room Björn is standing behind one of the armchairs, clutching its back with his hands. His eyes are dull, as if they were made from worn plastic.

'I've only seen hypnosis on television,' he says in a fragile voice. 'I mean, I'm not sure I really believe in it . . .'

'Just think of hypnosis as a way to help you feel better.'

'But I want her to leave,' he says, looking at Margot.

'Of course,' Erik says.

'Can you talk to her?'

Margot remains seated on the sofa, there's no change in her expression.

'You'll have to go and wait outside,' Erik says quietly.

'I've got symphysis, I need to sit down.'

'You know where the cafeteria is,' he replies.

She sighs and stands up, takes her mobile out and heads towards the door, opens it, then turns back towards Erik.

'Would you mind coming outside for a moment?' she says amiably.

'OK,' he says, and follows her into the corridor.

'We haven't got time to nursemaid him,' she whispers.

'I understand how you feel, but I'm a doctor and it's my job to help him.'

'I've got a job as well,' Margot says in a voice thin with irritation. 'And it involves stopping a murderer. This is serious, Björn knows things that—'

'This isn't an interrogation,' he interrupts. 'You know that, we've already talked about it.'

He watches the superintendent fighting her own impatience, then she nods as if she understands and accepts his words.

'As long as it doesn't harm him,' she says, 'from where I'm standing . . . well, every tiny detail could be of vital importance to the investigation.'

14

Erik shuts the door behind him, unfolds the stand and attaches the camera to it. Björn watches him, rubbing his forehead hard with one hand.

'Do you have to film it?' he asks.

'It's just a case of documenting what I do,' Erik replies. 'And I'd rather not have to be taking notes the whole time.'

'OK,' Björn says, as though he hadn't really listened to Erik's reply.

'You can start by lying down on the sofa,' Erik says as he goes over to the window and draws the curtains.

The room fills with a pleasant semi-darkness, and Björn lies back and shuffles down a little, then closes his eyes. Erik sits down on a chair, moves closer to him, and sees how tense he is. Thoughts are still racing through his head, as different impulses tug at his body.

'Breathe slowly through your nose,' Erik says. 'Relax your mouth, your chin and cheeks . . . feel the back of your head lying with all its weight on the pillow, feel your neck relax . . . you don't need to hold your head up now, because your head is resting on the pillow . . . Your jaw muscles are relaxing, your forehead is smooth and untroubled, your eyelids are feeling heavier . . .'

Erik takes his time, and moves through the whole body, from Björn's head to his toes, then back up to his weary eyelids and the weight of his head again.

With soporific monotony, Erik slips into the induction, speaking in a falling tone of voice as he tries to gather his strength in advance of what is coming.

Björn's body gradually begins to exhibit an almost cataleptic relaxation. A mental trauma can lead to increased receptivity to hypnosis, as if the brain were longing for a fresh command, a way out of an unsustainable state.

'The only thing you're listening to is my voice . . . if you hear anything else, it only makes you feel more relaxed, and more focused on my words . . . I'm about to start counting backwards, and for each number you hear, you'll relax a bit more.'

Erik thinks about what's coming, what's waiting inside the house, what Björn saw when he walked in through the door: the illuminated moment when the shock hit with full force.

'Nine hundred and twelve,' he says quietly. 'Nine hundred and eleven . . .'

With each exhalation Erik says a number, slowly and monotonously. After a while he breaks the logical sequence, but still carries on the countdown. Björn is now down at a perfect depth. The sharp frown on his brow has relaxed and his mouth looks softer. Erik counts, and sinks into hypnotic resonance with a curious shiver in his stomach.

'Now you're deeply relaxed . . . you're resting nice and calmly,' Erik says slowly. 'Soon you're going to revisit your memories of Friday night . . . When I finish counting down to zero, you will be standing outside your house, but you're completely calm, because there's no danger . . . Four, three, two, one . . . Now you're standing in the street outside your house, the taxi is driving away, the tyres are crunching on the grit covering the tarmac . . .'

Björn opens his eyes, his eyes gleaming, but his gaze is focused inward, into his memories, and his heavy eyelids close once more.

'Are you looking at the house now?'

Björn is standing in the cool night air in front of his house. A strange glow is lighting up the sky in time with the slow rhythm of his heartbeat. It looks like the house is leaning forward as the light expands and the shadows withdraw.

'It's moving,' he says almost inaudibly.

'Now you're walking up to the door,' Erik says. 'The night air is mild, there's nothing unpleasant . . .'

Björn starts as some jackdaws fly up from a tree. They're visible against the sky, their shadows move across the grass, and then they're gone.

'You're perfectly safe,' Erik says as he sees Björn's hand move anxiously over the seat of the sofa.

15

Deep in his trance, Björn slowly approaches the door. He keeps to the stone path, but something about the black shimmer of the window catches his attention.

'You've reached the door, you take your key out and put it in the lock,' Erik says.

Björn carefully pushes the handle, but the door is stuck. He tries harder, and there's a sticky sound when it eventually opens.

Erik sees that Björn's brow is sweating, and repeats in a soothing voice that there's nothing to be scared of.

Björn tries to open his eyes and whisper something. Erik leans forward, and feels his breath against his ear.

'The doorstep . . . something odd about it . . .'

'Yes, this doorstep has always been odd,' Erik replies calmly. 'But once you've crossed it, everything will be just as it was on Friday.'

Erik notes that the whole of Björn's face is covered with a sheen of sweat as his chin begins to tremble.

'No, no,' he whispers, shaking his head.

Erik realises that he needs to put him in deeper hypnosis if he's to be able to enter the house.

'All you have to do now is listen to my voice,' Erik says. 'Because soon you'll be in an even more relaxed state, and there's nothing to be worried about there . . . You're sinking deeper as I count: four . . . you're sinking, three . . . getting calmer, two . . . one, and now you're completely relaxed, and can see that the doorstep isn't any sort of barrier . . .'

Björn's face is slack, his mouth is hanging open, one corner wet with saliva: he's in a deeper state of hypnosis than Erik had intended.

'If you feel ready, you can . . . cross the threshold now.'

Björn doesn't want to, he's thinking that he doesn't want to, but he still takes a step into the hall. His looks along the corridor towards the kitchen. Everything is the same as usual, there's an advertisement from Bauhaus on the doormat, too many shoes piled up on the shoe-rack, the umbrella that always falls over does so again, and his keys jangle as he puts them on the chest of drawers.

'Everything is the same as usual,' he whispers. 'The same as . . .'

He falls silent when he notices a strange, rolling movement from the corner of his eye. He daren't turn to look in that direction, and stares straight ahead while something moves at the edge of his field of vision.

'There's something strange . . . off to the side . . . I . . .'

'What did you say?' Erik asks.

'It's moving, off to the side . . .'

'OK, just let it go,' Erik replies. 'Look straight ahead and keep going.'

Björn walks through the hall, but his eyes keep getting drawn to the side, towards the clothes hanging in the porch. They're moving slowly in the gloom, as if a wind were blowing through the house. The sleeves of Susanna's trenchcoat lift in a gust, then fall back.

'Look ahead of you,' Erik says.

Someone suffering mental trauma experiences a chaotic jumble of memories that press in on them from all sides: they lose all coherence, fade away and lurch into view, all mixed up.

All Erik can do is try to lead Björn through the rooms, towards the fundamental insight that he couldn't have prevented his wife's death.

'I'm in the kitchen now,' he whispers.

'Keep going,' Erik says.

There's a bag of newspapers for recycling in the passageway leading to the door of the cellar. Björn takes a cautious step forward, looking straight ahead, but he still sees a kitchen drawer slide open, and it rattles when it comes to a halt.

'One drawer is open,' he mutters.

'Which one?'

Björn knows it's the drawer containing the knives, and he knows that he's the one opening it, seeing as he washed a large knife several hours earlier.

'Oh, God . . . I can't . . . I . . .'

'There's nothing to be afraid of, you're safe, and I'll be with you as you go further in.'

'I'm walking past the door to the cellar, towards the living room . . . Susanna must have gone to bed already . . .'

It's quiet, the television is switched off, but something's different, the furniture seems to be in the wrong places, as if a giant had picked the house up and given it a gentle shake.

'Sanna?' Björn whispers.

He reaches out his hand towards the light switch. The room doesn't light up, but the glow fills the windows that look out onto the garden. He can't help thinking he's being watched, and feels an urge to close the curtains.

'God, oh God, oh God,' he suddenly whimpers, his face trembling.

Erik realises that Björn is there now, in the midst of his memory of the traumatic event, but he's barely describing anything, he's keeping it to himself.

Björn is getting closer, sees himself in the black window, sees the bushes outside move in the wind, far beyond the reflections.

He's gasping even though he's under deep hypnosis, his body tenses and his back arches.

'What's happening?' Erik asks.

Björn stops when he sees someone with a dark grey face looking back at him in the window. Right next to the glass. He takes a step back and feels his heart pounding hard in his chest. A branch of the rosebush sways and scrapes the window ledge. He realises that the grey face isn't outside. There's someone sitting on the floor in front of the window. He can see their reflection.

A calm voice repeats that there's nothing to be scared of.

He moves to the side and realises that it's Susanna. She's sitting on the floor in front of the window.

'Sanna?' he says quietly, so as not to startle her.

He can see her shoulder, some of her hair. She's leaning back against an armchair, looking out. He approaches cautiously and feels that the floor is wet beneath his feet.

'She's sitting down,' he mutters.

'She's sitting?'

Björn goes closer to the armchair by the window, and then the light in the ceiling comes on and the room is bathed in light. He knows he switched it on, but is still frightened when the bright light fills the room.

There's blood everywhere.

He's trodden in blood, it's splashed across the television and sofa, and up the walls, there are smears of blood on the floor, trickling into the gaps between the wood.

She's sitting on the floor in a dark-red pool. A dead woman wearing Sanna's kimono. Dust has settled on the pool of blood around her.

Erik sees Björn's face tense, and his lips and the tip of his nose turn white. As soon as Björn has realised that the dead woman is his wife, Erik is planning to bring him out of the hypnosis.

'Who can you see?' he asks.

'No . . . no,' he whispers.

'You know who it is,' Erik says.

'Susanna,' he says slowly, and opens his eyes.

'You can move back now,' Erik says. 'I'm going to wake you up in a moment, and—'

'There's so much blood, God, I don't want to . . . Her face, it's been destroyed, and she's sitting perfectly still, with—'

'Björn, listen to my voice, I'm going to count from—'

'She's sitting with her hand over her ear, and there's blood dripping from her elbow,' he says, panting for breath.

Erik feels an icy chill as adrenalin fills his veins for a few seconds, the hairs on his arms and the back of his neck stand up. With his heart pounding he glances towards the closed door of the treatment room and hears a trolley rattle as it moves away.

'Look at your own hands,' he says, trying to keep his voice steady. 'You're looking at your own hands and you're breathing slowly. With each breath you're feeling calmer—'

'I don't want to,' Björn whispers.

Erik can feel that he's forcing him, but he has to know the position Björn's wife was sitting in when he found her.

'Before I wake you up, we need to go deeper,' he says, swallowing hard. 'Beneath the house that you're in is another house, identical to the other one . . . but down there is the only place you can see Susanna clearly. Three, two, one, and now you're there . . . She's sitting on the floor in the pool of blood, and you can look at her without feeling frightened.'

'Her face is almost gone, it's just blood,' Björn says sluggishly. 'And her hand is stuck to her ear . . .'

'Keep going,' Erik says, glancing at the door again.

'Her hand is tangled up in . . . in the cord of her kimono.'

'Björn, I'm going to bring you up now . . . to the house above, and the only thing you know there is that Susanna is dead and that there was nothing you could have done to save her . . . That's the only thing you're going to take with you when I wake you up, you're going to leave everything else behind.'

16

Erik closes his office door and goes over to his desk. He feels that his back is wet with sweat when he sits down.

'It's nothing,' he whispers anxiously to himself.

He moves the mouse to wake his computer up, then logs in. With his hand trembling he pulls open the top drawer, presses a Mogadon out of a blister-pack and swallows it without water.

He quickly signs into the database of patients, and notices how cold his fingers are as he waits to be able to perform a search.

He jumps when Superintendent Margot Silverman opens the door without knocking. She walks in and stops in front of him with her hands clasped round her stomach.

'Björn Kern says he can't remember what you talked about.'

'That's natural,' Erik replies, minimising the document.

'How did you get on with the hypnosis, then?' she asks, running her hand over the wooden elephant from Malaysia.

'He was definitely receptive . . .'

'So you were able to hypnotise him?' she smiles.

'I'm afraid I forgot to start the camera,' Erik lies. 'Otherwise I could have shown you, he went into a trance almost instantly.'

'You forgot to start the camera?'

'You know that this wasn't an official interview,' he says, a touch impatiently. 'This was a first step towards what we call affective stabilisation, so that—'

'I don't give a damn about that,' she cuts him off.

'So that you can have a functional witness later on,' he concludes.

'How much later? Will he be able to say anything later today?'

'I think he's going to realise what happened fairly quickly, but talking about it is another matter.'

'So what happened? What did he say? He must have said something, surely?'

'Yes, but—'

'No fucking oath of confidentiality bollocks now,' she interrupts. 'I have to know, otherwise people will die.'

Erik goes over to the window and leans on the sill. Far below a patient is standing smoking, thin and bent-backed in his hospital gown.

'I took him back,' Erik says slowly. 'Into the house . . . it was rather complicated, because it was very recent, and full of fragments of terrible memories.'

'But he saw everything . . . could he see everything?'

'It was only to make him understand that he couldn't have saved her.'

'But he saw the murder scene, and his wife? Did he?'

'Yes, he did,' Erik replies.

'So what did he say?'

'Not much . . . he talked about blood . . . and the wounds to her face.'

'Was she in a particular position? A posture with sexual implications?'

'He didn't say.'

'Was she sitting up or lying down? How did her mouth look, where were her hands? Was she naked? Violated?'

'He said very little,' Erik replies. 'It can take a long time to reach details of that sort . . .'

'I swear, if he doesn't start talking I'll take him into custody,' she says in a loud voice. 'I'll drag him off to headquarters and watch him like a hawk until—'

'Margot,' Erik interrupts in a friendly voice.

She looks at him with a subdued expression, nods and breathes through her mouth, then pulls out a business card and puts it down on his desk.

'We don't know who his next victim's going to be. It could be your wife. Think about that,' she says, and leaves the room.

Erik feels his face relax. He walks slowly back to his desk. The floor is starting to feel soft beneath his feet. As he sits down in front of his computer there's a knock on the door.

'Yes?'

'That charming superintendent has left the building,' Nelly says, peering round the door.

'She's only trying to do her job.'

'I know, she doesn't really seem too bad . . .'

'Stop it,' he says, but can't help smiling.

'No, but she was pretty funny,' Nelly says and laughs.

Erik rests his head on his hand and she turns serious and walks in, closes the door behind her and looks at him.

'What is it?' she asks. 'What's happened?'

'Nothing,' he replies.

'Tell me,' she insists, sitting down on the corner of his desk.

Her red woollen dress crackles with static electricity against her nylon tights as she crosses her legs.

'I don't know,' Erik sighs.

'What's up with you?' she laughs.

Erik stands up, takes a deep breath and looks at her.

'Nelly,' he says, and she can hear how empty his voice sounds. 'I need to ask you about a patient . . . Before you started working here, Nina Blom put together a team for a complicated research project.'

'Go on,' she says, looking at him with obvious curiosity.

'I know I outlined my cases to you, but this may not have been included, I mean . . .'

'What's the patient's name?' she asks calmly.

'Rocky Kyrklund – do you remember him?'

'Yes, hang on,' she says tentatively.

'He was a priest.'

'Exactly, I remember, you talked about him quite a lot,' she says as she thinks. 'You had a file of pictures from the crime scene, and—'

'You don't remember where he ended up?' he interrupts.

'That was years ago,' she replies.

'He's still inside, though, isn't he?'

'We'd better hope so,' she replied. 'He'd killed people, after all, hadn't he?'

'A woman.' Erik nods.

'That's right, now I remember. Her whole face was destroyed.'

17

Nelly stands behind Erik as he makes his way through the patient database on his computer. He types Rocky Kyrklund's name, searches, and discovers that he was sent to Karsudden District Hospital.

'Karsudden,' he says quietly.

She brushes a strand of blonde hair from her cheek and looks at him, her eyes narrowing.

'Do you want to tell me why we're talking about this patient?'

'Rocky Kyrklund's victim had been posed. You won't remember, but she was lying on the floor with her face horribly disfigured, and her hand round her neck . . . I've just hypnotised Björn Kern, and . . . and he described details that were very reminiscent of the old murder.'

'The one committed by the priest?'

'I don't know, but Björn Kern said his wife's face had been completely destroyed . . . and that she was sitting with her hand over her ear.'

'What do the police say?'

'I don't know,' Erik mutters.

'I mean, you did tell that . . . lovely pregnant lady?'

'I didn't tell her anything.' Erik says.

'You didn't?' she asks, a sceptical smile playing at the corners of her mouth.

'Because it emerged while he was under hypnosis, and—'

'But he wanted to talk, didn't he?'

'I might have misheard,' Erik says.

'Misheard?' she laughs.

'It's just so sick – I can't think clearly any more.'

'Erik, it probably isn't important, but you have to tell the police, that's why they're here,' Nelly says gently.

He walks over to the window. The area where the patients stand and smoke is empty now. But he can still see the cigarette butts and sweet wrappers that have been tossed on the ground, and a blue shoe-cover that's been pushed into the ashtray.

'It's a long time ago, but to me . . . Do you know what those weeks were like? I didn't want Rocky to be released,' Erik says slowly. 'It was everything . . . the brutality, the eyes, the hands . . .'

'I know I read all about it,' Nelly says. 'I don't remember the details of your recommendation, but I know you said he was seriously bloody dangerous and that there was a severe risk of a relapse.'

'What if he's out? I've got to call Karsudden,' Erik says, then picks up his phone, checks his computer, and dials the number for Simon Casillas, the senior consultant in charge.

Nelly sits down on Erik's sofa while he talks to the doctor, and smiles at him when he looks at her as he exchanges the usual pleasantries and when he ends the conversation by repeating that the consultant's article in *Swedish Psychiatry* really was excellent.

The sun passes behind a cloud and darkness falls across the room, as if a huge figure were standing in front of the building.

'Rocky is still in Ward D:4,' Erik says. 'And he's never been let out on parole.'

'Does that feel better?'

'No,' he whispers.

'Are you losing your grip?' she asks, so seriously that he can't help smiling.

He sighs and puts his hands to his face, then slowly lowers them, feeling his fingertips press gently against his eyelids and down his cheeks before he looks at Nelly again.

Her back is straight as she looks at him carefully. A tiny, sharp little wrinkle has appeared between her thin eyebrows.

'OK, listen,' Erik says. 'I know this is completely wrong, but in one of the last conversations I had with Rocky, he claimed he had an alibi for the night of the murder, but I didn't want him to be released simply because he'd bought himself a witness.'

'What are you trying to say?' she asks quietly.

'I never passed that information on.'

'No way,' she says.

'He could have been released—'

'Bloody hell, you can't do that!' she interrupts.

'I know, but he was guilty and he would have killed again.'

'That's not our business, we're psychologists, we're not detectives, and we aren't judges . . .'

She takes a few agitated steps, then stops and shakes her head.

'Fucking hell,' she gasps. 'You're mad, you're completely—'

'I can understand you being angry.'

'Yes, I am angry. I mean, you know, if this gets out you'd lose your job.'

'I know what I did was wrong, it's tormented me ever since, but I've always been utterly convinced that I stopped a murderer.'

'Shit,' she mutters.

He picks up the business card from his desk and begins to dial the superintendent's number.

'What are you doing?' she asks.

'I need to tell her about Rocky's alibi, and the whole business about the hand and the ear, and—'

'Go ahead,' she interrupts. 'But what if you were right, what if his alibi wasn't real? Then any similarities are just coincidence.'

'I don't care.'

'Then ask yourself what you're going to do with the rest of your life,' she says. 'You'll have to give up being a doctor, you'll lose your income, you might even face charges, all the scandal and gossip in the papers—'

'It's my own fault.'

'Find out if the alibi checks out first – if it does, then I'll report you myself.'

'Thanks,' he laughs.

'I'm being serious,' she says.

18

Erik leaves the car in front of the garage, hurries up the path to his dark house, unlocks the door and goes inside. He turns the light on in the hall but doesn't take his outdoor clothes off, just carries on down the steep staircase to the cellar that contains his extensive archive.

In the locked steel cabinets he keeps all the documents from his years in Uganda, from the major research project at the Karolinska Institute, and about his patients at the Psychology Clinic. All the written material is collected in the form of logbooks, personal journals and extensive notes. The recordings of his sessions have been saved on eight external hard-drives.

Erik's heart is thumping as he unlocks one of the cabinets and searches back in time to the year when his life crossed paths with that of Rocky Kyrklund.

He pulls the file out of a black box and hurries upstairs to his study. He switches the lamp on, glances at the black window, removes the elastic band round the file, and opens it on the desk in front of him.

It was nine years ago, and life was very different. Benjamin was still in primary school, Simone was writing her dissertation in art history, and he himself had just started working at the Crisis and Trauma Centre with Professor Sten W Jakobsson.

He no longer remembers the exact details of how he was contacted and invited to join a team for a forensic psychology project. He had actually decided not to take part in anything like that again but, given the particular circumstances, changed his mind when his colleague Nina Blom asked for his help.

Erik remembers spending the evening in his new office, reading the material the prosecutor had sent over. The man who was going to be evaluated was a Rocky Kyrklund, and he was vicar of the parish of Salem. He was being held in custody on suspicion of having murdered Rebecka Hansson, a forty-three-year-old woman who had attended Mass and then stayed behind to speak to him in private on the Sunday before she was murdered.

The murder had been extremely aggressive, fuelled by hatred. The victim's face and arms had been destroyed. She was found lying on the linoleum floor of her bathroom, with her right hand around her neck.

There was fairly persuasive forensic evidence. Rocky had sent her a number of threatening text messages, and his fingerprints and strands of his hair were found in her home, and traces of Rebecka's blood were found on his shoes.

An arrest warrant was issued and he was eventually picked up seven months later in conjunction with a serious traffic accident on the motorway at Brunnby. He had stolen a car at Finsta and was heading for the airport at Arlanda.

In the accident Rocky Kyrklund suffered serious brain damage which led to epileptic seizures in the frontal and temporal lobes of his brain.

He would suffer recurrent bouts of automatism and memory loss for the rest of his life.

When Erik met Rocky Kyrklund, his face was criss-crossed with red scars from the accident, his arm was in plaster, and his hair had just started to grow again after several operations. Rocky was a large man with a booming voice. He was almost two metres tall, broad-shouldered, with big hands and a thick neck.

Sometimes he would faint, falling off his chair, knocking over the flimsy table holding glasses and a jug of water, and hit his shoulder on the floor. But sometimes his epileptic attacks were almost invisible. He just seemed a bit subdued and distant, and afterwards he couldn't remember what they had been talking about.

Erik and Rocky got on fairly well. The priest was undeniably charismatic. He somehow managed to give the impression of speaking straight from the heart.

Erik leafs through the private journal in which he made notes during their conversations. The various subjects can be traced from one session to the next.

Rocky had neither admitted nor denied the murder; he said he couldn't remember Rebecka Hansson at all, and couldn't explain why his fingerprints had been found in her home, or how her blood came to be on his shoes.

During the best of their conversations, Rocky would circle the small islands of memories in an attempt to discern a bit more.

Once he said that he and Rebecka Hansson had had intercourse in the sacristy, albeit interrupted. He could remember details, such as the rough rug they had been lying on. An old gift from the young women of the parish. She had begun to menstruate, leaving a small bloodstain, like a virgin, he said.

During the following conversations he couldn't remember any of this.

The conclusion of the examination was that the crime had been committed under the influence of severe mental disturbance. The team believed that Rocky Kyrklund suffered from a grandiose, narcissistic personality disorder with elements of paranoia.

Erik leafs past a circled note, 'paying for sex + drug abuse', in the journal, followed by some ideas for medication.

Naturally he shouldn't have had an opinion on the matter of guilt, but as time passed Erik became convinced that Rocky was guilty, and that his mental disorder constituted a serious risk of further crimes.

During one of their last sessions, Rocky was talking about a ceremony to mark the end of the school year in a church decked out with spring greenery, when he suddenly looked up at Erik and said he hadn't murdered Rebecka Hansson.

'I remember everything now, I've got an alibi for the whole of that evening,' he said.

He wrote down the name Olivia, and an address, then gave the sheet of paper to Erik. They carried on talking, and Rocky began to speak in broken fragments, then fell completely silent, looked at Erik, and suffered a severe epileptic attack. Afterwards Rocky didn't remember anything, he didn't even recognise Erik, just kept whispering about wanting heroin, saying he could kill a child if only he was given thirty grams of medical diacetylmorphine in a bottle with an unbroken seal.

Erik never took Rocky's claim of an alibi seriously. At best it was a lie; at worst Rocky could have bribed or threatened someone to support the alibi.

Erik threw away the scrap of paper, and Rocky Kyrklund was found guilty and sentenced to secure psychiatric care, with severe restrictions on any parole application.

And nine years later a woman is murdered in Bromma in a way

that was reminiscent of Rebecka Hansson's murder, Erik thinks, closing the file bearing Rocky's name.

Aggressive violence directed at the face, neck and chest.

But, on the other hand, murders of this sort aren't altogether unusual. They can be triggered by anything from the jealousy of an ex-husband, aggression linked to Rohypnol and anabolic steroids, so-called honour killings, or a pimp making an example of a prostitute trying to break away from him.

The only concrete connection is that Susanna Kern was left at the scene of the murder with her hand covering her ear, just like Rebecka Hansson was found on the floor with her hand round her own neck.

Perhaps Susanna Kern merely got tangled up in the belt of her kimono during the struggle.

The parallels certainly aren't unambiguous, but they are there, and they're forcing Erik to do something he should have done a long time ago.

He puts the file in his desk drawer and looks up the number of senior consultant Simon Casillas at Karsudden Hospital once more.

'Casillas,' the man answers in a voice like dried leather.

'Erik Maria Bark from the Karolinska.'

'Hello again.'

'I've checked my diary, and I could actually squeeze in a visit.'

'A visit?'

The sound of a squash court is audible in the background, a ball hitting the wall, the squeak of shoes.

'I'm taking part in a research project for the Osher Centre at the Institute which involves us following up on old patients, right across the spectrum . . . which means I'm going to have to interview Rocky Kyrklund.'

Before they end the conversation Erik hears himself babble about the fabricated research project, about health-service funding, tax declarations, online CBT, and someone called Doctor Stünkel.

He slowly puts his phone down on the desk. Watches the little screen turn black as it slips into dormancy. The room is perfectly still. His leather seat creaks quietly like a moored boat. Through the open window he can hear the hiss of an evening shower approach across the gardens.

He bends forward and rests his elbows on the desk, leans his head on his hands and asks himself what on earth he's doing. What did I just say? he thinks. And who the hell is Stünkel?

This could be a crazy idea, he knows that. But he also knows he has no choice. If Rocky's alibi was genuine, then he must be released, even if that would mean a media frenzy and a miscarriage of justice.

Erik skims through the logbook. There are no notes about an alibi, but towards the end one page has been torn out. He leafs forward, then stops. From that last session with Rocky there's a faint note in pencil that Erik doesn't remember. In the middle of the page, it says 'a priest with dirty clothes' across the lines, then the remainder of the book is blank.

He stands up and goes out into the kitchen to find something to eat. While he walks through the library he repeats to himself that he has to find out if Rocky's alibi was real.

If it was genuine, then this new murder could be connected to the old one, and Erik will have to confess everything.

19

Saga Bauer is driving slowly through the vast campus of the Karolinska Institute. As she approaches Retzius väg 5, she turns into the deserted car park and stops in front of the empty building.

Even though she's tired and not wearing any make-up, hasn't washed her hair and is wearing baggy clothes, most people would probably say she was the most beautiful person they had ever seen.

Recently there's been something hungry and hunted about her appearance: the bright blue of her eyes makes her creamy white skin look radiant.

On the floor in front of the passenger seat is a green holdall containing underwear, a bulletproof vest and five cartridges of ammunition: .45 ACP, hollow-tipped.

Saga Bauer has been on sick leave from her job with the Security Police for more than a year, and she hasn't visited the boxing club in all that time.

The only time she's missed work was during Barack Obama's visit to Stockholm. She stood at a distance and watched the President's cortège. Being constantly on the lookout for threats is an occupational hazard. She remembers the tingle that ran through her body when she identified a potential vantage point from which to fire a rocket-propelled grenade, an unguarded window, but a moment later the danger had passed and nothing had happened.

The Forensic Medicine Department is closed, all the lights in the red-brick building seem to be off, but a white Jaguar with a damaged front bumper is parked on the path right in front of the entrance.

Saga leans to the side, opens the glove compartment, takes out the glass jar and leaves the car. The air is mild and smells of freshly mown grass. She feels her Glock 21 bouncing under her left arm, and can hear a faint sloshing sound from the jar as she walks.

Saga has to clamber across the flowerbed to get past Nils Åhlén's car. The thorns of the wild rose make a scratching sound as they let go of her military trousers. The branches sway and a few rose petals drift to the ground.

The lock of the front door is prevented from clicking shut with the help of a rolled-up information leaflet.

She's been here enough times before to find her way. The grit on the poorly cleaned floor crunches as she heads down the corridor towards the swing-door.

She can't help smiling when she looks at the jar, and the cloudy liquid, the particles circling round.

The memory flashes through her, and her free hand goes involuntarily to one of the scars he left on her face, the deep cut just below her eyebrow.

Sometimes she thinks he must have seen something special in her, that that was why he spared her life, and sometimes she thinks that he simply considered death too easy – he wanted her to live with the lies he had made her believe, in the hell he had created for her.

She'll never know.

The only thing that is certain is that he chose not to kill her, and she chose to kill him.

She thinks of the darkness and the deep snow as she walks down the empty corridor of the Forensic Medicine Department.

'I hit him,' she whispers to herself.

She moistens her mouth, and in her mind's eye sees herself firing and hitting him in the neck, arm and chest.

'Three shots to the chest . . .'

She changed her magazine and shot him again when he'd fallen into the rapids, she held the flare up and saw the cloud of blood spread out around him. She ran along the bank, shooting at the dark object, and carried on firing even though the body had been carried off by the current.

I know I killed him, she thinks.

But they never found his body. The police sent divers under the ice, and checked both banks with sniffer-dogs.

Outside the office is a neat metal sign bearing his name and title: *Nils Åhlén, Professor of Forensic Medicine.*

The door is open, and the slight figure is sitting at his neat desk reading the newspaper with a pair of latex gloves on his hands. He's wearing a white polo-neck shirt under his white coat, and his pilot's sunglasses flash as he looks up.

'You're tired, Saga,' he says amiably.

'A bit.'

'Beautiful, though.'

'No.'

He puts the newspaper down, pulls off the gloves and notices the quizzical look in her eyes.

'To save getting ink on my fingers,' he says, as though it were obvious.

Saga doesn't answer, just sets the jar down in front of him. The chopped-off finger moves slowly in the alcohol, through a cloud of wispy particles. A swollen and half-rotten index finger.

'So you think that this finger belonged to . . .'

'Jurek Walter,' Saga says curtly.

'How did you get hold of it?' Nils Åhlén asks.

He picks up the jar and holds it up to the light. The finger falls against the inside of the glass as if it were pointing at him.

'I've spent more than a year looking . . .'

To start with Saga Bauer borrowed sniffer-dogs and walked up and down both banks of the river, from Bergasjön all the way to Hysingsvik on the Baltic coast. She followed the shoreline, combed the beaches, studied the currents of Norrfjärden all the way down to Västerfladen, and made her way out to every island, talking to anyone who went fishing in the area.

'Go on,' Åhlén said.

She looks up and meets his relaxed gaze behind the shimmering surface of his sunglasses. His latex gloves are lying on the desk in front of him, inside out, in two little heaps. One is quivering slightly, either from a draught or because of the rubber contracting.

'This morning I was walking along the beach out at Högmarsö,' she explains. 'I've been there before, but I gave it another go . . . the terrain on the north side is quite tricky, a lot of forest on the cliffs at the headland.'

She thinks of the old man walking towards her from the other direction with an armful of silver-grey driftwood.

'You've gone quiet again.'

'Sorry . . . I bumped into a retired church warden . . . he said he'd seen me the last time I was there, and asked what I was looking for.'

Saga went with him to the inhabited part of the island. Less than forty people live there. The warden's house is tucked behind the white chapel and freestanding bell tower.

'He said he found a dead body on the shore towards the end of April . . .'

'A whole body?' Åhlén asks in a low voice.

'No, just the torso and one arm.'

'No head?'

'No one can live without a torso,' she says, and can hear how agitated her voice sounds.

'No,' Åhlén replies calmly.

'The warden said the body must have been in the water all winter, because it was badly swollen, and very heavy.'

'They look terrible,' Åhlén said.

'He brought the body back through the forest in his wheelbarrow, and laid it on the floor of the tool-shed behind the chapel . . . but the smell drove his dog mad, so he had to take it to the old crematorium.'

'He cremated it?'

She nods. The crematorium had been abandoned for decades, but in the middle of the overgrown foundations was a sooty brick oven with a chimney. The warden used to burn rubbish in the oven, so he knew it worked.

'Why didn't he call the police?' Åhlén asked.

Saga thinks of the way the churchwarden's house stank of fried food and old clothes. His neck was streaked with dirt and the bottles of home-brew in the fridge had dirty marks from his fingers.

'He had a still at home . . . I don't know. But he did take a few pictures with his mobile in case the police showed up and started asking questions . . . and he kept the finger at the bottom of his fridge.'

'Have you got the pictures?'

'Yes,' she says, and pulls out her phone. 'It must be him . . . look at the gunshot wounds.'

Åhlén looks at the first picture. On the bare cement floor of the tool-shed lies a bloated, marbled torso with just one arm. The skin has split across the chest and slipped down. There are four ragged gunshot holes on the body. The water has made a black mark on the pale grey floor – a shadow that gets narrower towards the drain in the floor.

'That looks good, very good,' Nils Åhlén said, handing her phone back.

There is a tense look in his eyes as he gets to his feet and picks the glass jar up from the desk, and he looks at her as if he were about to say something else, but walks out of the room instead.

20

Saga follows Nils Åhlén through a dark corridor with narrow wheel-tracks on the floor, into the closest pathology lab. The chilly fluorescent lights in the ceiling flicker a few times before settling and lighting up the white tiled walls. Beside one of the metal tables is a desk with a computer and a large bottle of Trocadero.

The room smells of disinfectant and drains. A bright yellow hose is attached to one of the taps. A trickle of water runs from the end of the hose towards the drain in the floor.

Åhlén walks straight over to the long, plastic-covered post-mortem table with its double trough and drainage runnels.

He pulls over a chair for Saga, then places the glass jar on the slab.

She watches him put on protective overalls, a mask and latex gloves. Then he stops, quite still, in front of the jar, like an old person disappearing into a memory. Saga is on the point of saying something when Åhlén takes a deep breath.

'The right finger of a body found in brackish water, preserved in strong alcohol at a temperature of eight degrees for four months,' he says to himself.

He photographs the jar from various angles, then unscrews the lid bearing the words BOB *Raspberry Jam*.

Using a pair of steel tweezers he removes the finger, lets it drip for a while, then puts it down on the post-mortem table. The nail has come off, and is still lying in the murky liquid. A nauseating smell of rotten seawater and decaying flesh spreads through the room.

'It's certainly true that the finger was removed from the body long after death,' he says to Saga. 'With a knife or perhaps a pair of pliers or secateurs . . .'

Åhlén is breathing audibly though his nose as he carefully rolls the finger over so he can photograph it from every angle.

'We can get a good fingerprint from this,' he says seriously.

Saga has backed away, and is standing with her hand over her mouth, watching as Åhlén picks up the dead finger and holds it against a print-scanner.

The machine bleeps when the print has been scanned.

The tissue is swollen and pudgy, but the fingerprint that appears in the little screen is still very clear.

The papillary lines are really the ridges between the cells and sweat pores that develop in the epidermis while an embryo is still in the womb.

Saga stares at the oval containing a labyrinth of swirls.

The room feels full of suppressed anticipation.

Åhlén takes off his protective clothing again and logs into the computer, hooks up the scanner and clicks on the icon with the text *LiveScan*.

'I've got a private AFIS system,' he says straight out as he clicks another icon and types in a new password.

Saga sees him search for 'Walter', then click to bring up the digital image of the ID form that was compiled at the time of Jurek's arrest. The sharp reproductions of the thumb and fingerprints from both hands were made in ink.

Saga tries to control her breathing.

Sweat is trickling down her sides from her armpits.

Åhlén whispers something to himself, and drags the best image from LiveScan across to the search box of the AFIS system, then clicks the button saying *Analysis and Comparison*, and immediately gets a result.

'What's happening?' Saga says, and swallows hard.

The reflections of the fluorescent lights slide across his glasses. She sees his hand shake as he points at the screen.

'The details of the initial level are rather vague . . . mostly just patterns,' Åhlén explains, and clears his throat quickly. 'The second level are so-called Galton details . . . you can see the length of the papillary lines and the way they relate to each other. The differences are only the result of tissue breakdown . . . And the third level, that's primarily concerned with the layout of pores, and there the match is perfect.'

'Do you mean that we've found Jurek?' she whispers.

'I'll send the DNA to the National Forensics Lab in Linköping, but purely as a formality,' he replies with a nervous smile. 'You've found him, there's no doubt that it's him. It's over now.'

'Good,' she says, feeling hot tears well up in her eyes.

The initial relief is full of contradictory impulses and emptiness. Her heart is still pounding hard in her chest.

'You've said all along that you were sure you killed Jurek – why was it so important to find his body?' Åhlén asks.

'I couldn't try to find Joona before I'd found it,' she replies, rubbing her cheeks with her hand to wipe the tears away.

'Joona's dead,' Åhlén says.

'Yes,' she smiles.

Joona's jacket and wallet were found in the possession of a homeless man who hung around Strömparterren, at the end of the island housing the parliament building in Stockholm. Saga's watched the video of the interview plenty of times. The homeless man identified himself as Constantine the First. He usually borrowed one of the fishing boats and slept outside a heating vent.

He sat in the interview room with his big beard and dirty fingers, cracked lips and a wary look in his eyes. In a rattling voice he told them about the big Finn who told him to keep his distance, before taking his jacket off and swimming out into the water. He watched him swim out towards Strömbron until he reached the fast-flowing current and disappeared.

'You don't believe he's dead?' Åhlén asks calmly.

'Several years ago he phoned me . . . he wanted me to find out some information about a woman in Helsinki, in secret,' Saga says. 'At the time I thought the woman had something to do with the case at Birgittagården.'

'What about her, then?'

'She was seriously ill, she was in hospital for an operation . . . Her name was Laura Sandin,' Saga says, holding Åhlén's gaze. 'But she was really . . . really Summa Linna, his wife, wasn't she?'

'Yes,' he nods.

'I tried to get hold of Laura to tell her that Joona was dead,' Saga explains. 'Laura had been in a cancer hospice for palliative care, but two days after Joona's suicide she was discharged to spend her last days at home . . . but neither Laura nor her daughter are still at their address on Elisabetsgatan.'

'Really?' Åhlén says, his thin nostrils turning pale.

'They aren't anywhere,' Saga says, taking a step towards him.

'That's good to hear.'

'I think Joona arranged his suicide so he could go and pick up his wife and daughter and go into hiding with them.'

Nils Åhlén's eyes are red, and his mouth is twitching slightly with emotion when he speaks:

'Joona was the only person who believed that Jurek's reach extended beyond the isolation unit, and as usual, he was right . . . If we hadn't done this, Jurek would have killed Summa and Lumi, just as he killed Disa.'

'Nils, I need to find Joona and tell him that Jurek Walter is dead,' Saga says. 'He needs to know that the body's been found.'

She puts her hand on his arm and sees his shoulders slump when he makes his mind up.

'I don't know where they are,' he eventually says. 'But if Summa is dying, like you say . . . I know where you could try looking . . .'

'Where?'

'Go to the Nordic Museum,' he says in a thick voice, as if he were worried about changing his mind. 'There's a small bridal crown, a Sámi bridal crown made of woven roots. Look at it carefully.'

'Thanks.'

'Good luck,' Åhlén says seriously, then hesitates. 'No one wants to hug a pathologist, but . . .'

Saga hugs him hard, then leaves the room and hurries along the corridor.

21

Saga parks in front of the large flight of steps leading up to the Nordic Museum, drinks a sip of cold coffee from a 7-Eleven mug, and looks at the people around her, all dressed for summer. It's as if she hasn't really paid attention to her surroundings before now. Adults and children, tired from the sun or long picnics, or excited and expectant on their way to the amusement park or some restaurant.

She's barely noticed the summer passing her by again. Since Joona disappeared she has withdrawn from the world, searching for Jurek's body.

Now it's time to bring this to an end.

Saga gets out of the car and goes up the steps. There's a broken syringe on one of the top steps.

She walks in through the imposing entrance, buys a ticket, picks up a plan of the museum and carries on into the entrance hall. A colourful statue of Gustav Vasa sits on a huge wooden throne gazing off towards the replica of a post-war home that's been installed in the museum.

As she walks towards the staircase she catches a glimpse of a text about the *people's home* and the Social Democratic vision of a modern, supportive and equal Sweden in which all families had the right to a home with hot water, a kitchen and bathroom.

She jogs up the stone steps and carries on to the section for Sámi handicrafts. A few visitors are walking along the glass cabinets containing jewellery, knives with reindeer-horn handles, cultural artefacts and clothes.

She stops in front of a display featuring a bridal crown. This must be the one Åhlén meant. It's a beautiful piece of work, made of woven birch-root, with points that look like the fingers of two interlaced hands.

Saga looks at the small lock on the case, sees that it would be easy to pick, but the cabinet is alarmed and there's a risk that a guard would arrive before she had time to look at the crown.

An elderly woman stops next to her and says something in Italian to a man pushing a stroller a short distance away.

The man speaks to the guard and is helped towards the lifts. A girl with straight fair hair is looking at the ceremonial Sámi costumes.

There's a crackle of velcro as Saga pulls out her tiny dagger for hand-to-hand fighting from its sheath below her left armpit. She carefully slides the tip in next to the lock on the glass door, and jerks it. The door shatters and the splinters fall to the floor as an alarm goes off.

The girl looks at Saga in astonishment as she calmly puts the knife away, opens the door and removes the bridal crown.

It looks smaller outside the case, and weighs practically nothing. Saga stares at it as the alarm blares.

Åhlén told her that Summa's mother had woven the crown for her own wedding, and that Summa had worn it for hers, and then donated it to the museum of handicrafts in Luleå.

Saga sees the guard hurrying back, and carefully turns the crown over in her hands, looks inside it and sees that someone has burned the name 'Nattavaara 1968' into it with a brand. She puts the crown back in the case and closes the shattered door.

She knew there was some sort of family connection to Nattavaara, and assumes that that's where Joona is at the moment.

Saga feels her heart swell at the thought of being able to tell Joona Linna that it's all over.

The guard's cheeks are flushed as he stops five metres away and points at her with his radio without managing to get a word out.

22

The train pulls out of Stockholm Central Station, rocking noisily across the points as it rolls away from the dirty sidings. To the left, big white boats are gliding along on Karlbergssjön, while to the right is a concrete wall covered in badly painted-over graffiti.

Seeing as the bunks were all booked, Saga has had to take an ordinary seat. She shows her ticket to the conductor, then eats a sandwich with her eyes fixed outside the window. As the train passes Uppsala she takes off her military boots, folds her jacket around her pistol and uses that as a pillow.

The train journey to Nattavaara, over a thousand kilometres away, will take almost twelve hours.

The train rumbles on through the night. Lights pass by outside like tiny stars, fewer and fewer the further north they get. Warm air streams from the scorching-hot radiator by the panel beside her seat.

In the end the night outside the window is nothing but solid darkness.

She closes her eyes and thinks about what Nils Åhlén told her. When Joona and his partner Samuel Mendel caught Jurek Walter many years ago, Jurek announced his plan for revenge before he was isolated in the secure unit at the Löwenströmska Hospital. Samuel thought it was an empty threat, but somehow Jurek managed to reach out from his cell and snatch Samuel's wife and two sons.

Joona realised the threat was serious. With Nils Åhlén's help, he arranged for his wife and little daughter to die in a car accident. Summa and Lumi were given new identities and had no further contact with Joona. As long as Jurek was alive, there was a risk that his threat might be put into practice. In hindsight, Joona saved them from a terrible death by sacrificing their life together.

But Saga can reassure Joona now. She's going to find him and reassure him. Jurek Walter is dead, his remains have been found and identified.

At the thought of that, an almost erotic shiver runs through her body. She leans back in her seat, shuts her eyes, and falls asleep.

For the first time in ages, she sleeps properly.

When she wakes up the train is standing still and chill morning air is streaming into the carriage. She sits up and sees that she is now in Boden. She has been asleep for almost ten hours, and needs to change trains for the last part of the journey to Nattavaara.

She stretches, puts her boots on, tucks her gun in its holster, picks up her jacket and gets off the train. She buys a large cup of coffee at the station, then returns to the platform. She watches a group of young men in military fatigues and green berets getting on to a train heading in the other direction.

Someone has smeared chewing tobacco on the glass of the station clock.

A black locomotive with red undercarriage approaches with a squeal of brakes. Rubbish blows across the sleepers. The train stops and wheezes slowly at the deserted platform. Saga is the only person who gets on the train to Gällivare, and she has the carriage to herself.

The journey to Nattavaara is supposed to take less than an hour. Saga drinks her coffee, goes to the toilet, washes her face, then sits in her seat and watches the landscape go past, vast stretches of forest with the occasional red cottage.

Her plan is to go to the village shop or parish hall and ask about people who have moved in recently – there can hardly be that many.

It's almost eleven o'clock in the morning when Saga Bauer steps on to the platform. The station is little more than a shack with a sign on its roof. In the weeds in front of the shack is a bench with peeling paint and rusting armrests.

Saga starts to walk along the road through the dark green, whispering forest. There's no sign of anyone, but occasionally she hears dogs barking.

The road surface is uneven and cracked from frost.

She carries on, over a bridge that stretches across the valley of the Pikku Venetjoki, then she hears the sound of an engine behind her. An old Volkswagen pickup is heading towards her, and she waves her arms to stop it.

A suntanned man in his seventies, wearing a grey sweater, winds down his window and nods in greeting. Beside him sits a woman the same age, in a padded green jerkin and pink-framed glasses.

'Hello,' Saga says. 'Do you live in Nattavaara?'

'We're just passing through,' he replies.

'We're from Sarvisvaara . . . another metropolis,' the woman says.

'Do you know where the grocery store is?'

'It closed last year,' the old man says, picking at the wheel. 'But we've got a new shop now.'

'That's good,' Saga smiles.

'It's not a shop,' the old woman says.

'I call it a shop,' he mutters.

'But that's wrong,' she says. 'It's a service point.'

'Then I'd better stop doing my shopping there,' he sighs.

'Where's the service point?' Saga asks.

'In the same building as the old shop,' the woman replies with a wink. 'Jump up on the back.'

'She's hardly a high-jumper,' the man retorts.

Saga climbs up on to the wheel, grabs hold of the edge of the pickup and swings herself over, then sits down with her back to the cab.

During the drive she hears the old couple carry on arguing, to the point where the pickup almost drives into the ditch. The bumper thuds and grit flies up under the vehicle, which is surrounded by a cloud of dust.

They drive into the village and stop in front of a large, red building with a sign for ice creams outside, along with symbols showing that the shop acts as an agent for the Post Office, the National Lottery, as well as a pickup point for prescriptions and supplies from the state-owned alcohol monopoly.

Saga clambers down, thanks the pair for the lift, and goes up the steps. A little bell on the door rings as she walks in.

She finds a bag of dill-flavoured crisps, then goes over to the young man at the counter.

'I'm looking for a friend who moved here just over a year ago,' she says without further elaboration.

'Here?' he asks, then looks at her for a while before lowering his eyes.

'A tall man . . . with his wife and daughter.'

'Ah,' he says, blushing.

'Do they still live here?'

'Just follow the Lompolovaara road,' he says, pointing. 'Up to the bend at Silmäjärvi . . .'

Saga leaves the shop and heads in the direction he indicated. Tractor-tyres have furrowed the ground and the verge is virtually non-existent. There's a beer can in the grass. The wind in the trees sounds like a distant sea.

She eats some of the crisps as she walks, then puts the rest in her bag and wipes her hands on her trousers.

Saga has walked six kilometres by the time she sees a rust-red house at a point where the road bends round a broad tarn. There's no car in sight, but there's smoke coming out of the chimney. The garden around the house consists of tall meadow grass.

She stops and hears the insects in the ditch.

A man comes out of the house. She watches his figure move through the trees.

It's Joona Linna.

It's him, but he's lost weight, and he's leaning on a stick. He's got a curly blond beard and strands of hair are sticking out from his black woolly hat.

Saga walks towards him. The grit crunches beneath her boots.

She sees Joona stop beside a woodshed, lean his stick against the wall, pick up an axe and split a large log, then he picks up another one and splits that, then rests for a moment before picking up the pieces and carries on chopping.

She doesn't call out because she knows he's already seen her, probably long before she saw him.

He's wearing a moss-green fleece beneath an aviator's jacket made of coarse leather. The folds have cracked and the sheepskin lining of the collar has turned yellow.

She walks over and stops five metres away from him. He stretches his back, turns round and looks at her with eyes as grey as pale fire.

'You shouldn't have come,' he says quietly.

'Jurek's dead,' she says breathlessly.

'Yes,' he replies, and goes on chopping.

He picks up a new log and places it on the chopping block.

'I found his body,' Saga says.

His swing goes wrong, the axe catches and he loses his grip. He stands for a while with his head lowered. Saga looks down into the large wood-basket and sees that there's a sawn-off shotgun taped to one side of it.

23

Joona leads her through a dark entrance hall. He doesn't say anything, but holds a door opens and ushers her into a little kitchen with copper saucepans on the walls.

An elk-hunting rifle with telescopic sights is hanging under the windowsill, and on the floor are at least thirty boxes of ammunition.

The sun is shining through the drawn curtains. On the table is a coffee pot and two cups.

'Summa died last spring,' he explains.

'I'm so sorry,' she says quietly.

He puts the wood-basket down on the floor and slowly straightens his back. There's a faint smell of smoke in the kitchen, and she can hear the pine logs crackling behind the closed hatch of the iron stove.

'So you found the body?' he says, looking at her.

'I wouldn't have come otherwise,' she replies seriously. 'Call Åhlén if you want confirmation.'

'I believe you,' he says.

'Call him anyway.'

He shakes his head but doesn't say anything, then, leaning on the draining board, he makes his way to the other door, nudges it open and says something quietly into the gloom in Finnish.

'This is my daughter, Lumi,' Joona says as a girl comes into the kitchen.

'Hello,' Saga says.

Lumi has straight brown hair, a friendly, curious smile, but her eyes are as grey as ice. She's tall and thin, dressed in a simple blue cotton shirt and a pair of faded jeans.

'Are you hungry?' Joona asks.

'Yes,' Saga replies.

'Sit yourself down.'

She sits down on a chair and Joona gets out bread, butter and cheese, then starts chopping tomatoes, olives and peppers. Lumi heats some water and grinds coffee beans in a manually operated mill. Saga looks at the dimly lit room behind them, and sees a sofa and a stack of books on a table. Hanging from a drip-stand is a night-vision sight and a mount allowing it to be attached to a rifle for nocturnal hunting.

'Where was he?' Joona asks.

'He drifted ashore on Högmarsö,' Saga replies.

'Who?' Lumi asks, glancing at the control panel for some twenty motion detectors that's attached to the wall beneath the spice-rack.

'Jurek Walter,' Joona says, cracking twelve eggs into the frying pan.

'I've found his body,' Saga says.

'So he's dead?' she asks lightly.

'Lumi, can you take over for a minute?' Joona says, then leaves the kitchen.

His heavy steps echo through the hall, then the front door closes. Lumi gets some dried basil and rubs it between her palms.

'Dad says he had to leave me and Mum,' Lumi says, trying to keep her voice steady. 'He says Jurek Walter would have killed us if we'd had any contact with him at all.'

'He did the right thing, he saved your lives, there was no other way,' Saga says.

Lumi nods and turns towards the stove. A few tears drip on to the black metal range in front of her.

Lumi wipes her face, lowers the heat, and then carefully turns the omelette with a spatula.

Through the closed curtains Saga can see Joona standing out on the road with a phone pressed to his ear. She knows he's talking to Nils Åhlén. He's frowning, and his jaw muscles are tense.

Lumi turns the stove off and lays the table as she looks at Saga curiously.

'I know you're not going out with Dad,' the girl says after a while. 'He's told me about Disa.'

'We used to work together.' Saga smiles.

'You don't look like a police officer,' the girl says.

'Security Police,' Saga says curtly.

'You don't look like one of them either,' she laughs, sitting down opposite Saga. 'But if you say you're from the Security Police, then you must be Saga Bauer.'

'Yes.'

'Dig in,' Lumi says. 'It'll get cold.'

Saga thanks her, helps herself to some omelette, bread and cheese, and pours coffee for the two of them.

'How is Joona?' she asks.

'Yesterday I'd probably have said not good,' Lumi says. 'He's freezing most of the time and hardly sleeps, he keeps watch over me, makes himself stay awake . . . I don't know how he manages it.'

'He's very stubborn,' Saga says.

'Is he?'

They laugh.

'You know, I didn't have my dad for so many years,' the girl says, and her eyes grow moist. 'I barely remembered him. I mean, nothing can make up for that, but . . . we've spent more than a year sitting and talking . . . every day, for hours . . . I've told him about me and Mum, what we did and how we were . . . and he's talked about himself . . . There can't be many people who've talked so much with their dad.'

'Not me, that's for certain,' Saga says.

Lumi stands up when a motion sensor reacts to Joona's approach. She switches the alarm off and then they hear the front door open, followed by footsteps in the hall.

Joona comes into the kitchen, puts his stick down, leans against the table, then sinks on to a chair.

'Åhlén is certain,' he says, helping himself to some food.

'We're quits now,' Saga says, looking him in the eye. 'I don't care what you think, but we're quits . . . I killed him, and I found the body.'

'You've never owed me anything.'

Joona is leaning forward slightly, with his arms wrapped round his body, taking small mouthfuls of food. Lumi puts a thick blanket round his shoulders, then sits back down.

'Lumi's going to study in Paris,' Joona says, smiling at his daughter.

'We don't know that,' she says quickly.

A smile flits across her pale face. Saga sees Joona's hands shake as he picks up his cup and drinks some coffee.

'I'm cooking venison fillet tonight,' he says.

'My train back leaves in two hours,' Saga says.

'With chanterelles and cream,' he adds.

She smiles. 'I have to go.'

24

Erik is early for his piano lesson, and stands on the pavement opposite the door to Lill-Jans plan 4. The curtains on the ground floor are open, and he can see straight into Jackie Federer's flat. She's in the kitchen, she runs her hand along the wall-mounted cupboards, takes out a glass, then holds her finger under the tap. He can see that she's wearing a black skirt and an unbuttoned blouse. He walks across the street to see better, gets closer to the window and can now see that her wet hair has dripped down the back of her silk blouse. She drinks the water, wipes her mouth with her hand, then turns round.

Erik stretches and catches a glimpse of her stomach and navel through the opening of her unbuttoned shirt. A woman with a pushchair stops on the pavement and stares at him, and he suddenly realises how he must look. He hurries to reach the pavement and goes in through the entrance. Once again he stands in the darkness outside the door of her flat and moves his finger towards the bell.

Since the hypnosis session he has been thinking that Rocky's alibi may well have been genuine, and has had to double his nightly dose of Stilnoct in order to get any sleep. The earliest he has been able to book a visit to Karsudden Hospital is first thing tomorrow morning.

When Jackie opens the door her blouse is buttoned. She smiles calmly at him and the light in the stairwell reflects off her dark glasses.

'I'm a bit early,' he says.

'Erik,' she smiles. 'Welcome.'

They go inside and he sees that her daughter has pinned up a drawing of a skull under the no entry sign.

He follows Jackie along the passageway, watching her right hand trace the wall, and it strikes him that she seems to move with no obvious caution. Her shiny blouse is hanging outside her black skirt, across the small of her back.

As her hand reaches the door frame she switches the light on and heads out across the living-room floor until she comes to the rug, where she stops and turns towards him.

'Let's hear how far you've got,' Jackie says, and gestures to the piano.

He sits down, opens the score and brushes his fringe from his forehead. He puts his right thumb on the right key and spreads his fingers.

'Opus 25,' he says with jokey solemnity.

He starts to play the notes that Jackie set him for homework. Even though she's told him not to, he can't help looking at his hands the whole time.

'It must be awful for you to have to listen to this,' he says. 'I mean, if you're used to beautiful music.'

'I think you've been very good,' she replies.

'Can you get music scores in braille – you must be able to?' he asks.

'Louis Braille was a musician, so that happened fairly naturally . . . but in the end you have to memorise everything anyway, because of course you need both hands when you're playing,' she explains.

He puts his fingers on the keys and takes a deep breath, then the doorbell rings.

'Sorry, I'll just get that,' Jackie says, and stands up.

Erik watches her go out into the hall and open the door. Outside stands her daughter, next to a tall woman in gym clothes.

'How was the match?' Jackie asks.

'One-one,' the girl replies. 'Anna scored our goal.'

'But it was your pass,' the woman says kindly.

'Thanks for bringing Maddy home,' Jackie says.

'My pleasure . . . on the way we talked about not having to be the best in the world, but that maybe she could be a bit pushier.'

Erik doesn't hear Jackie's reply, but the door closes and then Jackie kneels down in front of her daughter and feels her hair and face gently.

'So you're going to have to be a bit pushier,' she says softly.

She returns to Erik, apologises for the interruption, sits down and explains what he should do next.

Erik struggles to get his hands to work independently of each other, and feels his back start to sweat.

After a while the little girl comes into the room. She's changed into a casual dress and sits down on the floor to listen.

Erik tries to play the section, but gets the fourth bar wrong, starts again, but makes the same mistake, and laughs at his own failure.

'What's so funny?' Jackie asks calmly.

'Just that I'm playing like a broken robot,' Erik replies.

'My hedgehog makes mistakes as well,' Madeleine says consolingly, holding up her stuffed toy.

'My left hand is the worst,' Erik says. 'It's as if my fingers don't want to hit the right bits.'

Madeleine blinks but manages to keep a straight face.

'Keys, I mean,' Erik says quickly. 'Maybe your hedgehog says "bits", but I say keys.'

The girl looks down with a broad grin. Jackie gets up from her chair.

'You need to rest,' she says. 'We'll run through the first bit of musical theory before we end the lesson.'

'I'll go and put the dishwasher on,' the girl says.

'You know it's bedtime soon – you'll have to make sure you've got time.'

They sit down at the table. Erik picks up the jug and pours two glasses of water. It feels impossible not to sneak glances at Jackie as she explains about G-clef, F-clef, and different overtones. Her blouse is creased at the waist, and her face looks thoughtful. He can make out her simple bra and breasts beneath the silk.

He feels a nervous temptation in being able to look at her without her knowing.

He carefully shifts position so he can see up between her thighs and catch a glimpse of her plain white underwear.

His heart beats faster as she parts her legs slightly, he has a feeling that she knows she's being looked at.

She takes a sip of water.

Her open eyes are only just visible behind her dark glasses.

He looks between her thighs again, leans a little closer, but the next moment she crosses her legs and puts the glass down.

Jackie smiles and then says that she imagines that he works as a lecturer at the university, or as a priest. Erik replies that the truth is somewhere in between, and tells her about his work at the Psychology Clinic, and his research into hypnosis, then falls silent.

She gathers together the various sheets of music theory, taps them on the table to neaten them, then puts them down in front of him.

'Can I ask you something?' Erik asks.

'Yes,' she says simply.

'You turn your face towards me when you talk – does that come naturally, or do you have to learn that?'

'It's a concession to what sighted people find pleasant,' she answers honestly.

'That's what I thought,' Erik says.

'Like switching the light on when you enter a room to alert sighted people that you're there . . .'

She falls silent and her slender fingers trace the rim of her glass.

'Sorry, I'm being horribly rude and embarrassing, asking about such things . . .'

'Most people prefer not to talk about their impaired vision. Which I can understand,' Jackie says. 'We'd all rather be seen as individuals and all that . . . but I think it's better to talk.'

'Good.'

He looks at her soft pink lipstick, the curve of her cheekbones, her boyish haircut and the green-tinted vein pulsing in her neck.

'Isn't it odd, being able to hypnotise other people and see into their secret, private thoughts?' she asks.

'It's not like I'm spying on them.'

'Isn't it?'

25

The bright sky is reflected in the cellophane covering the carton of ten packets of cigarettes on the seat beside Erik as he slowly drives into the area of parkland, past a sign saying that access is prohibited and that all visits must be announced in advance.

Karsudden District Hospital is the largest secure psychiatric facility in Sweden, with room for one hundred and thirty criminals who have been sentenced to treatment rather than prison as a result of mental illness.

His stomach is churning with anxiety. Soon he will be seeing Rocky Kyrklund, to ask him about his supposed alibi.

If it is genuine, then the latest murder could be connected to the old one, and Erik will have to tell the police everything.

Because if Rocky was innocent, there may well be parallels between the old murder and the new one. And it would be no coincidence that Susanna Kern was found with her hand strapped to her ear.

It's not inevitable that I'll lose my job, he tells himself. That will depend on whether the police decide to pass the case on to a prosecutor.

In front of the entrance to the administrative block is a sign showing a camera with a line across it. Yet at the same time this place is full of surveillance cameras, Erik thinks.

He picks up the cigarettes and starts to walk towards the white building.

A snail's trail shimmers across the path in front of the reception area.

In the sharp sunlight inside the doors, the dust is clearly visible as it drifts towards the battered furniture and worn floor.

Erik shows his ID, is given a name badge, and gets no further than the magazine rack next to the waiting area before a man with blond highlights in his hair comes in.

'Erik Bark?'

'Yes,' Erik replies.

The man stretches his lips into a semblance of a smile, and introduces himself as Otto. There's something exhausted about the man's face, a sadness that's impossible to hide.

'Casillas would have liked to have been here himself, but . . .'

'I understand, don't worry,' Erik says, and feels his face flush as he thinks of his lies about Dr Stünkel and the research project.

They set off, and the man explains that he's a care assistant, and has worked at Karsudden for years.

'We'll go the long way round . . . no one likes the tunnels,' Otto mutters as they head outside.

'Do you know Rocky Kyrklund?' Erik asks.

'He was here when I started,' Otto says, gesturing towards the high fences and dismal brown buildings.

'What do you make of him?'

'A lot of people are a bit frightened of Kyrklund,' he replies.

They go in through Entrance D, and over to a locker room where Erik has to leave any loose possessions.

'Can I take the cigarettes with me?' Erik asks.

Otto nods. 'They'll probably come in useful.'

The orderly puts Erik's keys, pen, mobile and wallet in a plastic bag, seals it and hands him a receipt.

Then he unlocks a heavy door that leads to another door with a coded lock. They pass through and walk down a corridor with a grey linoleum floor and secure doors leading to small rooms with beds in them.

The air is heavy with disinfectant and stale cigarette smoke.

From one room comes the sound of a porn film. The door is open and Erik sees a fat man lean forward on a plastic chair and spit on the floor.

They go through another airlock and find themselves in a shadowy exercise yard. Six-metre-high fences link two brick buildings, forming a cage around a yellowing patch of grass edged with cinder paths.

A skinny man in his twenties is sitting on a park bench, his face tense. Two carers are talking over by one of the brick walls, and at the far end a thickset man is standing facing the fence.

'Do you want me to come with you?' Otto asks.

'No need.'

The former priest is standing smoking as he faces the high fence. His eyes are roaming across the grass of the parkland towards the leafy trees. By his feet is a mug of instant coffee.

Erik walks along the path, which is littered with cigarette butts and discarded plugs of chewing tobacco.

I'm about to meet the priest I let down because I'd already judged him, he thinks. If Rocky Kyrklund does have an alibi, I'm going to confess what I did to the police, and take the consequences.

Dust from the path swirls around his legs, and he knows Rocky can hear him approaching.

'Rocky?' he says.

'Who wants to know?'

'My name is Erik Maria Bark.'

Rocky lets go of the fence and turns round. He's tall, one metre ninety. His shoulders are even broader than Erik remembers, he's got a full beard, specked with grey, and back-combed hair. His eyes are green, and his face radiates a chilly pride. He's wearing a pilled, camouflage-green sweater with worn elbows. His sturdy arms are hanging by his sides, a cigarette clasped between his fingers.

'The senior consultant said you liked Camels,' Erik says, and attempts to give him the cigarettes.

Rocky juts his chin out and looks down at him. He doesn't reply, and shows no sign of accepting the gift.

'I don't know if you remember me,' Erik says. 'I was involved in your trial nine years ago, I was part of the group that conducted the psychological assessment.'

'What conclusion did you reach?' Rocky says in a dark voice.

'That you needed neurological and psychiatric treatment,' Erik replies calmly.

Rocky flicks his glowing cigarette at Erik. It hits him in the chest and falls to the ground. A few sparks fly out.

'Go in peace,' Rocky says calmly, then purses his lips.

Erik stubs the cigarette out and sees that two carers are approaching across the grass, carrying an alarm.

'What's going on here?' one of them asks as they stop.

'It was an accident,' Erik says.

The men stay for a few moments, but neither Erik nor Rocky say anything. In the end the guards go back to their coffee.

'You lied to them,' Rocky says.

'I do that sometimes,' Erik replies.

Rocky's face remains impassive, but there's a flicker of interest in his eyes now.

'Have you received neurological and psychiatric treatment?' Erik asks. 'You have a right to it. I'm a doctor, do you want me to look at your notes and rehabilitation plan?'

Rocky shakes his head slowly.

'You've been here for a long time, but have never applied for parole.'

'Why would I do that?'

'Don't you want to get out?'

'I accept my punishment,' Rocky says in his deep voice.

'You had trouble remembering back then – is that still the case?' Erik asks.

'Yes.'

'But I remember our conversations, and sometimes it sounded like you thought you were innocent of the murder.'

'Naturally . . . I surrounded myself with lies in an attempt to escape, they crawled all over me like a swarm of bees, and I tried to avoid responsibility by blaming someone else.'

'Who?'

'That doesn't matter . . . I was guilty, but I let the lies crawl all over me.'

Erik bends over and puts the cigarettes down at Rocky's feet, then takes a step back.

'Do you want to talk about the person you wanted to blame?' he asks.

'I don't remember, but I know I thought of him as a preacher, an unclean preacher . . .'

The priest falls silent and turns back towards the fence. Erik goes and stands next to him and looks out at the trees.

'What was his name?'

'I can't remember names any more, I don't remember their faces, scattered like ashes . . .'

'You called him a preacher – was he a colleague of yours?'

Rocky's fingers clutch the fence and his chest rises and falls as he breathes.

'I only remember that I was scared, that was probably why I tried to blame him.'

'You were scared of him?' Erik asks. 'What had he done? Why were you . . .'

'Rocky? Rocky!' says a patient who has walked up behind them. 'Look what I've got for you!'

They turn round and see the skinny man holding out a jam biscuit in a napkin.

'Eat it yourself,' Rocky says.

'I don't want to,' the other inmate says eagerly. 'I'm a sinner, God and His angels hate me, and—'

'Shut up!' Rocky roars.

'What have I done? Why are you—'

Rocky takes hold of the man by the chin, looks him in the eyes, then spits in his face. The man loses his balance when Rocky lets go, and the biscuit falls to the ground.

The guards approach across the grass again.

'What if someone came forward and gave you an alibi?' Erik says quickly.

Rocky's green eyes stare into his without blinking.

'Then they'd be lying.'

'Are you sure about that? You don't remember anything from—'

'I don't remember an alibi, because there wasn't one,' Rocky interrupts.

'But you do remember your colleague – what if he was the one who murdered Rebecka?'

'I murdered Rebecka Hansson,' Rocky says.

'Do you remember that?'

'Yes.'

'Do you know anyone called Olivia?'

Rocky shakes his head, then looks towards the approaching guards and raises his chin.

'Before you ended up here?'

'No.'

The guards push Rocky up against the fence, hit the backs of his knees, force him to the ground and put handcuffs on him.

'Look out for him!' the other patient cries.

The larger of the guards puts his knee on Rocky's back while the other one holds his baton to his throat.

'Look out for him . . .' the other patient sobs.

As Erik follows one of the guards away from Ward D, he starts to smile to himself. There is no alibi. Rocky killed Rebecka Hansson, and there's no connection between the murders.

Out in the car park he stops and takes several deep breaths as he looks up past the trees in the park at the bright sky. A feeling of liberation is spreading through his body, as a longstanding burden is lifted from his shoulders.

26

Nils Åhlén, professor of forensic medicine, pulls in and parks his white Jaguar across two parking spaces.

The National Criminal Investigation Department want him to take a look at two homicides.

Both bodies have already been through post-mortems. Åhlén has read the reports. They're beyond reproach, far more thorough than is strictly necessary. Even so, the head of the preliminary investigation has asked him to take a second look at both bodies. They're still fumbling in the dark, and want him to try to identify any subtle similarities, signatures or messages.

Margot Silverman believes she's dealing with a narcissistic serial killer, and thinks the murderer is trying to communicate.

Åhlén leaves his car and breathes in the morning air. There's almost no wind today, the sun is shining and the blue blinds have been lowered in all the windows.

There's something next to the entrance. At first Nils Åhlén thinks someone's dumped rubbish behind the railing of the little concrete steps, but then he sees that it's a human being. A bearded man is asleep on the tarmac, with his back leaning against the cement foundations of the brick wall. He's wrapped in a blanket, and his forehead is resting against his tucked-up knees.

It's a warm morning, and Åhlén hopes the man is left to sleep in peace before the security guards find him. He adjusts his aviator's sunglasses and walks towards the door, but stops when he notices the man's clean hands and the white scar running across his right knuckles.

'Joona?' he asks gently.

Joona Linna raises his head and looks at him, as though he wasn't asleep, just waiting to be addressed.

Åhlén stares at his old friend. Joona is almost unrecognisable. He's lost a lot of weight, and is sporting a thick, fair beard. His pale face is grey, with dark rings under his eyes, and his hair is long and messy.

'I want to see the finger,' he says.

'I might have guessed.' Åhlén smiles. 'How are you? You look OK.'

Joona takes hold of the railings and pulls himself up heavily, then picks up his bag and stick. He knows how he looks, but he can't help it, he's still grieving.

'Did you fly or drive down?' Åhlén asks.

Joona peers at the lamp above the door. At the bottom of the glass under the bulb is a small heap of dead insects.

After Saga's visit, Joona went with his daughter Lumi to visit Summa's grave in Purnu. Then they walked down to the little sandy beach at Autiojärvi and talked about the future.

He knew what she wanted to do, without her having to say anything.

In order for Lumi not to lose her place at the Paris College of Art, she had to be there to enrol in two days' time. Joona arranged for her to live with his friend Corinne Meilleroux's sister in the eighth arrondissement. They didn't have time to make too many other arrangements, but he gave Lumi enough money to get by.

And a whole load of useful tips about close combat and automatic weapons, she joked.

He drove her to the airport, and it took a real effort not to go to pieces. She gave him a hug and whispered that she loved him.

'Or did you catch the train?' Åhlén asks patiently.

He returned to the house in Nattavaara, dismantled the alarm system, locked the weapons in the cellar, and packed a rucksack. Once he'd turned the water off and shut the house up, he walked to the railway station and caught the train to Gällivare, made his way to the airport and flew to Arlanda, then caught the bus in to Stockholm. He covered the last five kilometres to the campus of the Karolinska Institute on foot.

'I walked,' he replies, without noticing the look of surprise on Åhlén's face.

Joona waits, with one hand on the black iron railings as Åhlén unlocks the blue door. They walk together along the corridor with its muted colours and worn floor.

Joona can't walk quickly with his stick, and has to stop and cough several times.

They pass the door to the toilets and are approaching a window containing a large pot plant that seems to consist mainly of roots. Dandelion seeds are drifting through the air in the sunshine outside. Something moves unexpectedly out there. Joona's instinct is to duck down and draw his gun, but he forces himself to walk over to the window instead. An old woman is standing on the pavement, waiting for a dog that's running back and forth among the dandelions.

'How are you?' Åhlén asks.

'I don't know.'

Joona's body is trembling, and he goes into the toilet, leans over the basin and drinks some water straight from the tap. He straightens up and dries his face with a paper towel, then goes back out into the corridor.

'Joona, I've got the finger in the locked cabinet in the pathology lab, but . . . I'm meeting Margot Silverman in half an hour . . . You can wait in my room instead if you don't feel up to it—'

'It doesn't matter,' Joona interrupts.

27

Nils Åhlén opens the swing-door to the pathology lab, and holds it open for Joona. Together they walk into the bright room with its shimmering white tiles. Joona puts his rucksack down by the wall next to the door, but keeps the blanket round his shoulders.

A cloying stench of decay lingers over the room in spite of the whirring fans. There are two bodies on the post-mortem tables. The more recent one is covered, and blood is slowly trickling down the stainless steel gutter.

They go over to the desk with the computer. Joona waits quietly as Åhlén unlocks a heavy door.

'Sit down,' he says as he puts the glass jar on the table.

He pulls a folder out of a box, opens it and places the test results from the National Forensics Lab, the old ID documents, the fingerprint analysis and enlargements of the images from Saga's phone in front of Joona.

Joona sits down and stares at the jar. After a few seconds he picks it up, holds it up to the light, examines it closely, and nods.

'I've kept everything here because I had a feeling you'd show up,' Åhlén says. 'But, like I said on the phone, you'll see that it all checks out. The old man who found the body cut the finger off, as you can see from the angle of the cut . . . and that happened long after death, just as he explained to Saga.'

Joona carefully reads the report from the laboratory. They had built up a DNA profile based on thirty STR regions. The match was one hundred per cent, thus confirming the results of the fingerprint analysis.

Not even identical twins have the same fingerprints.

Joona lays out the photographs of the mutilated body in front of him and examines the violet-coloured entry-wounds.

He leans back and closes his burning eyelids.

Everything checks out.

The angles of the shots are just as Saga described. The size and constitution of the body, the size of the hand, the DNA, the fingerprint . . .

'It's him,' Åhlén says quietly.

'Yes,' Joona whispers.

'What are you going to do now?' Åhlén asks.

'Nothing.'

'You've been declared dead,' Åhlén says. 'There was a witness to your suicide, a homeless man who—'

'Yes, yes,' Joona interrupts. 'I'll sort it out.'

'Your flat was sold when your estate was wound up,' Åhlén explains. 'They got almost seven million for it, the money went to charity.'

'Good,' Joona says bluntly.

'How has Lumi taken everything?'

Joona looks over at the window, watching the slanting light and the shadows of the dirt on the glass.

'Lumi? She's gone to Paris,' he replies.

'I mean, how did she deal with you coming back after so many years, how has she dealt with the loss of her mother, and . . .'

Joona stops listening to Åhlén as memories spread out inside him. More than a year ago he made his way in secret to Finland. He thinks about the afternoon when he arrived at the gloomy Radiotherapy and Cancer Clinic in Helsinki to fetch Summa. She could still walk with a Zimmer frame at the time. He can remember exactly how the light fell in the foyer, reflecting off the floor, the windows and pale wood-work, as well as the row of wheelchairs. They walked slowly past the unstaffed cloakroom and the confectionery machine and emerged into the fresh winter air.

Åhlén's phone buzzes, and he pushes his sunglasses up onto his nose and reads the text message.

'Margot's here, I'll go and let her in,' he says, and heads towards the door.

Summa had chosen to have palliative care in her flat on Elisabetsgatan, but Joona took her and Lumi to her grandmother's house in Nattavaara, where they had six happy months together. After the years of chemotherapy, radiation, cortisone and blood transfusions, all that was left was pain relief. She had morphine patches that lasted for three days, and took another 80 milligrams of OxyNorm every day.

Summa loved the house and the countryside around it, the air and light that streamed into the bedroom. Her family was together at last. She grew thinner, lost her appetite, lost all the hair on her body, and her skin became as soft as a baby's.

Towards the end she weighed almost nothing, her whole body hurt, but she still liked it when Joona carried her round, and sat her on his lap so they could kiss.

28

Joona sits motionless, staring at the glass jar containing the amputated finger. The particles in the liquid have sunk to the bottom.

He really is dead.

Joona smiles to himself as he repeats the sentence in his head.

Jurek Walter is dead.

He disappears into recollections of his staged suicide, and is still sitting there with the blanket round his shoulders when Margot Silverman and Nils Åhlén come into the pathology lab.

'Joona Linna. Everyone said you were dead,' Margot says with a smile. 'Can I ask what the hell actually happened?'

Joona meets her gaze, and thinks that he was forced to do what he did, he was forced to take every step he had taken over the past fourteen years.

Margot stands still, staring into Joona's eyes, into their greyness, as she hears Åhlén remove the protective covering from his sterilised tools.

'I came back,' Joona replies in a deep Finnish accent.

'A bit too late,' Margot says. 'I've already got your job and your room.'

'You're a good detective,' he replies.

'Not good enough, according to Åhlén,' she says breezily.

'I just said you ought to let Joona look at the case,' Åhlén mutters, stretching the latex gloves before putting them on.

While Åhlén begins his external inspection of Maria Carlsson's body, Margot tries to explain the case to Joona. She recounts all the details about the tights and the quality of the film, but doesn't get the response or the follow-up questions she had been expecting, and after a while she starts to worry that he might not even be listening.

'According to the victim's calendar, she was about to go off to a drawing class,' Margot says, glancing at Joona. 'We've checked, and it's true enough, but there's a small "h" at the bottom of the page of the calendar that we don't understand.'

The legendary superintendent has aged. His blond beard is thick and his matted hair is hanging down over his ears, and curling at the back of his neck, over the padded collar of his jacket.

'The films suggest narcissism, obviously,' she goes on, sitting down on a stainless steel stool with her legs wide apart.

Joona is thinking about the perpetrator watching the woman through the window. He can come as close as he wants, but there's still a pane of glass between them. It's intimate, but he's still shut out.

'He wants to communicate something,' Margot says. 'He wants to make a point . . . or compete, match his strength against the police, because he feels so damn strong and smart while the police are still miles behind him . . . And that feeling of invincibility is going to lead to more murders.'

Joona looks over at the first victim, and his eye is caught by her white hand, resting beside her hip, cupped like a small bowl, like a mussel-shell.

He stands up with some effort, with the help of his stick, thinking that something attracted the perpetrator to Maria Carlsson, made him cross his boundary as an observer.

'And that's why,' Margot goes on. 'That strong sense of superiority is why I think there could be some sort of signature, that we haven't seen . . .'

She falls silent when Joona walks away from her, heading towards the post-mortem table with weary steps. He stops in front of the body and leans on his stick. His heavy leather aviator's jacket is open, its sheepskin lining visible. As he leans over the body, his holster and Colt Combat come into view.

She stands up, and feels the child in her belly has woken up. It falls asleep when she moves about, and wakes up if she sits or lies down. She holds one hand to her stomach as she walks over to Joona.

He's looking closely at the victim's ravaged face. It's like he doesn't believe she's dead, as if he wanted to feel her moist breath against his mouth.

'What are you thinking?' Margot asks.

'Sometimes I think that our idea of justice is still in its infancy,' Joona replies, without taking his eyes from the dead woman.

'OK,' she says.

'So what does that make the law?' he asks.

'I could give you an answer, but I'm guessing you have a different one in mind.'

Joona straightens up, thinking that the law chases justice the way Lumi used to chase spots of reflected light when she was little.

Åhlén follows the original post-mortem as he conducts his own. The usual purpose of an external examination is to describe visible injuries, such as swellings, discolouration, scraped skin, bleeding, scratches and cuts. But this time he is searching for something that could have been overlooked between two observations, something beyond the obvious.

'Most of the stab-wounds aren't fatal, and that wasn't the point of them either,' Åhlén says to Margot and Joona. 'If it was, they wouldn't have been aimed at her face.'

'Hatred is stronger than the desire to kill,' Margot says.

'He wanted to destroy her face,' Åhlén nods.

'Or change it,' Margot says.

'Why is her mouth gaping like that?' Joona asks quietly.

'Her jaw is broken,' Åhlén says. 'There are traces of her own saliva on her fingers.'

'Was there anything in her mouth or throat?' Joona asks.

'Nothing.'

Joona is thinking about the perpetrator standing outside filming her as she puts on her tights. At that point he is an observer who needs, or at least accepts, the boundary presented by the thin glass of the window.

But something lures him over that boundary, he repeats to himself, as he borrows Åhlén's thin torch. He shines it into the dead woman's mouth. Her saliva has dried up and her throat is pale grey. There's no sign of anything in her throat, her tongue has retracted, and the inside of her cheeks are dark.

In the middle of her tongue, at its thickest part, is a tiny hole from a piece of jewellery. It could almost be part of the natural fold of the tongue, but Joona is sure her tongue was pierced.

He goes over and looks at the first report, and reads the description of the mouth and stomach.

'What are you looking for?' Åhlén asks.

The only notes under points 22 and 23 are the injuries to the lips, teeth and gums, and at point 62 it says that the tongue and hyoid bone are undamaged. But there's no mention of the hole.

Joona carries on reading, but there's no mention of any item of jewellery being found in the stomach or gut.

'I want to see the film,' he says.

'It's already been examined tens of thousands of times,' Margot says.

Leaning heavily on his stick, Joona raises his face, and his grey eyes are now as dark as thunderclouds.

29

Margot signs Joona in as her guest at the reception of the National Criminal Investigation Department, and he has to put on a visitor's badge before they pass through the security doors.

'There are bound to be loads of people wanting to see you,' Margot says as they walk towards the lifts.

'I haven't got time,' he says, taking his badge off and throwing it in a waste-paper bin.

'It's probably a good idea to prepare yourself for shaking a few hands – can you manage that?'

Joona thinks of the mines he laid out behind the house in Nattavaara. He made the ANNM out of ammonium nitrate and nitromethane, so that he had a stable secondary explosive substance. He had already armed two mines with three grams of pentaerythritol tetranitrate as a detonator, and was on his way back to the outhouse to make the third detonator when the entire bag of PETN exploded. The heavy door was blown off, and knocked his right leg out of its socket.

The pain had been like a flock of black birds, heavy jackdaws landing on his body and covering the ground where he lay. They rose again, as though they'd been blown away, when Lumi ran over to him and held his hand in hers.

'At least I've still got my hands,' he says as they pass a group of sofa and armchairs.

'That makes it easier.'

Margot holds the lift door open and waits for him to catch up.

'I don't know what you think you're going to see on the video,' she says.

'No,' he says, and follows her in.

'I mean, you seem pretty bloody weird,' she smiles, 'but I almost think I like that.'

When they emerge from the lift the corridor is already full of their colleagues. Everyone comes out of their rooms, leaving a passageway open between them.

Joona doesn't look anyone in the eye, doesn't smile back at anyone, and doesn't answer anyone. He knows what he looks like. His beard is long and his hair scruffy, he's limping and leaning on his stick, and he can't stand up straight.

No one seems to know how to handle his return; they want to see him, but they mostly seem rather shy.

Someone's holding a bundle of papers, someone else a mug of coffee. These are people he saw every day for many years. He walks past Benny Rubin, who's standing eating a banana with a neutral expression on his face.

'I'll go as soon as I've seen the film,' Joona tells Margot as he carries on past the doorway of his old room.

'We're working in room twenty-two,' Margot says, pointing along the corridor.

Joona stops to catch his breath for a moment. His injured leg hurts and he presses the stick into the floor to give his body a break.

'Which rubbish tip did you find him on?' Petter Näslund says with a grin.

'Idiot,' Margot says.

The head of the National Criminal Police, Carlos Eliasson, comes towards Joona. His reading glasses are swinging on a chain round his neck.

'Joona,' he says warmly.

'Yes,' Joona replies.

They shake hands and patchy applause breaks out in the corridor.

'I didn't believe it when they said you were in the building,' Carlos says, unable to contain his smile. 'I mean . . . I can't really take it in.'

'I just want to look at something,' Joona says, and tries to walk on.

'Come and see me afterwards and we'll have a talk about the future.'

'What's there to say about that?' Joona says, and walks away.

His work there feels distant now, further away than his childhood. There's nothing for me to come back to, he thinks.

He wouldn't be here now if the first victim's hand hadn't been cupped like a little bowl by her hip.

That made a small spark begin to smoulder inside him.

Her slender fingers could have been Lumi's. A deep-seated curiosity woke up inside him, and he suddenly felt compelled to get closer to the body.

'We need you here,' Magdalena Ronander says as they shake hands.

It's no longer his job, but when he was confronted with the first victim, he felt a connection that he'd like to be able to control. Maybe he can give Margot a hand with the early stages, just until she can see a way through.

Joona stumbles as pain shoots down his leg, his shoulder hits the wall and he hears his leather jacket scrape against the rough wallpaper.

'I put a note on the intranet that you were going to be coming,' Margot says as they stop outside room 822.

Anja Larsson, his assistant for all those years, is standing in the doorway of her room. Her face is red. Her chin starts to quiver and tears well up in her eyes as he stops in front of her.

'I've missed you, Anja,' he says.

'Have you?'

Joona nods, and looks her in the eye. His pale grey eyes have a dull shimmer, as if he had a fever.

'Everyone said you were dead, that you'd . . . But I couldn't believe that . . . I didn't want to, I . . . I suppose I always thought you were too stubborn to die,' she smiles as tears run down her cheeks.

'It just wasn't my time,' he replies.

The corridor starts to empty as everyone returns to their rooms; they've already seen enough of the fallen hero.

'What do you look like?' Anja says, wiping her nose on the sleeve of her blouse.

'I know,' he says simply.

She pats his cheek.

'You'd better go, Joona. They're waiting for you.'

30

Joona enters the operations room and closes the door behind him. On the long wall is a huge map of Stockholm with the crime scenes marked on it. Next to the map pictures from the examination of the scenes have been stuck up: footprints, bodies, blood-spatter patterns. There's a large photograph of the porcelain deer's head, with its reddish-brown glazed fur and eyes like black onyx. Joona looks at the copy of Maria Carlsson's Filofax. The day she was murdered she had written 'class 19.00 – squared paper, pencils, ink', and underneath she had scribbled the letter 'h'.

On the other wall they've tried to map the victims' profiles. They've begun to identify family connections and other relationships. Their movements – workplaces, friends, supermarkets, gyms, classes, buses, cafés – have been marked with pins.

Adam Youssef stands up from his computer and walks over to Joona, shakes his hand, then pins a picture of a kitchen knife on the wall.

'It's just been confirmed that this knife was the murder weapon. Björn Kern washed it up and put it back in the drawer . . . but we had a number of stab-wounds through the sternum, so it was fairly easy to reconstruct the type of blade we were looking for . . . and it turned out that there were still tiny traces of blood on it.'

Youssef catches his breath, scratches his head hard a couple of times, then moves on to the enlargement of the deer's head.

'The porcelain figure is made of Meissen china,' he says, letting his finger linger over the animal's glistening black eye. 'But the rest of the deer wasn't at the crime scene . . . Björn Kern hasn't yet been able to give any sort of coherent statement, so we don't know if he was the one who put it in her hand . . .'

Joona stops and looks at the photograph of Maria Carlsson's body. The dead woman is sitting propped up against a radiator under a window, wearing a pair of tights.

He reads the report from the examination of the crime scene. There's no mention of any tongue-stud or similar item of jewellery being found in her home.

Adam shoots a questioning glance at Margot behind Joona's back.

'He wants to look at the film of Maria Carlsson,' she says.

'OK. What for?'

She smiles. 'We've missed something.'

'Probably,' he laughs, and scratches his neck.

'You can borrow my computer,' Margot says amiably.

Joona thanks her and sits down on her chair, adjusts the media-player to full-screen and starts the clip. Just as Margot has described, it shows a thirty-year-old woman filmed in secret through her bedroom window as she pulls on a pair of black tights.

He sees her face, completely unaware, her downturned eyes, the calm set of her mouth, which then switches to something approaching lethargy. Her hair is hanging round her face, it looks like it's just been washed. She's wearing a black bra and she's trying to get her tights to sit properly.

There's a lamp with a clouded white shade and alabaster base in the window, and her shadow moves across the chest of drawers and the flowery wallpaper. She slips her hand between her thighs and tries to pull the thin nylon material up towards her crotch, and he can see her breathing through her mouth as the film ends.

'Did you see what you were looking for?' Adam asks, leaning over Joona's shoulder.

Joona remains seated in front of the screen, then plays the film again, watches her struggle with her tights, then freezes the picture after thirty-five seconds and clicks to advance it frame by frame.

'We've done that too,' Adam says, stifling a belch.

Joona moves closer to the screen and watches Maria Carlsson as she moves very slowly, breathing with her mouth open. Her eyes blink and her long lashes cast shadows across her cheeks. Her right hand sinks weightlessly between her thighs to her crotch.

'This won't do,' Adam says to Margot. 'We need to get on.'

'Give him a chance,' she replies.

Maria Carlsson turns jerkily towards the camera, the grey shadow crosses her face, as if she were being lifted up from a bath full of lead. Her lips part, the light from the lamp in the window shines on her face, making her eyes glow, and there's a shimmer in her mouth, then the film ends.

Behind Joona, Adam and Margot have started to talk about investigating the people in the drawing class that Maria was about to set out for; they've already tried to find out if any of their names begin with 'H', but without success so far.

Joona moves the cursor and plays the last five seconds again. The light plays across her hair, her ear and cheeks, making her eyes shine, and then her mouth flashes.

He enlarges the image as far as he can without losing too much focus, then shifts the enlarged area so that it covers her mouth, and looks at the last few frames again. Her parted lips fill the screen, light shines in and the pink tip of her tongue becomes visible. He clicks to advance the image, frame by frame. The curve of her tongue comes into view, becomes lighter, and in the next shot it looks like a white sun fills the whole of her mouth. The sun contracts. And in the penultimate frame the glow has shrunk to a white dot on a grey pea.

'He took the jewellery,' Joona says quietly.

The two detectives fall silent and turn to look at him and the computer screen. It takes a few moments for them to interpret the enlarged image, the pink tongue and hazy stud.

'OK, we missed the fact that her tongue was pierced,' Adam says in a rasping voice.

Margot is standing with her legs apart and her hands round her stomach, and looks at Joona as he leans against the desk and gets up from the chair.

'You saw that she had a hole in her tongue and wanted to watch the film to see if the stud was there,' she says, picking up her phone.

'I just thought her mouth was important,' Joona says. 'Her jaw was broken, and she had her own saliva on her hand.'

'Impressive,' Margot says. 'I'll request an enlargement from Forensics at once.'

Joona stands still, staring at the pictures and maps on the wall as Margot speaks into the phone.

'We're collaborating with the BKA,' Margot explains once she's hung up. 'The Germans are way out in front when it comes to this sort of thing, in all forms of image enhancement . . . Have you met Stefan

Ott? Handsome guy, curly hair. He's developed his own programs, which J-lab . . .'

'OK, so we've got an item of jewellery on the film,' Adam says, thinking out loud. 'The degree of violence is aggressive, fuelled by hatred . . . probably jealousy, and . . .'

Margot's inbox bleeps and she opens the email and clicks on the image so that it fills the whole screen.

In order to improve the contrast of the stud itself, the image enhancement software has changed all the colours. Maria Carlsson's tongue and cheeks are blue, almost like glass, but at the same time the stud is clearly visible.

'Saturn,' Margot whispers.

At the end of the stud piercing Maria's tongue is a silver sphere with a ring around its equator, just like the planet Saturn.

'That's not an "h",' Joona says.

They turn and see that he's looking at the photograph of Maria's Filofax where it says 'class 19.00 – squared paper, pencils, ink', then on the line below the letter 'h'.

'That's the symbol for Saturn,' he says. 'It actually represents a scythe or sickle. That's why it's slightly crooked, and sometimes it's crossed up at the top.'

'Saturn . . . the planet. The Roman god,' Margot says.

31

Joona and Margot have taken their shoes off and are standing looking through a pane of glass. The room inside is warm and damp.

'I've tested for allergens, and it turns out that I'm allergic to mindfulness,' she says.

To the strains of Indian music, about thirty perspiring women are moving with mechanical symmetry on their yoga mats.

Margot got five officers to check through Maria Carlsson's Internet traffic once more: her email, Facebook and Instagram accounts. The stud in her tongue is only visible in a few pictures, and is only mentioned by one of her friends on Facebook before all communication between them ceased.

'You got lick it, before we kick it. Me too wanna pierce my tongue.'

The woman who had posted that was called Linda Bergman, and she was an instructor in Bikram yoga in the centre of Stockholm. They were in very regular contact for six months before she suddenly unfriended Maria.

Linda Bergman emerges from the staffroom dressed in jeans and a grey sweater. She's suntanned, and has quickly showered and put on some make-up.

'Linda? I'm Margot Silverman,' Margot says, shaking the woman's hand.

'You didn't say what this was about, and I can honestly say that I have absolutely no idea,' she says.

They walk along the pavement in the direction of Norra Bantorget while Margot tries to get Linda to relax by asking about Bikram yoga.

'It's a form of Hatha yoga, but takes place in a room with high humidity, at a temperature of forty degrees,' Linda explains.

They enter the former playground in front of the old Norra Latin School. The spherical fountain shimmers silvery white, and the wind keeps scattering showers of tiny droplets.

'The founder's name is Bikram Choudhury . . . he created a series of twenty-six positions that are actually the best I've ever tried,' she goes on.

'Let's sit down,' Margot says, patting her stomach.

They sit down on an empty park bench beside the fence facing Olof Palmes gata.

'You used to be friends with Maria Carlsson on Facebook,' Joona says, drawing a deep vertical line in the path, raising a little cloud of dust.

'What's happened?' she asks warily.

'Why did you unfriend her?'

'Because we no longer have anything to do with each other.'

'But you seem to have been in very close contact for several months,' Margot says.

'She came to a few classes, and we started talking, and . . .'

Linda tails off and her gaze flits anxiously from Margot to Joona.

'What did you talk about?' Margot asks.

'Can I ask if I'm suspected of having done something?'

'You're not,' Joona says.

'You knew that Maria had a piercing, that she had a tongue-stud?' Margot goes on.

'Yes,' Linda says, and gives a slightly embarrassed smile.

'Did she have several different studs?'

'No.'

'Do you remember what hers looked like?'

'Yes.'

Linda stares at the old school building and the play of the shadows under the trees for a moment before replying:

'It had a tiny model of Saturn at the top.'

'A tiny model of Saturn,' Margot repeats, very gently. 'What does that mean?'

'I don't know,' Linda says blankly.

'Is it to do with astrology?'

Linda looks over at the trees again, and kicks the ground with her trainers.

'Do you know where she got it from? It doesn't seem to be for sale anywhere, not from any of the usual Internet sites, anyway.'

'I don't understand where this is going,' Linda says. 'I've got another class soon, and—'

'Maria Carlsson's dead,' Margot interrupts, with quiet seriousness. 'She was murdered last week.'

'Murdered? She was murdered?'

'Yes, she was found on—'

'Why are you telling me?' Linda interrupts and stands up.

'Please, sit down,' Margot says.

'Maria's dead?'

Linda sits down, her eyes drift off towards the fountain, and she starts to cry.

'But I . . . I . . .'

She shakes her head and hides her face in her hands.

'Did you give her the stud?' Joona asks.

'Why the hell do you keep going on about that tongue-stud?' she snaps. 'Find the killer instead. This is completely sick!'

'Did you give her the stud?' Joona repeats, drawing a short line across the first one.

'No, I didn't,' she replies, wiping the tears from her cheeks. 'She got it from a guy.'

'Do you know the name of the guy?' Margot asks.

'I don't want to get involved,' she whispers.

'We respect that,' Margot nods.

Linda looks at her with bloodshot eyes, and purses her lips.

'His name is Filip Cronstedt,' she says quietly.

'Do you know where he lives?'

'No.'

'Was Maria going out with him?'

Linda doesn't answer, just stares down at the ground as the tears begin to fall again. Joona adds the last curve to the symbol with his stick and leans back.

'Why did she have a model of Saturn on her tongue-stud?' Margot asks carefully. 'What does it mean?'

'I don't know. Because it looked nice,' she says weakly.

'In Maria's diary there's a symbol written in ten different places – it's the old symbol for Saturn,' Margot says, and points to the ground.

32

Linda's cheeks turn red as she looks at the symbol drawn in the grit in front of Joona's feet. The stylised scythe has already begun to be erased by the wind. She says nothing, but her forehead is shiny with sweat.

'Sorry, but I'm expecting a phone call,' Joona says, and stands up with the help of his stick.

Margot watches him limp off towards the steps of the Norra Latin School and pull out his mobile. She understands that he's left them alone to give her a chance to create a more intimate atmosphere between her and Linda Bergman.

'Linda,' she says, 'I'm going to find out what all this is about sooner or later, but I'd rather you told me.'

The young woman has dark-grey sweat marks under her arms now, as she slowly brushes the hair from her face.

'It's just a bit personal,' she says, licking her lips again.

'I appreciate that.'

'They call it saturnalia,' Linda says, looking down at the ground.

'Is that some sort of role-play?' Margot asks gently.

'No, it's an orgy,' Linda replies as steadily as she can.

'Group sex?'

'Yes, although group sex sounds like . . . I don't know, it's not like some sort of tragic old swingers' club.' She smiles, embarrassed.

'You seem to know what you're talking about,' Margot goes on.

'I went with Maria a few times,' she replies, shaking her head almost imperceptibly. 'I'm single, it was nothing funny, you didn't have to sleep with everyone just because you were there.'

'But isn't that the point?'

'I don't have any regrets about trying it . . . but it's not exactly something I'm proud of either.'

'Tell me about the saturnalias,' Margot asks quietly.

'I don't know what to say,' Linda says, crossing her legs. 'I was carried along by Maria's . . . I don't know, completely open attitude about sex. Well, I thought I was, anyway . . .'

'Were you in love with her?'

'I did it for my own sake,' Linda said, without answering the question. 'To try something new, no obligation, to just let go and allow it to mean nothing but sex.'

'I can understand that.' Margot smiles gently.

'The first time,' Linda says, giving Margot a dark look, 'your whole body just shakes . . . You think, I can't be doing this. Several men at the same time . . . and there are loads of drugs, and you have sex with other girls and it goes on for hours . . . it's mad.'

She looks over towards Joona and brushes the sweat from her top lip with her forefinger.

'But you stopped going,' Margot says.

'I'm not like Maria, I wanted to be with her, and I tried doing it her way . . . and after a while I felt different, and brave and everything . . . But after the third time I started to think a whole load of things, it wasn't like I regretted it . . . more like: OK, why am I doing this? I don't have to feel ashamed, I'm allowed to do it . . . but why?'

'That's a good question.'

'It was my decision to go, but it sort of wasn't on my terms . . . I think I felt a bit exploited, in spite of all that.'

'Was that why you stopped?'

Linda rubs the end of her nose and says quietly:

'I'd had enough when it turned out that someone had filmed one of the saturnalias. You're not supposed to do that, no mobiles . . . Maria called and told me, she was really angry, but it just made me worried, I felt like I was going to be sick . . . The film clip was on a porn site for amateur films, it was shaky and dark, but I could still see myself, and that wasn't exactly a great feeling, I can tell you.'

A few drops from the fountain reach them, and Linda turns away from the hazy sphere and shakes her head.

'I can't believe she's dead,' she whispers.

'These saturnalias – how are they arranged?'

'It's two guys from Östermalm, Filip and someone called Eugene . . . It probably started out as them having parties where there was a lot of cocaine and Ecstasy . . . And then there was spice, monkey dust, Spanish fly and all the rest of it . . . and now it's been going on for at least two or three years . . . There are maybe a couple of saturnalias every month . . . exclusive, invite only.'

'Always on Saturdays?'

'You know where the English word Saturday comes from?' Linda replies, looking her in the eye.

Margot nods, and Linda kicks at the ground again.

'I'd just like to say that I never took any drugs,' she says.

'Good for you,' Margot says neutrally.

'I drank too much champagne instead.' She smiles.

'Where do they take place?'

'When I was involved, they had a suite at the Birger Jarl Hotel . . . All I remember is really weird, psychedelic rooms.'

'Tell me about the stud Maria had in her tongue.'

'Filip and Eugene gave studs to all the girls who belonged to the inner circle.'

'Did Maria want to leave as well? Do you know?'

'I don't think so . . . well, I . . .'

She falls silent and gathers her hair over one shoulder.

'What were you going to say?'

'Just that Filip fell in love with her, he wanted to see her on her own, didn't want her sleeping with other men. She just laughed . . . That was what she was like, Maria.'

Margot pulls out a photograph of Susanna Kern.

'Do you recognise this woman? Take a good look.'

Linda looks at Susanna Kern's smiling face, her warm, light-brown eyes and glossy hair, and shakes her head.

'No,' she replies.

'Was she at the saturnalias?'

'I don't recognise her,' Linda says, getting to her feet.

Margot remains seated on the bench, thinking that they still haven't found a connection between the victims. They're dealing with a serial killer who stalks his victims, but they have no idea where he finds them, or how he chooses them.

33

Madeleine Federer is walking with her mother along a path that cuts diagonally across Humlegården. After school she went with her to play in St Jacob's Church. Jackie takes all the extra work she can get as an organist so that they can manage financially.

Now Madeleine is walking along next to her mother, talking and keeping an eye on the path even though she knows that her mum doesn't need help.

Her mother walks with one foot nudging the edge of the grass, so she can feel the plants against her leg and at the same time listen to the stick tapping the path.

A compressor starts to rumble outside the Royal Library, and powerful drills begin digging at the asphalt with rapid metallic thuds. The noise means that her mother loses her bearings and Madeleine takes hold of her arm.

They pass the playground with the spiral slide she used to love when she was younger; it smelled so good, of plastic and warm sand.

When they reach the street her mother thanks her for her help, and they carry on towards the pedestrian crossing.

Madeleine can hear how the tapping of the stick against the stone pavement sounds harder than it did on the tarmac, but she can't tell how it sounds when they pass a pole close to the edge of the road.

'It's just a momentary gap in the noise of the cars,' her mother explains, and stops.

As usual, she puts the tip of her stick over the edge of the pavement so that she'll be prepared for the change in height when the cars stop and the ticking sound from the traffic lights speeds up.

They cross, and walk along in front of a large yellow building when her mother turns towards an open garage door and clicks her tongue. A lot of people with visual impairments do this to listen to the echo and identify potential hazards.

Once they're home Jackie closes the door, locks it and engages the security chain. Madeleine hangs up her coat and watches her mum go into the living room without switching the light on, and put her music scores on the table.

Madeleine goes to her room, says hello to Hoggy, and just has time to change into some home clothes before she hears her mother's voice.

'Maddy?' she calls from her bedroom.

When Madeleine enters the brightly lit room she sees her mother standing in just her underwear, trying to close the curtains in front of the window. Just outside the window a pink child's bicycle is lying on the grass. The curtain has got caught in the door of the wardrobe, and her mother runs her fingers down the fabric and manages to pull it free before she turns round.

'Did you turn the light on in here?' she asks.

'No.'

'I mean this morning.'

'I don't think so,' she replies.

'You need to make sure we don't leave any lights on when we go out.'

'Sorry,' she says, although she really doesn't think she had done so.

Her mum reaches for the blue dressing-gown on the bed, her hands fumbling and locating it up near the pillow.

'Maybe Hoggy got scared of the dark and came in and turned the light on.'

'Maybe,' she says.

Her mum turns the flimsy dressing-gown the right way round, puts it on, then kneels down and cups Madeleine's face with both her hands.

'Are you the prettiest girl in the world? You are, I know you are.'

'Haven't you got any pupils today, Mum?'

'Only Erik.'

'Aren't you going to put some clothes on?'

'Thanks for the suggestion,' she says, wrapping the silk gown round her body.

'Put the silvery skirt on, that's nice.'

'You'll have to help me find something.'

Her mother has a colour reader, but always asks Madeleine if her clothes look right, if the colours match.

'Shall I go and get the post?'

'Bring it to the kitchen.'

Madeleine walks through the hall, and can smell damp earth and stinging nettles as she picks the post up from the floor in front of the door. Her mother is already sitting at the kitchen table when she comes in and stops next to her.

'Are there any love-letters?' Jackie asks, like she always does.

'There's . . . an advert from an estate agent.'

'Throw it away. Throw all the adverts away. Anything else?'

'A reminder about the phone bill.'

'Nice.'

'And . . . a letter from my school.'

'What do they have to say?' Jackie asks.

Madeleine opens the envelope and reads out the letter, which has been sent to all parents. Someone has been writing rude words on the walls of the corridor and in the toilets. The headteacher asks parents and guardians to talk to their children about the matter, and tell them how much it costs to clean up, money which reduces the amount available for refurbishment of the playground.

'Do you know who's doing it?' her mother asks.

'No, but I've seen the graffiti. It's really stupid. Really childish.'

Her mother gets up and starts to take cherry tomatoes, crème fraiche and asparagus out of the fridge.

'I like Erik,' Madeleine says.

'Even though he called the keys "bits"?' her mum asks, filling a large saucepan with water for pasta.

'He said he played like a broken robot,' Madeleine giggles.

'Which is absolutely true . . .'

Madeleine can't help smiling, and sees her mum smile as she switches the hotplate on.

'A handsome little robot,' Madeleine goes on. 'Can't I keep him? My very own little robot . . . he could sleep in the doll's cot.'

'Is he really handsome?'

'I don't know,' she replies, thinking of his kind face. 'I think so, he looks a bit like one of those actors everyone keeps going on about.'

Her mother shakes her head, but looks happy as she adds some salt to the water.

34

Erik feels pleased with himself that he can play all the way to the eighteenth bar with his right hand, even if his left hand can only manage six. Jackie smiles to herself for a few seconds, but decides not to give him any praise, and asks instead if he's been practising the way she told him to.

'As often as I've been able to,' he assures her.

'Can I hear?'

'I've been practising, but it doesn't sound right.'

'There's nothing bad about making mistakes,' Jackie points out.

'But you won't want me as a pupil if I play too badly.'

'Erik, there's no danger of—'

'And I really love being here,' he goes on.

'That's nice to hear . . . But if you're going to learn how to play, you've got to . . .'

Jackie tails off in the middle of the sentence and blushes, before raising her chin again.

'Are you flirting with me?' she asks with a sceptical smile.

'Am I?' he laughs.

'OK,' she says seriously.

'I'll try playing the piece I practised, if you promise not to laugh.'

'What will happen if I laugh?' she asks.

'That will just prove that you've got a sense of humour.'

She smiles broadly just as Madeleine comes in, dressed in her nightie and a pair of slippers.

'Goodnight, Erik,' she says.

He smiles. 'Goodnight, Madeleine.'

Jackie gets up and follows her daughter to her bedroom. Erik watches them go, and has just put his left hand on the keys when he sees that Madeleine has forgotten her stuffed hedgehog on the armchair.

He picks it up and goes after them, turning right into the corridor.

The door of the girl's room is open and the light is on. He can see Madeleine's back, and Jackie turning back the covers.

'Maddy,' he says, opening the door. 'You forgot . . .'

He gets no further before the door slams into his face and bounces back. Madeleine is screaming hysterically and slams the door again. Erik tumbles backwards into the wall of the corridor and puts his hand to his nose as the blood starts to flow.

Madeleine is still screaming in her room, and he hears something fall to the floor and break.

He goes into the bathroom, puts the hedgehog down, squeezes his nose and hears the girl calm down. After a while Jackie emerges into the hall and knocks softly on the bathroom door.

'Are you OK? I don't understand what—'

'Tell her I'm sorry,' Erik interrupts. 'I forgot the sign, I just wanted to give her hedgehog back.'

'She was asking where it was.'

'It's on the cabinet in here,' Erik says, opening the door. 'I didn't want to get blood on it.'

'Are you bleeding?'

'Not really, just a slight nosebleed.'

Jackie takes the hedgehog and goes back to her daughter while Erik rinses his face. He returns to the piano as Jackie comes out again.

'Sorry,' she says, holding her hands out. 'I don't understand what got into her.'

'She's wonderful,' Erik says.

Jackie nods. 'Yes, she really is.'

'My son is eighteen, and he's still never managed to switch the dishwasher on . . . But now he's living with his mother, and she's a bit tougher than me . . .'

They fall silent. Jackie is standing in the middle of the room, she can smell Erik, a smell of clean clothes and warm wood from his aftershave. Her face is sombre as she wraps her knitted cardigan more tightly round her, as if she were cold.

'Would you like a glass of wine?' she asks.

35

Erik and Jackie are sitting opposite each other at the kitchen table. She's got out wine, glasses and bread.

'Do you always wear dark glasses?' he asks.

'My eyes are light-sensitive – I can't see anything, but they can hurt a lot,' she says.

'It's almost completely dark in here,' he says. 'Only the little lamp behind the curtain is switched on.'

'Do you want to see my eyes?'

'Yes,' he confesses.

She takes a small bite of bread and chews slowly, as if she were thinking about it.

'Have you always been blind?' he asks.

'I had retinitis pigmentosa when I was born. I could see fairly well for the first few years, but I was completely blind by the time I was five.'

'You didn't get any treatment?'

'Just Vitamin A, but . . .'

She falls silent, then takes off her dark glasses. Her eyes are the same sad, bright blue as her daughter's.

'You have beautiful eyes,' he says quietly.

It feels strange that they aren't staring at each other, even though he's looking into her eyes. She smiles and almost closes her eyes.

'Can you get scared of the dark if you're blind?' he asks.

'In the dark the blind man is king,' she says, as if she were reciting a quotation. 'But you get scared of hurting yourself, of getting lost . . .'

'I can understand that.'

'And earlier today I got it into my head that someone was looking at me through my bedroom window,' she says with a short laugh.

'Really?'

'You know, windows are strange things for blind people . . . a window is just like a wall, a cool, smooth wall . . . I mean, I know you can see straight through a window like it wasn't there . . . So I've learned to close the curtains, but at the same time you don't always know . . .'

'I'm looking at you now, obviously, but I mean, does it feel uncomfortable to have someone watching you?'

'It's . . . it's not without its challenges,' she says, with a brief smile.

'You don't live with Madeleine's father?'

'Maddy's father was . . . It wasn't good.'

'In what way?' Erik asks.

'He was damaged . . . I found out later that he'd tried to get psychiatric help, but was turned down.'

'That's a shame,' Erik says.

'It was for us . . .'

She shakes her head and takes a sip of wine, wipes a drop from her lip and puts the glass back on the table.

'There are different ways of being blind,' she goes on. 'He was my professor at music college, and I didn't realise how unwell he was until I got pregnant. He started saying it wasn't his child, called me all sorts of horrible things, wanted to force me to have an abortion, said he fantasised about pushing me in front of an underground train . . .'

'You should have reported him.'

'Yes, but I didn't dare to.'

'What happened?'

'One day I put Maddy in her pushchair and walked to my sister's in Uppsala.'

'You walked there?'

'I was just glad it was over,' Jackie says. 'But for Maddy . . . Obviously, it's impossible for anyone to know how much longing a child can live with. How much fantasising and magical thinking a child can manage, to explain why her dad never gets in touch . . .'

'All these absent fathers . . .'

'When Maddy was almost four and was able to answer the phone, she picked up once when he called . . . She was delighted, said he'd promised to come on her birthday, and bring a puppy, and . . .'

Her lips begin to tremble and she falls silent. Erik pours them both some more wine and puts her hand to the glass, feeling her warmth.

'But you're not an absent father?' she says.

'No, I'm not . . . but when Benjamin was small I had a problem with prescription drugs, things got pretty bad,' he replies honestly.

'And his mother?'

'Simone and I were married for almost twenty years . . .'

'Why did you split up?'

'She met a Danish architect. I don't blame her, I actually like John . . . And I'm genuinely happy for her.'

'I don't believe that.' She smiles.

He laughs.

'Sometimes you just have to pretend you're grown up, and do what you're supposed to, say the things that grown-ups say . . .'

He thinks about Simone, and their backwards ceremony where they gave their rings back to each other, retracted their vows, and then at the party afterwards had a divorce cake and a last dance.

'Have you met anyone else?' Jackie asks quietly.

'I've had a few relationships since the divorce,' he admits. 'I met a woman at the gym, and . . .'

'You go to the gym?'

'You should see my muscles,' he jokes.

'Who was she?'

'Maria . . . nothing came of it, she was probably a bit too advanced for me.'

'But you've never slept with your professor?'

'No,' Erik laughs. 'Almost, though. I did end up in bed with a colleague of mine.'

'Oops.'

'No, it was OK, actually . . . We were drunk, I was divorced and abandoned . . . she and her husband were taking a break, it wasn't a big deal . . . Nelly's wonderful, but I wouldn't want to live with her.'

'What about patients?'

'Occasionally you find them attractive,' Erik says honestly. 'That's unavoidable, it's an extremely intimate situation . . . but attraction and seduction are merely a way for the patient to avoid thinking about anything painful.'

He thinks of how Sandra used to stop in the middle of a sentence and feel her beautiful, intelligent face with her fingertips as tears welled up in her forest-green eyes. She wanted him to hold her, and when he did she dissolved in his arms, as though they were making love.

He doesn't know if it was premeditated, but he still asked Nelly to take her on instead. Sandra had already met her, and it seemed like the natural solution.

'So who are you seeing at the moment?' Jackie says.

Erik looks at her smile, the shape of her face in the soft light, her dark, short hair and white neck. Rocky Kyrklund suddenly feels a very long way away, and he can't understand how he managed to get so worried.

'I don't know how serious it is, but . . . Well, we've only met a few times,' he says. 'But I feel happy whenever I'm with her . . .'

'That's good,' Jackie mumbles, and blushes.

She picks up another piece of bread.

'When I'm with her I never want to go home . . . And I already like her daughter, and I'm also learning to play the piano like a robot,' he says, and puts his hand on hers.

'You've got soft hands,' she says, with a big smile.

He strokes her hands, wrists and lower arms, slides his fingers up to her face, following her skin. He leans forward and kisses her gently on the mouth, several times. He looks at her, her heavy eyelids, her chin, her long neck.

She smiles as she waits to be kissed again, and they kiss, open their mouths and feel each other's tongues, tentatively, breathing tremulously, when the doorbell suddenly rings.

They both start, and sit perfectly still, trying to breathe quietly.

The bell rings again.

Jackie hurries to stand up and Erik does the same, but when she opens the door there's no one there. The stairwell is completely dark.

'Mummy!' Madeleine calls from her room. 'Mummy!'

Jackie reaches out her hand and touches Erik's face.

'You should probably go now,' she whispers.

36

An old woman with plastic bags wrapped over her clothes casts an anxious glance at Joona Linna as he wobbles unsteadily beside her in the queue of homeless people.

He tried to get some rest on the green line of the underground, but met a Roma man who offered him somewhere to sleep. He's been lying on the floor of a caravan out in Huddinge, wrapped in a blanket, with his eyes closed, waiting for sleep, but his thoughts won't leave him alone.

He hasn't eaten or slept since Lumi left. He gave her all his money, keeping only enough to cover the journey to see Nils Åhlén.

Lack of sleep means that his migraines are coming more and more frequently. The pain is like a burning needle behind one eye, and his hip is getting even worse.

An Iranian man with friendly eyes is patiently pouring coffee for the hungry and giving them sandwiches. Most of the people here have probably been sleeping in the Central Station or in the nearby multi-storey car parks.

Joona no longer feels hungry, it's only there as a weight that makes his legs weak. When he's handed his coffee and sandwich, he feels like he's going to faint. He moves to one side, unwraps the bread, takes a bite and swallows it, but his stomach starts to cramp, trying to reject the food. He puts his hand over his mouth and turns his back on the others. Dizziness forces him to his knees. He spills his coffee on the ground, takes another bite, coughs and spits it out, and feels sweat break out on his forehead.

'How are you doing?' the Iranian man says, having seen what happened.

'I haven't got round to eating anything for a while,' he replies.

'A busy man.' The Iranian smiles gently.

'Yes,' Joona says, coughing again.

'Just let me know if you need help.'

'Thanks, but I'm fine,' Joona mutters, then picks up his stick and limps away.

'At one o'clock the soup kitchen in St Clara Church opens,' the man calls after him. 'Come along, you could do with sitting down and getting warm.'

Joona crosses the bridge towards the City Hall, feeds the sandwich to the swans, and walks with heavy steps up the long slope of Hantverkargatan. He stops and rests for a while outside Kungsholmen Gymnasium School, fingering the little stone in his pocket, and then carries on towards the fire station before turning off into Kronoberg Park. The foliage high above is drenched in sunlight, but the grass beneath the trees is shady, a soft moss-green.

Joona walks slowly up the hill, leaning on his stick, loosens the wire inside the railings, opens the gate and enters the old Jewish Cemetery.

'I'm sorry I look the way I do,' he says, putting the stone down on Samuel Mendel's family grave.

Joona pushes a sweet wrapper away with his stick and tells his former partner that Jurek Walter is dead at last. Then he stands in silence, listening to the wind through the trees, and the sound of the children in the nearby playground.

'I've seen the evidence,' he whispers, patting the headstone before he leaves.

Margot Silverman has asked Joona to attend an unofficial meeting today. She's probably just trying to be nice to him, letting him play at being a detective for a while.

On his way down towards Fleminggatan Joona thinks about the orgies Maria Carlsson attended.

Saturnalias, carnivals, drunken binges – they have always been part of human life. Every breath takes us closer to death, and we console ourselves with work and routines, but every so often we have to turn our regulated lives upside down, if only to prove to ourselves that we are free.

Maria Carlsson had evidently been planning to attend a saturnalia the day she was murdered. It's impossible to say if the orgies are the link between the victims, but on her calendar Susanna Kern had circled the same July Saturday that Maria Carlsson had booked for an orgy.

Childhood friends Filip Cronstedt and Eugene Cassel are joint owners of the company Croca Communication Ltd, which had a turnover of ninety-five million euros last year. Even though they're both registered as living abroad, it's very obvious that they spend most of their time in Sweden.

Neither of them has visited the office on Sibyllegatan in the past six months, and they haven't attended a board meeting in a very long time. The managing director has been in touch with Eugene, most recently just last week, but he hasn't heard from Filip since the start of the year.

Linda Bergman said she was still in contact with Maria Carlsson when Filip suddenly withdrew from the saturnalias.

But the orgies went on, attended by both Maria and Eugene.

There seem to be a number of regular participants who attend every time, while a limited number of new people are invited along for a trial.

According to Linda, passcards for the hotel suite double as entrance tickets.

The investigative team have little expectation of finding Filip at the hotel, but they're relatively confident that Eugene will be there.

According to Maria Carlsson's Filofax, there's an orgy planned for next Saturday, and another one in three weeks' time. These two dates may be their only hope of finding Eugene and tracing Filip.

37

Adam, Margot and Joona are sitting at a table in the new part of The Doors bar. A football match is playing on the television. Margot is eating a large hamburger and drinking water. Adam and Joona are both drinking black coffee.

'Filip doesn't seem to have left Sweden,' Adam says, arranging some printouts on the table. 'He's here, but he's not registered as living here, and he doesn't appear to have been in any of the homes owned by the company.'

Filip Cronstedt's face looks up at them from the table. The photograph shows a man in his forties with back-combed blond hair and pale eyebrows. He looks like a friendly, considerate banker. His furrowed brow and the set of his cheeks and chin suggest hard-living, but that only makes him look more sympathetic.

'I don't know if I believe that he killed Maria Carlsson,' Adam adds, pointing a finger at the picture. 'It doesn't make sense . . . I mean, he hasn't got a history of violence, he's got no criminal record, he's never even been suspected of anything, and there's no mention of him in Social Service records.'

'He can afford good lawyers,' Margot says.

'Yes, but even so,' Adam says.

A woman is dragging a fifty-litre barrel of beer across the floor. A family with three young girls walk past the scratched window overlooking Tulegatan.

'All we know is that Filip Cronstedt started to get jealous of Maria,' Margot says, and puts some French fries in her mouth. 'He wanted her to stop going to the saturnalias, but she kept going . . . and now she's dead, and that stud in her tongue is missing . . .'

'Yes, but . . .'

'I'm thinking,' she goes on. 'I'm thinking that he became obsessed with Maria Carlsson, stood on the sidelines watching her at the orgies . . . So far, so good – but is he a serial killer?'

'Or a spree killer,' Adam says. 'We've only got two murders, and that's not actually enough to—'

'But we're hunting a serial killer,' she interrupts.

'That doesn't really matter,' Joona says quietly. 'But Margot's right, because . . .'

He shuts his eyes as his migraine flares up behind his eye and he raises his hand slowly to his head. While the pain subsides he sits absolutely still and tries to remember what he was going to say about spree killers. The term refers to a murderer who has killed at least two people in different places, with barely any time between them. A spree killer doesn't have the serial killer's lifelong, sexualised attitude towards the dramaturgy of murder, but commits his murders as a direct response to a crisis.

'OK,' Adam says after a while.

'It's still too early to say anything about Filip,' Margot says with her mouth full. 'It could be him, I think that's a possibility, but . . .'

'In that case, the orgies form part of his fantasy about killing,' Joona says, opening his eyes.

'We'll carry on with what we've got,' Margot declares. 'This evening is the only time we know where Eugene Cassel is going to be . . . and if anyone can tell us where Filip is, it's Cassel.'

'Mind you, we can't just storm into a private orgy,' Adam says with a grin.

'Only one of us needs to go in. Find Eugene and talk to him, nice and calmly,' Margot says, then takes a large bite of her hamburger.

'You can't work out in the field, seeing as you're pregnant,' Adam says.

'Does it show?' she asks as she chews.

'OK, what the hell, I'll do it,' Adam says.

'This isn't a raid,' Margot says. 'There's no obvious threat . . . We'll call it a meeting with an anonymous informant, then we don't need to run it past management beforehand.'

Adam sighs and leans back.

'So now I've to go in among a load of . . .'

He falls silent, stares into space with glazed eyes, and shakes his head.

'Obviously it's a bit tricky, approaching people in a situation like that, but what can we do?' Margot says.

'I don't get it . . . What sort of people would want to go to an orgy?'

'I don't know, I haven't had group sex for at least ten years,' Margot says, dipping some fries in ketchup.

Adam stares at her open-mouthed as she chews, a slight smile on her face. She wipes her fingers on a napkin and then looks up at him.

'I was joking,' she says with a grin. 'I'm a nice girl, I promise, but I was actually involved in a raid on a swingers' club when I worked in Helsingborg . . . As I recall, it was mostly just men in their sixties, with big bellies and skinny legs—'

'Enough!' Adam said, slumping down in his chair.

'I'll give your wife a call tomorrow and ask what time you got home, just so you know.'

'Fine,' Adam sighs, then grins.

'Think of it as a job, nothing more,' Joona says. 'The other people are irrelevant, you just go straight in and talk to Eugene, get him to tell you where Filip is, and arrest him as soon as you're sure you've got the information.'

'Arrest him?'

'To stop him warning Filip,' Joona says, looking Adam in the eye.

'If you find out anything about Filip,' Margot says, 'then . . .'

'Then we call you,' Adam fills in.

'No, I'll be asleep,' she says, and puts the last of the food in her mouth. 'If you find out anything, hand it over to the rapid-response unit.'

The two men remain seated at the table after Margot has left the pub. A few elderly patrons get up from their table and go outside to smoke.

'Where are you staying?' Adam asks, looking at Joona.

'There's a campsite on the outskirts of Huddinge.'

'The Roma?'

Joona doesn't reply, takes a sip of coffee and looks out of the window.

'I've looked you up,' Adam says. 'I saw that . . . the year before you were injured you taught the Special Operations Unit in military Krav Maga . . . Sorry, but looking at you now, it's hard to believe you were a paratrooper.'

Joona looks at his own hands and thinks that what he liked most was jumping from a great height, plummeting down into a terrible storm.

'Have you ever been to Leeuwarden?' he asks Adam.

Joona was the only Swede to be sent to the Netherlands to be trained in unconventional close combat and guerrilla warfare. That was at a base north of Leeuwarden. He used to go for long runs along the sandy beaches of the Wadden Sea when the tide had gone out.

38

The psychedelic room at the Birger Jarl Hotel that Linda Bergman described is actually known as 'the Retro Room', and can be booked just like any other room.

The hotel underwent a complete renovation at the turn of the millennium. All the rooms were gutted and the décor completely changed. Once the workmen had left, it turned out that room 247 had been forgotten.

The room had somehow been ignored during every refurbishment since the hotel was built in 1974.

It's still intact, like a small time-capsule from a bygone age.

In 2013 a murder was committed at the hotel, after a sofa in room 247 was changed. Naturally, everyone claims that there was no connection between the two events, but now the staff refuse to make any adjustments to the layout of the room.

Adam has been sitting in his car in front of the old electricity works for five hours, watching the entrance to the hotel. Joona has been standing outside, wrapped in his blanket, holding out a cup with some coins in it.

Thirty-five guests have gone in during that time, but no Eugene.

Further down the street a grey-haired waiter is squatting down outside an Italian restaurant, smoking. When the church bells slowly strike eleven o'clock, Joona limps over to the car.

'You'd better go in,' he says to Adam.

'Can't you come with me?'

'I'll wait here,' Joona says.

Adam drums his thumbs on the steering wheel.

'OK,' he says, and rubs his chin a few times.

'Take it easy in there,' Joona says. 'Just because they're there doesn't make them criminals. You're likely to see quite a lot of drugs, but ignore that. You should intervene only if you see signs of forced sexual activity, or if there's anyone underage.'

Adam nods, and feels his stomach flutter as he gets out of the car and walks into the hotel.

The softly curved reception desk is empty except for a man talking on the phone.

Adam goes over to the desk, shows his ID, is given a passcard and continues towards the lifts. The Retro Room is at the end of the corridor, and on the door handle is a floppy plastic sign saying 'Do not disturb'.

Adam hesitates, then lowers the zip of his black leather jacket. His white T-shirt is tucked inside his black jeans, and his Sig Sauer is in a holster beneath his left armpit.

All he has to do is go in, nice and calmly, he tells himself. Find Eugene, take him to one side, and ask his questions.

Adam clears his throat and runs the card through the reader. The lock clicks and a little green light comes on. He opens the door, walks into a dark hallway, and shuts the door behind him.

He can hear music and muffled voices, and a bed creaking.

The light is weak, but it isn't completely dark. He looks around. He's in a small lobby where people have left their clothes.

A woman with a boyish blonde haircut comes out of the bathroom and blinks at him in the darkness. She's wearing nothing but a pair of skimpy black silk panties, and she's so beautiful that his heart starts to beat faster.

She's got traces of white powder stuck in the lip-gloss at one corner of her mouth. She looks at Adam with big, black pupils surrounded by a narrow ring of ice-blue. She moistens her lips and says something that he doesn't hear, before going back into the bedroom.

He follows her, unable to stop himself staring at her naked, glistening back.

Inside the dimly lit room there's a sweet, smoky smell.

Adam stops and looks over at the bed, then looks away again immediately. He shuffles sideways along the wall, passing a naked man with a glass of champagne in his hand, then stops.

No one has reacted to his presence.

A woman pushes past, her eyes focused on the floor. The wallpaper is pink and wavy, the carpet brown with a starburst pattern. There are no lamps on, but the light of the city outside reaches around the curtains, spreading across the ceiling.

The whole room is heavy with the smell of excited people. Wherever

Adam looks he can see glistening genitals, open mouths, breasts, tongues, buttocks.

Apart from the music, there's very little sound. The people having sex are concentrating on that, intent on their own or their partner's pleasure. Others are resting, watching the orgy with a hand between their legs.

His pulse thuds in his ears and he can feel himself blushing.

He needs to try to find Eugene.

Adam passes a beautiful woman in her thirties. He can't help looking at her. She's wearing a batik blouse, and is sitting on the desk with her eyes closed. Her exposed crotch looks like it's been powdered. It resembles polished marble, with a line drawn on it in pink chalk.

None of it is as desperate or grubby as he had imagined. It's more introverted, more self-aware.

Adam carries on round the bed, wondering if this is all simply part of these people's trendy lifestyle.

He's the same age as most of the people there, but he's only there to do his job, and then go home to his wife in Hägersten, no doubt to remember what he has seen forever. He knows already that he won't be able to talk to her about it – not seriously. He'll end up joking about it, or turning it into something disgusting.

He looks at the people around him, and thinks that he'll be able to tell himself that they're spoiled, that he feels sorry for them, but that isn't true, not right then.

A pang of envy runs through him.

39

Adam carries on through the open sliding door to the next room. The wallpaper is darker here, with big, bold patterns, like pale green crystals.

The music is louder. Two naked men have put an orange plastic armchair on top of the bed. A woman with straight black hair is sitting on the chair, laughing as the others rock the armchair on the mattress. More men join in, someone grabs hold of her feet and starts to laugh louder.

The woman with the boyish haircut is kneeling in front of a glass-topped table, dabbing at the remains of some white powder and rubbing her finger on her gums.

He steps aside and almost stands on a large tube of lubricant lying on the floor. Dust and strands of hair have stuck to the goo that's spilled out.

In the window are ten glasses full of champagne. Drops of condensation are running down the stems and forming small puddles on the marble sill.

Further into the room Adam reaches a windowless passageway containing wardrobes and a suitcase rack. The bathroom door is half-open. A naked woman is sitting slumped on the lid of the toilet, her stomach folded and one arm tensed.

'Are you all right?' Adam asks softly.

She lifts her head and looks at him. Her eyes are dark and moist, and he gets a strong feeling that he ought to leave the hotel.

'Help me,' she whispers.

'How are you feeling?'

'I can't stand up,' she mumbles.

A slim man comes towards them from the bedroom and stops in the doorway. His erect penis sways as he moves.

'Is Paula here?' he asks.

He looks at them through half-closed eyes, and then disappears the way he came.

'Help me up,' the woman says, breathing through her mouth.

Adam takes her hand and pulls her up on to her feet. He backs away and she stumbles out of the bathroom, managing to pull a towel down from the rail. Only now does he notice that she has a dildo strapped around her hips. She falls towards him and puts her hand round his neck.

The woman's breath smells of alcohol, and the dildo slips between his thighs. Her legs begin to give way and he holds her up, feeling her heavy breasts against his body.

'Can you stand?'

'I don't know if this thing is on right,' she mutters against his neck. 'Can you check the strap at the back?'

She turns round, leans one hand against the wall, knocking a brown wall-clock and making its plastic cover rattle.

'Have you seen Eugene?' Adam asks.

The black leather strap between her buttocks has become twisted, and she feels along it with tired fingers.

'It's twisted,' Adam says.

He doesn't know what to do, hesitates, then tries to help her. He twists the strap twice, but notices that it's tangled further down as well.

Her skin is hot and sweaty, he's trembling and can feel how cold his fingers are as he follows the strap down between her buttocks.

A naked man pushes past and weaves into the bathroom. He urinates without closing the door, or so much as glancing at them.

Adam can't help noticing that the leather strap between her legs is wet and slippery as he tries to adjust it. She stumbles again and leans her cheek against the wall, as the plastic clock sways on its hook.

A woman in the next room is whimpering, two men move through the passageway, and then he sees the beautiful woman with the boyish haircut in the doorway. She's no longer wearing her pants. She's walking slowly towards the next room when she catches sight of him. She raises her champagne glass towards him in a toast, and he sees pale lip-prints on the rim.

The woman in front of him leans her shoulder against the wall, then slides down on to the floor and rests her cheek on the carpet.

The woman with the boyish haircut comes over to Adam, her neck looks flushed, and she leans into him, pressing her forehead to his chest, then looks up at him with a smile.

Adam can't help himself. He kisses her, and she responds, and he can feel her tongue-stud against his tongue.

He tells himself that he couldn't help it. It's wrong and he already knows that he's going to regret it and will feel terrible afterwards, but all he wants right now is to have sex with her.

The woman on the floor mutters something about falling over, and pulls at his leg, making him sway.

When the woman with the boyish haircut opens his trousers, a wave of icy fear runs through him.

This is too easy, too tempting, he thinks.

But his hands are touching her breasts, they're warm and tense and powdered with something rough and glittery.

He's never seen such a beautiful woman.

He picks her up, pushes her back against the wall, and slides inside. Angst and lust spin through him. He groans, and sees her mouth open and Saturn sparkles on her tongue. Her body billows and her breasts quiver with his thrusts. She's smiling, eyes closed, but she makes no noise, no groaning, and she doesn't really seem interested in what's happening, maybe she's too drugged.

Two women come into the passageway and watch them for a while before they carry on.

The woman with the dildo has got to her feet, she's standing behind him and her hands are suddenly under his T-shirt, caressing his waist and back. He tries to pull away and doesn't know if she's felt his gun, but she suddenly stops, moves away from him, mutters something and lurches into the bedroom.

Adam knows his cover may have been blown, but he can't stop now. The woman says something to his neck, and he can smell a raspberry aroma from her mouth, she's trying to get him to slow down, puts her hand on his chest, but he moves her hand away and pushes her hard against the wall.

40

When Adam enters the third room he immediately catches sight of Eugene Cassel. He's wearing a black top hat, but nothing else. Five people are having sex with each other on the large bed. The shade of a table lamp is hanging askew and shaking in time with the movement of the bed. Eugene is on his knees behind a woman on all fours.

Her pearl necklace is swinging between her breasts.

The woman with the strap-on dildo comes staggering into the room after Adam. He watches her sit down on the edge of the bed, almost fall, then sit up again. Another woman takes hold of the dildo, says something and laughs. She replies, then coughs into her elbow.

'What did you say?'

'Tra-la-la-laa,' she smiles.

'OK.'

'The cops are here, tra-la-la-laa,' she repeats, and coughs again.

Eugene hears her words and stops, sits down on the bed and puts an arm on the woman's backside, and then turns to look at Adam.

'This is a private party,' he says with a look of disappointment.

'Is there somewhere we can talk in private?' Adam says, showing his police ID.

'Leave your card and I'll get my lawyers to call you on Monday,' Eugene says, and gets up from the bed.

Eugene is about forty years old, probably the oldest person in the suite of rooms. His naked, hairless body is in good shape, despite his protruding stomach. His erection has subsided. Beneath the rim of his hat a gold ring sparkles in his eyebrow, and his pupils are dilated.

'I need to find Filip Cronstedt,' Adam says.

'Good luck,' Eugene says, and raises his hat slightly. 'He isn't here, but I can give you a clue: follow the white rabbit.'

'Listen,' Adam says. 'We can leave the hotel nice and quietly, but if I have to, I'll put handcuffs on you in here and drag you all the way to the car.'

A woman with shimmering white skin and reddish-brown hair in two plaits over her breasts enters the room and comes over to Eugene.

'Shall I order some food?' she says, putting a joint to her lips.

'Still hungry?' he asks flirtatiously.

She nods and smiles, then exhales a narrow plume of smoke, and walks off towards the phone beside the bed.

'OK, I'm going to have to arrest you according to chapter twenty-four, paragraph seven of the penal code,' Adam says.

'It's not my fault you went to a bad school and ended up having to join the police,' Eugene says sternly. 'The world's unfair, and—'

'You know Maria Carlsson, don't you?' Adam butts in.

'I love her,' he replies slowly.

'Give her a kiss,' Adam says, pulling out a picture from the crime scene.

In the sharp light of the flash, the dead woman's ravaged face, gaping mouth and broken jaw are brutally visible. Eugene whimpers, staggers backwards and knocks over a table lamp, and its brown ceramic base shatters.

41

Eugene Cassel has put his clothes back on, and Adam has called for a patrol car. They're walking down the hotel corridor together.

'I'm really sorry . . . I'm shocked, just tell me what I can do, I want to help, as a point of honour . . . but I have to speak to my lawyer first.'

Eugene has washed his face, but his cheeks are white and shiny with sweat.

'I need to find Filip,' Adam says.

'He didn't do this,' Eugene says instantly.

'Filip isn't at any of the usual addresses, where is he?'

'I know, he's not doing too well,' Eugene says, scratching his forehead with his hat. 'Look, I'm not going to spread shit about Filip, but the way things are right now, I really don't want anything to do with him. I've tried to get him to seek help, but . . .'

'Help with what?' Adam says.

The lift door opens and they step aside to let a woman in an orange trenchcoat get out before going in.

'He's been taking a bit too much,' Eugene smiles, waving his hand towards his temple.

'Is he an addict?'

'Yes, but the problem with taking too much MDPV, MDPPP, MDPBP, MDAI . . . It doesn't work, you just get fucking paranoid, and then you get the wrong sort of high and end up feeling so bad you want to die.'

'Does it make you aggressive?' Adam asks as they step out of the lift on the ground floor.

'I mean, you're terrified the whole time, but sort of ultra-focused at the same time. You think too quickly, don't sleep at all . . . The last time I met Filip he was completely fucking manic, said he was on thousands of satellite pictures on Google, kept going on about Saturn being forced to eat his own children . . . He couldn't stand still for a second, he kept ranting, waving this little knife around, he cut my hand and yelled that I should be grateful . . . and then he cut himself, right across the arm. He was dripping with blood as he ran off into the underground.'

They pass the lobby and walk out of the doors on to Tulegatan at the very moment a patrol car pulls up.

'Right now I just need to know where I can find him,' Adam repeats, stopping Eugene.

'OK, I feel like a traitor, but he said they couldn't see him in the storerooms.'

'Storerooms?'

'He rents a load of storage over on Vanadisvägen – you know, that self-storage place. I think he's got more than half of the storerooms there.'

Two uniformed officers come over and say hello to Adam. One of them leads Eugene to the back seat of the car while the other one listens to Adam.

'Take him to the custody negotiation room,' Adam. 'Make sure he doesn't call anyone, buy us some time. Once his lawyer shows up we won't be able to hold him.'

42

Joona is driving fast as he ignores the red light and turns left into Odengatan.

A homeless woman with two overloaded shopping trolleys is sitting asleep outside the 7-Eleven.

Adam tells him how Filip has been overdosing on several different varieties of MDPV for a while now, and that Eugene thinks he's entered a paranoid psychosis.

The drug has caused a number of deaths in Sweden, and was referred to in the evening tabloids as 'the cannibal drug' after a man who'd taken it tried to eat the face of a homeless man.

'We haven't got much time, they won't be able to hold Eugene for long, he'll be out soon and I reckon he's likely to warn Filip,' Adam says in a tense voice.

Joona overtakes a taxi on the inside, pulls in front of it, then swerves into the oncoming lanes and turns into Vanadisvägen.

The bumper thuds as he drives up on to the pavement and stops in front of the pale mocha-coloured building with red garage doors.

Within central Stockholm the self-storage companies have had to make do with using existing basements so as not to change the visible appearance of the city. Huge areas of small, locked rooms spread out just below the ground, like old catacombs beneath cathedrals.

Joona and Adam get out of the car and head over to the closed office looking out onto the little car park. In the gloom through the window they can make out flat stacks of removal boxes, a reception desk, and a large monitor for security cameras on the wall.

'I want to look at a map of the storerooms, and I want to look at those cameras,' Joona says.

'It's closed, we're going to have to go through a prosecutor,' Adam replies.

Joona nods, taps his stick against the edge of the pavement and thinks how it feels to sink through broken ice. It's when you warm up that you start to freeze, he thinks as he picks up a heavy kerb-stone and throws it through the window. There's a loud crash as the glass shatters and a red light begins to flash over on the reception desk.

'The alarm will have gone off at their security company,' Adam says feebly.

Joona pushes some loose splinters from the window frame with his stick, then goes in. Adam looks round, then follows him.

There's a plan hanging on the wall, showing a grid system of wide and narrow passageways.

Every storeroom is numbered, and they're arranged in blocks. A list of staff codes for the stores is neatly pinned up alongside.

Joona sits down at the computer. The passageways between the storerooms are monitored by security cameras. Twenty-five small squares cover the screen. All the cameras are filming windowless darkness. It's night, and the lights have all been switched off.

'See if you can find a list of customers,' Adam says.

Joona minimises the security cameras, tries to open various programs but can't get anywhere. Everything apart from the cameras requires a password.

He quickly returns to the cameras and enlarges the first square and stares at the grey-black stillness, like a black square of linen. Then the next one. The camera is filming nothing but darkness. Adam shuffles nervously behind him. He looks at the plan on the wall.

Everything is quiet, sunk in darkness.

The third camera is pointed towards an emergency exit. A green sign above the door casts an algae-like glow across the flecked cement floor and corrugated metal walls.

There's some rubbish outside one of the storerooms, and the underwater lighting from the emergency exit illuminates an abandoned barrow.

Joona glances at the plan on the wall and locates the emergency exit, and works out where the camera is mounted. Everything is still quiet. A numbing feeling of exhaustion washes over him like a wave, forcing him to close his eyes for a couple of seconds.

The darkness on the computer screen is monotonous. Some of the cameras register light from coded locks, but nothing else.

'Dark,' Adam says.

'Yes,' Joona says, enlarging the fourteenth square.

He's just about to close it when there's a flicker in the bottom corner.

'Hang on,' he says.

Adam leans forward and looks at the dark image. There's nothing in sight, everything is still, but then the little light in the corner flashes again.

'What was that?' Adam whispers, leaning closer to the screen.

The little light flashes again. It's faint, and only manages to light up a small area of floor, revealing the pattern of the cement.

Joona clicks to enlarge the next camera image, then the next, and waits a while, but they show nothing but blackness. He looks at the overview, with all twenty-five cameras at the same time. Number fourteen flickers again, but the others remain lifeless.

'The source of the light ought to be here, or here,' Joona says, pointing at the plan. 'But it's not covered by one single camera, which makes no sense.'

'Where are we?' Adam asks, looking at the plan on the wall.

'Camera fourteen must be at the far end of corridor C,' Joona says.

He enlarges the images one by one. All black, still, but suddenly he stops.

'Did you see something?' Adam asks.

They both stare at the static black image.

'That's what I mean,' Joona replies. 'Where's the green light? This is the camera pointing at the emergency exit.'

'Try that one,' Adam says, pointing. 'That ought to pick up the light from the lock leading to the next section.'

Joona quickly enlarges the image. Also completely black. The door and lock can't be seen at all.

That can only be because there's something wrong with the camera. There seem to be an awful lot of faulty cameras down there.

'There's a huge area missing, loads of cameras,' he says, looking at Adam.

'Where?'

'The whole of this upper area, along corridors C, D and E . . . that's maybe fifty storerooms,' Joona says, looking back at the image from camera fourteen again.

The faint light flickers across the uneven floor, and remains on for a moment. He can just make out the bottom of the metal doors before the light goes off, then comes on again.

'That light's an emergency signal,' Joona says, getting up from the chair.

Security camera number fourteen is registering fragments of an emergency signal. Further along the corridor, where the cameras aren't working, someone is flashing a light. It's the international emergency signal using Morse code. SOS: three quick flashes followed by three longer ones, then three short ones again.

43

The automatic garage door whirrs shut behind them. The pain in his hip from walking down the slope makes Joona break out in a sweat. His heavy pistol is swinging against his ribs, and the sound of his stick echoes in the narrow tunnel leading down to the storage area.

'We ought to call for backup,' Adam says, drawing his Sig Sauer.

He pulls out the magazine, checks that it's full, pushes it back in and feeds the first bullet into the chamber.

'There's no time, but I can go in on my own,' Joona says.

'I was thinking of telling you to wait outside, you're not a police officer any more, and I can't take responsibility for you,' Adam explains.

They emerge into an underground garage, with metal doors leading to the storage area. Large ventilation pipes run across the ceiling.

'I can usually manage,' Joona says, stopping in front of the door.

He pulls out his large-calibre pistol. It's a Colt Combat, with new sights and an improved trigger coil. He's filed one side of the rosewood grip so that the gun sits snugly in his left hand.

Adam walks over to the keypad to the coded lock, and pulls out the list of staff codes. The little screen casts a blue light over his hand and up across the white concrete wall.

'Stay behind me,' he whispers, and opens the door.

They go inside, closing the steel door carefully behind them, and start to head along a dark side-passage. The monotonous grey metal walls and series of storeroom doors stretch off into the darkness.

They're approaching the first wider passageway which, according to the plan, runs the entire length of the basement.

They move across the cement floor almost silently. The only sound is from Adam's breathing, and the faint tapping of Joona's stick.

Adam is walking ahead, and slows down when he reaches the junction with the main passageway. His right shoulder rubs against the metal wall, he stops, then swings round the corner quickly with his pistol raised.

There's a buzzing sound as the ceiling lights come on ten metres away. It sounds like a large parrot climbing the bars of its cage. Adam lowers his gun and tries to breathe through his nose.

The barrel of his pistol is moving slightly in time with his raised pulse.

The sudden light makes Joona's migraine flare behind his eye. It's not serious, but he still has to lean against the wall for a moment before following Adam.

The lights in the main passageways are evidently activated by motion-sensors.

Joona looks up at one of the security cameras. The dark lens shimmers enigmatically.

The pipes running across the ceiling click. But otherwise the basement is completely quiet.

They reach a side-passage and once again there's a clatter of tiny claws as a section of lighting comes on in the main walkway.

They turn left, walking past rows of sealed storerooms, and pass two shabby sofas as the lights go out behind them.

'We ought to reach his area soon,' Adam whispers.

Indirect light from an electronic lock some way ahead makes the storerooms seem to bulge out into the passageway.

Adam pauses to listen.

There's a drumming, rattling sound somewhere. They can both hear something hard knocking against metal.

Then everything falls silent again.

They wait several seconds before continuing to move forward into the darkness.

There's a sudden scraping sound, then a metallic noise far in the distance. Joona points up at a camera in the ceiling: the lens has been covered with duct-tape.

Adam stops before he reaches the next main passageway, moves his pistol to his left hand, wipes his right palm on his trousers, gives his hand a shake, then takes a firm grip of his gun. He notices that some gold glitter from the woman in the hotel room has stuck to the sleeve of his jacket, and glances quickly at Joona, focuses and darts round the corner.

The ceiling clicks and ticks along the passageway as the lights come on in quick succession.

The walls, floor and ceiling are bathed in sharp light, but beyond the lights there's nothing but blackness. Even though the passageway runs another fifty metres or so, only the first ten are visible.

'Stop,' Joona says quietly behind Adam.

They both stand completely still in the illuminated passageway. A drop of sweat falls from the tip of Adam's nose. Joona leans on his stick, feeling strangely dizzy.

The brittle knocking sound starts up again in the distance, a high-frequency metallic buzz.

Suddenly the lights in the main passageway go out when the sensors can't detect any movement. The two men stand motionless, staring into the darkness. Up ahead there's a faint glow across the floor, from one of the side-passages.

The light vanishes, then returns in the same sequence: three longer flashes, followed by three short ones.

The strange drumming sound echoes again, followed by something hitting a metal wall. It's much closer now.

'What do we do?' Adam whispers.

Joona doesn't have time to answer before the ceiling lights at the very far end of the main passageway come on.

A young woman is standing in the middle of the gangway, swaying. She's wearing nothing but a pair of dirty tracksuit bottoms and a padded jacket. Her feet are bare, and her hair looks matted.

She's tied round the waist with thick steel wire, which snakes off into the side-passage next to her. When she takes a step forward the wire makes a metallic rattling sound against the walls behind her.

Her right arm is moving strangely, twitching and then moving away from her. There's a black band round her wrist. It looks like someone's tugging the band.

She steps towards them. Her arm sinks and suddenly there's a large shadow behind her. A huge dog with a bloody ear appears at her side. Its black leash hangs limp in her hand, and leads behind her back and up to the dog's neck.

The huge dog is a Great Dane. It reaches her chest and must weigh twice as much as her.

The dog moves nervously, twitching its head anxiously.

The woman says something and then drops the leash on the ground. The dog leaps forward and picks up speed rapidly in the passageway. The huge animal is getting closer to Joona and Adam with powerful, silent movements. Its muscles ripple across its back and loins as the lights come on, section by section.

They move back and raise their guns just as the lights go off at the far end of the passageway.

The young woman is no longer visible.

The sound of the animal's claws and its panting breath is getting louder.

They run into a side-passage, past padlocks that shimmer in the light from the main passageway, but fifteen metres in their way is blocked by a barricade of furniture and removal boxes.

Now they can hear barking from another direction.

A sharp pain flares behind one of Joona's eyes. It's as if a hot knife-blade is being pushed into his head, and when it gets pulled out again he can't see for a few seconds.

The pain of his migraine almost makes him drop his gun.

The dog slides on the cement floor, comes round the corner, catches sight of him and speeds up again.

Joona raises his pistol, blinks hard in an effort to see properly, but the sight on the barrel is trembling too much.

It's too dark, but he fires anyway. The sound of the shot multiplies off the metal walls and concrete. The bullet misses and ricochets between the walls.

The dog is approaching with powerful bounds.

Joona blinks and can just make it out in a series of flickering images, its pointed ears and shimmering muscles, shoulders and strong thighs. His stick clatters to the floor as he rests his shoulder against the corru-gated metal of a storeroom door and takes aim again.

'Joona!' Adam cries.

The sights quiver and slip past the beast's head. He squeezes the trigger. The sights slide down towards its dark torso, and the shot rings out as the bullet slams into the dog's chest just beneath its throat. The recoil sends Joona staggering backwards. He tries to keep his balance and throws his arm out, hitting the corrugated metal with the barrel of the pistol.

The dog's legs buckle. Its heavy body thuds to the floor, momentum carrying it forward. It slides across the cement floor and hits Joona's legs. He sinks to one knee and lets out a gasp. His vision flares, and jagged shapes flash and pulse in front of his eyes.

The dog's legs are still twitching as Joona gets to his feet and picks up his stick.

Some distance away Adam is clambering over the barricade of old furniture, rolled-up carpets and boxes. He gets tangled up in a bicycle and falls over the other side, hitting his head against a metal door.

In front of Joona is an upturned bed pushed against one wall. He shoves it over across the rest of the barricade and squeezes through the gap between it and the wall. Through piles of chairs, bags of clothes hangers and old-fashioned hairdryers on stands he sees Adam get to his feet just as the second dog launches itself at him.

44

Adam cries out in pain as Joona pushes through the gap between the bed and the storeroom wall. He hears something made of glass break under the pressure. The lights in the main passageway go out but Joona can still see that the huge dog has clamped its jaws round Adam's lower arm. It's pulling backwards hard, snarling as its claws scrabble on the cement floor.

Adam is gasping and trying to hit the animal.

Joona can't fire into the darkness, so tries to force his way through to them. A standard lamp with a broken shade, tucked into a pile of chairs, catches on his clothes.

The dog isn't letting go of Adam's arm. They crash into the metal wall together. Blood from Adam's arm is running from its locked jaws.

Its paws slip on the polished cement floor, its claws unable to get any grip.

The dog jerks backwards again, trying to knock Adam off balance, but he's managing to stay on his feet.

Joona shoves the lamp aside, its cord whips his cheek, but he makes it out past the bed and clambers over some boxes of books.

The dog makes a sudden downward jerk and when Adam stumbles forward it lets go and snaps at his neck. It misses and only catches part of the collar of his jacket, rips the fabric and tries to bite again. Adam throws himself back, falls and starts to kick out. The dog bites into his foot and tugs him towards it.

Joona pulls over a box of paperback books as he stumbles out on to the floor. He runs over with his pistol raised, but the dog suddenly lets go and disappears.

'Big dogs,' Joona says.

Leaning on his stick, he watches as Adam picks his pistol up off the floor and gets to his feet. Joona shuts his weary eyes for a moment, and can't help thinking that he might be about to break.

They carry on towards the next main passageway. The lights go on ahead of them, and the clicking sound is back.

'There,' Adam says.

They catch a glimpse of someone disappearing into one of the side-passages. There's a sound of clattering metal wire vibrating against the metal walls.

'Did you see? Was it the same woman?'

'I don't think so,' Joona replies, noticing how pale and sweaty Adam's face is. 'How are you doing?'

Adam doesn't answer, just shakes off the blood running down the back of his hand on to the floor. His lower arm is injured, but his leather jacket prevented it being completely torn apart.

They stick to the right-hand side of the passageway in order to be able to see into the side-passage on the left. The metal wire scrapes and rattles against the metal walls.

A young woman is standing in the passageway, swaying. It's not the same one as before. Her white jeans and chequered shirt are much dirtier.

'He said you'd come,' she mumbles in a brittle voice.

'We're police officers,' Adam says.

She staggers and fumbles for a little dog-whistle attached to a cord around her neck.

'Don't do it,' Adam says when he sees the second large dog get closer, crouching low with its ears folded down.

She's been crying, her make-up has run down her face and her hair is hanging in messy clumps.

There's blood around the waist of her shirt.

She rolls the dog-whistle between her fingers, then puts it to her lips.

Adam raises his pistol, takes aim and shoots the dog in the forehead. It collapses to the floor and the echo fades away.

She smiles at them through cracked lips, then staggers backwards when someone tugs on the metal wire round her waist.

'We saw an SOS signal,' Adam says.

'I'm smart, aren't I?' she says wearily.

She starts to move back along the passageway, and the metal wire pulling her clatters against the walls and floor.

'How many of you are there down here?' Adam asks as they follow her.

They step over the dog and the pool of dark blood spreading out across the floor.

'Where are you going?'

She doesn't answer, and they carry on round a corner. Further along the dimly lit passageway is a faint light. They pass an open storeroom and in the gloom they can see a mattress on the floor, boxes, some old skis, and stacks of tinned food.

Someone tugs harder on the wire and the young woman keeps stumbling on, opens the next door and staggers into the storeroom.

Light shines out on to the door opposite, and her shadow sways across the corrugated metal and smooth walls.

There's a growing stench of rotting rubbish.

Joona and Adam follow her with their pistols pointed at the floor. The light is coming from a pocket torch hanging from the ceiling, illuminating the nearest part of the large storeroom. Among a mass of removal crates and picture frames stands an emaciated man dressed in an unbuttoned mink coat.

It's Filip Cronstedt.

Joona and Adam raise their guns.

He's filthy, and has white froth at the corners of his mouth. His bare chest is covered with blood from a patchwork of cuts.

The first woman they saw, the one in the worn padded jacket, is sitting on a box in front of him, eating mushrooms from a jar with her fingers.

Filip hasn't seen them yet. He's carefully winding the retracted wire round a huge spindle, then scratches his neck and pulls the woman in the chequered shirt closer without looking up.

'Filip,' she whispers.

'I need you on guard, Sophia . . . I don't want to have to lock you up, but I've told you before, you can only have the light on when the door is closed.'

'Filip Cronstedt?' Adam says in a loud voice.

45

Filip Cronstedt looks up and stares at Adam with tired eyes and dilated pupils.

'I'm the hatmaker,' he says quietly.

Sweat is running down Joona's back, and he can't hold his pistol up any longer.

The torch hanging from the ceiling sways in a gust of air, and the shadows slide around the walls, its light reflecting off a large floor-mirror.

Joona moves to one side, blinks, and sees in the mirror that there's a knife sticking out of the box in front of Filip.

'We need to talk to you,' Adam says, moving forward cautiously.

'How many videos are you in every day?' Filip asks, staring at the floor. 'Where does it all go, what decisions does it lead to?'

'We can talk about that if you let the girls go.'

'I don't give a shit about Snowden and optic nerves,' he says slowly, pointing at the ceiling.

'Just let the girls go, and—'

'This isn't Prism or XKeyscore or Echelon,' he interrupts in a louder voice. 'This is a fuck of a lot bigger than that.'

Joona puts his pistol back in its holster and walks slowly towards the woman whose name is evidently Sophia. He can feel the last of his strength draining away, the way icy water makes everything sluggish, but scorchingly sleepy.

Filip's hand is getting closer to the knife sticking out of the box.

Sophia falters, and the wire rattles softly.

'Saturn ate his children,' Filip goes on, then sniggers. 'I mean, the NSA is much bigger . . . and we're their children . . .'

Joona just manages to see him put his hand on the knife before his vision flares again and he has to lean his own hand against the wall to stop himself falling.

Little dots are still floating before his eyes as he starts to loosen the coarse wire around Sophia's waist. He has to rest his forehead against her shoulder for a while before going on. He can hear her shallow breathing.

Without showing any sign of outward anxiety, he unwinds the wire some twenty revolutions before she's free.

'Are there more of you down here?' he asks in a subdued voice as he leads her out of the storeroom.

'Just me and my sister,' she replies.

'We're going to get you out. What's your sister's name?'

'Carola.'

The metal wire unravels on the cement floor with a scraping sound.

Filip tugs at the knife, making the side of the box bulge out before he loses his grip.

'We're here now, but who ends up in Guantánamo? You don't know, do you?' he says without looking at them.

'Carola,' Joona says in a normal tone of voice. 'Could you come over here, please?'

Sophia's sister puts the lid back on the jar of mushrooms and shakes her head without looking up.

'Carola, come to me,' Sophia says.

She sits there picking at the jar, as Filip looks at her and scratches his neck.

'Come on,' Joona says, feeling his gun rub against his chest.

'Eugene is with them, you know, GCHQ . . . the NSA. Same thing . . . I've been so badly fucking deceived, for years . . . Everyone's naked, everyone's having fun . . . but how can you protect yourself if you're completely naked, if everyone can film you from the fucking back?'

The torch spins round and dark shadows cross their faces and shoulders.

'Sophia wants you to come over here,' Joona says.

Carola looks up and smiles at her sister. Sophia brushes the tears from her cheeks and holds out her hand.

'Can we go home now?' Carola whispers, and stands up at last.

She's about to start walking when Filip grabs hold of her hair and pulls her back, tugs the knife from the box and holds it to her throat.

'Hang on, hang on, take it easy now,' Adam calls. 'Look, I'm putting my gun down.'

'Go to hell!' Filip screams and sticks the knife into his forehead before putting it to Carola's throat again.

'Do something!' Sophia whimpers.

Blood from the wound in Filip's forehead trickles through one eyebrow and drips down on to his cheek.

'I know you're only trying to protect her,' Joona says calmly.

'Yes, but you—'

'Listen to me,' Adam interrupts, breathing quickly. 'You need to put the knife down.'

Sophia is sobbing with her hand over her mouth. Filip looks at Adam and grins at him.

'I know where you're from,' he says, and presses the knife harder against Carola's neck.

'Put the knife down now,' Adam shouts, moving sideways to get a clear line of fire.

Filip watches Adam and licks his lips nervously. The room is gloomy, but blood is clearly running down the blade.

'Filip, you're hurting her,' Joona says, trying to conquer his dizziness. 'You don't have to do that, we're no threat to you . . .'

'Shut up!'

'We're just here to—'

'Shut up!'

'We're here to ask about Maria Carlsson,' Joona concludes.

'Maria? My Maria?' he says in a low voice. 'Why . . .?'

Joona nods and thinks that he could shoot Filip in the shoulder, disarm him and then lie down on the floor. He's waited too long. He can hardly see anything now, through the burning pain behind his eyes.

'Look, I'm taking my gun out and giving it to you,' Joona says, carefully drawing his Colt.

Filip stares at him with bloodshot eyes.

'Maria said the NSA have started creeping about in her garden,' he explains. 'I went over and saw for myself, a skinny man in yellow over-alls, like the Lofoten fishermen when I was little, he was filming her through the window, and . . .'

Joona wipes some blood from his nose and then his head explodes and his legs give way.

Sophia screams when he slumps on to his side, tries to get up, but falls on to his back and lies there with his eyelids quivering.

She goes over to him and kneels down. A bubbling, pulsing sensation behind one eye makes him hold his breath. Before it goes completely dark he feels her pull the pistol from his hand.

She stands up, straightens her back, takes a few shallow, panting breaths, then aims the pistol at Filip.

'Let my sister go!' she says sharply. 'Just let her go!'

'Put the gun down,' Adam says in a shaky voice, and moves between them. 'I'm a police officer, you need to trust me.'

'Get out of the way!' she yells. 'Filip's not going to let her go!'

'Don't do anything silly,' Adam says, holding out his hand.

'Don't touch me – I'll shoot!'

She's clutching the pistol with both hands, but the barrel is still shaking.

'Give me the gun and—'

There's a deafening explosion as the pistol goes off. The bullet grazes Adam's torso and hits Filip in the top of his arm. The knife falls to the floor and Filip stares at Sophia in astonishment as blood seeps through his fingers.

'Get out of the way!' she shouts again.

Adam lurches to the side, and feels warm blood pulsing out beneath his clothes. Sophia fires again, and hits Filip right in the chest. Blood spatters the boxes behind him and runs across the glass of the mirror. The empty cartridge falls to the ground with a tinkling sound.

Carola is still standing there with her head bowed, and slowly raises her hand to her neck. Sophia lowers the gun and stares blankly at Filip, who slumps down and sits on the floor, leaning back against a box.

He picks listlessly at the wound in his chest as blood pumps out, and his eyes flit about as he tries to say something.

46

On his way to his piano lesson, Erik stops at the ICA supermarket next to the Globe. He knows Madeleine loves popcorn, so he's thinking of buying a few bags. As he walks through the shop he catches sight of his former patient, Nestor, in the dairy section. The tall, slim man is dressed in pressed trousers and a knitted grey sweater over a white shirt. His thin, clean-shaven face and small head with its white hair and side-parting look exactly the same as ever.

Nestor has seen him, and smiles in surprise, but Erik doesn't go over to talk to him, just waves from a distance and carries on through the shop.

He picks up some popcorn and is on his way towards the checkout when he sees a popcorn machine on special offer. He knows he has a tendency to go over the top, but it doesn't weigh much, and isn't particularly expensive.

When he emerges into the car park with his bags of corn and the popcorn machine, he catches sight of Nestor again. The tall man is waiting at the crossing, on his way towards the underground. He has six full bags of shopping by his sides. They're so heavy that he can only carry them a few metres at a time.

Erik opens the boot of his car and puts the box inside. He's sure Nestor hasn't spotted him. The shy man is muttering to himself as he picks up the bags, shuffles a few metres, then puts them down again.

Nestor is standing blowing into his thin hands as Erik goes up to him.

'That looks heavy,' he says.

'Erik? No, it's f-fine.' Nestor smiles.

'Where do you live? I'll give you a lift.'

'I don't want to be a nuisance,' he whispers.

'You're not,' Erik says, picking up four of the bags.

As Nestor gets in the car beside him, he repeats that he could have managed. Erik replies that he knows that, and pulls out slowly from his parking space.

'Thanks for the coffee . . . but you shouldn't be buying things for me,' Erik says.

'You saved m-my life,' Nestor replies quietly.

Erik recalls how Nestor's psychotic breakdown happened when his seriously ill dog had to be put down three years ago.

When he was allocated to Erik as a patient, Erik had read the notes from the secure psychiatric unit where Nestor had been admitted. He used to talk to dead people: a grey lady who brushed dandruff from her hair, and a mean old man who twisted his arms in different directions.

During Erik's conversations with him, it emerged that Nestor was fixated upon his dog's death. He talked a lot about the syringe being stuck in his right front paw, and how the fluid was injected. The dog shook and urine spread across the bench as its muscles relaxed. He felt he had been tricked by the vet and the vet's wife.

Nestor responded well to treatment, but when he tried to cut down his daily dose of Risperdal, he began hearing strange voices again.

Erik was never sure if had actually managed to hypnotise Nestor, he may have belonged to the small group who weren't receptive, but during those relaxed sessions in the dimly lit treatment room they did at least begin to get to grips with things.

Nestor had grown up with his mother, younger brother, and a black Labrador. When he was seven, his five-year-old brother became seriously ill with a lung infection, which exacerbated his already bad asthma. The boys' mother told Nestor that his brother would die unless they had the dog put down. Nestor took the dog to Söderbysjön and drowned it in a trunk full of stones.

But his brother died anyway.

In Nestor's mind, the two events became intertwined. He had always suffered from the belief that he had drowned his brother in a trunk, and had no memory of the dog.

They worked on his anger with his mother's damaging manipulation, and after a month he finally let go of the idea of his own guilt, and the notion that his mother could sometimes control his actions from beyond the grave.

Nestor was living normally again now, didn't need to take any medication, and was incredibly grateful to Erik.

They pass St Mark's Church in Björkhagen and pull up outside Axvallsvägen 53.

Nestor unbuckles his seat belt and Erik helps him carry his food to the door of his ground-floor flat.

'Thanks for everything,' the former patient says in a tremulous voice. 'I've got ice cream, and time to—'

'I need to get going,' Erik says.

'But I have to offer you s-something,' Nestor says, opening the door.

'Nestor, I've got an appointment.'

'Walk across the dead without a s-sound. Walk across the dead and hear their murmuring resound.'

'I haven't got time for riddles now,' Erik says, and walks out of the door of the building.

'Promise!' Nestor calls after him.

47

Jackie and Madeleine are sitting together on the sofa eating popcorn while Erik tries to play his étude.

Madeleine says he's very good every time he makes a mistake. She's tired and her yawns are getting bigger and bigger.

Jackie tries to explain the quaver rests and the rhythmic pattern, and gets up and puts her right hand on top of his.

She asks him to start from the twenty-second bar with his left hand, then she suddenly falls silent, goes back to her daughter, and listens to her breathing.

'Could you manage to carry her to bed?' she asks. 'My elbow isn't up to it.'

Erik gets up from the piano and picks the child up. Jackie walks ahead of them, opens the door to the girl's room, turns the light out and pulls the covers back for Erik.

Erik carefully lays Madeleine down on her bed, and brushes the hair from her face.

Jackie tucks her daughter in and kisses her on the cheek, whispers something in her ear, and turns on the little pink nightlight on the bedside table.

Only now does Erik see that the walls of the child's bedroom are covered in rude words, curses and obscenities.

Some of the words are written in childish scribble in chalk, misspelled, whereas others are written in more confident handwriting. Erik presumes Madeleine must have been doing this for several years. Her mother is the only person unable to see what she's done.

'What is it?' Jackie says, noticing his silence.

'Nothing,' he says, closing the door gently behind him.

As they walk through the hall, Erik wonders if he should tell Jackie about what he saw, or just let it go.

'Should I leave?' Erik asks.

'I don't know,' Jackie replies.

She holds out her hands and feels his face, stroking his cheeks and chin.

'I'm just going to get some water,' she says hoarsely, then goes into the kitchen and opens a cupboard.

He helps her, standing close to her, filling the glass and passing it to her. She drinks, and then he kisses her cool mouth before she has time to wipe her chin.

They embrace, she stands on tiptoe and they kiss each other deeply, foreheads bumping together.

Erik's hands slide over her back and hips. The fabric of her skirt has a peculiar texture, and rustles like thin paper.

She pulls away slightly, turns her face and puts one hand on his chest.

'We don't have to,' he says to her.

She shakes her head and puts her hand behind his neck again, pulls him to her, kisses his neck, fumbles with the buttons of his trousers, then stops herself.

'Are the curtains closed?' she whispers.

'Yes.'

She goes to the door and listens for any sound in the corridor, then closes it carefully.

'Maybe we shouldn't do this here, not now.'

'OK,' he says.

She stands with her back to the draining board, one hand on the counter, her mouth half-open.

'Can you see me?' she asks, taking her dark glasses off.

'Yes,' Erik replies.

Her clothes are disordered, her blouse hanging outside her skirt, and her short hair is rather messed up.

'Sorry, I'm being difficult.'

'There's no rush,' Erik mumbles, and walks up to her, takes hold of her shoulders and kisses her again.

'Let's take our clothes off. Shall we?' she whispers.

They get undressed in the kitchen, and Jackie starts talking slowly about a radio report she heard about the persecution of Christians in Iraq.

'Now France is offering asylum to all of them,' she smiles.

He unbuttons his trousers and looks at her as she lays item after item on the chair, and undoes her bra.

Completely naked, Erik goes and stands beside her, thinking that he feels oddly natural. He doesn't even try to hold his stomach in.

Jackie's teeth glisten in the faint light as she pulls her underpants down, wriggles her legs and lets them fall.

'I'm not a shy person,' she says quietly.

Her nipples are pale brown, and in the darkness she looks luminous. A marbled tracery of veins is faintly visible beneath her pale skin. Her dark pubic hair makes her inner thighs look fragile.

Erik takes her outstretched hand and kisses her. She backs into the chair and sits down. He leans forward, kisses her on the lips again, then kneels down and kisses her breasts and stomach. He pulls her carefully to the edge of the chair and parts her legs. Her folded clothes fall to the floor.

She's already wet, and tastes of warm sugar to Erik. Her thighs quiver against his cheeks and her breathing grows heavier.

The salt cellar topples over on the table and rolls in a semi-circle.

She holds his head between her legs, gasping faster, the chair slides backwards and she slips gently on to the floor with a smile.

'I'm not sure I'm any good at relationships,' she says, resting the back of her head uncomfortably against the seat of the chair.

'I'm just a pupil,' he whispers.

She rolls over on to her stomach and starts to crawl under the table. He follows her and grabs hold of her behind just as she rolls on to her back.

She pulls him gently to her, between her thighs, hears him hit his head on the table and feels the heat of his bare skin against hers.

Jackie holds his back hard and gasps for breath as he slowly slides into her and then pauses.

'Don't stop,' she whispers.

Her heart is pounding and the torrent of thoughts has finally fallen silent. She moves her hips, presses herself towards him and feels the silky heat from her crotch.

The hard floor disappears behind her, her thighs tremble and stretch, and Erik moves faster. She tenses her buttocks and toes and whimpers against his shoulder as her orgasm pulsates through her body.

———

Erik wakes up in the darkness to the sound of gentle piano music. It sounds strangely muted, like a piano buried under the ground. At first he thinks he's dreaming. He reaches out his hand but can't feel Jackie. Moonlight filters through the fabric of the curtains, casting strange, long shadows across the room. With a shiver he creeps out of bed and into the flat. Jackie is sitting naked on the piano stool in the living room. She's placed a thin blanket over the piano to muffle the sound.

Through the gloom he sees her body swaying gently, her hands seem to be slipping through water. Her bare feet move over the brass pedals. She is sitting on the edge of the stool, and he can see her slender waist and the shadowy groove down the centre of her upright back.

'*Nam et si ambulavero in medio umbrae mortis,*' she murmurs to herself.

He thinks she knows that he's there, but she still plays to the end of the piece before turning towards him.

'The neighbours have complained,' she says quietly. 'But I need to learn a fairly hard piece for a wedding tomorrow.'

'It sounded wonderful.'

'Go back to bed,' she whispers.

He returns to the bed and is just about to fall asleep when he finds himself thinking of Björn Kern. The police still don't know that the dead woman was sitting with her hand to her ear. The thought snaps Erik awake when he realises that he could be hindering the police investigation.

After an hour the music falls silent and Jackie comes back to the bedroom. It's already light outside by the time he falls asleep again.

In the morning the bed is empty. Erik goes to the bathroom, showers, then gets dressed. When he emerges he can hear Jackie and Madeleine in the kitchen.

He walks in and gets a cup of coffee. Madeleine is eating breakfast cereal with milk and fresh raspberries.

Jackie explains that she has to be in Adolf Fredrik Church in a little while to rehearse for the wedding.

As soon as she leaves the kitchen to get changed, Madeleine puts her spoon down and turns towards Erik.

'Mum says you carried me to bed,' she says.

'She asked me to help her.'

'Was it dark in my room?' she asks, looking at him with bottomless eyes.

'I haven't said anything to your mum . . . that would be better coming from you.'

The girl shakes her head, and tears start to run down her cheeks.

'It's not as bad as you think,' Erik says.

'Mum will be really sad,' she hiccoughs.

'It'll be all right.'

'I don't know why I have to ruin everything,' she sobs.

'You don't.'

'Yes I do, I can't get rid of that,' she says, wiping her cheeks.

'I did far worse things . . .'

'No,' she sobs.

'Maddy, it's not a problem . . . Listen, now,' he says. 'We can . . . Why don't you and I paint your walls?'

'Can you do that?'

'Yes.'

She looks at him with a trembling chin and nods several times.

'What colour would you like?'

'Blue . . . blue, like Mum's nightie,' she smiles.

'Is that light blue?'

'What are you talking about?' Jackie asks.

She's standing in the doorway, already dressed in her black skirt and jacket, a pale pink blouse, round sunglasses and pink lipstick.

'Maddy thinks it's time to repaint her room, and I said I'd be happy to help.'

'OK,' Jackie says, with a slightly bemused expression.

48

Margot sees Adam waiting for her in the underground garage of Police Headquarters. His T-shirt is bulging because of the bandage round his chest. She walks towards him, but has to stop when the baby pushes upwards. The plastic-covered trestle tables are covered with objects seized from Filip Cronstedt's storeroom, lined up and numbered, ready for analysis.

Another colleague approaches from the other direction, she hears him say something appreciative to Adam, then he carries on towards the lifts.

Adam's weary face, with its dark shadow of stubble, looks brittle in the harsh lighting.

Behind him she can see that the work of cataloguing the vast amount of material seized is proceeding. On the first table lies a gilded bed-head, a wooden crate containing starched, folded linen, battered books and three pairs of trainers.

'How are you feeling?' Margot asks when she reaches Adam.

'It's nothing,' he replies, putting his hand to his ribs. 'My mind's spinning, though, I keep seeing it all and thinking that I would have been dead if she'd angled the gun just a tiny bit more, three milli-metres to the left.'

'You should never have gone down there without backup.'

'I made the decision that we had to go in . . . but I don't think I really appreciated the state Joona was in – he collapsed on the floor and dropped his gun.'

'He shouldn't have been there anyway.'

'It was a fuck up.' He nods. 'There's going to be an internal inquiry . . . obviously, seeing as I was shot . . . but it will probably end up with the National Police-Related Crimes Unit, so we'll need to talk that through.'

Margot looks at a faded school poster of the female anatomy. The eyes have been coloured in with blue chalk.

'But without Joona, we'd never have caught Filip,' she says.

'I caught Filip, I was the one who did that. Joona was lying on the floor . . .'

The harsh glare from the fluorescent lights and magnifying lamps reflects off the plastic between the objects on the tables. Margot stops beside three video cameras with crushed lenses wrapped in ESD-proof packaging in a spacious cardboard box.

'Is anyone trying to match Filip's cameras with the videos of the victims?' she asks.

'I presume so.'

'But you haven't found the tongue-stud or the rest of the deer?'

'Give it time,' Adam smiles. 'This is just the material from the storeroom. There's no rush, the important thing is that it's over, that we've got him.'

They pass a pile of hand-painted tin soldiers and Margot can't help thinking that the rest of the little porcelain deer and the Saturn stud ought to be here, given that Filip was living in the storage facility at the time of the murders.

'How sure are we that it's him?' she asks.

'Filip's in the operating theatre at the Karolinska, but as soon as he can talk we'll get a confession out of him.'

'Have you got anyone on guard there?' she asks.

'He was shot in the chest, one lung is wrecked, so I hardly think that's necessary.'

'Do it anyway.'

There are about twenty polaroid photographs of young women with bare chests in a small plastic folder.

'If it will calm you down, I'll sort it out as soon as I get upstairs,' Adam replies.

'I spoke to Joona in the hospital, and he seems to think that Filip didn't commit the murders, and—'

'What the fuck?' Adam interrupts with an irritated smile. 'I let Joona come with me because I felt sorry for him – that was a mistake I'm not going to repeat. We can't let him play at being a detective.'

'I agree,' she says quickly.

'He messed up, and he's not coming anywhere near this investigation again.'

'I'm just trying to say that this feels too easy,' Margot says calmly, carrying on along the tables.

'Filip was on the point of confessing when he was shot. He said he'd been creeping about outside Maria Carlsson's windows,' Adam says, turning to her with a grin. 'He's got no alibi for the evenings of the murders, he's extremely violent, paranoid, and completely obsessed with cameras and surveillance—'

'I know, but . . .'

'He'd locked himself away with two women, you should have been there, he had them tied up with steel wire.'

Even though he is hollow-eyed and clearly short of sleep, there's an underlying fire in his eyes, and his cheeks are flushed.

Adam stops and catches his breath, leans his knuckles on the nearest table for a while with his eyes closed.

The stress and exertions of the night come back to hit him like a heavy pendulum. He thinks about the ringing in his ears after the last shot, as blood trickled down his side and under the waist of his jeans before he managed to disarm one of the sisters.

He thinks of the huge dog that tried to rip him apart, and the orgy in the Birger Jarl Hotel, the unprotected sex with an unknown woman.

Tears well up in his eyes as he thinks about how little control he has, how little he knows about himself.

He suddenly feels an intense desire to go home to his wife, to curl up in his warm bed behind Katryna, to the smell of her hand cream and her ugly bed socks and the liver spots on her back that look almost like the Plough.

Margot walks past an old-fashioned gramophone, and stops in front of some jewellery on a piece of cardboard. She gets out a pen and pokes through the tarnished silver rings, brooches, broken chains and crucifixes. She picks up a heart-shaped charm with her pen just as her mobile rings.

Margot lets the heart fall back on to the cardboard, pulls out her phone and answers by giving her surname.

Something in her voice makes Adam turn towards her.

Margot will always remember this moment, the way they were standing in the bright light among Filip's possessions, and how her heartbeat drowned out absolutely everything else for a few moments.

'What is it?' Adam says.

She stares at him, she can't talk, her throat is so dry, and she realises that her jaw is trembling.

'A film,' she hisses. 'We've received another film.'

'Fuck,' Adam swears, and starts running towards the lifts.

'Call the hospital!' Margot gasps as they hurry past the tables towards the lifts. 'Check if Filip's escaped.'

Adam presses the lift-button, then clutches his phone to his ear as she catches up with him. The machinery rumbles slowly. She's moved too quickly and her pelvis is burning.

Adam holds the phone to his ear and shakes his head in her direction.

'Has he gone?' she gasps.

'No answer,' he says anxiously.

The lift stops two floors up and Margot presses the button again, whispering angry curses to herself.

Finally someone picks up at the hospital. A sluggish voice tells Adam that he's reached the Intensive Care Unit.

'My name is Adam Youssef, I'm a detective with the National Criminal Investigation Department, and I need to know if one of your patients, Filip Cronstedt, is still with you.'

'Filip Cronstedt,' the man at the other end says.

'Listen, you have to listen,' Adam pleads, and realises how incoherent he sounds. 'I want you to go and see him and check that he's there.'

The man sighs, as though he were indulging some sort of ridiculous whim, but Adam hears him put the phone down on his desk and walk away.

'He's gone to check,' Adam tells Margot.

'Make sure they confirm his identity,' she says, as the lift doors close behind them.

They shuffle about like caged animals as they're sucked up inside the building. Adam's shoulder crumples a poster advertising a concert by the police choir.

'Filip Cronstedt is still sedated,' the slow voice finally tells Adam.

'Filip's sedated,' Adam repeats.

49

Adam runs down the corridor ahead of Margot. Filip Cronstedt was given emergency sedation when he was brought into A&E early that morning, and has been kept like that ever since.

The real serial killer is still on the loose.

Margot follows Adam into their office and sees the treetops of Kronoberg Park in the pale sunlight through the small windows.

'Have we got a copy?'

'It looks like it,' he replies.

Margot is gasping for breath as she sinks onto the second chair in front of the computer while Adam clicks the video file. The base of her spine is stinging and she leans back, her shirt pulling up over her bulging stomach.

'The film has been online for two minutes,' he whispers, and starts the media-player.

The camera is moving quickly through the outer fringes of a bird cherry. The leaves obscure the view for a moment, then a bedroom window appears on the screen, with condensation along the bottom.

The garden is shady, but the white sky shimmers in the windowsill.

The camera moves backwards again when a woman dressed in her underwear comes into the room. She hangs a white towel with old hair-dye stains over the back of a chair, then stops and leans one hand against the wall.

'One minute left,' Adam says.

The room fills with soft light from the lamp in the ceiling. They can make out fingerprints on the mirror, and a slightly tilted framed poster from the Picasso exhibition at Moderna Museet.

The camera moves to one side, and now they can both see a reddish-brown porcelain deer on the bedside table.

'The deer,' Margot pants, leaning towards the screen as her plait falls over her shoulder.

The snapped deer's head that Susanna Kern was clutching in her hand must have come from an ornament exactly like that one.

The woman in the bedroom is holding one hand to her mouth, and walks slowly over to the bedside table, opens the drawer and takes something out of it. Her face is more visible in the glow of the bedside lamp. She has pale eyebrows and a straight nose, but her eyes are hidden behind the reflection in her dark-framed glasses, and her mouth is relaxed. Her bra is red and worn, and her underpants white, with some sort of sanitary pad. She rubs something over one of her thighs and then takes out a small, white stick and presses it to her muscle.

'What's she doing?' Adam asks.

'That's an insulin injection.'

The woman holds a swab against her thigh and screws her eyes shut for a moment, then opens them again. She leans forward to put the syringe back in the drawer, and manages to catch the little deer, knocking it over. Small fragments fly up in the sharp lighting as the head snaps off and falls to the floor.

'What the hell is this?' Adam whispers.

With a weary look on her face the woman bends over and picks up the porcelain head, puts it on the bedside table, then goes round the bed towards the steamed-up window. Something makes her stop and peer out, searching the darkness beyond.

The camera moves slowly backwards, and some leaves brush over the lens.

The woman looks worried. She puts out her hand, takes hold of the cord of the blinds and loosens the catch by tugging it to the side. The slats slide down, but end up crooked and she pulls the cord and lets them fall again, then gives up. Through the damaged blinds she can be seen turning back towards the room and scratching her right buttock before the film suddenly comes to an end.

'OK, I'm a bit tired,' Adam says in an unsteady voice, and stands up. 'But this is crazy – isn't it?'

'So what do we do? Watch the film again?'

Her phone buzzes on the desk, Margot turns it over and sees that it's one of the forensics team.

'What have you got?' Margot says as soon she answers.

'Same thing, impossible to trace either the film or the link.'

'So we're waiting for someone to find the body,' Margot says, and ends the call.

'She's maybe one metre seventy tall, weighs less than sixty kilos,' Adam says. 'Her hair is probably dark blonde when it's dry.'

'She's got type-1 diabetes, went to see the Picasso exhibition last autumn, single, regularly colours her hair,' Margot adds in a monotone.

'Broken blinds,' Adam says, printing out a large colour picture where the whole of the woman's face is illuminated.

He goes over to the wall and pins the photograph up as high as he can. A solitary picture, no name, no location.

'Victim number three,' he says weakly.

To the left of the photograph are pictures of the first two victims, stills taken from the YouTube clips. The difference is that below those two first pictures are names and photographs of the murder scenes, as well as reports from the forensic analysis of the scenes and the post-mortems.

Maria Carlsson and Susanna Kern.

Multiple stab and knife-wounds to their faces, necks and chests, severing their aortas, lungs and hearts.

50

Sandra Lundgren leaves the bedroom, and feels a shiver run down her spine, as if someone were watching her from behind.

She tightens the belt of her dressing-gown, which is so long it reaches the floor. Her medication leaves her feeling drowsy long into the day. She goes into the kitchen, opens the fridge and takes out the remains of the chocolate cake and puts it on the worktop.

She adjusts her glasses and her dressing-gown falls open again, uncovering her stomach and sagging underwear. She shivers, pulls the wide-bladed knife from the block, cuts a small slice of cake and puts it in her mouth without bothering to get a spoon.

She's started using Stefan's striped dressing-gown even though it actually makes her feel sad. But she likes the way it weighs upon her breasts, its drooping shoulders, the threads hanging off the sleeves.

Beside the candleholder on the drop-leaf table is the letter from Södertörn University College. She looks at it again, even though she's already read it thirty times. She's on the reserve list for creative writing. Her mum helped her fill in the application. Back then she didn't feel up to doing it herself, but her mother knew how much it would mean to her to be accepted onto the course.

She cried in the spring when she was told she hadn't got a place. That was probably a bit of an overreaction. Nothing had really changed, after all. She would just carry on with her fourth term on the career-counselling programme instead.

She doesn't know how long the letter had been lying there among all the old post on the hall floor, but she's read it now, and it's sitting on the kitchen table.

She decides to phone her mum and tell her the news.

Sandra glances at the window and sees two men walking towards Vinterviken on the other side of the road. She lives on the ground floor, but still hasn't got used to the fact that people sometimes stop and look right in through her windows.

The wooden floor out in the hallway creaks. She thinks it sounds like a grown person trying to creep quietly.

Sandra dials the number as she sits down on one of the kitchen chairs. She holds the phone to her ear as the call goes through, pinching the corner of the letter.

'Hi, Mum, it's me,' she says.

'Hello, darling, I was just going to call you . . . Have you thought any more about this evening?'

'What?'

'About coming over for a meal.'

'Oh yes . . . I don't think I feel up to it.'

'You still have to eat, you know. I could come and pick you up in the car, I'll give you a lift both ways.'

Sandra suddenly hears something rustling and looks over towards the dark hallway, and its clothes and shoes.

'Will you let me do that? Darling?'

'OK,' she whispers, looking at the letter in her hand.

'What would you like?'

'I don't know . . .'

'Shall I do beef á la Rydberg? You usually like that, you know, cubes of steak and—'

'OK, Mum,' she interrupts, and goes into the bathroom.

The blister-pack of Prozac is on the edge of the basin. The green-and-white capsules shimmer in their plastic rows.

Sandra looks at her own reflection in the mirror. The bathroom door is open behind her and she can see right out into the hall. It looks like there's someone standing there. Her heart skips a beat, even though she knows it's only her black raincoat.

'The three musketeers went out for lunch today . . .'

Sandra leaves the bathroom while her mother tells her that she and her sisters went out to the Waxholm Hotel and had fried Baltic herring with mashed potatoes and lingonberry jam, melted butter, and nice cold low-alcohol beer.

'How is Malin?' Sandra asks.

'She's amazing,' her mother replies. 'I don't know how she manages to be so positive the whole time . . . she's had her last session of radiotherapy, and feels pretty good . . . It makes you glad you live in Sweden . . . she'd never have been able to pay for the treatment on her own . . .'

'Isn't there anything else they can do now?'

'Karolina thinks we should all move to Jamaica and sit around smoking cannabis and eating good food until the money runs out.'

'I'll come with you,' Sandra smiles.

'I'll let her know,' her mum laughs.

The phone feels warm and sticky against her cheek. Sandra moves it to her other ear and walks to the bedroom, but stops suddenly. She can't help staring at the window. The big bird cherry is moving through the broken blinds.

'I had a look at the list of course literature for your fourth term,' her mum says. 'It's all about the politics of the job market.'

'Yes,' Sandra says weakly.

She isn't sure why she doesn't just tell her mum about her place at Södertörn.

Slowly she forces herself to look away from the window, and catches sight of herself in the mirror. Her dressing-gown has fallen open again. She stands there in her underwear, looking at herself, her pale skin, rounded breasts, her smooth stomach, and the long, pink scar across her right thigh.

She and Stefan had rented a cottage in Åre over the Easter holiday. She was driving and Stefan was asleep as they got close to Östersund. It was dark, and the box of skis on the roof was making a lot of noise. They had been stuck behind a timber truck for several kilometres through the black fir-forest. The wide rear tyres of the swaying trailer were churning up masses of snow from the edge of the road. In the end she pulled out to the left to overtake, but saw the lights from an oncoming bus and pulled in again.

After the bus there were three cars, then nothing again. Sandra pulled out again and accelerated. They had just reached a long downward slope and the timber-truck was going faster. She sat beside the huge trailer, clutching the wheel with both hands and felt the car lurch in the turbulence.

Sandra accelerated a bit too hard to get past, and her wheels slid in the ridge of snow in the middle of the road. She lost control of the car and ended up underneath the timber truck. They got stuck and were dragged along, the metal screeching and shaking. She had blood in her eyes but saw the huge wheels thud into the side of the car. The metal gave way and crumpled on top of Stefan. There was a whirlwind of glass and the truck jack-knifed as the driver braked and the trailer lurched forward with a screech.

She was alive, but Stefan was dead. She had seen the photographs and read what little had been reported about the evening when her life was thrown off course.

'Are you taking your pills like you should?' her mum asks gently, and Sandra realises that she must have stopped talking again.

'Leave it, Mum, I can't talk now,' she says.

'But you'll come this evening?' her mum says quickly, unable to conceal her concern.

'I don't know,' Sandra replies, sitting on the bed and screwing her eyes as tightly shut as she can.

'It would be lovely if you did. I'll come and get you, and if you change your mind I can take you back whenever you want.'

'We'll talk later on,' Sandra says, and ends the call.

She puts the phone down on the bedside table, next to her blood-sugar monitor.

Outside the window the verdant foliage of the bushes is swaying about.

Sandra takes off the dressing-gown and lays it on the bed, pulls on her jeans and opens the chest of drawers. The broken deer is lying beside the pile of neatly folded clothes. The funny thing is that the little head has disappeared. She takes off her glasses and pulls on a clean T-shirt. Once again she feels like she's being watched, and glances at the broken blinds, the shadowy garden, the leaves moving in the wind.

She hears a thud from the hall and jumps. It's probably just more adverts, despite the sign on the door. She picks up the phone to call her mum back and apologise, and try to explain that she's actually happy, but that being happy dredges up a load of sadness too.

She goes out into the kitchen again, looks at the letter on the table and walks over to the worktop to cut herself another slice of cake, but the knife isn't there.

She has time to think that her medication has made her confused, that she must have put the knife down in the bathroom or bedroom, when someone dressed in yellow comes towards her from the hall with long strides.

Sandra just stands still, this can't be happening.

She doesn't manage to say a word, just hold her left hand up to protect herself.

The knife comes from above, and hits her in the chest.

Her legs collapse and the knife is jerked out as she falls backwards and sits down hard on the floor. She hits her head against the table, dislodging the candle from its holder, and it rolls over the edge.

Sandra feels hot blood pulsing down over her stomach. She has a terrible pain deep inside her chest, it feels like her heart is shaking.

Sandra just sits there, unable to move, unable to understand, when she feels a blow to her head, then a terrible pain in her cheek. She falls backwards and loses consciousness. Everything becomes dark and warm, she can hear burbling water, then a burning pain in her lungs. She comes round and starts coughing up blood, stares up at the ceiling for a few seconds, feels the blade of the knife moving about inside her chest.

Her heart quivers a few times, then stops. It all goes quiet, it feels as if she's wading out into warm water. A silver-grey river that's flowing gently on into the night.

51

The police have only had the third film for eighty minutes when the emergency call centre receives a phone call from a woman who says in a monotone that her daughter has been murdered.

The time is quarter to five when Margot parks her Lincoln Towncar in front of the fluttering tape of the police cordon.

The policeman who went inside to see if the victim could be saved is sitting on the step of the neighbouring doorway. His face is grey, and there's a dark look in his eyes. A paramedic puts a blanket round his shoulders and checks his blood pressure as Adam talks to him. The woman who found her daughter is in hospital with her sister. Margot makes a mental note to go and talk to her later, once the tranquillisers have softened the burning layer of pain and shock.

While Margot was driving to Hägersten she'd called Joona at the hospital to tell him about the third murder. He sounded very tired, but listened to everything she told him, and for some strange reason that made her feel calmer.

Margot passes the inner cordon and enters the hallway of the block of flats. Floodlights illuminate the stairwell, reflecting off the glass covering the list of residents' names.

Margot pulls on some shoe-protectors and carries on past the forensics officers who are setting out stepping-plates in silence.

She stops in the harsh glare of the floodlights. The metal clicks as it heats up. The smell of warm blood and urine is overpowering and acrid. A forensics officer is filming the room according to a set procedure. On the linoleum floor sits a woman with an utterly ravaged face, her chest split open. Her glasses have fallen off into the pool of blood beside the table.

She's lying with her hand over her left breast. Her soft skin shimmers pearly white beneath her blood-blackened hand.

She has evidently been placed in that position after death, but it doesn't look particularly sexual.

Margot stands there for a few moments, looking at the devastating scene, at the display of brutality, the blood sprayed out by a stabbing knife, the arterial spatter on the smooth door of a kitchen cupboard, and the smeared blood left by the victim's struggle and the spasmodic jerking of her body.

They know far too little about the second murder, but this one seems to follow the pattern of the first exactly. The level of brutality is inconceivable, and appears to extend far beyond the moment of death.

Once the fury of the attack subsided, the body was arranged slightly before being left at the scene of the murder.

In the first case the victim's fingers had been inserted into her mouth, and this time her hand is covering her breast.

Margot steps aside to make way for one of the forensic officers who is laying out boards on the floor.

With her hand on her protruding stomach, she carries on into the bedroom and looks down into the open drawer at the porcelain deer, chestnut-brown, except for the break where the head should be. After a while she returns to the victim.

She stares once again at the carefully staged arrangement of the hand on her chest, and a thought flits through her head and vanishes.

There's something she recognises.

Margot stands for a while and thinks before leaving the flat and going back to her car. She starts the engine and holds one hand on the wheel and the other on her stomach, moves it down to counter the baby's rapid movements with her fingertips, the small nudges from the other side, from the beginning.

She tries to make herself more comfortable, but the steering wheel presses against her stomach.

What is it I can't quite remember? she thinks. It could have been five years ago, in a different police district, but I definitely read something.

Something about the hands, or the deer.

She can't help thinking that she won't get any sleep tonight if she doesn't work out what it is.

Margot turns into Polhemsgatan and pulls up beside the rock face.

Her phone rings and Margot sees the picture of Jenny in her cowboy hat from Tucson on the screen.

'National Crime,' Margot answers.

'I need to report a crime,' Jenny says.

'If it's urgent you should call 112,' she says, parking more neatly. 'But otherwise—'

'This is about a crime against public decency,' Jenny interrupts.

'Can you be a bit more specific?' Margot asks, opening the car door.

'If you come here, I can show you . . .'

Margot has to take the phone from her ear as she gets out of the car and locks it.

'Sorry, what did you say?'

'I just called to find out where you'd got to,' Jenny says in a different tone of voice.

'I'm on Kungsholmen, I've got to—'

'You haven't got time – you need to come home straight away,' she cuts in.

'What's happened?'

'Seriously, Margot . . . this is hopeless. For God's sake, you were the one who picked Sunday, they'll all be here any minute—'

'Don't be cross with me . . . I just can't let go of this case before—'

'You're not coming?' Jenny interrupts. 'Is that what you're saying?'

'I thought it was next weekend,' Margot replies.

'How the hell could you think that?'

Margot had completely forgotten about dinner with her family. The idea was for her and Jenny to thank everyone for their support during the Pride festival. Everyone who had marched with banners saying 'Proud Parents and Families'.

'You'll just have to explain that I'll be a bit late,' she says, stopping ten metres from the entrance to Police Headquarters.

'Look . . . this isn't on,' Jenny says, then takes a deep breath. 'I'm actually feeling pretty let down . . . You got a career opportunity, and I was happy to support you, and . . .'

'Look after the children while I worked – and now I'm working, just like—'

'But you're working the whole bloody time, and—'

'That was what we agreed,' Margot interrupts.

She starts walking towards the entrance as a colleague comes out and unlocks the heavy chain around the rear wheel of a motorbike.

'OK . . . that was what we agreed,' Jenny says quietly.

'I've got to go now, but I'll be home as soon as—'

Margot stops when she realises that Jenny has hung up on her. She carries on into the lobby, passes the security doors and heads towards the lifts.

Maria Carlsson, the first victim, had her hand in her mouth, Margot thinks once more.

That wasn't enough for her to discern a pattern. But when she saw Sandra Lundgren lying there with her hand over one breast, she had a fleeting sense of a connection.

It didn't look natural, it was arranged.

She walks along the empty corridor to her office, closes the door behind her and sits down at the computer, and searches for arranged bodies.

She can hear sirens from emergency vehicles somewhere.

Margot kicks off her shoes as she clicks through the results. Nowhere does she find any similarity to her murders. Her stomach feels tight and she undoes her belt altogether.

She expands the search to cover the whole country, and when the list of results appears she knows she's found what she was looking for.

A murder in Salem.

The victim was found with her hand round her own neck.

She had been arranged like that after she died.

The preliminary investigation had been conducted by the Södertälje Police District.

As she read, she remembered more details. Far too much had leaked to the press. The extreme level of brutality had been focused primarily on the victim's face and upper body.

The dead woman had been found in her bathroom with her hand around her own throat.

The victim's name was Rebecka Hansson. She had been wearing pyjama bottoms and a sweater, and according to the post-mortem she had not been subjected either to rape or attempted rape.

Margot's heart is pounding in her chest as she finds the information about Rocky Kyrklund, a priest. She reads that an arrest warrant was issued for him in his absence, and he was subsequently apprehended in connection with a traffic accident. The forensic evidence against him was compelling. Rocky Kyrklund underwent a forensic psychiatric examination and was consigned to Karsudden District Hospital with specific restrictions placed on any parole application.

I've found the murderer, Margot thinks, and her hand is trembling as she reaches for the phone and calls Karsudden Hospital.

When she finds out that Rocky Kyrklund is locked up and that he has never been let out on licence, she demands an immediate meeting with the head of security.

Barely two hours later Margot is sitting in the office of the head of security, Neil Lindegren, in the gleaming white main building, discussing the security arrangements for Section D:4.

Neil is a thickset man with a fleshy forehead and neat, stubby hands. He leans back in his chair as he explains the secure perimeter fences, the alarm system, the airlock and passcards.

'That all sounds very good,' Margot says when Neil falls silent. 'But the question is: could Rocky Kyrklund have managed to get out anyway?'

'You're welcome to meet him, if that would make you feel any better,' he smiles.

'You're absolutely sure you'd have noticed if he escaped and came back the same day?'

'No one's escaped,' Neil says.

'But hypothetically,' Margot goes on. 'If he got out immediately after you did your round at eight o'clock – when would he have to be back today in order for his absence not to be noticed?'

Neil's smile fades and his hands fall to his lap.

'Today is Sunday,' he says slowly. 'He wouldn't need to be back before five o'clock, but you know . . . the doors are locked and alarmed, and the whole area is covered by surveillance cameras.'

52

On a large monitor, thirty squares show what's being picked up by the facility's security cameras.

A technician in his sixties shows Margot the system of CCTV cameras, motion-activated cameras, their locations, and the laser and infrared barriers.

Recordings from the surveillance cameras are stored for a maximum of thirty days.

'This is Section D:4,' he says, pointing. 'The corridor, dayroom, exercise yard, fence, the outside of the fence, the outside of the building . . . and these show the park and the driveway.'

The monitor shows an image of the hospital as it was at five o'clock that morning. The static glow from the lamps make the park look strangely lifeless. The clock in the corner of the screen moves on, but everything remains perfectly still.

When the man speeds up the replay, a few trees appear to move in the wind. The night-time security guard walks along the corridor and disappears into the staffroom.

Suddenly the technician stops the film and points at an area of grass that spreads out like a patch of grey water. Margot leans forward and sees a number of dark shapes against the bushes and trees.

The technician enlarges the image and plays the footage. Three deer appear in the glow of a lamp. They walk across the grass, all stop at once, stand still with their necks craned, then carry on.

He shrinks the image and hits fast-forward again. Daylight arrives and the transparent shadows grow sharper as the sun rises.

Cars arrive and staff go inside and spread out through the corridors and tunnels.

The technician stops the recordings to show the night-staff leaving. Margot watches the morning round in the various sections in silence.

There's very little activity, given that it's Sunday. There's no sign of

Rocky Kyrklund among the patients who have opted to go out into the exercise yard.

They carry on fast-forwarding, stopping occasionally to look more closely at anyone in the corridors, but everything seems to be calm as the hours tick by.

'And there you are,' the technician says with a smile.

He enlarges one square to show her struggling to get out of her car, and her wrap dress slips open, revealing her pink underwear.

'Whoops,' she mumbles.

Margot sees herself walk across the car park with her big leather bag over her shoulder, her hands round her stomach. She goes round the corner of the building and disappears from view, but the next camera picks her up outside the entrance. At the same time she is visible from another angle on a camera above the reception desk in the lobby.

'I disappeared for a few seconds as I went round the corner of the building,' she says.

'No,' he says calmly.

'It felt like it,' she insists.

He goes back to the image of her getting out of her car, flashing her underwear, follows her across the car park, and stops the recording as she walks round the corner of the building and disappears from that screen.

'We've got a camera here that ought to . . .'

He enlarges another square, showing the end of the building, and lots of leaves, but not her. He plays the footage slowly, and she comes into view outside the entrance.

'OK, you're gone for a few seconds,' he eventually says. 'There are always going to be tiny gaps in the system.'

'Could someone exploit them to escape?'

The technician leans back, and the wad of chewing tobacco beneath his lip slips down over one of his teeth as he shakes his head.

'Not even theoretically,' he says firmly.

'How certain are you of that?'

'Pretty much one hundred per cent,' he replies.

'OK,' Margot says. She gets up laboriously from her chair and thanks him for his help.

If Rocky couldn't have escaped, she's going to have to think again. The murder he committed has to be linked to the recent killings.

There are no coincidences on that level.

The priest must have had someone helping him, an apprentice on the outside, she thinks to herself.

Unless they're dealing with a completely independent copycat, or someone with whom Rocky Kyrklund has been communicating.

The technician leads her back through the deserted corridors to Neil Lindegren's room. The head of security is talking to a woman in a white coat when Margot walks in.

'I need to talk to Rocky Kyrklund,' she says.

'But it's not even certain that he'll be able to remember what he's been doing today,' Neil says, gesturing towards the doctor.

'Kyrklund has a serious neurological injury,' the doctor explains. 'His memories only come back to him as tiny fragments . . . and sometimes he does things without being aware of them at all.'

'Is he dangerous?'

'He would already be getting prepared for rehabilitation back into society if he'd shown any indication that that's what he wants,' Neil says.

'He doesn't want to get out – is that what you're saying?' Margot asks.

'We start socialising most of our inmates fairly early . . . they get a chance to meet people outside the hospital, have supervised excursions, but he mostly keeps to himself and won't accept any visitors . . . He never phones anyone, writes no letters, and doesn't use the Internet,' the doctor says.

'Does he talk to the other patients?'

'Sometimes, as I understand it,' Neil replies.

'I need to know which patients have been discharged from Section D:4 during the time he's been there,' she says, sitting down on the chair she sat on earlier.

She looks round Neil's tidy office while he searches his computer. He's got no photographs on display, no books or ornaments.

'Have you found anything?' she asks, and can hear how anxious her voice sounds.

Neil turns the screen to show her.

'Not much,' he says. 'That section has a very low turnover of patients. There are a few who have been moved to other psychiatric institutions, but we've only had two inmates discharged in the time Rocky has been here.'

'Two in nine years?'

'That's normal,' the doctor says.

Margot opens her leather bag, takes out her notebook and writes the names down.

'Now I want to see Rocky Kyrklund,' she says.

53

Two guards with emergency alarms, batons and tasers on their belts accompany Margot through the airlocks and into the corridor where Rocky Kyrklund's section is located.

He's sitting on the bunk in his room watching a Formula 1 race on a television fixed to the wall up near the ceiling.

The shimmering cars move round the track like dragonflies, with their bursts of speed and metallic colours.

'My name is Margot Silverman, I'm a superintendent with the National Criminal Investigation Department,' she explains, leaning back against his desk chair.

'Adam fucked Eve and then she got pregnant and gave birth to Cain,' Rocky says, looking at her stomach.

'I've come here from Stockholm to talk to you.'

'You're not observing the day of rest,' Rocky states, then looks back at the television.

'Are you?' she asks, pulling the chair out and sitting down. 'What have you done today?'

His face is calm, his nose looks like it was broken at some point, his cheeks are covered by a grey beard, and there are folds in his thick neck.

'Have you been out today?' she asks, and waits a moment before going on. 'You haven't been out in the exercise yard – but perhaps there are other ways of getting out.'

Rocky Kyrklund shows no reaction. His eyes are following the cars on the screen. One of the guards by the door shifts his weight and the keys on his belt jangle.

'Who have you been in contact with on the outside?' she asks. 'Friends, relatives, other patients?'

The turbo engines roar. They sound like chainsaws cutting through dry wood, over and over again.

Margot looks at his stockinged feet, the worn heels and clumsy darning of one sock.

'I've been told that you don't see any visitors?'

Rocky doesn't answer. His stomach rises and falls calmly under his denim shirt. One hand is resting between his legs, and he's leaning back against two pillows.

'But you do have personal contact with the staff? Some of them have worked here for many years . . . you must have got to know each other. Haven't you?'

Rocky Kyrklund remains silent.

On the television a Ferrari driver comes into the pits at speed. Before his car has even stopped the crew are ready to change his tyres.

'You have your meals with patients from other sections, and you share the exercise yard . . . Who do you like best? If you had to say a name?'

A bible with about sixty bookmarks in the form of red thread is lying on the bedside table. Beside it stands a dirty milk-glass. Light filtered by the trees comes through the vertical bars on the window.

Margot shifts position uncomfortably on the chair and takes the notebook containing the names of the two discharged patients out of her bag.

'Do you remember Jens Ramberg? Marek Semiovic?' she asks. 'You do, don't you?'

One car collides with another and spins round in a cloud of smoke while parts of the car fly across the track.

'Do you have any memory of what you were doing earlier today?'

She waits a while, then stands up again as the accident is replayed on the screen, its glow reflecting off Rocky's face and chest.

The guards don't meet her gaze as they leave the room together. Rocky doesn't seem to notice her departure.

As she walks back towards the car park, she can feel the technician watching her on one of the thirty cameras.

Before she drives back, she sits in the car and reads through the material about the murder of Rebecka Hansson, and thinks that Rocky Kyrklund must be involved in the new murders in some way, if only as a sort of distant *rodef*.

Margot sees that Erik Maria Bark was part of the team that conducted the forensic psychiatric evaluation of Kyrklund. Their conclusions, which formed the basis of the sentence, were based upon long conversations between Erik and Rocky. Erik evidently managed to gain his trust. She notes that he has taken part in almost one hundred forensic psychiatric evaluations and has been called as an expert witness during forty trials.

54

Adam Youssef is sitting in his car next to his wife Katryna. She's massaging her hands, and the smell of her hand cream is spreading through the car. It's starting to get dark, and the traffic on Valhallavägen is fairly light. They've been to the Dramatic Institute to watch her brother Fuad's performance about post-punk group The Cure.

The middle-aged singer, Robert Smith, was depicted sitting without any make-up on a carousel horse, talking about his years at Notre Dame Middle School.

Adam stops at a red light and looks at Katryna. She's plucked her eyebrows a bit too much, making her face look rather cruel.

'You're not saying anything,' he says.

She shrugs her shoulders. He looks at her nails. She's painted them in a colour that shifts from violet to pink at their tips. He ought to say something about them.

'Katryna,' he says. 'What is it?'

She looks him in the eye with a seriousness that makes him scared.

'I don't want to have the baby,' she explains.

'You don't?'

She shakes her head and the red light disappears from her face. He turns back towards the traffic light. It's turned green, but he can't bring himself to drive on.

'I'm not sure I want children at all,' she whispers.

'You've only just got pregnant,' he says helplessly. 'Can't you wait, see if you change your mind?'

'I'm not going to,' she says simply.

He nods and swallows. A car blows its horn a couple of times before overtaking on the right, and then the light goes red again. He looks at the switch for the hazard-warning lights, but can't be bothered to press it.

'OK,' he says.

'I've made up my mind, I've booked an appointment to have an abortion next week.'

'Do you want me to come with you?'

'There's no need.'

'But I could wait in the car while—'

'I don't want you there,' she interrupts.

He stares at the cars driving across the junction in front of them, then at some black birds flying overhead; they're describing a wide arc in front of Stockholm's Olympic Stadium.

He's losing her, it's already happening.

Recently he's been trying to show her he loves her every day. They love each other, after all, they really do. Or at least he thought they did.

What if she's lying when she says she's going out with her workmates at Sephora after work every Thursday? She never talks about it, and he hasn't been interested enough to ask or go along.

The light goes green again and he moves his foot on to the accelerator and drives on. They're approaching Sveavägen when his phone rings.

'Can you look and see who it is?'

She picks up the phone from the pocket by the gearstick and turns it over.

'It's your boss.'

Adam looks away from the traffic for a moment before taking the phone.

'Margot?' he says in a weak voice.

'It's the same deer,' she says.

The broken edge of the deer in Sandra's room has been matched with the little head found in Susanna Kern's hand, one hundred per cent.

'It seemed completely mad when we saw it on the video,' Margot says, sounding like she's panting for breath. 'But all it means is that the murders are planned long before they take place, that someone has recorded them and then waited – possibly for weeks.'

'But why?' Adam asks, feeling his hand sweating on the wheel.

The murders are following each other like a string of pearls, a ring of roses, he thinks. The order of death is ordained long before anyone pulls the trigger. That ought to give us more time, in theory, but not in practice, seeing as the murderer doesn't upload the videos until it's too late for us to identify the scene or the woman.

'I've found some similarities with an old case,' Margot says.

'What did you say?'

'Are you listening?'

'Yes, sorry . . .'

He looks at Katryna's face, turned away from him, as he listens to Margot tell him about the similarities with an old murder in Salem, about the priest who was found guilty, about Rebecka Hansson's ravaged face and arranged posture.

She explains that she's checked the security arrangements at Karsudden, and that it seems impossible that anyone could have got out without it being discovered.

'So he must have an accomplice, a disciple . . . unless it's a copycat.'

'OK,' Adam says hesitantly.

'Do you think I'm making too much of this?'

'Maybe,' he says honestly.

'I can understand that, but right now it doesn't matter. You'll see what I mean when you take a look.'

'Do you want us to go and have a word with the priest?' Adam asks.

'I'm on my way back from there now.'

'Weren't you and Jenny supposed to be having some sort of big dinner today?'

'That's next weekend,' she says curtly.

'So what did he say, then?'

'Nothing. He didn't even look at me,' she says. 'It appears I'm completely devoid of interest.'

'Nice,' Adam says.

'That seems to be par for the course with him,' she says tolerantly. 'That was why they brought Erik Maria Bark into the team conducting the forensic psychiatric examination, he gets people to talk . . .'

'Apart from our witness,' Adam points out.

'Practically the entire investigation had its foundations in his conversations with Kyrklund,' Margot explains. 'It's a huge amount of material, we're going to have to get people to examine every last detail.'

'How long's that going to take?'

'That's why I'm on my way to see Erik Maria Bark now,' Margot says.

'Now?'

'Well, I'm already in the car, so . . .'

'So am I,' Adam laughs. 'But I'm certainly not thinking of—'

'I have to say, it would be brilliant to have you there,' she interrupts amiably.

55

Erik is sitting in his reading chair with a copy of the Swedish Psychiatric Association's journal in his lap, thinking about dinner at Nelly and Martin's. They invite him round fairly often to their huge modernist house with its curved windows and a terrace that looks like the bridge of an old sailing yacht.

After dinner Martin took off his tie and led them through the house clutching a glass of Calvados in his hand. In his study he had a fairly small oil painting he had just been given by his aunt in Westphalia. It was of a gloomy-looking angel. Nelly thought it was horrible and tried to offer it to Erik. Martin agreed with her, but Erik declined the offer because it was obvious that he wanted to keep it really.

When Martin had to take a call from Sydney, Erik and Nelly went to the billiard room. Nelly poured more wine, she was already fairly drunk. Her eyes were moist and she was leaning against the raised edge of the table.

'Martin looks at porn,' she slurred.

'Why do you think that?' Erik asked, rolling a ball across the green baize.

'I don't care, it's nothing perverse.'

'Does it make you sad?'

'Not jealous, but . . . I don't know, you should see the women . . . They're young and beautiful and they do things I'd never dare to try,' she said, reaching out and touching his lips.

'Talk to him.'

'Is youth the only thing that counts?' she drawled.

'Not to me.'

'What does matter, then? What do you want? What does any man really want?' she said, swaying slightly.

He helped her to her bedroom, but left before she took off her mocha-coloured dress.

When Nelly called him to discuss two Iranian patients from the unit for survivors of torture out in Danderyd, he took the opportunity to thank her for dinner. She just laughed and said he should be grateful she didn't get too drunk and embarrassing.

Now Erik leans back in his armchair and thinks about the bottle of champagne in the fridge that he opened earlier, all alone. He sealed it with some argon, a noble gas that will have kept it tasting like new if he were to have a glass now.

That would get rid of my headache, Erik thinks, as he sees the car headlights sweep in through the large glass window.

With a short sigh he gets up and puts the journal on the smoking table, leaves his slippers on the floor and goes to open the door. He watches Margot struggle out of her car and wave to him, then another car pulls into the drive.

A younger man with short dark hair hurries over to Margot and exchanges a few words with her. Behind the pair of them comes a beautiful young woman with clear eyes and a serious face.

Erik shakes hands with Margot and the young man, whom she introduces as a colleague working on the murder investigation with her.

The young woman hesitates in the doorway. Her black coat is shiny with rain, and she looks frozen.

'I didn't have time to take my wife home,' Adam explains, looking unexpectedly awkward. 'This is Katryna.'

'Adam didn't want me to wait in the car,' she says softly.

'You're more than welcome to come in,' Erik says, shaking her hand.

'Thank you.'

'What wonderful fingernails,' he says, holding on to her hand to look at them for a few seconds.

She smiles in surprise and her dark eyes warm up instantly.

Erik invites them to take their coats off, then steps into the porch to close the front door properly. The gentle rain is dripping rhythmically through the leaves of the lilac. The road is shimmering under the streetlights, and suddenly he imagines he can see the silhouette of a tall figure in his own garden. He switches the outside light on, thinking that it must have been the scrawny juniper next to the wheelbarrow.

Erik shuts the door and shows them into the library, where Katryna stops, looking a little embarrassed.

'I'm probably not supposed to overhear your conversation,' she says.

'You can sit here if you like,' Erik says, pulling a folio off the shelf. 'I don't know about you, but I'm a bit addicted to Caravaggio.'

He puts the art book down on the table, then shows the detectives into his study. Adam closes the door behind them.

'We found a third victim today,' Margot says at once.

'A third victim,' Erik says.

'We were expecting it, but it's still a blow.'

She looks down towards her stomach, and the corners of her mouth twitch slightly, possibly from exhaustion. She has a deep frown on her forehead that stretches down between her eyebrows.

'What can I help you with?' Erik asks neutrally.

'Do you know a man called Rocky Kyrklund?' Margot asks, looking up at him.

'Should I?'

'You ought to know that he was sentenced to psychiatric care after a forensic psychiatric evaluation nine years ago.'

'Of course, I'm sure that's right,' Erik says gently.

As soon as she mentioned Rocky's name, it occurred to him that she might know everything, that he's been found out.

'You were part of the team,' Margot explains.

'OK,' Erik says.

He's spent hours conjuring up different scenarios in which he's confronted with what happened, and then imagining possible reactions and answers that couldn't be regarded as lies even though they keep him out of it.

'And we have reason to believe that he confided in you . . .'

'I don't remember that, but—'

'He had murdered a woman in Salem in a way that's reminiscent of the murders that I'm currently investigating,' Margot says, without further elaboration.

'If he's been released and is killing again, then something has gone very wrong with the parole process,' Erik replies, just as he had planned.

'He hasn't been released. He's still in Karsudden and he hasn't left the facility at all,' she says. 'I've just been out there and spoken to the head of security.'

56

Margot opens her leather bag and hands Erik a copy of the verdict, and the forensic psychiatric evaluation.

The standard lamp shines warmly off the polished oak floor and leather binding of the volumes in the built-in bookcases. It's so dark outside the leaded windows that the fruit trees' dense network of branches is completely invisible.

Erik sits down opposite Adam at the little octagonal table, leafs through the material, nods and looks up.

'Yes, I remember him.'

'We think he has an apprentice, a disciple . . . maybe a copycat.'

'That's possible . . . if the similarities are that strong . . . well, I can't actually give an opinion.'

Margot shakes her wrist to get her watch in the right place.

'I spoke to Rocky Kyrklund today,' she says. 'I asked him a lot of questions, but he just sat there in silence on his bed, staring at the television.'

'He suffered serious brain damage,' Erik says, gesturing towards the old evaluation.

'He could hear and understand everything I said, he just didn't want to answer.' Margot smiles.

'It's often rather difficult to start with when you're dealing with this sort of patient.'

She leans forward, so that her stomach ends up resting on her thighs.

'Can you help us?'

'How?'

'Talk to him. He trusted you before, you know him.'

Erik's heart starts to beat faster. He mustn't show any feelings, so slowly clasps his hands together to stop them shaking.

They're probably going to find the tape recordings of the forensic psychiatric evaluation in which Rocky talks about his alibi.

But because Rocky is guilty, Erik can always say that he didn't take the idea of an alibi seriously if it comes up.

'What do you want to know?'

'We want to know who he was working with.'

Erik nods, and thinks that he'll be free at last after this, he'll no longer have to carry the burden of knowledge that he can't offload. He can tell them about the person Rocky blamed, whether or not Rocky just sits there in silence. He could even hypnotise Björn Kern again and then tell them about the hand clasped to Susanna's ear.

'Naturally, this is rather outside my usual remit,' he begins.

'Of course we'd pay . . .'

'That's not what I meant . . . I need to know the outline of the task, so I know what to say to my employers.'

Margot nods, with her lips half-open, as though she were about to say something, but decides against it.

'And I need to know what to say to the patient,' Erik goes on. 'I mean, am I allowed to let him know that you think his former associate has started killing again?'

Margot waves her hand. Erik notes that her colleague seems to have stiffened slightly as he sits there with his arms folded.

'We'll have to see if we can give any room for negotiation,' Margot says. 'We don't know yet, of course, but you might be able to offer him supervised excursions outside the hospital.'

She falls silent, as if she's run out of breath. Her hand goes to her stomach. Her thin wedding ring sits tightly around her swollen finger.

'What did you say to him today?' Erik asks.

'I asked which people he had most contact with.'

'Does he know why you were asking?'

'No . . . he didn't react at all to anything I said.'

'He has epileptic activity in his brain which affects his memory, and, according to his diagnosis, he suffers from a narcissistic, paranoid disorder . . . But all the evidence suggests that he's intelligent . . .'

Erik falls silent.

'What are you thinking?' Margot asks.

'I'd like the authority to be able to tell him why I'm asking him these questions.'

'Tell him about the serial killer?'

'He'll probably work out that I'm lying otherwise.'

'Margot,' Adam says. 'I have to—'

'What?'

He looks troubled as he lowers his voice.

'This is police work,' he says.

'We haven't got a choice,' she says curtly.

'I just think you're going too far now,' Adam says.

'Am I?'

'First you get Joona Linna mixed up in this, and now you're going to let a hypnotist do police work.'

'Joona Linna?' Erik asks.

'I'm not talking to you,' Adam says.

'He's back,' Margot says.

'Where?'

'Back probably isn't the right word,' Adam says. 'He's living with the Romanian Roma out in Huddinge, he's an alcoholic, and—'

'We don't know that,' she interrupts.

'OK, Joona's best,' Adam says.

Margot meets Erik's quizzical gaze.

'Joona fainted and ended up in A&E at St Göran's,' she says.

'When?' Erik asks, getting to his feet.

'Yesterday.'

Erik immediately picks up his phone and dials the number of a colleague in the hospital's intensive care unit, and waits as the call goes through.

'When can you talk to Rocky?' Margot asks, standing up.

'I'll head out there first thing tomorrow,' Erik says, as his colleague answers the phone.

57

After a short conversation with the doctor at St Göran's Hospital, Erik accompanies the two detectives to the door. Katryna and Adam don't look at each other as they walk out into the hall, and Erik gets the distinct impression that they've had a row.

The three of them leave the house and are swallowed up by the darkness as soon as they move beyond the circle of light in front of the door. Erik hears their footsteps on the gravel path leading to the drive, then they come into view again when the insides of their cars light up. He returns to his study and sees that the fax of the emergency records has arrived, and that – in line with correct procedure – the patient's name and ID number have been blanked out.

Joona arrived by ambulance after a priority-1 call from the emergency command centre. Erik glances through the records of his blood pressure, heartbeat, breathing frequency, oxygenation, temperature and level of consciousness.

He was suffering from malnutrition, fever, confusion and poor circulation.

The triage nurse made the right call from the available evidence when she suspected that he was suffering from blood poisoning.

After checking his blood-gases and lactic acid, she allocated him triage level orange, the second highest level of priority.

Because of his variable vital signs, Joona Linna was placed in a room under close supervision and attached to a monitor.

While they were waiting for the results of his blood analysis they gave him broad-spectrum antibiotics and a colloid solution to help his circulation and fluid balance.

But Joona disappeared before the antibiotics could take effect.

He hadn't given an address.

Given his symptoms, his condition was life-threatening unless he received treatment.

Erik leaves his study and picks up his jacket in the hall. He doesn't bother to switch the lights off.

It's no longer raining. The night air is cool and the car windows are covered with condensation. He turns the windscreen wipers on and waits for them to clear the screen before he drives off.

It's close to midnight and the streets are almost empty. Beyond the yellow glow of the streetlamps, beyond the speed cameras and barriers and noise-reduction screens, the late summer night is as dark as heavy velvet.

He drives down Storängsleden, turns on to Centralvägen towards Dalhemsvägen, heading into an industrial area with high fences, then emerges into a patch of woodland.

There never used to be any beggars in Sweden, but over the past few years migrants from the EU have become visible in Swedish towns and cities. They've come here to plead for help, on their knees in the snow outside supermarkets, with outstretched hands and empty paper cups.

It's struck Erik several times that modern Swedes have reacted with unexpected generosity to this change, considering the country's dark history of discrimination and enforced sterilisation.

There are faint lights between the trees. He slows down and drives towards them, turning on to a gravel track, and the tiny monkey attached to his ignition key bounces up and down.

In a clearing he can see sheets flapping on a rope strung between two trees. Lengths of plywood have been nailed together, and covered with tarpaulin and plastic.

Erik turns round and parks with two wheels on the verge. He locks up and walks away from the car, staring in amongst the trees.

The air smells of potatoes and liquid gas. Four battered caravans are standing in a row, with crooked wooden shacks between them. Smoke is rising from a buckled oil-drum; glowing embers drift up, spreading a stench of burning plastic.

Joona Linna is here somewhere, Erik thinks. He's got advanced blood poisoning and is going to die unless he gets the right antibiotics very soon. No other person on the planet has done as much for Erik as the tall detective.

A woman with a shawl over her head gives him a wary look and hurries away as he approaches.

He carries on towards the first caravan and knocks on the door. On a beautiful rug beneath the caravan stand five shabby pairs of trainers of various sizes.

'Joona?' Erik says loudly, and knocks again.

The caravan sways slightly and then the door is opened by an old man with eyes made cloudy by cataracts. Behind him sits a child on a mattress. On the floor a woman is asleep, fully dressed in a woolly hat and a winter coat.

'Joona,' Erik says in a subdued voice.

A thickset man in a padded tunic suddenly appears behind him and asks what he wants in broken Swedish.

'I'm looking for a friend of mine, his name is Joona Linna,' Erik says.

'We don't want problems,' the man says with an anxious look.

'OK,' Erik says, and walks over to the second caravan and knocks on the door. It's covered with circular scorch marks, as if people had stubbed cigarettes out on it.

A young woman in glasses cautiously opens the door. She's wearing a thick sweater and baggy sweatpants with damp knees.

'I'm looking for a sick friend,' Erik says.

'Next house,' she whispers with a frightened look in her eyes.

A tired child has come over and pokes at Erik with a plastic crocodile.

Erik steps across two crutches lying on the ground and walks up to the third caravan. The windows are broken and covered with pieces of cardboard.

In the darkness between the trees an unshaven, tired-looking man is smoking a cigarette.

Erik knocks on the door and opens it when there's no answer. In the glow of a clock-radio he sees his friend. Joona Linna is lying on a damp mattress with a folded blanket as a pillow. An old woman in an old-fashioned quilted jacket is sitting beside him, trying to get him to drink some water from a spoon.

'Joona,' he says quietly.

The floor creaks as Erik climbs inside the caravan. The water in a plastic bucket sloshes with the movement. The carpet on the floor is wet with rain by the door, and there's a strong smell of damp and cigarette smoke. There are scraps of bluish-grey cloth covering the cardboard-patched windows. As Erik moves further inside he sees a crucifix on the wall.

Joona's face is emaciated, covered by a grey beard, and his chest looks unnaturally sunken. His eyes look yellow, and his gaze is so unfocused that Erik isn't sure if he's actually conscious.

'I'm going to give you an injection before we leave,' Erik says, putting his bag down on the floor.

Joona barely reacts when Erik pulls his sleeve up, wipes the crook of his arm with a swab, looks for a vein and then injects a mixture of benzyl-penicillin and aminoglycoside.

'Can you stand up?' he asks as he puts a plaster where he stuck the needle.

Joona lifts his head slightly and coughs emptily. Erik helps him get up on one knee. A tin can rolls across the floor. Joona coughs again, points at the woman and tries to say something.

'I can't hear,' Erik says.

'Crina needs to be paid,' Joona hisses, and stands up. 'She's . . . helped me.'

Erik nods and takes his wallet out. He gives the woman a five-hundred-kronor note, and she nods and smiles with her lips closed.

Erik opens the door and helps Joona down the steps. A bald man in a crumpled suit stands outside and holds the caravan door open for them.

'Thanks,' Erik says.

From the other direction a blond man in a black, shiny jacket is approaching. He's hiding something behind his back.

Beside the next caravan stands a third man with a soot-stained saucepan in his hand. He's wearing jeans and a denim waistcoat, and his bare arms are dark with tattoos.

'You've got a nice car,' he calls out with a grin.

Erik and Joona start to walk towards the road but the blond man blocks their path.

'We need some rent,' he says.

'I've already paid,' Erik says.

The bald man shouts into the caravan and the old woman comes to the door and holds up the money she has just been given. The man snatches the note, says something angrily, then spits at her.

'We have to collect rent from everyone here,' the blond man explains, showing the length of metal pipe in his hand.

Erik mutters in agreement and thinks it would be best just to try to get to the car, when Joona stops.

'Give the money back to her,' he says, pointing at the bald man.

'I own the caravans,' the blond man says. 'I own all this, every mattress, every single fucking saucepan.'

'I'm not talking to you,' Joona says, and coughs into the crook of his arm.

'It's not worth it,' Erik whispers, his heart pounding in his chest.

'For fuck's sake, we've got a deal with them,' the tattooed man shouts.

'Erik, get in the car,' Joona says, and limps over to the men.

'It costs more now,' the blond man says.

'I've got a bit more money,' Erik says, taking his wallet out.

'Don't do it,' Joona says.

Erik gives a few more notes to the blond man.

'That's not enough,' he says.

'Give it all back,' Joona tells the blond man feebly.

'It's only money,' Erik says quickly, and pulls out the last couple of notes.

'Not to Crina,' Joona says.

'Run home and hide before we change our minds,' the blond man grins, and points at them with the metal pipe.

58

Joona stands still with his arms wrapped round him, leaning forward slightly. He sees the blond man change his grip on the pipe and move to the side. The bald man takes off his jacket and hangs it over a plastic chair.

Joona slowly raises his head and looks the bald man in the eyes.

'Give the money back to Crina,' he repeats.

The bald man grins with surprise and steps sideways into the darkness. There's a click as he unfolds the blade of a flick-knife.

'I'm going to hurt you if you don't drop the knife on the ground now,' Joona says in his melancholic Finnish accent, and takes a step forward.

The bald man crouches down and moves aside, holding the knife in a classic hammer-grip, then reaches forward and takes a few trial stabs.

'Be careful,' Joona says, and coughs gently.

The knife is sharp, and glimmers in the weak light. Joona watches it with his eyes and tries to read the man's irregular movements.

'Do you want to die?' the man grunts.

'I may look slow,' Joona says. 'But I'm going to take that knife and break your arm at the elbow . . . and if you don't lie still after that, I'll puncture your right lung.'

'Stab the Finn!' the blond man shouts. 'Stab the fucking Finn.'

'And I'll deal with you next, once I've got the knife,' Joona says, stumbling into a rusty bicycle.

The bald man swings the knife to the side unexpectedly and the blade catches Joona across the back of his hand, which starts to bleed.

The blond man backs away with a forced smile.

Joona wipes the blood from his hand on his trousers. The bald man shouts something to the blond one. A baby starts crying in one of the caravans.

The blond man moves in behind Joona's back; he notices, but is too weak to move.

When Joona glances over his shoulder the bald man mounts an attack. He aims low, towards Joona's kidneys. The white blade jabs forward like a lizard's tongue.

It happens fast, but everything is still there as a physical memory. Joona doesn't think as he deflects the knife, grabs the man's hand and closes his fingers over his cold knuckles.

Everything happens in rapid succession. Joona bends the man's wrist, puts his other hand under his elbow, and jerks upward.

When the man's arm breaks there's a cracking sound, like standing on a twig beneath deep snow. Splinters of the radial bone pierce through ligaments and tissue, and a squirt of blood spatters a filthy bucket. The man sinks to his knees, screaming, and bends double on the ground.

'Behind you!' Erik shouts.

Joona turns. Suddenly giddy, he stumbles in a pool of water, stares up at the tops of the pines against the sky, but manages to keep his balance.

He spins the knife between his fingers, changes his grip and hides it behind his body as he approaches the blond man.

'Leave me the fuck alone!' the man shouts, and swipes at the air with the pipe.

Joona goes straight in, takes the next blow on his shoulder, cuts the man across the forehead, and rams his lower arm up into the man's armpit, knocking his arm out its socket as the pipe falls to the ground.

The blond man gasps as he clutches the top of his arm, moves backwards, but can't see anything for the blood running into his eyes. He stumbles over a pile of wood and remains there, lying on his back.

The man with the saucepan has disappeared into the darkness behind the camp. Joona walks over, leans down and takes the money from both men, panting as he does so.

He knocks on the door of the caravan, leaning against the frame to stop himself falling. Erik runs over and holds him up when he staggers.

'Give the money to Crina,' Joona says, and sits down on the step.

Erik opens the caravan door, sees the woman in the gloom at the far end, looks her in the eye and shows her where he hides the money under her carpet.

Joona slips down onto the grass with his head resting against one of the concrete blocks holding the caravan up.

The tattooed man comes back round the first caravan. He's holding a shotgun and is approaching with long strides.

Erik realises that Joona is in no condition to run, so crawls beneath the caravan and tries to pull him in behind him.

'Try to help,' he whispers.

Joona kicks his legs and slowly slides in. The grit catches his jacket and they can hear steps nearby.

They hear the man with the gun open the caravan door and shout at the old woman. The floor above them thunders as he goes inside.

'Come on,' Erik says, crawling further in. He hits his head on a cable tray.

Joona shuffles after him, but catches his jacket on a strut. Erik emerges on the other side of the caravan and hides among some nettles.

Beneath the caravan Joona watches as the tattooed man steps down on to the ground again.

They hear voices and suddenly the man bends down, puts his hands on the ground and stares right at Joona as he lies under the caravan.

'Get them!' the blond man shouts.

Joona tries to pull himself free and the seams of his jacket creak. The tattooed man starts to walk round the caravan, through the rough undergrowth.

Erik slips hurriedly underneath again, crawls over to Joona and frees his jacket.

They roll sideways, crawl between the concrete blocks and emerge into the weeds, toss aside a rusty sheet of tin and take cover beside a shack.

The tattooed man comes round the caravan, slips on the wet ground, raises his gun and takes aim.

Erik pulls Joona out of his line of fire.

The man follows them with his gun raised. They crouch down beside a kitchen sink mounted between two trees.

The gun goes off and a stack of crockery on the draining board explodes. Broken shards rain down on them.

There's shouting and voices echo through the trees now. Erik leads Joona in behind the shack. The tattooed man follows them, the broken crockery crunching beneath his feet. The gun sighs as he expels the cartridge and feeds in a new one.

Erik can feel his legs shaking as he pulls Joona after him into the forest.

They hurry across the uneven ground, pushing through tight thickets of pine scrub and getting caught on branches.

Joona's back is wet with sweat, his hip is burning and he's lost all feeling in one foot. He can't focus properly and fever is rolling through him in waves, rushing icily through his veins and making him shiver with cold.

Erik is holding him firmly by the arm as they move through the edge of the woods towards the car. Between the trees they can see the flickering light of pocket torches, and a dozen migrants arguing after they disarm the tattooed man with the gun.

Joona has to rest for a while before he and Erik cross the road to the car.

His legs give out and he all but falls into the passenger seat and closes his eyes, coughing so badly that it makes his lungs burn.

Erik runs round the car, gets in and locks the doors as there's a sudden thud on the windscreen. The blond man with the blood-smeared face is lit up by the headlights. He's holding a heavy branch, and raises it again as Erik starts the engine and puts his foot down. The front wheel spins on the verge, and grit and small stones fly up beneath the car.

There's another crash and the wing mirror comes loose and dangles from its wires as they lurch back onto the road. They can already hear the sound of emergency vehicles beyond the patch of woodland.

59

Erik took a double dose of pills that night to get to sleep, but still wakes early and gets up at first light. He thought he had hung a blue shirt over the back of the chair the night before in advance of his trip to Karsudden, but now he can't find it, and has to get another one from his wardrobe.

The three new murders are reminiscent of the old one, but Rocky has been locked up the whole time and the police believe he had a partner, a disciple, who for some reason has become active again. Erik has been asked to find out what Rocky remembers, and ask him about the 'unclean preacher'.

Joona is still asleep in the guestroom when he leaves the house, performs a makeshift repair on the wing mirror with some duct tape, and drives away.

As Erik overtakes a horsebox, he thinks about how he helped Joona take his clothes off, got him into the shower, then put him to bed in the guestroom. The towel ended up covered in blood as he cleaned the knife-wound to the Finn's hand and taped the edges of the cut together. Joona was awake the whole time, looking at him calmly. Erik gave him an intramuscular tetanus injection, some more penicillin, intravenously, got him to drink a glass of water, and then examined the injury to his hip. The old wound had caused a lot of internal bleeding, which had run down into his leg beneath the skin. Nothing was broken. Erik injected some cortisone into the muscle just above his hip, and tucked him in.

On his way back from Karsudden Hospital he needs to stop at a chemist and pick up some topiramate for Joona's migraines.

The roads are quiet, and it's still early in the morning as he drives past Katrineholm and approaches the large institution.

Casillas is standing on the steps outside reception, tapping his pipe against the railing. He holds out his hand to greet Erik as he approaches along the path.

'We've conducted numerous neurological examinations,' he explains as they head towards the gloomy brick buildings. 'This isn't my area, but the experts have ruled out surgery. They say the damage to his brain tissue is permanent . . . he can function, but he just has to accept the blackouts and erratic memory.'

After checking in to Section D:4 they are met by a female member of staff with laughter lines around her eyes.

'Rocky Kyrklund is waiting for you in the calm room,' she says, shaking hands with Erik.

Regardless of the outcome of this meeting, Erik will tell Margot about the unclean preacher, the man Rocky tried to blame nine years ago.

They stop and Casillas explains to the guard that she should wait outside the calm room and then escort Erik to the exit when he's finished.

Erik pushes the bead curtain aside and goes in. Rocky is sitting in the middle of one of the sofas with his arms stretched out along the back of it, as if he's been crucified. There's a mug of coffee and a cinnamon bun on the low table in front of him. Gentle classical music is streaming from two loudspeakers.

Rocky scratches the back of his head against the wall, then looks at Erik with a completely relaxed expression.

'No cigarettes today?' he says after a while.

'I can arrange that,' Erik replies.

'Get me a pack of Mogadon instead,' Rocky says, tucking his hair behind his ears.

'Mogadon?'

'Then Jesus will forgive you your sins.'

'I can have a word with your doctor if—'

'You're on Mogadon,' Rocky interrupts. 'Or is it Rohypnol?'

Erik reaches into his inside pocket and gives him a whole blister-pack. Rocky presses one pill out and swallows it without drinking anything.

'Last time I was here I asked you about someone, a colleague of yours,' Erik says, sitting down in an armchair.

'I don't have any colleagues,' Rocky says darkly. 'Because God lost me somewhere along the way . . . and didn't come back to look for me.'

He moves his white plastic mug and picks up a piece of pearl sugar on his index finger.

'Do you have any memory of having an accomplice in the murder?'

'Why are you asking?' Rocky wonders.

'We talked about it last time.'

'Did I say I had an accomplice?'

'Yes,' Erik lies.

Rocky closes his eyes and nods slowly to himself.

'You know . . . I can't trust my memory,' he says, and opens his eyes again. 'I can wake up in the middle of the night and remember a day twenty years ago and write it all down, then when I read what I wrote a week later it feels like I made it all up, like it never happened . . . and of course I don't really know . . . It's the same thing with my short-term memory, half the days disappear, I take my medicine, play billiards, talk to some idiots, eat lunch, then it's all gone.'

'But you haven't said if you had an accomplice when you murdered Rebecka.'

'I don't give a damn about that, you tell me you were here, but I've never met you before—'

'I think you remember that I was here.'

'Do you?'

'And I think you lie sometimes,' Erik says.

'Are you saying I tell lies?'

'Just now you referred to the cigarettes I gave you last time.'

'I wanted to see if you were keeping up,' Rocky says with a smile.

'So what do you remember?'

'Why should I tell you?' he asks, taking a sip of coffee then licking his lips.

'Your accomplice has starting murdering on his own.'

'Serves you right, in that case,' Rocky mutters, and suddenly starts to shake.

The mug falls from his hand, spilling the last of the coffee across the floor, and his chin trembles. His eyes roll backwards, his eyelids close and twitch. The epileptic attack lasts just a few seconds, then he straightens up, wipes his mouth and looks up, apparently unaware of what just happened.

'You told me before about a preacher,' Erik says.

'I was alone when I murdered Rebecka Hansson,' Rocky says in a low voice.

'So who's the unclean preacher?'

'What difference does it make?'

'Just tell me the truth.'

'What do I get out of it?'

'What do you want?'

'I want pure heroin,' Rocky says, and looks Erik in the eye.

'You can get permission to go out if you help,' Erik says.

'I don't remember, anyway, it's all gone, this is pointless.'

Erik leans forward in the soft armchair.

'I can help you remember,' he says, after a pause.

'No one can help me.'

'Not in a neurological sense, but I can help you remember what happened.'

'How?' he asks.

'I can hypnotise you.'

Rocky sits still, leaning his head back against the wall. His eyes are half-closed and his mouth slightly pursed.

'There's nothing to be concerned about – hypnosis is merely a way of accessing another level of consciousness by being in a deep state of relaxation.'

'I read the journal, *Cortex*, and I remember a long article about neuropsychology and hypnosis,' Rocky says, waving his hand.

60

They have moved to Rocky's room, with the door closed and the lighting turned down. The weak lamplight is reflecting off a Playboy calendar. Erik has set up his tripod, attached the video camera and adjusted the angle and exposure, and has made sure the microphone is pointing in the right direction.

A small red dot indicates that the camera is recording.

Kyrklund is sitting on a chair, his broad shoulders are relaxed, rounded, like a bear's. His head is drooping. He slid into deep relaxation very quickly, and responded well to the induction.

The difficult part isn't the act of hypnosis, but finding the right level and placing the patient in a state where the brain is as relaxed as possible, yet still able to distinguish between real memories and dreams.

Erik is standing just behind Rocky, slowly counting backwards as he prepares Rocky to examine his memories.

'Two hundred and twelve,' Erik says in a monotone. 'Two hundred and eleven . . . you will soon find yourself standing outside Rebecka Hansson's house . . .'

When a patient is placed in deep hypnosis, the hypnotist often enters a sort of trance as well, in what is known as hypnotic resonance.

It's vital that Erik manages to differentiate between his absolutely present self, and a clearly observing self.

The observing self, in his own personal trance, is always underwater. That's become his internal image of hypnotic immersion.

While his patients are led through their memories, Erik sinks into a warm sea, past steep cliffs and coral.

In this way Erik can remain utterly present in the patient's experience, yet still maintain a protective distance.

'Eighty-eight, eighty-seven, eighty-six,' Erik goes on in a somnolent voice. 'The only thing that exists is my voice, and your desire to listen to it . . . With each number you're sinking deeper and deeper into relaxation . . . eighty-five, eighty-four . . . there's nothing dangerous here, nothing to be worried about . . .'

As Erik counts down, he sinks through strangely pink water together with Rocky Kyrklund. They're following the chain of an anchor. The rusty links are covered in stringy algae. Above them, on the silvery surface, is the hull of a large ship with motionless propellers.

They drift lower.

Rocky's eyes are closed and small air-bubbles are rising from his beard. He's got his arms by his sides, but the water passing them makes his clothes sway.

'Fifty-one, fifty, forty-nine . . .'

Out of the violet darkness sticks the top of a vast underwater mountain, grey-black, like a heap of ash.

Rocky raises his face and tries to look, but only the whites of his eyes are visible. His mouth opens, and his eyes close again. His hair is drifting above his head as bubbles emerge from his nostrils.

'Eleven, ten, nine . . . You will be able to remember all your real memories of Rebecka Hansson when I say so . . .'

As Erik sinks through the water, simultaneously he observes Rocky on the chair in his room. A string of saliva is hanging from his mouth, and the seams of his white vest are coming loose under his arms.

'Three, two, one . . . Now you open your eyes and can see Rebecka Hansson the way she was when you last saw her . . .'

Rocky is standing in front of him on top of the underwater mountain, his clothes moving in the gentle current, his hair floating like slow flames above his head. He opens his mouth and large bubbles stream out and float up in front of his face.

'Tell me what you can see,' Erik says calmly.

'I see her . . . I'm standing in the garden at the back of the house . . . Through the terrace door I see her sitting on the sofa watching television. Her knitting needles are moving and a ball of blue wool is slowly unravelling beside her hip . . . She's said she doesn't want to see me, but I think she'll open her legs anyway . . .'

'What's happening?'

'I knock on the glass door, she takes her glasses off and lets me in . . . she says she has to go to bed because she's working in the morning . . . but that I can stay the night if I like . . .'

Erik doesn't interrupt, just waits for the next segment of memories, waits for the images to join up.

'I sit down on the sofa and touch her necklace . . . There's an old knitting pattern in a women's magazine on the floor . . . Rebecka puts her knitting down on the table and I slip a hand between her thighs . . . she pulls away, says she doesn't want to . . . but I pull her night-dress up again . . .'

Rocky is breathing heavily.

'She resists, but I know she's changed her mind, I can see it in her eyes, she wants this now . . . I kiss her, and put my hand between her legs.'

He's smiling to himself on the chair, then turns serious.

'She says we should go to her bedroom, and I put a finger in her mouth and she sucks it, and . . . Outside.'

Rocky stops himself and just stares, his eyes wide open.

'There's someone outside! I can see a face. There's someone at the window.'

'Outside the house?' Erik asks.

'It was a face, I go over to the glass door but I can't see anything . . . just darkness, and the room reflected in the glass . . . and then I see someone standing behind me . . . I spin round, ready to lash out, but it's only Rebecka . . . she gets scared and tells me to leave . . . she means it, so I go into the hall and take all the money she's got in her bag, and . . .'

He falls silent, breathing more heavily, and the energy in the room changes, slowly becomes more dangerous.

'Rocky, I want you to stay with Rebecka,' Erik says. 'It's the same evening, you're at home with her, and—'

'I've gone to the Zone,' Rocky interrupts in a slurred voice.

'Later that evening, you mean?'

'I ignore the strippers on the main stage,' he whispers. 'I ignore the dealers, because what I'm looking for . . .'

'Do you go back to Rebecka's?'

'No, we sit in the disabled toilet so we can be alone.'

'Who are you talking about?'

'My girlfriend . . . the woman I love. Tina, who . . . She gives me a blow job without a condom, she doesn't care, she's in a hurry now, she's sweating all over.'

Erik wonders if he ought to bring the patient out of hypnosis, he can feel Rocky moving too quickly through his memories, and no longer knows if it's possible to keep him at the right level.

'Tina coughs over the basin and looks at me in the mirror with fear in her eyes . . . I know she's in a bad way, but . . .'

'Is Tina your accomplice?' Erik asks, looking at Rocky's open face.

'For fuck's sake, they owe me a hundred thousand, I'll be getting it next week,' he mutters. 'But right now I can only afford . . . shitty brown shoe-scrapings, have to dissolve it in acid so I can shoot up.'

Rocky starts to shake his head anxiously, and is breathing unevenly through his nose.

'There's no danger here,' Erik says, as calmly as he can. 'You're quite safe, you can talk about everything that happens.'

Rocky's body relaxes again, but his face is lined and sweaty.

'I sit there, let her have the spoon . . . I'm not getting a kick any more, but I feel great and start to nod off, and I see her use a cable as a tourniquet round her arm . . . the adapter's whirring and getting all tangled, and she can't sort it out afterwards . . . I'm too out of it to help her, I hear her ask for help with a sob in her voice . . .'

Rocky whimpers slightly and the atmosphere seems to contract to a single dark pinprick.

'What's happening now?' Erik asks.

'The door opens,' Rocky replies. 'Some bastard has picked the lock . . . I shut my eyes, I've got to rest, but I know it's the preacher, the preacher's found me . . .'

'How do you know that?'

'I can tell because of the filthy smell of old gear. It's withdrawal, it smells metallic, like fish-guts . . .'

Rocky shakes his head again, his breathing is getting too quick, and Erik thinks he should start to bring Rocky out of his hypnosis, but holds back.

'What's happening?' he whispers.

'I open my eyes and the preacher looks a fucking wreck,' he says. 'Hepatitis, probably, completely yellow eyes . . . The preacher snorts back some snot, then starts to speak in a really high voice.'

Rocky is breathing shallowly, twisting on his chair and moaning in anguish between his words.

'The preacher goes over to Tina . . . she's shot up, but can't get the cable loose . . . Dear God in heaven, have mercy on my soul, dear God in heaven . . .'

'Rocky, I'm going to start to wake you up, and—'

'The preacher's holding a machete, and it sounds like when you stick a spade into mud—'

Rocky starts to retch, he's panting heavily now, but goes on talking.

'The preacher chops her arm off at the shoulder, loosens the tourniquet and drinks . . .'

'Listen to my voice now.'

'And drinks the blood from her arm . . . while Tina lies bleeding to death on the floor . . . Dear God in heaven . . . Dear God—'

'Three, two, one . . . now you're above the disabled toilet, you're high above it, and nothing you can see is going to hurt you . . .'

'Dear God,' Rocky sobs, hanging his head.

'You're still in a state of deep relaxation, and you're going to tell me how much of what you've just said to me was a dream . . . You've taken drugs, and have been having nightmares . . . You're looking down at yourself on the toilet floor. What's really going on?'

'I don't know,' Rocky says slowly.

'Who is he?'

'The preacher's face is covered in blood . . . shows me a polaroid picture of Rebecka . . . just like Tina the week before, and . . .'

His hoarse voice disappears, but his mouth keeps moving for a while until it stops. He leans his big head to one side, and looks straight through Erik with empty eyes.

'I didn't hear what you said.'

'It's my fault . . . I should pluck out my eye, for it has offended me, it would be better to pluck my eye out than this.'

Rocky tries to stand up, but Erik holds him down with a gentle hand on his shoulder, and feels the big body vibrate, trembling with fear.

'You're in a state of deep relaxation,' Erik says, as sweat trickles down his back. 'But before you wake up, I want you to look straight at the preacher and . . . tell me what you see.'

'I'm lying on the floor, I can see boots . . . I can smell blood, and I shut my eyes.'

'Go back a little.'

'I can't do any more,' Rocky says, and starts to come round from his hypnosis.

'Stay there, just for a moment . . . There's no danger, you're relaxed, you're telling me about the first time you saw the unclean preacher.'

'It's in the church . . .'

He opens his eyes for a moment, then shuts them again, and mutters something inaudible.

'Tell me about the church,' Erik says. 'What's happening?'

'I don't know,' Rocky gasps. 'It's not a sermon . . .'

'What can you see?'

'He's wearing make-up over his stubble . . . and his arms are so fucking riddled with holes that—'

Rocky tries to stand up, but his chair falls over and he collapses and hits the back of his head on the floor.

61

Rocky rolls on to his side and Erik helps him to his feet. He stretches his back, rubs his mouth with his hand, pushes Erik away and goes over to the window, looking through the gaps between the vertical bars.

'Do you remember anything from when you were hypnotised?' Erik asks, picking the chair up off the floor.

Rocky turns round and looks at him through narrowed eyes.

'Was I entertaining?'

'You talked a lot about the preacher. You do know what his real name is – don't you?'

Rocky purses his lips and slowly shakes his head.

'No.'

'I think you do, and I don't understand why you're protecting him . . .'

'The preacher is just a scapegoat, a—'

'Give me a name, then,' Erik persists.

'I can't remember,' Rocky says.

'A place, then. Where is he? Where's the Zone?'

Sunlight from behind shines through his beard onto his furrowed cheeks.

'Was this the first time you've hypnotised me?' Rocky asks.

'I've never hypnotised you before.'

'As far as I'm concerned, the evaluation was a waste of time,' Rocky says, without listening. 'But I liked talking to you.'

'You remember that? It's almost ten years ago . . .'

'I remember your brown cord jacket, that must have been pretty damn retro even then . . . We used to sit on opposite sides of a table . . . chipboard, with a birch veneer, you can tell by the smell . . . Paper cups of water, Dictaphone, notebook . . . and my head was really hurting again, I needed morphine, but I wanted to tell you about my alibi first . . .'

'I don't remember that,' Erik says, taking a step back.

Rocky picks at the window between the bars.

'I wrote down Olivia's address, but that was never mentioned in court.'

'But you confessed to murdering—'

'Just tell me what happened to my alibi,' he interrupts.

'I didn't really take it seriously.'

Rocky turns round, walks closer, hunches up slightly and lowers his head, as if to see Erik better.

'So you never mentioned it to my defence lawyer?'

Erik glances quickly over his shoulder and can see that the guard outside the door has disappeared. Rocky shoves the chairs between them out of the way with his foot.

'I don't remember being given an address,' Erik says quickly. 'But if I was, I'm sure I would have handed it to your defence team.'

'You threw it away – didn't you?' Rocky says darkly and steps closer.

'Calm down,' Erik replies, moving towards the door.

'You sentenced me to this,' Rocky shouts. 'It was you! You were the one who did this to me!'

Erik is standing with his back to the door, and raises his hands to hold Rocky back, but he doesn't stand a chance of defending himself. Rocky just brushes his arms aside and punches him in the chest with his fist. The blow feels like a sledgehammer. All the air goes out of his lungs and he can't breathe. The next punch strikes exactly the same place and Erik's head slams back against the door with a dull thud.

He is struggling to stay upright. The zip on his jacket catches on the textured wallpaper as he moves sideways to get away. He raises a hand to fend Rocky off, coughs and tries to breathe.

'Do you want me to look into your alibi?' he hisses.

'Liar!' Rocky roars, grabbing Erik by the chin and pressing his mouth closed.

Rocky pulls him towards him and slaps the side of his head so hard that his vision goes black. Erik staggers to one side with the force of the blow, falls over the plastic chair and careers into the metal bed-frame with a force that makes his back creak. He pulls the covers off the bed as he slides down on to the floor, his cheek burning.

'That's enough, now,' Erik gasps, shuffling backwards.

'Shut up,' Rocky yells, and shoves the plastic chair aside.

As he leans forward Erik kicks out at him and hits him in the chest. Rocky catches hold of his foot and Erik kicks out with the other one. His shoe comes off and Rocky stumbles back just as the guard comes in holding a taser.

'Stand against the wall, Rocky! Hands behind your head, feet wide apart.'

Erik gets slowly to his feet and adjusts his clothes. He picks up the covers from the floor with trembling hands, and puts them back on the bed.

'It might look a bit odd,' he gasps, tasting blood in his mouth. 'But I had cramp in my leg and Rocky was helping me take my shoes off.'

The guard stares at him.

'Cramp?'

'It feels better already.'

Rocky is standing quietly to the side with his fingers laced behind his neck. The back of his white vest is wet with sweat.

'What have you got to say, Rocky?'

He lowers his hands and turns round slowly, scratches his beard and nods.

'I was helping the doctor with his shoe,' he says gruffly.

'We did shout, but no one heard,' Erik explains. 'I tried lying down on the bed, but slipped off onto the floor.'

'Is it feeling better now?' Rocky asks, picking Erik's shoe up from the floor.

'Much better, thanks.'

The guard stands there with the taser in his hand, looks at them, then nods, although something obviously isn't right.

'The visit's over,' the guard says.

'If you can just tell me Olivia's surname, I can find her,' Erik says, meeting Rocky's gaze.

'Her name is Olivia Toreby,' he says simply.

Erik leaves with the guard, follows him along the corridor, and sees that Casillas is talking to the head of section in the dayroom.

'Did it go OK?' Casillas calls.

Erik stops in the doorway, his cheek still stinging from the force of the blow.

'I have to say, you've done a remarkable job with the patient,' he replies.

'Thanks,' Casillas smiles. 'I'm pretty sure he'd have been released if he'd applied for parole . . . but he doesn't seem to think he's done his penance yet.'

Erik limps towards his car, gets out his phone and dials Margot's number to tell her about Olivia Toreby.

62

Joona opens his eyes and looks up at the white ceiling. Daylight is filtering into the room around the edges of the dark-blue roller-blind. The window is open slightly, and fresh air is streaming in, cooling the clean sheets.

There are blackbirds singing in the garden.

He looks at the alarm clock and sees that he has slept for thirteen hours. Erik has left him a phone, and on the bedside table are two pink capsules and three tablets on top of a note saying 'Eat us now, drinks loads of water, and have a look in the fridge'.

Joona swallows the drugs, empties the glass of water, then groans as he stands up. But he can at least bear to put some weight on his leg. The pain is still there, but it's far from severe. The nausea and pain in his stomach have vanished as though they never existed.

He goes over to the window and looks out at the apple trees as he dials Lumi's number.

'It's Dad,' Joona says, feeling his heart tighten.

'Dad?'

'How are you getting on? Do you like Paris?'

'It's a bit bigger than Nattavaara,' his daughter replies in a voice that could be Summa's.

'How's college?'

'I'm still finding it confusing, but I think it's pretty good . . .'

Joona reassures himself that she's got everything she needs, and Lumi tells him to shave off his beard and join the police again, and then they end the call.

Erik has left him a pair of black sweatpants and a white T-shirt. The clothes are too small, the trousers flutter round his calves and the T-shirt is tight across his chest. By the bed is a pair of white slippers, the sort you get in hotels.

Joona thinks that mysteries are only mysteries until you have discounted all the impossibilities.

When he was in hospital Margot told him that the videos had been recorded long before the murders took place.

Maria Carlsson owned nothing but black underwear, but the seams of the tights she was wearing when she died were different to the ones in the video. The spoon found in the tub of ice cream in Susanna Kern's home wasn't the same one that was in the video, and the post-mortem will probably show that Sandra Lundgren hadn't injected herself with insulin in her thigh on the day she was murdered.

Classic stalking. The women have been watched and their behaviour mapped over a long period.

Joona leans against the walls as he walks through the house towards the kitchen. He tells himself that he'll call the police in Huddinge and follow up the previous day's events as soon as he's had something to eat.

He drinks some more water, puts coffee on, and looks in the fridge, where he finds half a pizza and a tub of yoghurt.

On the kitchen table, next to Erik's empty coffee cup, are printouts relating to an almost ten-year-old case that was tried in Södertälje District Court.

Joona eats the cold pizza as he reads the verdict, the post-mortem analysis and the entire preliminary investigation report.

The old murder has striking similarities to the recent ones.

The vicar of the parish of Salem, Rocky Kyrklund, was arrested and convicted for the murder of a woman called Rebecka Hansson.

Joona was pretty out of it yesterday when Erik was taking care of him, but he can remember what Erik said. Margot Silverman had asked him to go and talk to a guy who had been sentenced to secure psychiatric care. She wanted Erik to find out if he had any accomplices or disciples.

She must have meant Rocky Kyrklund.

Margot's thinking along the right lines, Joona thinks, bracing his arms on the table as he stands up again. He walks barefoot into the back garden, sits down on the cushionless garden swing for a while, then walks over to the shed.

On one end is a water-damaged dartboard. Joona opens the door and gets out the cushions for the swing-seat. He goes back to the shed to close the door, but stops and looks at the neat arrangement of DIY tools and gardening implements on the wall.

In the turning circle at the end of the road an ice-cream van starts to play its jingle. Joona picks up an old Mora knife with a red wooden handle and tests its weight, then takes down a smaller knife in a plastic sleeve, walks out and shuts the door behind him.

He puts the smaller knife on the ground beside the swing-seat, then stands in the middle of the lawn and weighs the Mora knife in his right hand. He changes his grip, tries to find some sort of balance, a sense of lightness, puts the knife down by his hip and stretches out the other arm, feeling it tug at his wound.

Cautiously he tries to perform a kata against two opponents with the knife. He doesn't follow through on all the elements, but his legs still feel frustratingly heavy when he finishes.

Joona twists his body and moves his legs in the reverse order, leaving his attacker's torso unguarded. He performs a diagonal cut, starting at the bottom, blocks the second attacker's hand and diverts the force of the assault as the knife moves downward, then glides out of danger.

He repeats the pattern of movements, slowly, perfectly balanced. His hip hurts, but his level of concentration is the same as before.

The different elements of the kata are only complicated because they don't come naturally, but against untrained opponents they can be extremely effective. In nine coordinated movements the attackers are disarmed and rendered harmless. It works like a trap – if anyone chooses to attack, the trap is sprung.

Katas and shadow-boxing can never replace sparring and real-life situations, but they're a way to get the body used to the movements, and, by repetition, train the body to think that certain movements belong together.

Joona rolls his shoulders, finds his balance, hits out a few times, follows through with his elbow, then repeats the kata, but faster this time. He performs the vertical cut, deflects the imaginary attack, changes grip, but drops the knife in the grass.

He stops and straightens his back. Listens to the birdsong and the wind in the trees. He takes some deep breaths, bends over, picks up the knife and blows some grass off it, and finds its centre of gravity. Then he takes the knife in his right hand, throws it past the hammock at the dartboard, which wobbles, and the old darts come loose and fall off into the grass.

Someone claps, and he turns round and sees a woman in the garden. She's tall and blonde, and is watching him with a calm smile on her face.

63

The woman looking at Joona has a self-aware but relaxed posture, reminiscent of a mannequin. Her arms are slender and her hands very freckly. She's wearing make-up, but not too much, tasteful. It looks like she might be blushing slightly.

Joona bends down and picks up the second knife from the ground, weighs it in his hand, then throws it over his shoulder towards the dartboard. It ends up in the branches of the weeping birch and falls to the grass next to the shed. She claps her hands again and walks over to him, smiling.

'Joona Linna?' she asks.

'It's not easy to see with a beard like this, but I think so,' he replies.

'Erik said you were confined to bed, and—'

The veranda door opens and Erik comes out into the garden with a worried look on his face.

'You should be careful with that hip until we've had it X-rayed,' he says.

'It's fine,' Joona says.

'I gave him cortisone in—'

'So you said,' the smiling woman interrupts. 'It seems to have worked.'

'This is Nelly,' Erik says. 'She's my closest colleague . . . an excellent psychologist, the best in the country for traumatised children.'

'That's all empty flattery,' she smiles, shaking Joona's hand.

'How do you feel?' Erik asks.

'Fine,' he replies quietly.

'The penicillin will kick in properly tomorrow, you'll feel much stronger,' Erik says, smiling at Joona's tight clothes.

Joona groans as he sits down on the swing-seat. The others sit down beside him and they swing together gently. The springs creak and the cushions give off a damp, musty smell.

'Did you read the report of the preliminary investigation?' Erik asks after a while.

'Yes,' Joona says, glancing at him.

'I went and talked to Rocky this morning . . . he's had terrible problems with his memory since the accident, but he was willing to try hypnosis . . .'

'You hypnotised him?' Joona asks with interest.

'I wasn't sure if it would work, given the damage to brain tissue and his epileptic attacks . . .'

'But he was receptive?' Joona asks, leaning his head back and looking up at the sky.

'Yes, but it wasn't easy working out what were real memories . . . Rocky used to take a lot of drugs in those days, and some of the things he said under hypnosis – which ought to have been proper memories – sounded more like nightmares . . . delirium.'

'God, that's difficult,' Nelly said, stretching her ankles.

Erik stands up, making the swing-seat move again.

'I was really only going to ask about the murder of Rebecka Hansson to find out if he had an accomplice,' he says. 'But under hypnosis it sounded more like he was completely innocent.'

'In what way?' Joona asks.

'Rocky keeps returning to a man he calls the preacher . . . the unclean preacher.'

'That sounds creepy,' Nelly says.

'And now, all of a sudden, he remembers that he's got an alibi for the night of the murder,' Erik says in a low voice.

'He said that under hypnosis?' Joona asks.

'No, he was awake then.'

'Is there anyone who can confirm the alibi?'

'Her name is Olivia Toreby . . . he remembered it at the time, but he's probably already forgotten it again,' Erik says, looking away.

'An alibi,' Nelly says.

'It's worth checking out, anyway,' Erik says.

'Have you spoken to Margot about this?' Joona asks.

'Of course.'

'Psychologists lead, one-nil,' Nelly says, slapping the cushion beside her to get him to sit down again.

Erik does so, and they spend a little while swinging, drifting off to the sound of the slow creaking of the metal springs, the birdsong, and some children playing in a nearby garden.

Then Erik's mobile buzzes on the cushion. It's Margot, and Joona takes the call.

'I presume you've checked criminal records, any previous suspicions and the police database?'

'Good to hear that you're feeling better,' Margot's rough voice says.

'The murderer may have done time, or simply been out of the country for all these years,' Joona goes on. 'I've got pretty good contacts with Europol and—'

'Joona, I can't discuss the preliminary investigation with you,' she interrupts.

'No, but I was just trying to say that nine years is one hell of a long cooling off period for a—'

'OK, now I understand . . . I understand what you mean, but Rocky Kyrklund's alibi doesn't stand up.'

'You found her?'

'Olivia Toreby had no idea what we were talking about. She was living in Jönköping at the time, and we can't see any connection between her and Rocky Kyrklund.'

'So you still think he had an apprentice? That he's mixed up in the murders?'

'That's why I'm calling Erik,' Margot says calmly. 'I want him to go back and ask Rocky properly about accomplices.'

'I'll pass you over to him,' Joona says, and hands over the phone.

While Erik is talking to Margot, Joona goes and picks up the knives and puts them back in the shed. He rests against the handle of a lawnmower for a moment. There's a small wasps' nest up by the roof, and in the far corner a homemade toy truck behind some folding chairs.

When he comes out again Erik is no longer on the phone, and has stretched out next to Nelly.

'Do you normally phone witnesses to ask about alibis?' Erik asks him.

'It depends,' Joona replies.

'I just mean . . . You don't know if people are prepared to get involved,' Erik says. 'You don't know if people tell the truth when the police phone them so many years later.'

'No,' Joona says.

'I need to talk to her if I'm going to be able to go back to Rocky and look him in the eye,' Erik says.

64

Joona wanted to go with Erik to talk to Olivia Toreby, but accepted that it was too soon. Erik gave him some more penicillin, another cortisone injection in his hip, and made sure he took 50mg of topiramate to forestall further migraines.

Nelly gets in the passenger seat, and as Erik drives off he looks in the rear-view mirror and sees Joona sit down on the swing-seat again.

'Shall I drive you home?' Erik asks.

'Didn't you say she lived in Jönköping?'

'Apparently she moved to Eskilstuna five years ago.'

'That's about an hour away, isn't it?'

'Yes.'

'Martin said he'd be working late today,' says Nelly. 'So I won't have to sit in the house alone with all those windows . . . I keep getting the feeling that someone's spying on me . . . It's just because of you talking about this murderer. I know that, but still.'

'Is someone watching you, then?'

'No,' she laughs. 'I'm just scared of the dark.'

They head down Enskedevägen towards Södertälje, and sit in silence as they drive past a long, grey noise-proof fence.

'You said you were sure the priest was guilty,' Nelly says, looking at him.

'He said so himself, he said he'd killed Rebecka . . . but after hypnosis he suddenly remembered.'

'Remembered what, though? Suddenly remembered a woman who could confirm his alibi?' she asks sceptically.

'At first he remembered telling me about the alibi.'

'Shit,' she says. 'What happened? Did he get angry?'

'Yes, my chest feels a bit painful . . .'

'Did you have a fight? Can I see?'

She tries to pull his shirt up, and he holds the wheel with his left hand as he fends her off with the right.

'We'll end up in the ditch,' he laughs.

She loosens her seatbelt and turns in her seat so she can look at him.

'But are you in pain?' she asks, undoing his buttons. 'God, you're black and blue. What the hell did he do? That must really hurt . . .'

She leans over and kisses Erik's chest, kisses his neck, and then quickly on the mouth before he turns his face away.

'Sorry,' she says.

'I can't, Nelly.'

'I know, I didn't mean . . . it's just that I sometimes think about that time we slept together.'

'We were incredibly drunk,' Erik reminds her.

'I don't regret a thing,' she says gently, with her face right next to his.

'Nor do I,' he replies, tucking his shirt back in his trousers with one hand.

They drive along the E20 for a while in silence. A few emergency vehicles race past with their sirens blaring. Nelly picks up her handbag, folds down the sun-visor to use the mirror, and touches up her lipstick.

'We could do it again, if we wanted to,' she suddenly says.

'That would never work.'

'No, I know . . . I say things I don't mean, it was just a fantasy about how different everything could be in another universe,' Nelly says.

'All the lives we haven't lived,' Erik says quietly.

'Thinking like that is bound to be a sign of getting older.' She smiles.

'The tiniest choice closes a thousand doors and opens a thousand more,' Erik says. 'I lied about an alibi, and nine years later the lie catches up with me and I risk—'

'Yes, but you're an idiot,' Nelly interrupts, leaning back. 'I don't believe in that alibi, but I mean, if this woman confirms it, then I ought to report you.'

He gives her a sideways glance.

'If you want to report me, go ahead,' he says.

'Rocky's been locked up for nine years, locked up and medicated, and—'

'Please, Nelly,' Erik interrupts. 'I'm sorry, but I can't handle this conversation. I'm not going to ask you for anything, you can do whatever you like, whatever you think is the right thing to do.'

'Then I'll report you,' she says firmly.

'I don't care,' he mumbles.

'But it would be a lot easier if you weren't so sweet when you get angry,' she smiles.

'I dare say I need therapy,' Erik sighs.

'You need medication,' she says, and pulls a pack of Mogadon from her bag.

She presses out two capsules, takes one and gives Erik the other. He murmurs 'Cheers,' tips his head back and swallows.

65

When Erik parks the car beside the school where Olivia Toreby works as a teacher, Nelly hesitates with her hand on the door handle.

'Do you want me to come?' she asks. 'Say what you think.'

'I don't know . . . no, maybe it would better if you wait here.'

'So you can use your charm?' she smiles.

'Exactly!'

'I'll stay here with your dream woman,' she says, pointing at the little monkey in the pink skirt, hanging from the ignition key.

Erik walks across the playground, asks a caretaker for Olivia Toreby, and he points her out.

Olivia is in her fifties, a thin woman with a pale, worn face. She's standing with her arms folded, watching the children on the climbing frame. Now and then one of them calls out to her, or runs over wanting help with something.

'Olivia? My name's Erik Maria Bark, and I'm a doctor,' Erik says, handing her his card.

'A doctor,' she repeats, putting the card in her pocket.

'I need to talk to you about Rocky Kyrklund.'

Her thin face hardens for a moment, then reverts to neutral.

'The police again,' she says simply.

'I've spoken to Rocky Kyrklund, and he—'

'I've already said, I don't know anyone of that name,' Olivia interrupts.

'I know,' Erik says patiently. 'But he talked about you.'

'I've got no idea how he managed to get hold of my name.'

She looks at some children with skipping ropes round their necks, playing horses, and hurries over and puts the ropes round their waists instead.

'I'm supposed to have finished work, really,' she says when she returns to Erik.

'Just give me a few minutes.'

'Sorry, I have to get home and prepare appraisals for twenty-two children,' she says, and starts to walk off towards the school building.

'I believe Rocky Kyrklund was convicted of a murder he didn't commit,' Erik says, hurrying after her.

'I'm sorry to hear that, but—'

'He was a priest, but he was also addicted to heroin at the same time. He exploited the people around him . . .'

She stops in the shade in front of the steps and turns towards Erik.

'He was utterly ruthless,' she says in a toneless voice.

'So I understand,' Erik replies. 'But he still doesn't deserve to be convicted of a murder he didn't commit.'

Olivia's greying hair falls over her forehead and she blows it away.

'Will anything bad happen to me if I lied to the police before?'

'Only if you lied under oath in a court.'

'Of course,' she says, and her thin mouth quivers nervously.

They sit on the steps. Olivia looks down at her trainers, picks something off her jeans and clears her throat.

'I was a different person then, and I don't want to get mixed up in anything,' she says quietly. 'But it's true, I did know him back then.'

'He says you can give him an alibi.'

'I can,' she admits, and swallows hard.

'Are you sure?'

She nods, her chin starts to tremble and she looks down again.

'Nine years have passed,' Erik says.

She tries to swallow the lump in her throat, rubs her top lip, then looks up with shiny eyes and swallows hard once more.

'We were in the rectory in Rönninge . . . that's where he lived,' she says in an uneven voice.

'We're talking about the evening of April fifteenth,' Erik reminds her.

'Yes,' she replies, and quickly brushes some tears from her cheeks. 'How can you remember that?'

Her mouth starts to quiver and she bites her bottom lip to pull herself together before she answers.

'We were on a bender together,' she says in a whisper. 'We started on the Friday, and . . . it was at its worst on Sunday night . . .'

'You're sure about the dates?'

She nods and loses control of her voice:

'My little boy died in his cot on the fifteenth . . . I only found him the next day. It was sudden infant death syndrome – that was medically proven, it wasn't my fault, but if he'd been with me then it might not have happened . . .'

'I'm sorry to—'

'Oh, God,' she sobs, and gets to her feet.

Olivia turns away from the playground, wraps her arms tightly around herself, and forces herself to be quiet, to stop her grief pouring out. Erik tries to give her a handkerchief, but she doesn't see it. She takes a few trembling breaths and wipes her tears away.

'For years after that I just wanted to die,' she says, swallowing hard again. 'But I've never touched drugs since, I haven't had sex with anyone . . . I must never get pregnant again, I don't have the right, I . . . He took everything with him . . . I hate him for getting me to try heroin, I hate him for everything . . .'

They are interrupted by a ball rolling under the bench. A child comes running over to fetch it and Erik hands Olivia his handkerchief.

'Don't worry, Marcus,' she says warmly to the little boy, who's standing looking at her with the ball under his arm. 'I just need to blow my nose.'

The child nods and runs off with the ball. Erik thinks about Rocky's erratic memory. At some moments during his years at Karsudden he must have known that he had been wrongly convicted, because of Erik's betrayal.

'Olivia,' Erik says quietly, 'I appreciate that this isn't easy, but are you prepared to swear on oath that you were with Rocky when the murder took place?'

'Yes,' she says, looking him in the eye.

Erik thanks her, and at that moment notices Nelly standing behind the climbing frame, watching them. He starts to walk back, and wonders if she's going to report him when she finds out. Maybe he himself could file a report about a patient suffering harm while receiving treatment before she does.

66

Before the paint dries completely, Erik and Madeleine carefully pull off the masking tape from the skirting boards and around the door and window, fold up the stiff protective paper and pull the plastic off the furniture that they stacked in the middle of the room. Although he's taken two tranquillisers, he still feels overwhelmed with remorse whenever he thinks about the priest who has been locked up for longer than Madeleine has been alive, because of his lie.

They carry on cleaning until the pizza delivery guy rings the bell. Madeleine holds Erik's hand as they go out into the hall to open the door.

'How does it look?' Jackie asks when they come into the kitchen.

'Great,' Madeleine says, looking up at Erik.

Outside in the street rain is falling through the thin sunlight and the day feels pleasantly slow, like something from childhood. Erik cuts up the pizza and puts it on their plates.

'Robots eat pizza,' Madeleine says happily.

Her face is totally relaxed, she's so relieved that she starts to sing a song from the Disney film, *Frozen*, even though Jackie tries to tell her several times that she shouldn't sing at the dinner table.

'Clever robot,' Madeleine keeps saying to Erik.

'But what if he starts to get rusty?' Jackie smiles, as she feels something against her foot.

'He won't,' the little girl says.

'Maddy, what's this?' she asks, carefully shaking a blister-pack of Morfin Meda that must have fallen out of Erik's jacket as it hung over the back of the chair.

'That's mine,' he says. 'It's just some headache pills.'

He takes the pills from her hand and puts them in his pocket.

'Erik,' Jackie says. 'Can I ask you for a favour . . .? Maddy's got a match on Wednesday, and I'm playing at the evening service in Hässelby

Church . . . I don't like to ask, it feels wrong, but Rosita who usually brings Maddy home has been ill all week.'

'You'd like me to pick her up?'

'I can walk on my own, Mum – it's only at Östermalm Sports Club,' Madeleine says quickly.

'You're certainly not walking on your own,' Jackie snaps.

'I'll pick her up,' Erik says.

'It's actually a lethal road,' Jackie says seriously.

'Lidingövägen and Valhallavägen are completely mad,' Erik agrees.

'She's got her own key, and you don't have to stay if you can't – I'll be back by eight.'

'I might have time to watch the match,' Erik says hopefully to Madeleine.

'Erik, I'm incredibly grateful, and I promise I won't ask again.'

'Don't say that, I'm only too happy to help.'

Jackie whispers a silent thank you to him, and he gets up to clear the table just as his mobile buzzes in his shirt pocket.

It's Casillas, from Karsudden District Hospital. After his meeting with Olivia Toreby, Erik called him to discuss the chances of Rocky Kyrklund being allowed on excursions outside the hospital, and beginning his rehabilitation.

'I've spoken to the Administrative Court today,' Casillas tells him. 'And you won't be surprised to hear that you and I are in complete agreement.'

'That's great,' Erik says.

'The big problem is that Rocky refuses to sign . . . he says he murdered a woman, and that he doesn't deserve to be free.'

'I can talk to him,' Erik volunteers quickly.

'It's just that there's not much time if it's going to be considered at the next quarterly meeting.'

One and a half hours later Erik passes through the security doors of Section D:4, is shown through the corridor and out into the fenced exercise yard. The patients in Rocky's section have all committed serious violent crimes under the influence of severe mental disorders, but most of them are doing relatively well with their medication and are no longer considered particularly dangerous.

On the other side of the high fence is a low hedge. The bushes press against the fence as if they wanted to get inside the yard.

Rocky Kyrklund squints at him in the broken sunshine as he approaches along the path.

'No nice pills today, Doctor?'

'No.'

A man shouts something at Rocky from a distance, but Rocky ignores him.

'I've spoken to Olivia Toreby,' Erik begins.

'Who's she?'

'We talked about her last time . . . and she confirms your alibi.'

'My alibi for what?'

'For the murder of Rebecka Hansson.'

'Good,' Rocky smiles, and runs his huge hand through his steel-grey hair.

'She was addicted to heroin at the time, and I don't think her evidence would have affected the verdict against you, but I wanted you to know that all the evidence suggests that you're innocent.'

'You mean this is really happening?' he says sceptically.

'Yes.'

'An alibi,' Rocky repeats to himself.

'Olivia Toreby is living a different life these days, and she's sure of what she says. You were together at the time of the murder.'

Rocky focuses his eyes on Erik's.

'So I didn't murder Rebecka Hansson?' he says quietly.

'I don't think so,' Erik replies, without looking away.

'How sure is she?' Rocky asks, and his jaw muscles tense.

'She knows, because you were high on the night of the murder . . . and it was the same night her son died of sudden infant death syndrome.'

Rocky nods and stares straight up at the white sky.

'And that matches the register of deaths,' Erik concludes.

'So all this crap has been for nothing,' Rocky says, taking a crumpled packet of cigarettes from his pocket.

'She was a drug addict, and I don't think the court would have believed her testimony at the time,' Erik repeats.

'I might still have ended up here, but I'd have felt completely different if I'd known . . .'

The air currents between the buildings are picking up dust and loose particles in the sunlit park. The man who shouted is walking towards them across the yard. Erik looks at his face, swollen with medication, at the clumsy tattoos on his cheeks and forehead, as he passes them, whispering to himself.

'It's time for you to give your consent to the application for permission to leave the hospital . . .'

'Maybe.'

'What are you going to do when you get out?' Erik asks.

'What do you think?' Rocky smiles, pulling a half-smoked cigarette from the packet.

'I don't know,' Erik says.

'I'm going to fall to my knees and thank God,' he says sarcastically.

'You'll be free, but your alibi also means something else that I need to talk to you about.'

'Nice.'

'The reason why I've been coming here is that the police are hunting a serial killer whose methods are reminiscent of what Rebecka Hansson was subjected to.'

'Say that again . . .'

A gentle breeze fills an empty plastic bag with air and sends it tumbling across the exercise yard, as if it were unfettered by time itself.

67

Rocky clenches his teeth and leans back against the fence, so that the light shining through the links changes.

'The police are hunting a serial killer,' Erik repeats. 'And the murders are reminiscent of that of Rebecka Hansson.'

'I'm trying to take in the fact that I'm innocent,' Rocky says in a loud voice. 'I'm trying to understand that I haven't killed another person . . .'

'I can appreciate that . . .'

'I've been living with a fucking killer for nine years now,' he concludes, pointing to his own heart.

'Rocky?' the guard calls as he approaches.

'Isn't a person allowed to be happy?'

'What's going on?' the guard asks, stopping in front of them. 'Are you going back inside?'

'Do you know, I've been wrongly convicted,' he says.

'Then we're back to one hundred per cent innocent here at Karsudden,' the guard says, and goes in.

Rocky watches him with a smile, and puts his packet of cigarettes in his pocket.

'Tell me why I should try to help the police,' he says, cupping his hands around a match.

'Innocent people are dying.'

'That's debatable,' he mutters.

'The real murderer was responsible for you ending up in here,' Erik says. 'You understand? He did this to you, no one else.'

Rocky inhales the smoke and wipes the corners of his mouth with his big, nicotine-stained thumb. Erik looks at his worn face and deep-set eyes.

'You could end up getting a complete pardon in the Appeal Court,' Erik says tentatively. 'And maybe get your job as a priest back.'

Rocky smokes for a while, then flicks the cigarette towards another patient, who thanks him and picks it up off the ground.

'What could I do for the police?' he asks.

'You might be a witness. It's possible that you knew the perpetrator,' Erik goes on. 'From what you've said, it sounds like he could be a colleague of yours.'

'How do you mean?'

'You've spoken about a preacher,' Erik says, watching Rocky closely. 'An unclean preacher who could have been a heroin addict, just like you.'

The priest seems lost in the view of the trees. A prison service van is visible in the distance, driving along the road between the tree trunks.

'I don't remember that,' Rocky says slowly.

'You seemed frightened of him.'

'The only people you're frightened of are the dealers . . . Some are completely crazy, I know, there was one whose mouth was full of gold teeth . . . I remember him because he loved the fact that I was a priest . . . so I always had to do loads of crap . . . money wasn't enough, he wanted me on my knees, denying the existence of God before he would let me buy any gear, that sort of thing . . .'

'What was his name?'

Rocky shakes his head and shrugs.

'It's gone,' he says in a low voice.

'Could the preacher have been the name you gave the dealer?'

'No idea . . . But I used to feel like I was being stalked in those days. Presumably it was withdrawal, but you know . . . once when I was supposed to pick up some new liturgical vestments . . . It was morning, and the light was coming in through the Christening window . . . there were a thousand colours on the altar rail and along the aisle . . .'

Rocky falls silent and just stands there with his arms hanging by his sides.

'What happened?'

'What?'

'You were talking about the church.'

'Yes, the vestments had been dumped in front of the side-altar . . . someone had pissed on them, it had run all over the floor, in the cracks around the flagstones.'

'It sounds like you had an enemy,' Erik says.

'I know I thought people were creeping around outside the rectory at night. I used to turn the lights off, but I never saw anyone . . . But once I did find big tracks in the snow outside the bedroom window.'

'But did you have an enemy who—'

'What do you think?' Rocky asks impatiently. 'I knew a thousand idiots, and practically all of them would have killed their own brothers and sisters for a couple of wraps . . . and I'd smuggled a load of amphetamines from Vilnius and was waiting for the money.'

'Yes, but this is a serial killer,' Erik persists. 'The motive isn't money or drugs.'

Rocky's pale green eyes stare at him.

'I might have met the murderer, like you say. But how am I supposed to know? You're not telling me anything . . . give me a detail, it might trigger my memory.'

'I'm not involved in the investigation.'

'But you know more than I do,' Rocky says.

'I know that one of the victims was called Susanna Kern . . . Before she got married, she was Susanna Ericsson.'

'I don't remember anyone of that name,' the priest replies.

'She was stabbed in . . . in the chest, neck and face.'

'Like they said I'd done to Rebecka,' Rocky says.

'And the body was arranged so that her hand was covering her ear,' Erik goes on.

'Is it the same with the others?'

'I don't know . . .'

'Well, I can hardly help unless I know more,' he says. 'My memory has to have something to latch on to.'

'I understand, but I don't—'

'What were the other victims' names?'

'I don't have access to the preliminary investigation,' Erik concludes.

'So what the hell are you doing here, then?' Rocky roars, and marches off across the grass.

68

It's already five o'clock in the afternoon as Erik walks down the corridor of the Psychology Clinic with a cup of coffee in his hand. He can see a tall figure standing quite still against the ribbed glass of the stairwell. As he pulls out his keys and stops outside his door, he realises that it's his former patient, Nestor.

'Are you waiting for me?' Erik asks, walking over to him.

'Thanks for the lift.'

'You've already thanked me.'

The thin hand moving across his chest stops, as grey as silk.

'I just wanted to s-say that I'm thinking of getting another d-dog,' he said in a low voice.

'That's great, but you know you don't have to tell me.'

'I know,' Nestor replies, blushing slightly. 'But I was here anyway, checking M-Mother's grave, so . . .'

'Was that OK?'

'Would it be p-possible to b-bury her any deeper, do you think?'

He falls silent and takes a step back when Nelly approaches down the corridor. She gives Erik a cheery wave, but when she sees he's busy she stops outside her own office and starts looking for her keys in her shiny bag.

'We can make an appointment for you to come and talk, if you like,' Erik says, glancing at his door.

'There's n-no need, it's just . . .' Nestor says quickly. 'A d-dog is a big step for me, so . . .'

'You're better now, so you can do whatever you like.'

'I know how I w-was when I came to you, I . . . You can ask me for anything, Erik.'

'Thanks.'

'You need to get on,' Nestor says.

'Yes.'

'I walked and walked and suddenly it c-came to me,' Nestor says with unexpected intensity in his voice. 'I bent down and—'

'No riddles, now,' Erik interrupts.

'No, sorry,' the tall man says, and walks off.

Erik checks his watch. He's only got a few minutes before he's due to meet Margot Silverman, but he might just have time for a word with Nelly before then. He goes over to her room and knocks on the open door.

Nelly's already sitting at her computer, and for once she's got her reading glasses on. She's wearing a white tie-neck blouse with black spots, and a tight burgundy skirt.

'What did Nestor want?' she asks, without looking up from the screen.

'He's going to get a dog, and wanted to talk about it.'

'Maybe you need to tell him about the umbilical cord and the pair of scissors?'

'He's sweet,' Erik says.

'I'm n-not so sure,' Nelly says.

Erik can't help smiling as he walks over to the window and tells her that her idea for restructuring the crisis groups is already working well.

'Yes, it feels pretty good,' she says, taking her glasses off.

'I've got a meeting with the police, but . . .'

She smiles. 'It's a shame I haven't got time to join you.'

'Nelly, I just wanted to say that you're right,' Erik says. 'There are always problems once you start telling lies.'

'Can we do this later?' she asks.

'It's just . . . I want you to know that I'm going to do all I can to get Rocky out of Karsudden as soon as possible, and—'

'Hang on,' she interrupts. 'I don't want you to be upset, but I've spoken to Martin, and you know he likes you, he really does, but he says I have to report you to both the police and the Healthcare Inspectorate.'

'Good,' he says, and starts walking towards the door.

He leaves the room and sees that Margot Silverman and her colleague are waiting outside his door. They say hello and follow him to the floor below.

The meeting room has a glass wall facing the corridor, and new chairs that smell of plastic. Erik opens the window to let some air in and invites them to sit down. Margot fills a mug from the water dispenser, drinks, then refills it.

'Well, of course you know that Olivia Toreby has changed her mind,' he begins.

'Rocky remembers a nine-year-old alibi, but not a single damn thing we can actually use,' Margot says, sitting down heavily.

'You wanted me to ask him about an accomplice, only we've ended up with the opposite . . . Rocky was wrongly convicted, and—'

'What if he's just faking his memory loss?' she says.

'He isn't, but—'

'He's involved. He's mixed up in this somehow.'

'If I could just continue,' Erik says, running his hand over the surface of the table. 'The real murderer was never caught, and has suddenly started killing again . . . Both in conversation and under hypnosis, Rocky keeps coming back to a preacher who—'

'A priest?' Adam says.

'A preacher who there's probably good reason to take seriously, in light of the alibi.'

'But you've got no name, no location . . .'

'It takes time to find a way through the chaos . . . but under hypnosis he described how the preacher killed a woman by chopping her arm off . . . the problem is that I'm not completely sure how much of that is nightmares and how much genuine memories.'

'But you believe there's some truth in this?' Adam asks, leaning forward.

'He's mentioned the preacher several times, even when he's not hypnotised.'

'But nothing about the murder?'

'Rocky says he's prepared to help the police if he can – at least, he was prepared to do so before, even if it was actually a fairly absurd situation. I'm trying to help him remember, but I don't know anything.'

'Everything is strictly confidential,' Margot explains.

'If you want his help,' Erik says, 'then you're going to have to go and see him, and give him some details: names, locations, things that could trigger the process of remembering.'

'It's probably best if you carry on talking to him,' she says.

'I can do that, but—'

'What do you need to make progress?' Margot says.

'That's your decision.'

'We're still trying to hold the media at bay, even if our press officer doesn't think that's sustainable any more,' Adam says.

'It's just that . . . We have no idea how the serial killer will react to a load of publicity,' Margot says. 'He might simply vanish, or—'

'So we need to move fast,' Adam says.

'You can have some pictures of the victims to show Rocky,' she says. 'We've done a perpetrator profile, and I can tell you about his modus operandi and specific characteristics.'

'Will you be including any fake information?'

'Of course,' she says.

'As long as I know,' Erik says.

Margot takes a deep breath, then begins to describe the killer's methods and choice of victim.

'So far it's been women who are alone in their homes,' she says quietly. 'First he films them through a window, then he plans his attack, and then, once he's decided to murder them . . .'

'He sends the video to us,' Adam says, in a heavy voice. 'The killer finds his murder weapon at the scene and always leaves it behind.'

He leans over and takes three photographs out of his case, and puts them on the table, picture-side down.

'As soon as you've shown these to Rocky, we need you to destroy them.'

Erik looks at the back of the pictures, which are inscribed with the names of the victims: Maria Carlsson, Susanna Kern, Sandra Lundgren.

'Sandra Lundgren?' Erik says, turning the picture over and gasping.

'What is it?' Margot asks.

'She's a patient of ours . . . God . . . She's dead?'

'You knew her?'

69

Erik's mouth is completely dry as he sits in the meeting room and stares at the large colour photograph. It's a recent picture, and he can see that Sandra is struggling to look happy. The light is reflecting off her glasses, but her green eyes are clearly visible. Her dark blonde hair is slightly longer, settling on her shoulders.

'God,' he repeats. 'She was in a car accident . . . her boyfriend was killed and . . . We were a bit late starting her treatment . . . she was very badly depressed, survivor's guilt, kept having panic attacks . . .'

'She was your patient?' Margot says slowly.

'To start with . . . but one of my colleagues took over.'

'Why?'

He forces himself to tear his eyes from Sandra Lundgren's symmetrical face and looks up at Margot again.

'That often happens,' he tries to explain. 'It's to do with different stages of the treatment.'

He turns over the next photograph and his heart starts beating faster when he sees Maria Carlsson. He recognises her too. Before he met Jackie, he had a brief fling with Maria. She used to go to the same gym as him, they started walking to the bus stop together, went to the cinema, and slept together once. He remembers her pierced tongue, and the hoarse laugh he found so attractive.

A sudden lump of discomfort makes it hard for him to breathe and he knows that if he hadn't taken a Mogadon earlier his hands would be shaking and he wouldn't be able to hide how upset he is.

'I . . . I think I've seen her too, at the gym . . . This feels a bit creepy,' he says, and tries to smile at Margot.

'Which gym do you go to?' Adam asks, taking out a notebook.

'SATS, on Mäster Samuelsgatan,' he replies, and swallows hard, but the lump of anxiety keeps growing.

Adam looks at him with a blank expression.

'And you'd seen her there?' he says, pointing at the picture of Maria Carlsson.

'I've got a good memory for faces,' Erik says hollowly.

'It's a small world,' Margot says, without taking her eyes off him.

'Have you met Susanna Kern as well?' Adam asks, reaching for the last photograph.

'No,' Erik laughs.

But when Adam turns the picture he's sure he's seen her before somewhere. He doesn't know where. The name Susanna Kern meant nothing to him when he heard it, but he recognises her face.

Erik shakes his head and tries to make sense of this. He was brought in to talk to her husband after her murder. He hypnotised Björn Kern and went with him into his memories of the blood-soaked villa, but he never saw a picture of her.

'Are you sure?' Adam says, holding up the photograph.

'Yes,' Erik replies.

The picture of Susanna smiling folds back over Adam's hand. Erik takes it and looks at her face, then shakes his head as his mind races and the room shrinks around him.

He realises that he's on the verge of a panic attack. His mouth is getting drier, and he slowly puts both hands on his lap to stop them shaking.

'Tell me about . . . about the perpetrator profile,' Erik says in a voice that sounds like it belongs to someone else.

He forces himself to sit still while they explain that the evidence suggests that the perpetrator is divorced, with a relatively high socio-economic status.

He tries to concentrate on what they're saying, but his heart is pounding and thoughts are racing through his head in an attempt to find some sort of pattern, some sort of sense.

How is this possible? he asks himself, trying to see any kind of system in this. He had a brief affair with Maria Carlsson, Sandra Lundgren was his patient, and he knows he's met Susanna Kern.

Three pictures of three women he's met.

It's like a recurring dream; he can't work out what it is that he recognises in this terrible situation. Across the table Margot picks up her ringing mobile. Adam stands and walks over to the window. Someone's left a coffee cup on the windowsill.

Suddenly Erik realises that the feeling of similarity is to do with Rocky.

During hypnosis Rocky described how the unclean preacher had shown pictures of Tina and Rebecka.

Rocky had blamed himself, bellowing with pain and repeating words from the Bible: I should pluck out my eye, for it has offended me.

And now he's lied to the police again. It felt impossible to say that he'd met all three of them.

When Erik feels he can control his voice and body, he stands up.

'I have to go, I've got an appointment with a patient now,' he says quietly.

'When can you next talk to Rocky?' Margot asks, looking at him.

'Tomorrow, I think.'

'Don't forget the pictures,' Adam reminds him, passing them to him.

As Erik reaches out his hand to take the photographs from Adam he sways slightly, as it strikes him that he's a mirror-image of Rocky. Damnation brushes past him like a wind presaging a storm, and for a moment he sees himself gazing out through the six-metre-high fence surrounding the exercise yard at Karsudden.

70

Joona is practising his knife techniques, his fist and elbow exercises, as well as skipping, weight-training and running. He's still a long way from his old level, but is getting stronger all the time. His hip ached after his five-kilometre run, and he walked the last bit.

It's seven o'clock when he sees Erik's BMW turn into the drive. Joona puts the meat in the oven and pours two glasses of Pomerol as he hears the front door close and the sound of keys being put down on the chest of drawers.

Joona takes the glasses and goes to the library. Pushes the door open with his foot and walks in.

Erik's jacket is lying on the floor. He's in his study, searching through the papers on his desk.

'Food will be ready in forty minutes,' Joona says.

'Great,' Erik murmurs, glancing up with a stressed look in his eyes. 'You've shaved . . . nice.'

'It felt like it was time.'

'How are you?' Erik asks, switching his computer on.

'Good,' Joona says, walking into the room.

'How's your hip?' Erik says, looking at the screen.

'I've done some exercise, and I'm—'

'Can we talk?' Erik interrupts, looking Joona in the eye. 'I've just had a meeting with Margot and Adam, and . . . I'm not prone to paranoia . . . but I've met all three victims . . . It's crazy, I don't understand anything, but that can't be a coincidence – can it?'

'How do you know—'

'What are the chances of that?' Erik asks, staring at Joona.

'How do you know the victims?' Joona prompts, and puts the glasses of wine down on the desk.

'It feels like this is directed at me. Maybe it's just my imagination, but if that is the case, then . . .'

'Sit down,' Joona says gently.

'Sorry, I'm just . . . I'm pretty shocked,' Erik says, sinking down on to his chair and taking a deep breath.

'How do you know the victims?' Joona repeats, for the third time.

'I had a brief fling with Maria Carlsson earlier this summer . . . Sandra Lundgren was a patient at the clinic . . . And I recognise Susanna Kern . . . I've met her, but I don't know where.'

'What does Margot say?'

'Well, I was so surprised that I didn't say anything about Susanna Kern . . . but I'm going to, obviously . . .'

His mobile rings, making Erik jump.

'It's work. I'll leave it,' he mutters, clicks to reject the call and drops his phone on the floor.

'And I couldn't tell her I'd slept with Maria,' he goes on, picking up his phone. 'I just said we went to the same gym.'

'Anything else?'

'I said that Sandra had been a patient of mine, but not . . . I still don't think this is relevant,' he smiles, scratching his forehead. 'But I'll say it anyway . . . It's not unusual for patients to want to control the situation by trying to seduce their therapist . . . There's always a connection, that's only natural, but in this instance the patient went so far that I passed her on to Nelly.'

'But nothing happened between you?'

'No . . .'

Erik's hand is shaking as he picks up the wine glass, raises it to his lips and takes several large gulps.

'Could it be a patient taking revenge on you for—'

'I no longer work with dangerous patients,' Erik interrupts.

'But when you were doing research on—'

'That's fifteen years ago,' he says.

'How far back do your records go?'

'I record and archive everything.'

'Can you go through it?'

'Only if I know what to look for.'

'Some sort of parallel, a connection, anything – stalking, violence directed at the face, the arrangement of bodies . . . And we're probably dealing with trophies of some sort . . .'

Erik is standing up now, and starts walking back and forth across his study. He runs his hand through his hair and is muttering to himself:

'This is crazy, it's completely sick . . .'

'Sit down and tell me what—'

'I don't want to sit down!' Erik snaps. 'I've got to—'

'Listen,' Joona says. 'You're welcome to stand, but I need to know as much as possible . . . and, to be honest, you look like you need to sit down.'

Erik reaches for his glass, drinks on his feet, then pulls a pack of pills from his inside pocket, presses a couple out and swallows them with some more wine.

'Shit,' he sighs.

'Have you started on the pills again? I'd never have believed that,' Joona says, looking at him with sharp grey eyes.

'I'm keeping an eye on it, it's fine.'

'Good.'

Erik sits down on his desk chair, wipes his forehead and tries to breathe more calmly.

'I can't get my thoughts together,' he mutters. 'I've been trying to work out if Rocky had an accomplice or an apprentice.'

'You've only just seen him.'

'Trying to uncover real memories is one of my areas of expertise . . . but hypnotising Rocky was unusually complex. I managed to get past his organic amnesia, and ended up in a world of heroin highs and delirium . . .'

'What happened?'

'I don't really know how to interpret it,' Erik says in an unsteady voice. 'But today, when I was sitting there with Margot and Adam and realised that I'd met all three victims, when I saw the photographs . . . I started to think back to the hypnosis again . . . This is completely sick.'

'I'm listening,' Joona says, sipping his wine.

Erik nods, and screws his eyes up as he tries to describe what happened.

'Rocky was in a state of deep hypnosis when he said the preacher had shown him a picture of a woman he had already killed in front of his eyes . . . and after that he showed him a picture of Rebecka Hansson . . . I could have sworn that was just a nightmare.'

'But it's the same killer,' Joona says. 'The preacher is back, it's the same pattern.'

Erik's face has turned grey.

'In that case, I'm playing Rocky's role this time,' he whispers.

'Did Rocky have relationships with the two women?'

'Yes.'

'Call Simone at once,' Joona says seriously.

Erik picks up his phone, clears his throat, then stands up anxiously.

'Simone,' the familiar voice says in his ear.

'Hi, Simone, it's Erik.'

'What's happened – you sound upset?'

'I need to ask you for a favour . . . Are Benjamin and John there?'

'Yes, but why do you—'

'I think I've got a patient who's stalking me, and I just don't want you and Benjamin to be on your own at home until this is sorted out.'

'What's happened?'

'I can't tell you.'

'Are you in danger?'

'I just don't want to take any risks, please, just do as I say . . .'

'OK, I'll try to bear it in mind,' Simone says.

'Promise.'

'You're scaring me, Erik.'

'Good,' he replies, and hears her laugh wearily.

71

Erik has washed his face and is standing in the kitchen recounting everything Rocky said about the unclean preacher – that he wore make-up over his stubble, was a heroin addict and showed him pictures – while Joona puts the food on the table.

He's roasted the lamb in the oven with root vegetables and garlic. He scatters some herbs over the dish, then pours more wine in their glasses.

'This is great,' Erik says, sitting down.

'I just wanted to say . . . Summa's last months,' Joona begins, and looks up at him. 'We had half a year together, the whole family . . . That wouldn't have been possible without you, Erik, without the medication you prescribed for her and everything . . . I knew I could trust you, and I'll never forget that.'

They touch glasses, drink, and then chat about how they first met, but are soon back on the subject of Rocky and the photographs.

'Margot needs to take the preacher seriously,' Erik says.

'She will,' Joona assures him. 'The profilers have come up with a—'

'I've seen it.'

'I'm not involved in the case, obviously, but Anja told me that they've done a first sweep . . . She started with the parish of Salem, then nearby parishes and congregations,' Joona says, pushing the serving dish towards Erik. 'Roman Catholic, Assyrian, Russian and Greek Orthodox . . . the Scientologists, Mission Church, Salvation Army, Jehovah's Witnesses, Latter-day Saints, Methodists, Pentecostalists . . . and now they're expanding the search to look at all the priests in the country that work with drug addicts, in prisons, institutions and hospitals . . .'

Erik's hands have almost stopped shaking, but he's moving slowly, as if he doesn't quite trust himself as he helps himself to food.

'How many names are there on the list?' he asks, pushing the dish towards Joona.

'More than four hundred, already. But if you can get Rocky to remember the preacher's name . . . a first name, a description, a parish, then—'

'It's just so difficult,' Erik interrupts. 'His brain damage and addiction—'

'Why don't we talk about it tomorrow?' Joona says, and starts to eat.

'His memory follows its own patterns,' Erik says, cutting his meat.

'But he seems to remember much better under hypnosis.'

'Yes, although the door between nightmares and memory seems to be open . . .'

'But some of what he's told you has to be real memories?' Joona says.

'It should all be real, in theory . . . it's just that it sounds psychotic,' Erik points out.

'If Rocky agrees to be hypnotised again, do it at once . . . try to get hold of concrete details, like names and places.'

'I can do that, I know I can.'

'If you can, I'll be able to stop this serial killer,' Joona says.

'I'll go down there first thing tomorrow morning,' Erik says.

They eat in silence. The glazed root vegetables lend an earthy sweetness to the acidity of the redcurrant sauce, the salad is dressed with balsamic vinegar and truffle oil, the lamb spiced with coarsely ground black pepper and cut in slightly pink slices.

'You really do look much better already,' Erik says as Joona helps himself to more food. 'Six injections of penicillin and a bit of cortisone . . .'

He tails off when his mobile starts to ring in his pocket. He pulls it out and sees from the screen that it's Margot.

'Yes, Erik here.'

'Is Joona there?' she asks in a shaky voice.

'What's happened?'

'Rocky Kyrklund has escaped.'

Erik passes the phone to Joona, then sits with his hands over his face, trying to gather his thoughts.

Joona listens as Margot tells him that the senior consultant at Karsudden decided that Rocky should begin his rehabilitation that evening, before being formally granted parole.

Rocky was supposed to try ordering food at the Pizzeria Primavera on Storgatan in Katrineholm. Two guards were seated at another table a short distance away, so as not to put him off. Rocky ate his pizza, drank a large glass of water, ordered coffee, then went into the toilet and climbed out through the window.

Some youngsters saw him running along the railway line towards the forest beyond Lövåsen, but after that there had been no sign of him.

'We're not making a public appeal,' Margot says. 'The administrative court has already decided that he's eligible to apply for parole, so Karsudden are looking after this themselves.'

'How?' Joona asks.

'By not doing a thing,' she replies. 'I've spoken to the senior consultant, and he's so relaxed I almost nodded off . . . Apparently it's not uncommon for patients to run off the first time they get the chance. They almost always come back of their own accord when they realise how much things have changed, that their friends, flat, wife are all gone.'

Joona ends the call, wipes his mouth on a napkin, puts it on his plate and meets Erik's tired gaze.

'I was the one who recommended he be let out on supervised excursions,' Erik says, running his hand through his hair. 'But he'll come back, they nearly always do.'

'We haven't got time to sit and wait,' Joona says. 'We need to find him and get him to talk before the preacher kills again.'

'He doesn't have any family, and he's never mentioned any friends . . . And the rectory isn't there any more . . .'

'Couldn't he hide in the church itself, or somewhere nearby?'

'I'm pretty sure he's going to try to make his way to somewhere called the Zone before too long . . . That was where he used to get hold of heroin, and it sounded like he thought someone owed him money there.'

'I don't know about this Zone,' Joona says.

'It sounds like somewhere for heavy drugs . . . a fairly large place, given that there's a stage and a load of prostitutes.'

'I'll find out where it is,' Joona says, and stands up.

'Thanks for dinner.'

'There's ice cream for dessert,' Joona says, heading towards the hall.

Erik starts to clear the table, but exhaustion hits with such ferocity that he leaves everything and staggers off to the library. His silver glasses case is no longer beside the stack of books on the smoking table. He shudders and turns to look out of the window, which is rattling on its catch. It's still light out, but it will soon be dark, he thinks, as he sinks into the leather armchair and closes his eyes.

He needs to pull himself together and try to understand what's happening to him.

Without opening his eyes he pops an Imovane from the pack on the table, holds it in his sweaty palm for a moment, then puts it in his mouth.

Milky stillness empties his thoughts and he feels sleep rising up like a heavy wave when the phone rings. He can't manage to focus his eyes enough to see who's calling, and almost drops the phone but somehow catches it.

'Hello?' he says hoarsely, putting the mobile to his ear.

'You won't forget Maddy, will you?'

'What?'

'Erik, what's wrong?' Jackie asks seriously.

'Nothing, I was just sitting . . . and . . .'

He loses his train of thought and clears his throat instead.

'You're picking Maddy up – but you knew that?'

'Of course, no problem . . . it's on the calendar.'

'Thanks,' she says warmly.

'I've been practising,' he slurs, and shuts his eyes.

'Call me if there's a problem and I'll come, they'll have to manage without an organist. Promise you'll call me.'

72

Joona is sitting in Erik's car, driving towards the centre of Stockholm
while he waits for Anja Larsson of the National Criminal Investigation
Department to call him back. He's passed the Globe and is on his way
into the tunnels beneath Södermalm when his phone lights up.

Anja's fingernails are still tapping at the keyboard of her computer
as she tells him she hasn't managed to find anything yet.

'The Zone isn't in our register, it never has been,' she says in a
resigned voice.

'Maybe its real name is something different?'

'I've tried the border control agency, the security section, IT, and
Surveillance . . . I've started asking questions on a load of really nice
online forums and sex websites.'

'Can you get hold of Milan?' he asks.

'I'd rather not,' Anja replies bluntly.

The car windows sigh as Joona heads into the narrow mouth of the
tunnel. The lights in the roof and along the walls pulse towards him
and Anja's voice disappears.

'We've got to find Rocky Kyrklund,' he says, unsure if the connection has been lost altogether.

'Wait outside the front door,' she says distantly. 'I'll come down
and . . .'

Then silence, and Joona drives deeper into the tunnel as he thinks
about everything Erik has told him.

Ten minutes later he parks on the steep hill leading to the park,
gets his stick and walks down to the glazed entrance of the National
Police Headquarters.

Through the layers of glass he sees Margot pass the airlocks and
head outside with heavy steps.

'I happened to hear that Anja has arranged a meeting between you
and Milan on the steps below Barnhusbron,' Margot says.

'You'll have to stay at a distance.'

They walk down Bergsgatan together, past the solid façade of the Kronoberg swimming pool and the heavy metal gate to the prison.

'When can I have my pistol back?' Joona says, leaning on his stick with each step.

'I'm not even allowed to talk to you,' she points out.

As they pass the oldest parts of Police Headquarters, where the regional police chief has his offices, Margot tells him that Björn Kern has started to talk. Apparently his hypnosis had the effect that Erik was hoping for, providing him with a key to help him past the shock and find a way of structuring his memories.

'Björn says his wife was sitting on the floor with her hand over her ear when he found her.'

'The same pattern,' Joona nods.

'We've got nothing but the murders and the recurring modus operandi. We've gathered a hell of a lot of questions, but no answers at all so far.'

They cut across Rådhusparken. Joona is limping and Margot holds both hands around her big stomach.

'The act of filming them through windows is central,' Joona says after a while.

'What are you thinking? I'm not getting anywhere,' she admits, glancing sideways at him.

The trees are shimmering grey with damp, and there are yellow leaves in their crowns.

Joona is thinking that the murderer is a voyeur, a stalker who gets to know his victims, and chooses to capture a recurrent moment of life in his films.

'And the hands,' he mutters.

'Yes, what the hell is going on with the hands?'

'I don't know,' he replies, thinking that the hands are used to mark different places on the body.

It wasn't Filip Cronstedt who took the Saturn tongue-stud from Maria, it was the murderer, the person Filip had caught a glimpse of in the garden, filming in the rain.

Maybe the tongue-stud was the reason why the preacher went in, the incitement that was needed for him to cross the boundary?

They walk past a 7-Eleven shop. The tabloids' flysheets are offering a test to check if your boss is a psychopath.

Joona thinks that the preacher kills the woman, takes her jewellery, marks the place he took it from with the victim's hand to let us know why, and maybe understand the nature of the accusation.

It's a sort of announcement of the accusation, like the one hung on Jesus's cross.

Rebecka Hansson was found sitting with her hand around her neck, Maria Carlsson with her hand in her mouth, Susanna Kern with her hand over her ear, and Sandra Lundgren with her hand over her breast.

'He's taken something from each and every one of them . . . It could be jewellery, it could be something else,' he says.

'But why?' Margot asks.

'Because they've broken the rules.'

'Joona, I know you go your own way,' Margot says. 'But if you do track Rocky down at that place and find something out, it would be nice if you shared it.'

'I'll call you privately,' he replies after a brief pause.

'I don't care how you go about it,' she says. 'But I'd really like to stop this fucking killer before we have any more victims . . . and preferably without losing my job.'

As they cross Fleminggatan and approach the location for his meeting with Milan, he tells her to wait.

'Keep your distance now,' he repeats.

'Who the hell is this Milan, anyway?'

Milan has steered clear of Police Headquarters for the past six years. The only time Joona has seen him was on a film from a surveillance camera. He was in the background of a shady underworld fight, acting weirdly and then shooting a man in the back.

Milan Plašil works for the drugs squad, usually on long-term surveillance and infiltration jobs, and he has the largest network of informants in the whole of Stockholm.

'He's pretty smart,' Joona replies.

There are rumours that he has a child with a woman in the Bosnian mafia, but no one really knows. Milan has become a grey, shadowy figure. Always living in the liminal world of the infiltrator, and always having a hidden agenda, has made him a stranger to everyone.

'You might think he's unarmed, but he's probably got a Beretta Nano strapped round his ankle,' Joona says.

'Why are you telling me this?'

'Because he'd sacrifice us if we posed a risk to his undercover work.'

'Should I be worried?' Margot wonders.

'Milan's kind of unusual, so it would be best to keep your distance,' Joona repeats.

He leaves her on the other side of the street and carries on alone past the imposing buildings, to the end of the bridge, then down the steps to the bottom of the first flight, where the addicts usually hang out.

The air is thick with the smell of stale urine, the ground covered with cigarette butts and the remnants of a broken green-glass bottle.

The steel arches of the bridge are covered with spikes to stop pigeons landing there, but the entire concrete foundations are still hidden beneath a thick layer of droppings.

A shadow approaches along the walkway. Joona realises that it's Milan, leans his stick against the wall and waits for him to climb up to the landing.

Milan Plašil is thirty years old, with shaved hair and dark, canine eyes. He's thin as a teenager, and dressed in a shiny black tracksuit and expensive trainers.

'I've heard about you, Joona Linna,' Milan says, glancing down towards the water.

'I need to find a place called the Zone.'

'You usually carry a forty-five.'

'Colt Combat.'

'She can't stand up there,' Milan says, nodding up the steps.

Joona sighs when he realises that Margot has followed him, and turns round to call to her.

'Margot? Come down!'

She looks over the railing, hesitates, then comes down the steps with her hand on the rail.

'The Zone,' Milan repeats.

'It's somewhere that's existed for more than ten years, probably south of Stockholm, but we don't know for sure . . .'

'You can stop there,' Milan says to Margot when she has almost reached the landing.

'It's a place where you can buy serious drugs and sex,' Joona says.

'If I say something, I want a kiss on the lips,' Milan smiles.

'OK,' Joona says.

'Her too, she needs to do it as well.'

'What?' Margot asks, peering at them.

'I want a kiss,' Milan says, pointing at his lips.

'No,' she laughs.

'Then you have to look at my cock,' he says seriously, and pulls his trousers and underpants down.

'Sweet,' she says without batting an eyelid.

'Shit, I'm only messing about, yeah? I get it, you're National Crime, aren't you?'

'Yes.'

'Armed?' he asks, pulling his trousers back up.

'Glock.'

Milan laughs silently and looks down at the walkway. A swarm of tiny insects is hovering in the air by the side of the steps.

'The only place that's at all like your description used to be out in Barkarby,' he says, giving Joona a quick glance. 'Club Noir, that was its name. But it's gone now . . . This is neither the country nor the time for big brothels. The most usual sort these days is a flat with a couple of girls from Eastern Europe, all done on the Internet, loads of links in the chain, no one's ever guilty of a fucking thing . . .'

'But this place did exist?' Joona says.

'Before my time. It's not there any more, it can't be, no one ever mentions it . . .'

'Who do we ask?'

Milan turns towards him. A faint shadow of a moustache makes his lips look even thinner. His small black eyes are set deep, close together.

'Me,' he replies. 'If it's possible to buy heroin there, I'd know about it . . . unless it's a tiny Russian enclave.'

'So where do people buy heroin?' Margot asks.

'If you don't have any contacts, Sergels torg is still the place to go. Nothing changes . . . Medborgarplatsen and Rinkeby shopping centre too . . . A lot's been getting through lately . . . from Afghanistan, but it gets repackaged several times along the way. Once again, no one's ever guilty . . .'

Milan rubs his nose hard, spits close to Margot's feet, then repeats that the Zone doesn't exist.

73

Erik has had a terrible headache for two days. He's spent the morning reading Rainer Maria Rilke's poetry while a morose man tunes the grand piano that's just been brought in through the terrace doors.

Erik looks up as Joona Linna emerges from the study. He's changed into a tracksuit and disappeared into the hall when there's a ring on the door.

'Erik's bought a grand piano,' an excited girl's voice says.

'You must be Madeleine,' Joona says.

Erik puts his book down when he hears their voices, and quickly goes into the toilet and rinses his face. His hands are shaking, and he feels a pang of angst as he looks into his own bloodshot eyes. The three photographs, the smell of plastic in the meeting room, Sandra's green eyes and Maria Carlsson's generous smile are chasing through his mind.

When he returns Jackie and Madeleine are already standing in the living room in front of the piano, whispering and giggling. Jackie folds her white stick away and puts her hand on her daughter's shoulder when he walks in.

'Are you trying to impress me?' she asks.

'It's really, really lovely,' Madeleine says.

'Try it,' Erik says shakily.

'Has it been tuned after the move?' Jackie asks.

'That was part of the deal,' he replies.

Madeleine sits down on the stool and starts playing one of Satie's nocturnes. She moves her fingers softly, and her little body is upright and focused. When she finishes the last note she turns round with a big smile on her face. Erik applauds and can almost feel tears welling up in his eyes.

'Wonderful . . . how can you be so good?'

'It's going to need to be tuned again fairly soon,' Jackie says.

'OK.'

She smiles and runs her fingers over the shiny black of the closed lid. Her hand looks like it's made out of stone in the reflection in the varnish.

'But it sounds very nice.'

'Good,' Erik says.

Madeleine tugs at his arm.

'Now I want to hear the robot play,' she says.

'No,' Erik protests.

'Yes!' both Madeleine and Jackie laugh.

'OK, but you've set a very high standard,' Erik mumbles, and sits down.

He puts his fingers on the keys, feels himself shaking and stops himself before he's even started.

'I mean, Maddy . . . I'm so impressed,' he says.

'You're good too,' she says.

'Are you this good at football?'

'No . . .'

'I bet you are,' Erik says warmly. 'I was thinking of coming early, so I have time to see you score a goal tomorrow.'

The girl's face stiffens and she looks upset.

'What?' Jackie asks.

'When I pick Maddy up after her match,' Erik replies.

Jackie's face goes pale and turns hard.

'That was yesterday,' she says in a heavy voice.

'Mum, I . . . I can make my own . . .'

'Did you walk on your own?' Jackie asks.

'I don't understand,' Erik says. 'I thought—'

'Be quiet,' she interrupts. 'Maddy, did Erik not turn up after the match?'

'It was fine, Mum,' the little girl says, and starts to cry.

Erik merely sits there with his hands hanging, feeling his headache throb. He suddenly feels sick again.

'I'm so sorry,' he says quietly. 'I can't understand how—'

'You promised me!'

'Mum, stop,' Madeleine cries.

'Jackie, I've had such a ridiculous amount to—'

'I don't care!' she yells. 'I don't want to hear!'

'Stop shouting,' Madeleine sobs.

Erik kneels down in front of her and looks her in the eye.

'Maddy, I thought it was tomorrow, I got it wrong.'

'It's OK—'

'Don't talk to him!' Jackie snaps.

'Please, I only want to—'

'I knew it,' she says, and her dark glasses flash angrily. 'Those pills, they weren't Alvedon, were they?'

'I'm a doctor,' Erik tries to explain, standing up. 'I know what I'm doing.'

'Fine,' Jackie mutters, as she pulls Madeleine towards the door.

'But this time it—'

She walks into a table that had to be moved to make room for the piano. A vase of dried flowers falls and breaks into three large pieces.

'Mum, you broke—'

'I don't care!' Jackie snaps.

Madeleine looks scared as she follows her mother, crying and hiccoughing.

'Jackie, wait!' Erik pleads, trying to follow them. 'I'm having a bit of trouble with my pills, I don't how it happened, but—'

'Do you think I care? Am I supposed to feel sorry for you now? Because you take drugs and put my daughter in danger? I can't trust you now, you must see that, surely. I don't want you anywhere near her.'

'I'll call a taxi,' Erik says heavily.

'Mum, it wasn't his fault. Please, Mum—'

Jackie doesn't answer, tears are streaming down her cheeks as she leads her daughter outside.

'I'm sorry, I ruin everything,' Madeleine sobs.

74

Where Mäster Samuelsgatan crosses Malmskillnadsgatan, the tall buildings form a canyon that forces the wind to become gusty and hard. Dust and rubbish swirl about restlessly around the little bronze girl whose downturned eyes have been surrounded by prostitutes for more than three decades.

Erik has come with Joona so that he's close at hand if they manage to find Rocky. He's sitting in the Mozzarella restaurant and has just ordered a cup of coffee.

He's already called Jackie and left two messages for her, apologising and then trying to explain that there might be a patient stalking him.

He takes a sip of his coffee, and sees his worried face reflected in the window facing the street. He can't understand how he's managed to ruin everything. Being alone after Simone left hadn't scared him, but then he'd been given another chance, Cupid had crept to the edge of his cloud and fired another arrow his way.

He gets out his phone, looks at the time, then calls Jackie for a third time. When her recorded voice asks him to leave a message, he closes his eyes and speaks:

'Jackie . . . I'm so very sorry, I've already said that, but people do make mistakes . . . I'm not going to make any excuses, but I'm here . . . I'll wait for you, I'll practise my étude . . . and I'm prepared to do whatever it takes to make you start trusting me again.'

As Erik puts his phone down on the table, alongside his cup, Joona stops next to two women standing against a blank concrete wall. Leaning on his stick, he tries to strike up a conversation with them, but when they realise he isn't a customer they turn their back on him and begin talking to each other in low voices.

'Do you know somewhere called the Zone?' he asks. 'I'll pay well if you can tell me where it is.'

They start to walk off and Joona limps after them, trying to explain that the Zone might be called something else officially.

He stops and turns to walk in the opposite direction. Further ahead, close to the Kungsgatan towers, a thin woman gets into a white van.

Joona passes some scaffolding, and sees a pile of discarded latex gloves and condoms beside the wall.

A woman in her forties is sitting in the next doorway. Her hair is pulled up into a messy ponytail and she's wrapped in a thick jacket. She's wearing a pair of stained red shorts, and her legs are bare and covered in scabs.

'Excuse me,' Joona says.

'I'm going,' the woman slurs.

She stands up with the manner of someone who is used to being moved on, her coat falls open, revealing her cropped T-shirt, and she looks up.

'Liza?' Joona says.

Her eyes are watery, and her face is wrinkled and tired.

'They told me you were dead,' she says.

'I came back.'

'You came back.' She laughs hoarsely. 'Doesn't everyone?'

She rubs her eyes hard, smearing her make-up.

'Your son?' Joona says, leaning on his stick. 'He was with a foster-family, you were going to start seeing him again.'

'Are you disappointed in me?' she asks, turning her face away.

'I just thought you'd packed this in,' he replies.

'So did I, but what the hell . . .'

She takes a few unsteady steps, then stops and leans on an over-flowing rubbish bin.

'Can I get you a coffee and a cheese roll?' Joona asks.

Liza shakes her head.

'You have to eat, don't you?'

She looks up and blows some strands of hair from her face.

'Just tell me what you want to know.'

'Do you know a place called the Zone? It sounds like a lot of girls work there, it's pretty Russian, it's existed for ten years or so, and you can get hold of heroin fairly easily there . . .'

'There used to be a place out in Barkarby – what the fuck was it called?'

'Club Noir . . . that's gone now.'

A flock of sparrows takes off from the trees.

'There's the massage parlour out in Solna, but . . .'

'That's too small,' Joona says.

'Try the Internet,' she suggests.

'Thanks, I'll do that,' he says, and starts to walk off.

'Most men are OK,' she mutters.

Joona stops and looks at her again. She's standing unsteadily with her hands on the rubbish bin, licking her lips.

'Do you know where Peter Dahlin hangs out these days?' he asks.

'In hell, I hope.'

'I know . . . but if he hasn't got there yet?'

She bends over and starts scratching her leg.

'I heard he'd moved back into his mum's flat in the Fältöversten building, over at Karlaplan,' she says quietly, and stares at her nails.

75

Erik pulls up in the car park beneath the shopping centre at Fältöversten, and as they walk towards the lifts Joona explains that he's not allowed to be there.

'I've got a restraining order,' he says, and his smile makes Erik shiver.

On the sixth floor they walk along a dull corridor with names on letterboxes, dusty doormats, prams and trainers.

Joona rings on a door bearing an ornate brass sign with the name Dahlin on it.

After a while a woman in her twenties opens the door. There's a frightened look in her eyes, she's got bad skin and her hair is in old-fashioned rollers.

'Is Peter watching television?' Joona asks, walking in.

Erik follows him and closes the door. He looks around the drab hall with floral embroidery on the walls, as well as colour photographs of an old woman with two cats in her lap.

Joona pushes the glass door open with his stick, walks straight into the living room and stops in front of an older man sitting on a brown leather sofa with two tabby cats. He's wearing thick glasses, a white shirt and red tie, and his wavy hair has been combed over a bald patch in the middle of his head.

An old episode of *Columbo* is showing on television. Peter Falk puts his hands in the pockets of his crumpled raincoat and smiles to himself.

The man on the sofa gives Joona a quick glance, pulls a cat treat from a dusty bag, throws it on the floor and then smells his fingers.

The two cats jump down on to the floor without much enthusiasm and sniff the treat. The young woman limps off to the kitchen and squeezes out a dishcloth.

'Did you do your usual?' Joona asks.

'You don't know anything,' Peter Dahlin says in a nasal voice.

'Does she have any idea that this is only the start?'

Peter Dahlin smiles at him, but the corners of his eyes are twitching nervously.

'I've undergone voluntary sterilisation, you know that,' he says. 'My conviction was overturned in the Court of Appeal, I was awarded damages, and you're not allowed to come anywhere near me.'

'I'll leave as soon as you answer my question.'

'You can count on me reporting this,' he says, scratching his groin.

'I need to find a place called the Zone.'

'Good luck.'

'Peter, you've been to all the places people aren't supposed to go, and . . .'

'I'm so very, very bad,' the man says sarcastically.

The girl in the kitchen puts her hand against her stomach and closes her eyes for a moment.

'She's not wearing any pants,' Peter says, putting his feet up on the end of the sofa. 'They're soaking in vinegar under the bed.'

'Erik,' Joona says. 'Get her out of here, explain that we're from the police, I think she needs to see a doctor.'

'I'll only find another one,' Peter says nonchalantly.

Erik leads the girl into the hall. She's holding her hand to her stomach, and sways as she pulls her boots on and picks up her bag.

Before they've even closed the door Joona grabs hold of one of Peter's ankles and starts walking towards the kitchen. The older man manages to grab hold of the arm of the sofa, which moves with him, crumpling the Persian carpet.

'Let go of me, you're not allowed . . .'

The sofa catches on the threshold of the kitchen and Peter slides over the armrest and groans loudly as he hits the floor. Joona drags him across the linoleum kitchen floor. There's a clatter of cats' paws as they scuttle away. Peter tries to grab hold of one leg of the table, but can't quite reach.

Joona leans his stick in the corner, opens the door to the balcony and drags Peter out on to the green plastic grass before letting go.

'What are you playing at? I don't know anything, and you're not—'

Joona grabs him and heaves him over the railing, and he thuds into the outside of the red balcony screen. He doesn't let go until he sees that Peter is holding on properly.

'I'm slipping, I'm slipping!' Peter cries.

His knuckles are turning white and his glasses tumble to the ground far below.

'Tell me where the Zone is.'

'I've never heard of it,' he gasps.

'A large place, could be Russian . . . with prostitutes, a stage, plenty of drugs circulating.'

'I don't know,' Peter sobs. 'You have to believe me!'

'Then I'm leaving,' Joona says, and turns away.

'OK, I've heard the name, Joona! I can't hold on any longer, I don't know where it is, I don't know anything.'

Joona looks at him again, then pulls him back over the railing. Peter's whole body is shaking as he tries to get into the kitchen.

'That's not enough,' Joona says, pushing him back towards the railing.

'A few years ago . . . there was a girl, she mentioned some guys from Volgograd,' he says quickly, moving along the railing to the wall. 'It wasn't a brothel, it sounded more like a ring . . . you know, tough as hell, everyone watching each other . . .'

'Where was it?'

'I've got no idea, I swear,' he whispers. 'I'd tell you if I knew.'

'Where can I find the woman who told you about it?'

'It was in a bar in Bangkok. She'd spent a few years in Stockholm, I don't know what her name is.'

Joona returns to the kitchen. Peter Dahlin follows him, and closes the door to the balcony.

'You can't just do this,' he says, pulling himself together and wiping his tears with kitchen roll. 'You'll get the sack, and—'

'I'm not in the police any more,' Joona says, picking up his stick from the corner. 'So I've got plenty of time to keep an eye on you.'

'What do you mean, keep an eye on me? What do you want?'

'If you do as I say, you'll be fine,' Joona replies, turning his stick over in his hands.

'What do you want me to do?' Peter Dahlin asks.

'As soon as you've been to the hospital, you go to the police and . . .'

'Why would I be going to the hospital?'

Joona hits Peter Dahlin across the face with his stick. He staggers backwards, clutching both hands to his nose, stumbles into a chair, falls on his back and hits his head on the floor so hard that blood splatters the cat food in the bowls.

'When you've been to the hospital, you go to the police and confess to all the assaults,' Joona says, pushing the stick on to the pit of his throat. 'Mirjam was fourteen years old when she killed herself, Anna-Lena lost her ovaries, Liza got caught in prostitution, and the girl who was here just now—'

'OK!' Peter cries. 'OK!'

76

Erik picks Joona up from Valhallavägen after driving the young woman to a gynaecologist he knows at the Sophia Hospital.

'Now we know that the Zone exists,' Joona says as he gets in the car. 'But it seems to be a Russian set-up . . . where you buy membership by contributing to their illegal activities.'

'And that way you're bound to keep quiet,' Erik says, drumming his fingers on the wheel. 'That's why no one knows anything.'

'We're never going to be able to track it down, and it would take several years to infiltrate.'

Joona looks at his phone and sees that Nils Åhlén has called him three times in the last hour.

'Now we've only one lead to follow if we're going to find the Zone,' Joona says. 'And that's the woman Rocky called Tina.'

'But she's not alive any more – is she?'

'She not in the database, no one's been murdered that way in Sweden,' he replies. 'Having an arm chopped off isn't the sort of thing that's likely to get missed.'

'Maybe it was just a nightmare?'

'Do you believe that?' Joona asks.

'No.'

'Right, let's go and see Nils Åhlén.'

The Forensic Medicine Institute has a number of lecture rooms, but only one room for the display of bodies. The hall is reminiscent of an anatomy theatre. The room is circular, with banks of seating rising higher and higher around the small stage containing the post-mortem table.

From the lobby they can hear Nils Åhlén's sharp voice through the closed doors. He's just finishing a lecture.

They go in as quietly as they can and sit down. Åhlén is dressed in his white coat, and is standing beside the blackened body of a man who froze to death.

'And out of everything I've said today, there's one particular thing that you mustn't forget,' Nils Åhlén says in conclusion. 'A human being isn't dead until it's both dead and warm.'

He puts a gloved hand on the chest of the corpse and gives a bow as the medical students applaud.

Joona and Erik wait until the students have left the room before going down to the central dais. The corpse is giving off a strong smell of yeast and decay.

'I've checked our records as well,' Åhlén says. 'But there's no mention of that sort of injury . . . I've been through the databases covering violent crime, accidents and suicide . . . She doesn't exist.'

'But you also checked for me,' Joona says.

'So the obvious answer is that the body hasn't been found,' Åhlén mutters, taking off his glasses and polishing them.

'Of course, but—'

'Some are never found,' Åhlén interrupts. 'Some are found many years later . . . and some are found but never identified . . . We try dental records and DNA, and keep the bodies for a couple of years . . . The people at the National Board of Forensic Medicine are good, but even they have to bury a few unidentified bodies each year.'

'The injuries would still be recorded, though, wouldn't they?' Joona persists.

Nils Åhlén has a strange glint in his eye as he lowers his voice.

'I've thought of another possibility,' he says. 'There used to be a group of forensic medical officers who collaborated with certain detectives . . . They were known as the "Tax Savers", and they believed they could identify in advance the cases that were never going to lead anywhere.'

'You've never told me about that,' Joona says.

'It was back in the eighties . . . the Tax Savers didn't want Swedish taxpayers to be burdened with the cost of pointless police investigations and hopeless attempts to identify bodies. It wasn't a major scandal, a few people got ticked off, but it made me think . . . When you described Tina as a heroin addict, a prostitute, possibly a victim of human trafficking . . .'

'You're wondering if the Tax Savers are still active?' Joona asks.

'No paperwork,' Nils Åhlén says, clicking his fingers. 'No investigation, no Interpol, the body gets buried as an unknown, and the resources are used elsewhere.'

'But in that case Tina would still be in the database of the National Board of Forensic Medicine,' Erik says.

'Try looking for an unidentified body, natural cause of death, illness,' Åhlén says.

'Who do I talk to?' Joona asks.

'Talk to Johan in Forensic Genetics, mention my name,' he says. 'Or I could give him a call, seeing as we're here . . .'

He scrolls through his contacts, then puts his mobile to his ear.

'Hello, this is Professor Nils Åhlén, I . . . no, thank you, it was very enjoyable . . . Just offbeat enough, I'd say . . .'

Åhlén circles the body twice as he talks. When he ends the call he stands in silence for a moment. His mouth twitches slightly. The empty benches spread out around them like the growth rings of a huge tree.

'There's only one unknown woman from Stockholm who matches Tina's age during the period in question,' Åhlén says eventually. 'Either it's her, or her body was never found.'

'So could it be her?' Erik asks.

'The death certificate says heart attack . . . there's a reference to another file, but that file doesn't exist . . .'

'There's no description of the body?'

'Obviously they kept a DNA sample, fingerprints, dental records,' Åhlén replies.

'Where is she now?' Joona asks

'She's in Skogskyrkogården, buried among the trees of the Forest Cemetery.' Åhlén smiles. 'No name, grave number 32 2 53 332.'

77

Skogskyrkogården, to the south of Stockholm, is a Unesco World Heritage site, and holds more than one hundred thousand graves. Erik and Joona walk along the well-tended paths, past the Woodland Chapel, and notice the yellow roses in front of Greta Garbo's red headstone.

Block number 53 is located further away, close to the fence facing Gamla Tyresövägen. The cemetery workers have unloaded a digger on caterpillar tracks from a council truck, and have already dug out the earth above the coffin. The grass is lying alongside the heap of soil, a tangle of fibrous roots and plump worms.

Nils Åhlén and his assistant Frippe are approaching from the other direction, and the four of them greet each other in subdued voices. Frippe has had a haircut and his face looks a bit rounder, but he's still wearing the same old studded belt and washed-out T-shirt with a black Hammerfell logo.

The cab of the digger rotates gently and the hydraulics hiss as the scoop sinks and moves forward, carefully scraping the soil from the lid of the coffin.

As usual Nils is giving Frippe a short lecture, this time about how ammonia, hydrogen sulphide and hydrocarbons are released when proteins and carbohydrates break down.

'The final stage of the decomposition process leaves the skeleton entirely exposed.'

Nils signals to the digger driver to back away. Clumps of clay soil fall from the blade of the scoop. He slides down into the grave with his hand on the edge. The lid of the coffin has given way under the weight of the soil.

He scrapes around the edge of the coffin with a spade, then brushes it clean with his hands, inserts the blade of the spade under the lid and tries to prise it open, but the chipboard snaps. There's no strength left in it, it's like wet cardboard.

Nils whispers something to himself, tosses the spade aside and slowly starts removing it, piece by piece, with his hands. He passes the pieces to Frippe, until the contents of the grave are entirely uncovered.

The dead body isn't remotely unpleasant, it just looks defenceless.

The skeleton in the coffin looks small, almost like a child's, but Nils Åhlén assures them that it belonged to a grown woman.

'One metre sixty-five tall,' he murmurs.

She was buried in a T-shirt and briefs, the fabric is clinging to the skeleton, the curve of the ribcage is intact, but the material has sunk into the pelvis.

An image of a cobalt-blue angel is still visible on the T-shirt.

Frippe walks round the grave taking photographs from every angle. Åhlén has taken out a small brush which he uses to remove soil and fragments of chipboard from the skeleton.

'The left arm has been chopped off close to the shoulder,' Åhlén declares.

'We've found the nightmare,' Joona says in a low voice.

They watch Åhlén carefully turn the skull. The jaw has come loose, but otherwise the cranium is in one piece.

'Deep incisions across the front of the cranium,' Åhlén says. 'Forehead, zygomatic bone, cheekbone, upper jaw . . . the incisions continue across the collarbone and sternum . . .'

'The preacher's back,' Erik says with an ominous feeling in the pit of his stomach.

Nils Åhlén goes on brushing soil away from the body. Next to the hipbone he find a wristwatch with a scratched face. The leather strap is gone, turned to grey dust.

'Looks like a man's watch,' he says, picking it up and turning it over.

The back is inscribed with Cyrillic letters. Åhlén takes out his mobile and takes a picture of the lettering.

'I'll send this to Maria at the Slavic Institute,' he mutters.

78

Joona's just had another cortisone injection, and is in Erik's back garden practising combat techniques with a long wooden pole.

Nils Åhlén is trying to track down the colleague who signed Tina's death certificate while they wait for the translation of the engraving on the watch, to find out if it can help them make progress.

Erik is sitting at the grand piano, watching his friend's repetitive pattern of blocks and attacks as shadows cross the thin linen curtain.

Like a Chinese shadow-theatre, he thinks, then looks down at the piano keys in front of him.

He was planning to practise his étude, but can't bring himself to try. His mind is too unfocused. He still hasn't got hold of Jackie, and Nelly called him from work an hour ago to ask if she could come over.

Slowly he puts his little finger on a key and strikes it, making the first note echo as his phone starts to ring.

'Erik Maria Bark,' he answers.

'Hello,' a high voice says. 'My name is Madeleine Federer, and . . .'

'Maddy?' Erik gasps. 'How are you?'

'Fine,' she says quietly. 'I've borrowed Rosita's phone . . . I just wanted to say it was nice when you were here with us.'

'I loved spending time with you and your mum,' Erik says.

'Mum misses you, but she's silly and pretends that—'

'You need to listen to her, and—'

'*Maddy,*' someone calls in the background. '*What are you doing with my phone?*'

'Sorry I ruined everything,' the girl says quickly, then the call ends.

Erik slips off his piano stool and just sits on the floor with his hands over his face. After a while he lies back and stares up at the ceiling, thinking that it's time to get a grip on things again and stop taking pills.

He's used to helping patients move on.

When everything is at it darkest, it can only get brighter, he usually says.

He gets up with a sigh, goes and rinses his face, then sits down on the steps outside the glass door.

Joona groans as he turns round, strikes low with the stick, then jabs behind him before he stops and looks into Erik's face.

His face is wet with sweat, his muscles are pumped with blood and he's breathing hard, but isn't exactly out of breath.

'Have you had time to look into your old patients?'

'I've found a few who were the children of priests,' Erik says. Then he hears a car pull in and stop at the front of the house.

'Give their names to Margot.'

'But I've only just started going through the archive,' he says.

Nelly walks round the house, waves, and comes over to them. She's wearing a fitted riding jacket and tight black trousers.

'We ought to be at Rachel Yehuda's lecture,' she says, sitting down next to Erik.

'Is that today?'

Joona's phone rings and he walks over towards the shed before answering.

It strikes Erik that Nelly seems tired and subdued. The thin skin below her eyes is grey and she's frowning.

'Can't you report yourself?' she asks.

'I've thought about it.'

She just shakes her head and looks wearily at him.

'Do you think my mouth is ugly?' she asks. 'Your lips get thinner as you get older. And Martin . . . he's very sensitive when it comes to mouths.'

'So how does Martin look, then? Hasn't he got older?'

'Don't laugh, but I'm thinking of having surgery . . . I'm not prepared to get older, I don't want anyone thinking he's being kind by sleeping with me.'

'You're very attractive, Nelly.'

'I'm not fishing for compliments, but that's not the way it feels, not any more . . .'

She falls silent as her chin starts to tremble.

'What's happened?'

'Nothing,' she says, gently rubbing beneath her eyes before looking up.

'You need to talk to Martin about those porn films if it's upsetting you.'

'It isn't,' she says.

Joona has finished his call and is heading towards them with his phone in his hand.

'The Slavic Institute have managed to decipher the lettering on that watch. The writing's Belarusian, apparently.'

'What does it say?' Erik asks.

'In honour of Andrej Kaliov's great achievements, Military Faculty, Yanka Kupala University.'

They follow Joona into the study and listen to him as he tracks the name down in less than five minutes. Interpol has one hundred and ninety member countries, and he is put through by the unit for international police cooperation to the office of the National Central Bureau in Minsk.

He finds out that there's no indication that Andrej Kaliov is missing, but that a woman by the name of Natalia Kaliova from Gomel has been reported missing.

In British-accented English the woman on the phone explains that Natalia – the woman Rocky called Tina – was believed to have been a victim of human trafficking.

'Her family say that a friend of hers called from Sweden and encouraged her to go there via Finland, without a residence permit.'

'Is that everything?' Joona asks.

'You could try talking to her sister,' the woman says.

'Her sister?'

'She went to Sweden to look for her big sister, and is evidently still there. It says here that she calls us regularly to find out if there's any news.'

'What's the sister's name?'

'Irina Kaliova.'

79

The central kitchen of the NBA on Kungsholmen in Stockholm smells of boiled potatoes. The cooks are standing at their stoves dressed in protective white clothing and hairnets. The sound of a slicing machine echoes off the tiled walls and metal worktops.

Erik asked Nelly to go with them to meet Irina Kaliova. It could be useful to have a female psychologist on hand when the woman finds out that her sister had been a victim of the sex-trafficking industry before she was murdered.

Irina is dressed like all the others, in a hairnet and white coat. She's standing by a row of huge saucepans hanging from fixed hooks. She's staring at a display panel with a look of concentration, taps a command and pulls a lever to tip one of the pans.

'Irina?' Joona asks.

She lifts her head and looks inquisitively at the three strangers. Her cheeks are red and her forehead sweaty from the steam rising from the boiling water, and a strand of loose hair is hanging over her brow.

'Do you speak Swedish?'

'Yes,' she says, and carries on working.

'We're from the police, the National Criminal Investigation Department.'

'I've got a residence permit,' she says quickly. 'Everything's in my locker, my passport and all my documents.'

'Is there somewhere we could go and talk?'

'I need to ask my boss first.'

'We've already spoken to him,' Joona says.

Irina says something to one of the women, who smiles back. She puts her hairnet in her pocket, then leads them through the noisy kitchen, past a row of food trolleys and into a small staffroom with a sink full of unwashed mugs. There are six chairs around a table with a bowl of apples at its centre.

'I thought I was about to get the sack,' she says with a nervous smile.

'Can we sit down?' Joona asks.

Irina nods and sits on one of the chairs. She has a pretty, round face, like a fourteen-year-old. Joona looks at her slender shoulders in her white coat, and finds himself thinking of her sister's white skeleton in the grave.

Natalia used the name Tina as a prostitute, and she was murdered and buried like so much rubbish because she was alone, had no papers, and no one to help her. She was used up by Sweden, and afterwards wasn't even worth the cost of proper identification.

There's nothing so hard in police work as having to inform a relative about a death in the course of an investigation.

There's no way to get used to the pain that fills their eyes, the way all the colour drains from their faces. Any attempt to be sociable, to laugh and joke vanishes. The last thing to go is an effort to appear rational, to try to ask sensible questions.

Irina gathers together some crumbs on the table with a trembling hand. Hope and fear flit across her face.

'I'm afraid we've got bad news,' Joona says. 'Your sister Natalia is dead, her remains have just been found.'

'Now?' she asks hollowly.

'She's been dead for nine years.'

'I don't understand . . .'

'But she's only just been found.'

'In Sweden? I looked for her, I don't understand.'

'She had been buried, but couldn't be identified before, that's why it's taken so long.'

The small hands keep moving the crumbs, then slip on to her lap.

'How did it happen?' she asks, her eyes still wide-open and empty.

'We're not sure yet,' Erik replies.

'Her heart was always . . . she didn't want to worry us, but sometimes it would just stop beating, it felt like an eternity before it . . .'

Irina's chin begins to tremble, she hides her mouth with her hand, looks down and swallows hard.

'Have you got anyone to talk to after work?' Nelly asks.

'What?'

She quickly wipes the tears from her cheeks, swallows again and looks up.

'OK,' she says, in a more focused voice. 'What do I have to do, do I have to pay anything?'

'Nothing, we'd just like to ask a few questions,' Joona says. 'Would that be OK?'

She nods, and starts picking at the crumbs on the table again. They hear a metallic sound from the kitchen and someone tries the door.

'Did you have any contact with your sister while she was in Sweden?'

Irina shakes her head, her mouth moves slightly, then she looks up.

'I was the only person who knew she was heading to Stockholm, but I promised not to say anything. I was young, I didn't understand . . . She was very stern with me, said she wanted to surprise Mum with her first wages . . . Nothing ever came, but I spoke to her on the telephone once, she just said that everything would be all right . . .'

Irina falls silent and drifts off.

'Did she say where she was living?'

'We haven't got any brothers,' she replies. 'Dad died when we were little, I don't remember him but Natalia did . . . and after Natalia had gone, there was just me and Mum left . . . Mum missed her so much, she used to cry and worry about her weak heart, and said she just knew that something terrible had happened. So I thought if I could find my sister and take her back home, then everything would be fine . . . Mum didn't want me to leave, and she was alone when she died.'

'I'm so sorry,' Joona says.

'Thank you. Well, now I know that Natalia is dead,' Irina says, getting to her feet. 'I suppose I suspected as much, but now I know.'

'Do you know where she was living?'

'No.'

She takes a step towards the door, clearly keen to get away from the whole situation.

'Please, sit down for a moment,' Erik asks.

'OK, but I need to get back to work.'

'Irina,' Joona says, with a dark resonance in his voice that makes the young woman listen. 'Your sister was murdered.'

'No, I just told you, her heart—'

Irina's coat catches on the back of the chair, dragging it backwards with her. As the truth sinks in, she loses control of her face. Her cheeks turn white, her lips quiver and her pupils dilate.

'No,' she whimpers.

She leans back against the worktop, shakes her head, fumbles across the front of the fridge for something to hold on to. Nelly tries to calm her down, but she pulls free.

'Irina, you need to—'

'God, no, not Natalia!' she cries. 'She promised . . .'

She grabs hold of the handle of the fridge, and the door swings open as she falls, dislodging a shelf full of ketchup and jam. Nelly hurries across to her and holds her slender shoulders.

'*Nje maja ciastra*,' she gasps. '*Nje maja ciastra* . . .'

She curls up in Nelly's lap and tries to hold her hand over her mouth as she cries, screaming into her palm and shaking uncontrollably.

After a while she calms down and sits up, but she's still breathing unevenly between sobs. She wipes her tears and clears her throat weakly, trying to control her breathing.

'Did someone hurt her?' she asks in a ragged voice. 'Did they hit her, did they hit Natalia?'

Her face contorts again as she tries to hold her tears back, but they run down her cheeks.

Joona takes some napkins from a pack on the worktop and hands them to her, then pulls a chair over and sits down in front of her.

'If you know anything at all, it's very important that you tell us,' he says sternly.

'What could I know?' she says, looking at them in confusion.

'We're just trying to find the person who did this,' Nelly says, brushing the hair from Irina's face.

'You spoke to your sister on the phone,' Joona goes on. 'Did she tell you where she lived, or what her job was?'

'There are those men who trick girls from poor countries, who say they're going to get good jobs, but Natalia was smart, she said it wasn't anything like that, that it was real. She promised me, but I've been to the furniture factory . . . no one there had heard of Natalia, *durnaja dziaŭtjynka* . . . They're not employing anyone, haven't done for years.'

Her eyes are red from crying, and tiny red spots have appeared on the fair skin of her forehead.

'What's the name of the factory?' Erik asks.

'Sofa Zone,' she says blankly. 'It's out in Högdalen.'

Nelly remains seated on the floor with Irina, stroking her head and promising to stay with her for as long as she wants. Erik exchanges a quick glance with Nelly, then walks back out through the noisy kitchen with Joona.

80

Margot Silverman is sitting in front of a computer in the investigation room, looking at Erik's recording of Rocky's hypnosis again.

His large head is drooping forward as he describes his visit to the Zone in a languid voice. He talks about the dealers and strippers, and the fact that he thought he could pick up some money there.

As Margot listens her eyes drift along the walls of the room. The victims' patterns of movement are marked in three different colours on the large map.

Every place, every street where they could have come into contact with the preacher is marked.

On the screen, Rocky shakes his head as he says that the preacher smells of fish-guts.

Margot sees the pin in the map marking Rebecka Hansson's home in Salem.

Serial killers usually stick to their home patch, but in this case the locations are spread out across the most densely populated metropolitan district in Scandinavia.

'The preacher snorts back some snot, then starts to speak in a really high voice,' Rocky says, breathing unevenly.

Margot shudders, and watches the big man squirm on his chair and howl with angst as he describes the way the preacher cuts the woman's arm off.

'It sounds like when you stick a spade into mud . . .'

After the discovery out in Skogskyrkogården, no one doubts that the preacher is the serial killer that they're all looking for.

She knows it was Joona who persuaded Nils Åhlén to order the body to be exhumed. It would have been much easier if she could work with Joona openly, but Benny Rubin and Petter Näslund are backing up Adam, resisting his involvement.

Margot doesn't have the authority to let Joona join the investigation, but she's sure as hell not going to stop him from conducting his own inquiries.

Rocky shakes his head and his shadow moves across the glossy Playboy pinup on the wall behind him.

'The preacher chops her arm off at the shoulder,' Rocky gasps. 'Loosens the tourniquet and drinks . . .'

'Listen to my voice now,' Erik says.

'And drinks the blood from her arm . . . while Tina lies bleeding to death on the floor . . . Dear God in heaven . . . Dear God . . .'

Inside Margot's womb the baby moves so violently that she has to lean back and close her eyes for a while.

The preliminary investigation is proceeding systematically according to established routines, but no one really believes that's going to produce results in time.

The police have knocked on doors and questioned many hundreds of neighbours, they've examined all the footage from surveillance and traffic cameras around the crime scenes.

Unless Rocky returns to Karsudden Hospital soon, so that Erik can question him properly, they'll have to make a public appeal for information about him.

Margot switches the video off, and has a strong feeling that she's being watched, so gets up and closes the curtains over the window looking out on to the park.

She opens her bag and takes out her powder compact, looks at herself in the little mirror, and puts some more powder on. Her nose has got shiny and the rings under her eyes look darker. She reapplies her lipstick, blots her lips on a letter from the National Police Board, adjusts her hair, then calls Jenny on Skype.

She can see herself on the screen, and as the call is connected she undoes one button on her blouse and moves backwards slightly so that her cheeks are framed better.

Jenny answers almost immediately. She looks cross but attractive, with her messy black hair tumbling over her thin shoulders. She's wearing a washed-out vest and the little golden heart is shimmering against her neck.

'Hi, baby,' Margot says quietly.

'Have you caught the bad guy yet, then?'

'I thought I was the bad guy?' Margot says.

Jenny smiles and stifles a yawn.

'Did you call the bank about that ridiculous charge?'

'Yes, and apparently there's nothing wrong with it,' Jenny replies.

'That can't be right.'

'So call them yourself.'

'I just meant . . . OK, never mind . . . It's so irritating when they deduct payments for . . . oh, what the hell.'

'What did you want?' Jenny asks, picking at her armpit.

'How are the girls?' Margot asks.

'Fine,' Jenny says, glancing off to one side. 'But Linda's still a bit down. She needs to learn to make new friends . . . she's far too nice.'

'Being nice is a good thing, surely?' Margot points out.

'But she doesn't know what to do when her best friend says she's got fed up of her. She just gets upset and sits and waits.'

'She'll learn.'

Margot would like to be able to tell Jenny about the investigation, about the meaningless hatred and her feeling that the preacher is close by, watching them all.

She feels worried for herself, because she keeps forgetting all the things that normal people know, and the fact that she's going to have a baby, and that people can be happy and secure.

'You look nice,' Margot says, tilting her head to one side.

'No, I don't.' Jenny grins, then yawns loudly. 'Right, I'm going to carry on watching a repeat of the Stockholm Horse Show.'

'OK, I'll call again later.'

Jenny blows her a kiss and ends the call, leaving Margot looking at her own face. Her father's nose and those thick, colourless eyebrows. I look like someone's aunt, she thinks. Like my dad, if he'd been a woman.

The suspicion that there's something wrong between her and Jenny is snaking its way through Margot's head when Adam Youssef comes into the room and opens the window facing the park.

He's been in a meeting with Nathan Pollock and Elton Eriksson from the National Murder Unit in an attempt to prune the list of potential perpetrators and help move the preliminary investigation forward.

'I had Pollock as one of my lecturers when I was training,' Margot says.

'Yes, he said,' Adam replies as he sits down and leafs through a bundle of papers.

'Have you got the new profile there?' Margot asks.

Adam runs his hands through his thick hair in frustration.

'They just keep repeating things we already know . . .'

'That's how it works, setting up things that seem obvious as the parameters,' she replies, leaning back.

'The murders are characterised by a high degree of risk-taking, forensic awareness and excessive brutality,' he reads. 'The victims are women of child-bearing age, the crime scenes are the victims' homes . . . The motive is instrumental and the violence probably expressive.'

Margot listens to the generalisations and thinks about the fact that Anja's list of names has grown even longer.

Considering that Sweden is the most secular country in the world, she can't help thinking that there are an awful lot of priests and preachers.

They've now got almost five hundred people with direct connections to various faith organisations in the Stockholm area who match the general profile.

This investigation has ground to a halt, she finds herself thinking once more.

If only they had one sighting, just one decent piece of information to go on.

They need to bring things into focus.

There isn't enough time to check out more than five hundred men. Given the murderer's momentum so far, the video of his next victim could appear at any time.

In order to limit the search as things stand, we need to add in some uncertain parameters, she thinks. Previous violent crimes, for instance, or personality disorders.

'There are forty-two men who've been suspects in other cases, nine have been convicted of violent crimes, none for stalking, none for murder, and none for brutality that bears any resemblance to our serial killer's,' Adam says. 'Eleven have convictions for sexual offences, thirty for drugs . . .'

'Just give me someone to shoot,' she says wearily.

'I've got three names . . . none of them is a perfect match, but two of them have been investigated for crimes of violence against more than one woman . . .'

'Good.'

'The first one is a Sven Hugo Andersson, a vicar in the parish of

Danderyd . . . the other one's a Pasi Jokala, he used to be active in the Philadelphia Church, but now he's got his own congregation, known as the Gärtuna Revivalists . . .'

'And the third one?'

'I'm not sure, but he's the only one of these five hundred who has a documented personality disorder that matches the profile. A twenty-year-old diagnosis for borderline psychosis. But he's got no criminal record, doesn't feature in either police or social service registers . . . and he's also been married for ten years, which doesn't fit the profile at all.'

'Better than nothing,' she says.

'Anyway, his name's Thomas Apel, and he's the so-called stake president of the Church of Jesus Christ of Latter-day Saints, out in Jakobsberg.'

'We'll start with the violent ones,' she says, and stands up.

Adam goes to his office to call his wife and tell her he's got to work late, and Margot stops in the kitchen, looks in the cupboard and pops Petter Näslund's packet of jam biscuits in her bag before she walks out.

Adam's account of the perpetrator profile has made her think about stalker and serial killer Dennis Rader, whom she wrote an essay about when she was training. He used to call the police and media to tell them about his murders. He even used to send the police objects he'd taken from his victims.

In his case, the perpetrator profile was completely wrong. They had been looking for a divorced, impotent loner whereas Rader was married, had children, and was active in both the church and the scouting movement.

81

They go together in Margot's comfortable Lincoln. To make room for her stomach she's had to move the seat so far back that she can barely reach the pedals with her feet.

Only two of the three names are left. It turns out that Sven Hugo Andersson was in Danderyd Hospital for a bypass operation when Sandra Lundgren was murdered.

Once they're past Södertälje they head along the 225 motorway, through fields of yellow rape, past a large industrial area dominated by Astra Zeneca's pale grey facility. They pass beneath some tall electricity pylons, then head into a forested area.

Margot puts a biscuit in her mouth, chews, tasting the crumbly mixture of sugar and butter, then the chewy, tart jam.

'Are those Petter's biscuits?' Adam asks.

'He gave them to me,' she says, popping the next biscuit in her mouth.

'He wouldn't even offer one to his wife.'

'But he was very insistent that you have a couple,' she says, passing him the packet.

Adam takes a biscuit and eats it with a smile, holding one hand under his mouth so as not to drop crumbs in Margot's car.

The road gets narrower, grit flies up behind them and Margot has to slow down. They can make out the occasional cottage down by the lake.

Pasi Jokala was convicted of aggravated assault, rape and attempted rape.

Margot hasn't been on operational duty since she got pregnant, but she's choosing to see this as an extension of office work, given that Pasi Jokala has no listed phone number.

'Do you think he's dangerous?' Adam asks.

The two of them know that they shouldn't have come out here

without the National Task Force if they really believe they've found the unclean preacher. But, just to be on the safe side, Margot has brought her Glock and four extra magazines.

'He has problems with aggression and a lack of impulse control,' she says. 'But who the hell hasn't?'

Pasi Jokala is registered as living at the same address as the Gärtuna Revivalist Church.

Margot turns off onto a narrow gravel road through sparse forest, and can see the lake again. Some fifty cars are parked along the side of the road, but she drives all the way to the fence before stopping.

'We don't have to do this now,' Adam says.

'I'm just going to take a look,' Margot says, checking her gun before putting it back in its holster and struggling out of the car.

They're standing in front of a rust-red cottage with a white cross made of LED lights covering the gable end. The light inside looks like it's filtering out of the building through narrow gaps in the wood. Behind the house a wild meadow stretches down towards the lake.

The windows are covered on the inside.

A loud voice can be heard through the walls.

A man shouts something and Margot feels a sudden pang of unease.

She keeps walking, her holster rubbing against her. It's sitting too high, now that her stomach has grown. They walk past a water-butt, thistles a metre tall, and a rusty lawnmower. Dozens of slugs lurk in the shadowy grass beside the wall.

'Maybe we should wait here until they've finished?' Adam wonders.

'I'm going in,' Margot says curtly.

They open the door and walk into the hall, but now everything is completely silent, as if everyone were waiting for them to arrive.

On the wall is a poster about meetings beside the lake, and a group trip to Alabama. On a table is a bundle of printouts about fundraising for the Gärtuna Revivalists' new church, next to a buckled cashbox and twenty copies of the Redemption Hymnal.

Adam is hesitant, but she waves him towards her. It may be a church, but she still wants him in the right position if there's going to be any gunfire.

Margot holds her stomach with one hand as she walks through the next door.

She can hear the sound of murmuring voices.

The rest of the building is a single white church hall. The beams of the roof are held up by pillars, and everything is painted brilliant white.

There are rows of white chairs on the white floor, and up at the front is a small stage.

A couple of dozen people have stood up from their seats. Their eyes are fixed on the man on the stage.

Margot realises that the man in front of them is Pasi Jokala. He's wearing a blood-red shirt with open cuffs that are hanging down over his hands. His hair is sticking up from one side of his head, and his face is sweaty. His chair is lying on its side behind him. The members of the small choir are silent, looking at him with their mouths open. Pasi raises his head wearily and gazes out across the congregation.

'I was the mud beneath His feet, the dust in His eye, the dirt under His nails,' he says. 'I sinned, and I sinned on purpose . . . You know what I have done to myself, and to others, you know what I said to my own parents, to my mother and father.'

The congregation sighs and shuffles uncomfortably.

'The sickness of sin was raging in me . . .'

'Pasi,' a woman whimpers, looking at him with moist eyes.

They all start to mutter prayers.

'You know that I mugged a man, and beat him with a rock,' Pasi goes on with growing intensity. 'You know what I did to Emma . . . and when she forgave me, I left her and Mikko, you know that I drank so much that I ended up in hospital . . .'

The congregation is moving agitatedly now, chairs scrape the floor, some topple over, and one man falls to his knees.

The atmosphere grows more tense, and Pasi's voice is hoarse from chanting. The meeting seems to be reaching a crescendo. Margot retreats towards the door, as she sees two women holding each other's hands and speaking a strange language, incomprehensible, repetitive words, faster and faster.

'But I put my life in the Lord's hands and was baptised in the Holy Spirit,' Pasi goes on. 'Now I am the drop of blood running down Christ's cheek, I am the drop of blood . . .'

The congregation cheers and applauds.

The little choir starts to sing with full force: 'The chains of sin are broken, I am free, I am free, I am delivered of my sin, I am free, saved

and free, hallelujah, hallelujah, Jesus died for me! Hallelujah, hallelujah, I am free, I am free . . .'

The congregation joins in, clapping along, and Pasi Jokala stands
there with his eyes closed, sweat running down his face.

82

Margot and Adam wait outside the church and watch the congregation emerge. They're smiling and chatting, switching their phones on and reading messages as they head towards their cars, waving and saying their goodbyes.

After a while Pasi comes out alone.

His red shirt is unbuttoned down his chest and the fabric is dark with sweat under the arms. He's holding a plastic bag from Statoil in his hand as he carefully locks the door.

'Pasi?' Margot says, taking a few steps towards him.

'The pallets are in the garage . . . but I need to get to the Co-op before they shut,' he says, heading towards the gates.

'We're from the National Criminal Investigation Department,' Adam says.

'Would you please stop!' Margot says in a sharper tone of voice.

He comes to a halt with one hand on the gatepost and turns towards Margot.

'I thought you were here because of the advert . . . I've got five pallets of Polish Mr Muscle that I usually sell to a discount store, but they've cut their order . . .'

'Do you live here?'

'There's a smaller cottage a little way away.'

'And a garage,' Margot adds.

He doesn't answer, just prods a rusty pipe that's been stuck into the ground.

'Can we take a look?' Adam asks.

'No,' Pasi leers.

'We'll have to ask you to come with us . . .'

'I haven't seen any ID,' he says, almost in a whisper.

Adam holds his badge up in front of Pasi, but he barely looks at it. He just nods to himself and pulls the pipe from the ground.

'Drop that now!' Margot says.

Holding the pipe with both hands, Pasi walks slowly towards her. Adam moves aside and draws his Sig Sauer.

'I have sinned,' he says softly. 'But I—'

'Stop!' Adam shouts.

Something lets go of Pasi's tense frame. He stops and tosses the pipe into the grass.

'I have actively sought out sin, but I am forgiven,' he says wearily.

'By God, maybe,' Margot replies. 'But I need to know where you've been for the past two weeks.'

'I've been in Alabama,' he explains calmly.

'In the USA?'

'We were visiting a church in Troy. We were there two months, I got home the day before yesterday . . . there was a revivalist meeting on a wooden bridge with a roof,' Pasi smiles. 'Like the barrel of a cannon filled with prayer and song, that in itself made the whole trip worthwhile.'

Margot and Adam keep hold of Pasi while they confirm what he says with the passport authority. It all checks out, and they apologise for troubling him, get back in the car and drive off through the dark forest.

'So, did you see the light?' Adam says after a while.

'Almost.'

'I need to go home.'

'OK,' she says. 'I can talk to Thomas Apel on my own.'

'No,' Adam says.

'We know he isn't violent.'

Thomas Apel is the stake president of the Church of Jesus Christ of Latter-day Saints, out in Jakobsberg. Of the five hundred names on their list, he's the only one who has suffered from a borderline psychotic personality disorder.

'Let's do that tomorrow,' Adam pleads.

'OK,' she lies.

He glances sideways at her.

'It's just that Katryna doesn't like being at home on her own,' he confesses.

'Yes, you've been away a lot recently.'

'It's not that . . .'

She drives slowly along the winding forest track. The baby in her stomach moves and stretches out.

'I could have a word with Jenny,' Margot says. 'I'm sure she could go and be with Katryna.'

'I don't think so,' he says with a smile.

'What?' she laughs.

'No, stop it . . .'

'Are you worried Katryna might lose her virginity?'

'Stop it,' Adam says, squirming in his seat.

Margot picks up a biscuit and waits for him to say whatever he's trying to say.

'I know Katta, and she wouldn't want me to arrange for someone to keep her company. She just wants me to prove that I care about our relationship . . . . I'll go home as soon as we've spoken to Thomas Apel.'

'OK,' Margot says, and can't help feeling relieved that Jenny isn't going to have to spend the night with Katryna.

83

The private limited company, Sofa Zone, turns out to be based on Kvicksundsvägen in Högdalen industrial estate, close to the railway depot.

Erik and Joona are driving along next to a barbed-wire fence, towards thirty or so parked dustbin lorries. Grey drizzle is falling, sparkling like sand.

The little monkey girl is swinging beneath the ignition key.

In the distance white smoke is billowing from a chimney on the far side of some tall electricity wires.

They pass wide, empty roads between low industrial buildings bearing corporate flags and signs about private security companies, alarms and camera surveillance.

Barbed-wire fences glint in front of car parks full of articulated lorries, vans and containers.

The windscreen wipers sweep the rain aside mechanically, leaving a dirty triangle beyond the reach of the blades.

'Pull over,' Joona says.

Erik drives round an old tyre by the side of the road, slows down and stops the car.

On the other side of the road weeds and dandelions are growing in front of a tall fence crowned with four rows of barbed wire.

They stare at the big, corrugated-metal building. Rust has trickled down from the screws holding up the large sign bearing the name: *Sofa Zone*.

'This is the Zone, isn't it?' Erik says seriously.

'Yes,' Joona says, and drifts off in thought.

Rain covers the windscreen as soon as the wipers stop. The tiny drops quickly form little streams.

The Zone's only window is in the office at the front; it's grimy and covered with bars. In the parking spaces next to the fence stand nine private cars and two motorbikes.

'What are we going to do?' Erik says after a while.

'If Rocky is here, we try to get him out,' Joona says. 'And if he doesn't agree to that, you'll have to question him here, but . . . it's not enough for him to say that the preacher takes drugs, wears make-up and—'

'I know, I know.'

'We need an address, a name,' he concludes.

'So how do we get inside?'

Joona opens the door and cool air brings a smell of wet grass into the car. The noise of the huge railway yard can be heard over the sound of the worsening rain.

They leave the car and cross the road. The rain is cooling the ground and mist is rising from the tarmac.

'How does your hip feel?' Erik asks.

'Fine.'

They go through the gates into the industrial estate. There's wet cardboard on the ground, with disintegrating labels for three-seat sofas and double divans. Through the filthy window they can see that the office is dark.

A car stops in the car park and a man in a dark-grey suit gets out and walks round the far end of the building.

They wait a few moments, then follow him along the windowless façade. Joona takes out his phone and films the car's registration number as he passes.

On the end of the warehouse is a concrete loading bay with metal steps. Beside the large, rolling door for goods is a smaller, buckled steel door.

They carry on to the end of the building, crossing the shimmering black tarmac, past a stack of wooden pallets.

The man has disappeared.

Erik and Joona exchange a glance, then continue round the corner.

Pieces of polystyrene packaging swirl across the wet ground.

At the back of the warehouse is a skip surrounded by bindweed and thistles. All the way to the fence are mounds of sand.

Their feet leave prints in the wet sand. The man they were following evidently didn't come this way.

The steel door by the loading bay must be the entrance to the building.

They carry on along the rear of the building, across the sand, feeling the rain drip down their necks. Close to the far corner is another metal door at the bottom of a flight of steps, with metal rails to help move wheelie-bins up and down.

'Give me the car keys.'

Erik hands them to him and he removes the metal ring, hands back the little monkey and key, straightens out the metal and makes a hook at the end, pulls a ballpoint pen from his pocket, snaps off the clip and sticks it into the lock, then inserts the straightened keyring, pushes the clip upwards and turns the lock.

84

The bulb hanging from the ceiling of the waste-storage room is broken. The floor is stained from leaking rubbish, and four bins reek of rancid food. The tattered remnants of a list of rules and regulations hangs off the wall. In the weak light from outside, Joona can see another door at the far end of the room.

'Come on,' he says to Erik.

He cautiously opens the door and peers into a small kitchen with a buckled draining board. Rhythmic thuds echo through the walls. The ceiling lamp is on but there's no one about. On a table there's a chopping board with a grease-stained paper bag, surrounded by crumbs and sugar crystals.

There are two closed wooden doors in the far wall. The first is locked, but the second one has no lock.

Joona tries the handle, and they walk slowly into an empty changing room. They can hear music through the walls.

The door to the bathroom is closed.

They walk cautiously across the concrete floor, past three shower cubicles, a mirrored make-up table, and a row of clothes lockers.

Someone flushes the toilet, and they hurry through the room and find themselves in a narrow corridor lined with ten doors. The small rooms off the corridor have no windows, and are furnished with thin beds with shiny plastic mattresses.

Behind a closed door someone is moaning mechanically.

The only light comes from strings of fairy lights draped across the ceiling. Little hearts and flowers illuminate the bare walls in weak, flickering colours.

The corridor leads to a large storeroom with foil-covered ventilation pipes running across the ceiling.

In the flashing lights from a stage they can make out some thirty men and maybe ten women. There are sofas and armchairs every-

where. Along one wall is a row of plastic-wrapped pallets full of
furniture.

It's so dark that it's difficult to discern any faces.

The throbbing music keeps repeating one particular musical phrase,
over and over again.

On the stage a naked woman is dancing round a vertical metal
pole.

Joona and Erik walk forward carefully in the weak light. The room
smells of damp clothes and wet hair.

They keep an eye out for Rocky's bulky frame. He ought to be
visible against the light of the stage if he stands up.

They know this is a gamble. Rocky may already have been here
and left. But if he managed to get hold of any money, he's probably
bought some heroin, in which case he could well still be here in the
Zone.

A drunk is trying to negotiate a price with a woman, and one of
the guards appears quickly and says something that leaves the man
nodding.

The music changes, blending seamlessly into a different rhythm.
The woman on the stage squats down with her thighs spread wide on
either side of the pole.

A guard is standing by the bar, gazing out at the room with a
motionless face.

Joona sees a black German Shepherd moving among the furniture;
it looks accustomed to being there as it eats something from the floor,
sniffs and moves on.

A large man emerges from the corridor. He blows his nose and
heads towards the bar. Joona moves aside and tries to keep an eye on
him.

'It's not him,' Erik says.

They stop by the wall not far from the stage. It's almost dark, but
the reflected glow from the lights rigged up on the ceiling is illuminating an assortment of shirts and faces.

Right in front of the stage sits a man in black-rimmed glasses on a
red armchair with a label hanging from its arm. On the back of the
man's hand is a tattoo of a cross with a shining star at its centre.

On a low table two bottles are clinking together with the rhythm
of the bass. There are very few drugs in sight. Someone is snorting

cocaine, a couple more slip pills between their lips, but sex is clearly the main commodity being traded here.

A young woman in a black latex bikini and a studded collar comes over to Erik, smiles and says something he can't make out. She runs a hand through her short blonde hair as she bats her eyelids at him. When he shakes his head she moves on to the next man.

A film is showing on a television screen behind the bar: an aggressive man is walking round a room, hitting doors and pulling drawers open. A woman is shoved into the room, turns and tries to open the door again. The man goes over to her, pulls her backwards by her hair, and hits her face so hard that she falls to the floor.

Just off to one side of Erik and Joona stands a man with a coarse face and fleshy forehead. The shoulders of his grey jacket are wet with rain.

'Anatoly? I handed my money over when I was searched,' he says in a gruff voice.

'I know, welcome,' says a voice that sounds adolescent.

Joona moves sideways and sees that the voice belongs to a tall and very young man with yellowish skin and dark rings under his eyes.

'I was thinking of going to the room – can I buy two wraps of brown?'

'You can buy whatever you like,' the young man replies. 'We've got some top quality from southern Helmand, the usual from Iran, Tramadol, or . . .'

Their conversation tails off as they move away between the sofas and people.

The dog trots after them and licks the young man's hand. Joona falls in behind them, and sees them turn off to the right at the side of the stage.

Erik manages to stumble into a low lounge table. A beer bottle topples over and rolls onto the floor. He goes a different way, stands on a wet umbrella and carries on round a leather sofa.

The guard by the stage watches him walk.

A young woman with round, pockmarked cheeks is sitting astride a man in a leather vest. He twines a lock of her dark hair around his index finger as he talks on his phone.

In the darkness Joona can no longer see the young man who was dealing heroin. There are too many people everywhere now. He looks round and sees the black dog slip through a swaying beaded curtain. The beads settle long enough to form the Mona Lisa's face briefly before they part again and a young woman with bare breasts and a pair of tight leather trousers walks out.

85

The small beads tinkle as Erik and Joona pass through the Mona Lisa. The air is suddenly thick with sweet smoke, sweat and dirty clothes. All over the coarsely polished cement floor are worn and battered sofas and armchairs. The music from the stage is still audible, but only as the thud of the heavy bass.

Semi-naked people are sitting on the sofas or on the floor itself. Most of them look as though they're asleep, while others move lethargically.

They're all moving with ghostly slowness, drifting through the realm of the stoned.

They walk past a middle-aged woman sitting on a stained sofa with no cushions. She's wearing jeans that are too big for her and a flesh-coloured bra.

Her face is thin and focused as she holds her lighter under a crumpled piece of tinfoil and then hurriedly inhales the smoke through a small plastic straw. A slender curl of smoke twines up towards the corrugated metal roof.

The cement floor is littered with cigarette butts, sweet wrappers, plastic bottles, syringes, condoms, empty packs of pills and a bundle of fabric samples.

Through the smoke Joona can see the man named Anatoly sitting with the new guest on a sofa that's been sliced open, its stuffing hanging out.

Joona and Erik weave through the furniture.

A skinny man in his seventies is sitting on a stained flowery sofa with two young women.

On the floor behind it a man lies unconscious in just his underpants and white socks. He looks almost like a child, but his eyes and cheeks are sunken. The syringe is gone, leaving the needle with its little plastic end sticking out of a vein in the back of his hand. On an armchair beside him sits a woman with an apathetic expression on her face. After a while she bends forward and pulls the needle from his hand, but drops it on the floor.

Joona sees a guard dragging a man who has thrown up, and can't help thinking that this place is the complete opposite of the rich kids' saturnalias.

No wishes come true in the Zone. Here there are only prisoners and slaves, and the money only flows in one direction. Everyone is alone in their addiction, drained of all they have until they die.

He glances behind him and sees Anatoly stand up and walk through the room. The black dog follows him.

A fat man in camouflage trousers and a black jacket pushes away a woman in pink underwear and high heels. She goes back and tries to kiss his hands as she begs him for a fix. The man is impatient, tells her to pull herself together, that she hasn't earned enough.

'I can't, they hurt me, they—'

'Shut up, I don't give a fuck – you need to do three more customers,' he says.

'But, darling, I don't feel good, I need—'

She tries to stroke his cheek, but he grabs hold of her hand, pulls her little finger and bends it sharply backwards. It happens so quickly that at first the woman doesn't seem to realise what's going on. She stares wide-eyed at her broken finger.

A man with a salt-and-pepper moustache walks over to them, exchanges a few words with the other man, then pulls the sobbing woman through the room towards the curtain. She stumbles and loses a shoe, then he hits her and she falls over, dragging a standard lamp down with her.

Joona and Erik move out of the way.

The man drags the woman to her feet, and the lamp rolls away and shines straight into the face of a large bearded man.

It's Rocky Kyrklund.

He's sitting completely naked in a red armchair, asleep. His head is leaning forward and his beard looks like it has grown into the hair on his chest. He's injected himself in his right leg, and dark blood is trickling down his ankle.

Rocky isn't alone. Beside him, on a sofa bed with no mattress, sits a woman with bleached-blonde hair, wearing a brown bra. Her pale blue panties are on the floor next to her. A plaster is hanging half off her knee.

She holds a lighter under a sooty spoon, and stares with glassy eyes at the small bubbles forming in the water. She licks her lips as she waits for the powder to dissolve, leaving the spoon full of pale yellow liquid.

Erik steps over a footstool and walks over to them, smelling the insipid aroma of heroin and hot metal as he comes to a halt.

'Rocky?' Erik says in a low voice.

Rocky slowly raises his head. His eyelids are heavy, his pupils like pinpricks of black ink.

'Judas Iscariot,' he mumbles when he sees Erik.

'Yes,' Erik says.

Rocky smiles happily and slowly closes his eyes. The woman beside him puts a ball of cotton-wool in the solution, holds her syringe on top of it and sucks up the solution, then attaches a needle to the syringe.

Joona notices that the man in camouflage trousers is sitting on a chair outside the staffroom again, looking at his phone. At the other end of the room the man with the grey moustache disappears through the beaded curtain with the woman.

'Do you remember telling me about the unclean preacher?' Erik asks, squatting down in front of Rocky.

Rocky opens his tired eyes and shakes his head.

'Is that supposed to be me? The preacher?'

'I don't think so. I think you meant someone else,' Erik says. 'You talked about a man in make-up with scarred veins.'

Next to them the woman uses her briefs as a tourniquet round her arm, tightening them as hard as she can by twisting a pen through them a couple of times.

'Do you remember him killing a woman here at the Zone?'

'No,' Rocky grins.

'She was known as Tina, but her real name was Natalia,' Erik goes on.

'Yes, that . . . that was him, that was the preacher,' Rocky mutters.

The woman on the sofa bed looks for a vein in the usual places, a soft spot without too many scars.

'I need to know . . . are we talking about a real preacher, a priest?'

Rocky nods and closes his eyes.

'Which church?' Erik asks.

Rocky whispers to himself and Erik leans forward until he can smell his rancid breath.

'The preacher is jealous . . . just like God,' he whispers.

The woman inserts the needle and a drop of blood mixes with the yellow liquid before she injects it. With nimble fingers she undoes the tourniquet and lets out a long groan as the kick washes through her. Erik watches her stretch her legs, tense her ankles, then relax as her body goes completely soft.

'We believe the preacher has murdered at least five women, and we need a name, a parish, or an address,' Erik says.

'What are you saying?' Rocky mutters, closing his eyes again.

'You were going to tell me about the preacher,' Erik persists. 'I need a name, or—'

'Stop banging on,' the woman says, lying back against Rocky's hairy thigh.

'Say hello to Ying,' Rocky murmurs, stroking her head clumsily.

While Erik tries to get Rocky to remember, Joona is keeping an eye on the room. The fat man in the camouflage trousers gets up from the chair outside the staffroom and peers out across the room. Joona watches him put his phone in his pocket and set off through the sofas. He stops by one man who's lying with his eyes closed, a lit cigarette between his lips, then returns to his place.

'You want me to tell you things,' Rocky says. 'But all I remember from purgatory is that I was sitting in a little monkey cage . . . and there were long wooden poles with glowing ends—'

'Blah, blah, blah,' Ying interrupts with a hoarse laugh.

'I howled, tried to get away, tried to protect myself with my food bowl . . . blah, blah, blah,' he smiles.

'Seriously, though,' Erik says in a louder voice. 'I won't disturb you any more, if you can just tell me something that will help us find him.'

It looks as though Rocky's dozed off. His mouth slips open a few millimetres and a string of saliva dribbles into his beard.

The man with the grey moustache comes back from the other side of the room. The curtain sways behind him, letting a yellow glow into the room before the Mona Lisa's face reforms.

'We can't stay here much longer,' Joona tells Erik.

Ying tries to put her briefs on but they catch between her toes and she leans back and rests with her eyes shut.

'My brain is mush,' Rocky mumbles. 'You need to . . .'

'Blah, blah, blah,' Ying says.

'Give me a name,' Erik persists.

'You're probably going to have to hypnotise me if . . .'

'Can you stand up?' Erik asks. 'Let me help you.'

Joona sees the fat man in the camouflage trousers get up from his chair again. He's speaking on his phone as he sets off towards them.

The woman in the studded collar is standing in the doorway leading to the stage, holding the curtain open. She seems to be hesitating about whether to come in or not.

Behind her Joona can see a tall figure in a yellow oilskin coat. The sort fishermen used to wear.

At first he doesn't understand how he knows that he's staring at the preacher, but his mind suddenly brings a moment from the past into sharp focus.

'Erik,' Joona says quietly. 'The preacher is here, he's standing over there by the curtain, in a yellow raincoat.'

The woman in the studded collar waves to someone and stumbles into the room. The beads of the curtain swing back and sway in front of the yellow figure.

And now Joona remembers how Filip Cronstedt described the man who was filming Maria Carlsson.

The last thing he heard before he collapsed in the storeroom was that the thin man with the camera was wearing yellow oilskins, like the fishermen in Lofoten.

Joona starts walking, but the man in the camouflage trousers steps round the flowery sofa and stops him.

'I have to ask you and your friend to come with me,' he says.

'Erik,' Joona says. 'You saw him, didn't you? Over there by the curtain. That's the preacher. You have to follow him, try to get a look at his face.'

'This club is for members only,' the man says.

'We were thinking of buying a sofa,' Joona says, as he sees Erik hurry away towards the curtain.

86

The fat man shouts at him to stop, but Erik carries on, weaving quickly between the sofas. The man yells at Joona to move out of the way. An armchair gets shoved backwards, making a scraping sound on the floor.

'Pydään anteeksi,' Joona says in Finnish, stopping him again.

The man brushes Joona's hand away, steps back and pulls out a projectile taser.

'Nyt se pian sattuu,' Joona goes on with a smile.

He takes a step forward, sliding out of the line of fire, pushes the taser aside with his hand and kicks the man in the knee, making his leg buckle. The man gasps and two projectiles with spiral wires slam into the back of a sofa. Joona twists the taser out of the man's hand and hits him in the collarbone with it, then wraps the wires round his neck and pulls. The man collapses to the floor, rolls over and tries to get up again. Joona forces him back down with his foot, winds the wires round his hand and pulls them tighter until the man loses consciousness and slumps to the floor.

Erik disappears through the bead curtain beside the stage.

The door of the staffroom at the other end of the room opens. A broad-shouldered man in a shiny jacket emerges with a phone to his ear, and looks round.

Joona sits down to stay out of sight, but knows he has to stop the man from going after Erik.

Rocky still has his eyes closed, but he's now got a cigarette between his lips.

The prostitute with the studded collar pushes a used tissue between the cushions of a sofa and walks over to Joona in her high heels.

'Shall we go to a room? I can show you a good time,' she says, moving closer.

'Stay out of the way,' he replies abruptly.

She wipes her mouth and starts to walk towards the beaded curtain.

The man in the shiny jacket has seen Joona. He heads towards him, pushing a chair over as he approaches. Joona stands up and sees that the man is hiding a weapon by his hip, a high-calibre pistol with a short barrel.

The fat man is lying on his back, untangling the wires from his neck, coughing and trying to get up.

The man in the shiny jacket stops in front of Joona, with the flowery sofa between them, and screws a silencer on to his Sig Pro.

'I'll shoot you in both knees unless you come with me,' he says.

Joona holds up one hand in a calming gesture and tries to back away, but the fat man on the floor grabs hold of his legs.

'I didn't know this was a private club,' Joona says, trying to pull his legs free.

The armed man has finished fitting the silencer, raises the gun and squeezes the trigger. Joona throws himself aside, lands on his shoulder and hits his temple on the floor.

There's no sound as the gun goes off, but the powder is hanging in the air, and a naked man behind Joona stands up with blood streaming from a bullet hole in his stomach. A woman screams and hurries to move away from him, and falls on all fours.

'Time to die,' the man with the gun pants, climbing up on to the sofa to see over the back of it.

Joona grabs hold of the toppled lamp and swings the heavy base in a semi-circle. It hits the man in the shoulder and he staggers to one side. The cable clatters on the floor as it snakes along behind. The man leans against the back of the sofa and Joona reaches him before he has time to fire, knocking the pistol aside and punching him squarely in the throat.

He grabs the warm barrel of the gun and feels a heavy blow to his cheek as he bends the weapon upwards.

The man recoils, clutching his throat. He can't breathe and saliva is dribbling from his gaping mouth.

Joona takes a step back as he twists the gun round and shoots the man through his right lung.

The only sound is a sharp click, instead of a loud bang.

The empty shell bounces off the cement floor.

The man staggers, trying to cover the entry hole with his hand, coughs, then slumps back onto the sofa.

The fat man gets unsteadily to his feet with a knife in his hand. One of his shoulders is drooping and the taser is still dangling from the wires around his neck.

Joona moves away and glances quickly towards the bead curtain.

The man takes a couple of steps and jabs with the knife. Joona backs into a table as he feels the tip of the blade touch his jacket. He follows the knife as it moves, holds it aside with the pistol, twists his body and rams his right elbow into the man's cheek with immense force. His head snaps sideways, spraying droplets of sweat in the direction of the blow. Joona moves with him, takes a long stride to keep his balance and feels a stab of pain from his hip.

As the man slumps unconscious to the floor, Joona moves out of the way and scans the room.

Very soon it will be impossible to get out. Crouching down, Joona moves towards the curtain with the pistol pointing at the floor.

The new customer who bought heroin from Anatoly is lying lifeless beside his sofa. His lips are grey and his eyes open.

Joona steps round a low glass table and sees the woman in the studded collar heading towards him between the sofas.

'Take me away from here with you,' she whispers, with a desperate look in her eyes. 'Please, I'm begging you, I have to get away from here . . .'

'Can you run?'

She smiles at him and then her head suddenly jerks. A cascade of blood squirts from her temple.

Joona spins round as a bullet slams into the back of the chair next to him and stuffing sprays out across the floor. The man with the grey moustache is approaching between two women with a raised pistol.

Smoke rising from the barrel.

Joona takes aim, lowers the barrel a couple of millimetres, then fires three times. It sounds like the gun isn't loaded, but a cloud of blood explodes behind the man.

The man takes another two steps before collapsing on top of the two women, dropping his pistol and putting his hand out towards a footstool.

The woman in the studded collar is still standing. Blood is pumping from her temple and running down her body. She looks at Joona and her mouth opens as if she's trying to speak.

'I'll get help,' he says.

Bewildered, she touches her bloody hair, then falls sideways on to an armchair and curls up as if she wants to sleep.

In the distance a round-shouldered man is approaching at a crouch, using the sofas as cover. Joona runs the last part of the way. A bullet hits the wall beside him, throwing out a shower of plaster. He ducks through the curtain, tucks his gun close to his body and walks as fast as he can towards the passageway.

A fat man is dancing on the stage with his shirt outside his trousers.

There's no sign of Erik, and Joona starts running as soon as he reaches the narrow corridor.

He can hear his pursuers behind him as he enters the changing room and quickly locks the door. Someone is in the shower, and the plastic tray creaks with their weight. Joona runs past two women standing in front of the make-up table.

In the kitchen a short man is frying frozen meatballs on the stove. He barely has time to snatch up a knife before Joona shoots him in the thigh.

The man falls to the floor and Joona hears him scream as he runs across the old cardboard boxes in the waste-storage room and emerges out of the back of the building. He runs round the warehouse as fast as he can, through tall weeds, then out through the gates, along a barbed-wire fence and round a van before he sees that Erik's car has gone. He sets off at a limp towards Högdalsplan to alert the police and emergency services.

87

There's barely any traffic, and Erik is taking care to keep a safe distance between him and the car in front all the way through the industrial estate and up on to Älvsjövägen. The preacher is driving a blue Peugeot which is so dirty it's impossible to see what the registration number is. Erik has no other plan beyond following it as long as he can without being seen.

The amber glow of the streetlights fills the car, then vanishes between the lampposts, like slow breathing.

Erik wonders if the preacher was at the Zone to buy drugs or to meet Rocky.

Concern about what has happened to Joona flutters in his chest. Erik didn't look back, just did what he had to do: he left the room full of addicts, passed through the bead curtain and carried on through the crowd.

The heavy bass of the music grew louder as the beat was turned up and the throb of the music reached deep inside his body.

In the flickering light from the stage he suddenly caught sight of the yellow raincoat. The preacher was heading for the exit and Erik followed him. A woman tried to stop him, but he just shook his head and forced his way past.

No one gave him a second glance as he passed the search area and hurried on through the metal door and out onto the loading bay.

Joona seemed so sure of what he had said that the only thing on Erik's mind was that he mustn't lose the preacher now that they were so close.

The yellow oilskin glinted in the darkness over by the cars, and Erik followed as quickly as he could without being heard. The preacher walked out through the gates and stopped in front of the blue car.

He has now been following the red tail-lights for quarter of an hour, and keeps telling himself that he mustn't let too much of a gap form.

He speeds up a little on a long straight past a bare-grit football pitch and a school. The sparse lights of a large housing estate flicker through the greenery.

A night bus pulls out from a stop and Erik has to slow down. He loses sight of the preacher, puts his foot down and overtakes the bus on the wrong side of a central reservation.

A set of traffic lights ahead turns red. Erik speeds up, swerves and just makes it past the back of a car crossing his path.

It's already too late, though, as he realises that the blue Peugeot has turned off to the right. He sees its lights flickering between the houses.

There's no time to think if he isn't to lose the preacher altogether.

Erik turns into the next road, and in the boot a bag of empty bottles for recycling falls over. He's trying to double-guess the other car's likely direction as he drives past lush gardens and dark houses.

He brakes and turns left, glancing the side of a letterbox and accelerating hard past a number of villas, then realises that there's a dead end up ahead, beyond the next junction, and brakes hard, sending the tyres skidding across the tarmac, jerks the wheel and swerves sharply to the right.

The back wheels lose their grip and there's a crash as the rear wing hits an electricity pole. The bottles in the boot shatter as Erik lurches out on to the main road again.

He accelerates hard up a hill, reaches the top and just manages to spot the preacher driving into the tunnel under the motorway bridge.

He slows down and feels his hands shaking on the steering wheel. The wing mirror has come loose again and is dangling from its wires.

Someone has sprayed the words 'Another world is possible' on the concrete walls of the tunnel.

Everything goes dark, then a moment later he emerges into an area of attractive four-storey buildings.

The blue Peugeot passes a bin lorry emptying dustbins with measured mechanical movements, and Erik wonders if the preacher lives here in Hökmossen.

Even though he has a reasonable grasp on reality, the idea of the preacher having an ordinary life seems incredible: a man who stabs knives into the faces of his victims long after they're dead, then goes home to his lovely villa with apple trees and lawn-sprinklers and sits down to watch television with his family.

Erik follows the blue car as it turns right off Korpmossevägen and into Klensmedsvägen.

The preacher slows down and stops just after the third side-street.

Without changing his speed, Erik drives past the blue car and looks in the rear-view mirror as the light inside the car goes out. He passes a small patch of woodland, turns into the next road, stops and hurries back. The yellow raincoat is disappearing into the forest to the left of the road, and Erik stops on the pavement and realises how badly his legs are shaking.

88

The Church of Jesus Christ of Latter-day Saints is located on Järfallavägen, next to a large, tarmacked car park. It's a low building with a terracotta-coloured façade, panelled roof and a red tower rising from the centre of a circular stone foundation.

Stake president Thomas Apel lives with his wife and two children in a cement-grey villa very close to the temple. From the garden's wooden decking with its covered barbeque, the red tower is visible above the trees and tiled roofs.

Adam and Margot are sitting in the living room with glasses of lemonade. Thomas Apel and his wife Ingrid are sitting opposite them. Thomas is a skinny man, dressed in grey trousers, a white shirt, and a pale grey tie. His face is clean-shaven and thin, with fair eyebrows and a narrow, crooked mouth.

Margot has just asked Thomas where he was at the times of the murders, and he's replied that he was at home with his family.

'Is there anyone else who could vouch for that?' Margot asks, looking at Ingrid.

'Well, of course the children were at home,' Thomas's wife says in an amiable voice.

'No one else?' Adam asks.

'We lead a quiet life,' Thomas replies, as if that explained everything.

'You have a lovely home,' Margot says, glancing round the smart room.

An African mask is hanging on the wall next to a painting of a woman in a black dress with a red book in her lap.

'Thank you,' Ingrid says.

'Each family is a kingdom,' Thomas says. 'Ingrid is my queen, the girls princesses.'

'Naturally.' Margot smiles.

She looks at Ingrid's face, free of make-up, at the small pearls in her earlobes, and the long dress that reaches up to her neck and halfway over her hands.

'You probably think we dress in a very old-fashioned, boring way,' Ingrid says when she sees Margot looking.

'It looks nice,' Margot lies, and tries to find a comfortable position on the deep sofa with crocheted antimacassars on the back.

Thomas leans forward, pours more lemonade in her glass, and she thanks him soundlessly.

'Our lives aren't boring,' Thomas says calmly. 'There's nothing boring about not using drugs, or alcohol or tobacco . . . or coffee or tea.'

'Why not coffee?' Adam asks.

'Because the body is a gift from God,' he replies simply.

'If it's a gift, then surely you can drink coffee if you want to?' Adam retorts.

'Of course, it isn't set in stone,' Thomas says lightly. 'It's just guidance . . .'

'OK,' Adam nods.

'But if we listen to this guidance, the Lord promises that the angel of death will pass our home and not kill us.' Thomas smiles.

'How quickly does the angel come if you mess up badly?' Margot asks.

'You said you wanted to look at my diary?' Thomas says, the veins in his temples darkening slightly.

'I'll get it,' Ingrid volunteers, and rises to her feet.

'I'll just get some water,' Margot says, and follows her.

Thomas makes a move to stand up but Adam stops him by asking about the role of the stake president.

Ingrid is standing at a bureau looking for the diary when Margot walks into the immaculately tidy kitchen.

'Could I have some water?' Margot asks.

'Yes, of course,' Ingrid says.

'Were you here last Sunday?'

'Yes,' the woman replies, and a tiny frown appears across the bridge of her nose. 'We were at home.'

'What did you do?'

'We did . . . the usual, we had dinner and watched television.'

'What was on television?' she asks

'We only watch Mormon television,' Ingrid says, checking that the tap is properly turned off.

'Does your husband ever go out alone in the evening?'

'No.'

'Not even to the temple?'

'I'll have a look in the bedroom,' the woman says, her cheeks flushing as she leaves the kitchen.

Margot drinks, then puts the glass down on the worktop and goes back out to the living room. She can see the tension in Adam's face, and a tiny hint of sweat above his top lip.

'Are you on any medication?' Adam asks.

'No,' Thomas replies, wiping his palms on his pale grey trousers.

'No psychoactive drugs, no anti-depressants?' Margot asks, sitting down on the sofa again.

'Why do you want to know that?' he asks, looking at her with calm, blank eyes.

'Because you received treatment for mental illness twenty years ago.'

'That was a difficult time for me, before I listened to God.'

He falls silent and looks warmly at Ingrid, who's just come back in. She's standing in the doorway with a red Filofax in her hand.

Margot takes the book, puts on her reading glasses and starts leafing through the dates.

'Do you have a video camera?' Adam asks as Margot skims through the diary.

'Yes,' he replies, with a quizzical look at Adam.

'Can I take a look at it?'

Thomas's Adam's apple bobs above the knot of his tie.

'What for?' he asks.

'Just routine,' Adam replies.

'OK, but it's being repaired.' Thomas smiles, stretching his crooked mouth.

'Where?'

'A friend's mending it for me,' he says softly.

'Can I have the name of the friend, please?'

'Of course,' Thomas murmurs and Adam's phone rings inside his jacket.

'Excuse me,' he says, standing up and looking for his mobile as he turns his back on Thomas.

Through the window at the back he sees a neighbour standing on the other side of the fence looking at them. In the reflection he can also see himself, his thick hair and heavy eyebrows. He finds his phone: Adde, an IT technician with National Crime, who also happens to live in Hökmossen.

'Adam,' he says as he answers.

'Another film,' Adde practically screams.

'We'll be there as soon as—'

'It's your wife on the video, it's Katryna—'

Adam doesn't hear anything after that, he walks straight into the hall, leans against the wall and manages to pull down a framed photograph of two smiling girls.

'Adam?' Margot calls. 'What's going on?'

She leaves the book on the sofa, stands up and accidentally knocks over a glass of lemonade on the low table.

Adam has already reached the front door. Margot can't see his face. She feels sick, clutches her stomach and follows him out.

Adam runs down the path to the car.

He's started the engine before she's even out of the door. She stops, panting for breath, and watches him rev the engine, perform a sharp U-turn in the road, skid and drive into a hockey-goal that some children have erected on the side of the road. She walks down to the road and is gesturing for him to stop when her phone rings.

89

The house at Bultvägen 5 only has three rooms, but the kitchen has a nice dining area and there's a basement, and a small garden that backs on to a patch of forest. They bought it fairly cheaply and were able to move closer to the city, but the house won't make it through many more winters without some serious renovation work.

Katryna Youssef is sitting on the white sofa in front of the television. She's wearing her soft blue Hollister sweatpants and a pink T-shirt.

She knows the varnish on her new nails dried a long while ago, but she still spreads her fingers out as she reaches for her glass of wine. Seeing as Adam isn't home, she's taken the opportunity to do her nails. Otherwise he goes out and sits in the car to avoid getting a headache.

She takes a sip, then looks down at the iPad in her lap. Caroline hasn't updated her status yet. She hasn't said anything for an hour now, and she can't have been in the shower all that time, surely?

Katryna is watching an old film called *Face/Off* on television, but is finding it rather far-fetched.

She's got to work tomorrow, so shouldn't really sit up and wait for Adam.

I'm not going to either, she thinks, and glances at the window as a bush in the garden brushes hard against the glass.

She slips her hand inside her loose sweatpants and starts to masturbate, shuts her eyes for a few seconds, then stares out at the garden through the window, still masturbating, but stops when it occurs to her that their neighbour might bring back the rake he borrowed earlier that evening. She can't be bothered to close the curtains, and anyway, she's more bored than horny.

Katryna yawns and scratches her ankle. Even though she ate a tuna salad earlier she's hungry again. She carries on looking at the iPad, scrolls back and reads her own comments, then writes another one.

With peculiar persistence she looks at the latest pictures of Caroline Winberg, the woman she's practically stalking.

Caroline was discovered on an underground train on her way to football practice, and is now a supermodel. It's rumoured that she won't get out of bed for less that 25,000 dollars.

Katryna follows her on all the forums there are, and always knows where she is and what she's doing.

It's just turned out that way.

She reaches for the glass of wine again and shivers when she realises that the garden lights aren't working. The bushes look black against the glass. She's not sure if the lights have worked at all that evening. It's not the first time they've gone wrong. Adam will have to check the fuse-box. There's no way she's going down into the cellar. Not after the break-in.

She sees her own reflection in the dark window, drinks some more wine and looks at her nails.

Someone broke in last Thursday when she and Adam were both at work, and now the lock on the cellar door is broken. They've tied a piece of rope around it so it feels locked if you pull it. Nothing of value was stolen, not the home cinema centre, the stereo or games console.

Maybe they realised that Adam is in the police and changed their minds? It's possible that they saw his framed diploma from the Police Academy and got out as fast as they could.

Adam thinks it was just some bored youngsters.

But it's still a bit odd, Katryna thinks. They could have taken their whisky and wine, or her jewellery. The Prada clutch-bag that Adam gave her two years ago was lying out in the bedroom.

She's only discovered one missing object. A little cloth embroidered by her grandmother. Adam doesn't believe her, he reckons it will turn up, and refused to mention it in the police report.

Lamassu, the protective deity that her grandmother embroidered in pale red thread on white fabric, has always sat on the bookcase next to the silver crucifix on a stand.

Katryna knows someone has taken it.

When she was little she didn't like the embroidery at all. Her mum said that Lamassu watched over their home, but she could only see a monster. The close-stitched cloth depicted a man with a plaited beard, with the body of a bull and enormous angel's wings arching out from his back.

Once again she thinks of the rope that Adam wound round the handle of the cellar door and then tied to the water pipe leading to the washing machine. She's made him look through the house several times.

Apart from the cellar, the part of the house she finds creepiest is the large cleaning cupboard between the living room and the kitchen.

It's like a dressing room, with two unusually thick wooden doors. It used to be locked from the outside with a revolving wooden catch, but that's come loose. Now she and Adam just push the doors shut, but they move, rubbing against each other and opening slightly, as if someone's trying to peer out.

A car's headlights reflect off the gilded icon on the bedroom wall, then the glass covering Adam's framed match jersey.

Every home has its creepy corners, she thinks with a shudder. Rooms and corners that have stored up childhood fears of the dark over the ages.

She drinks the last of the wine and gets up to go to the kitchen.

90

Katryna moves the wine-box to the edge of the worktop, then fills her glass under the little tap, splashing some tiny red droplets on her hand.

The wind is rattling the kitchen air vent. Through the glass door she can see the empty street through the branches of the viburnum.

The two wooden doors of the cleaning cupboard in the hall leading to the living room knock against each other, then close tighter.

She puts her glass down on an advert from Sephora, sucks the drops of wine from the back of her hand, looks at the glass, at the blonde woman on the flyer, and decides to keep the baby and not go through with the abortion.

Katryna leaves her wine glass in the kitchen, thinks that she should send Adam a text message telling him she's changed her mind. She walks slowly, keeping her eyes on the heavy wooden doors the whole time. She feels almost compelled to look at them, and stops when the far one starts to open slightly. Katryna takes a deep breath and hurries past. She forces herself not to run, but can feel the movement of the door as a shiver down her spine.

She sits on the sofa and carries on watching the film.

John Travolta has swapped faces with Nicolas Cage, but they just look like themselves.

She can't help thinking about their neighbour. He gave her a funny look when he borrowed the rake, and she wonders if he knew she was at home on her own.

Her iPad has gone dark, and she puts her finger on the screen and finds herself pointing straight at Caroline's smiling face when the screen comes back to life.

Katryna knows that if she turns her head to the left she can see the cupboard doors reflected in the window at the back of the house.

She needs to stop this, it's turning into an obsession.

What if it was their neighbour who broke in and stole the cloth and a pair of her pants from the washing basket?

If you knew that the cellar door was only held shut by a rope, you could get in without making any noise at all.

Katryna stands up and goes over to the window, and is drawing the curtains when she thinks she can see someone running across the grass.

She leans closer.

It's hard to see in the dark.

A deer, it must have been a deer, she thinks, and closes the curtain with her heart pounding.

She sits down on the sofa, switches the television off and starts to text Adam. In the middle of a sentence her phone rings, scaring her so much that she jumps.

She doesn't recognise the number.

'Katryna,' she says warily.

'Hello, Katryna,' a man says quickly. 'I'm one of Adam's colleagues at National Crime, and—'

'He's not—'

'Listen now,' the man interrupts. 'Are you at home?'

'Yes, I'm—'

'Go to the front door and leave the house, don't worry about clothes or shoes, just go straight out into the street and carry on walking.'

'Can I ask why?'

'Are you on your way out?'

'I'm going now.'

She stands up and starts to walk through the room, looking towards the cupboard doors as she goes round the sofa and turns towards the front door.

A person wearing yellow rain-clothes is standing on the doormat with their back to her, closing the front door behind them.

Katryna quickly moves backwards, goes round the corner and stops.

'There's someone in here,' she whispers. 'I can't get out.'

'Lock yourself in somewhere, and leave your phone on.'

'God, there's nowhere to—'

'Don't speak unless you absolutely have to, go to the bathroom.'

She's walking on unsteady legs towards the kitchen when she sees that the doors to the cleaning cupboard have slid open slightly. She can't think straight, and opens one of the doors, slips quickly inside and stands beside the vacuum cleaner, and pulls the door closed behind her.

It's hard to close it properly when her fingers won't fit in the gap. She tries to get hold of the edge with her nails and pull it towards her.

Katryna holds her breath when she hears footsteps outside the cupboard. They move off in the direction of the kitchen, the doors knock against each other the other door slips open a couple of millimetres.

She stands in the darkness with her eyes open wide, and hears a kitchen drawer being opened. There's a metallic clattering sound, and she's breathing in short gasps, and suddenly thinks about the relic in the church in Södertälje. Adam didn't want to go in with her, but she went and looked at it anyway. It was a fragment of bone belonging to Thomas, one of the apostles. The priest claimed that the Holy Spirit was still present in the relic, in the yellow fragment of bone inside the glass tube on the marble table.

She reaches out her hand and tries to close the door, but can't get any grip, her nails just slide over the wood. She moves carefully to the side, but the mop and bucket are in the way. The handle of the mop touches her winter coat, and a few empty hangers rattle softly on the rail.

She manages to pull the door closed, but loses her grip again. It swings open slightly and she can see a dark figure standing right outside the cupboard.

91

The door is yanked open and a man with a pistol steps backwards. His mouth is half-open and his dark brown eyes are staring at her. A smell of sweat reaches her. She registers every detail at that moment. His worn jeans with turned-up cuffs, the grass stain on his right knee, his padded black nylon jacket, and the logo of the New York Yankees sewn badly on to his cap.

'I'm a police officer,' he says in a gasp, and lowers his gun.

'Oh, God,' she whispers, and feels tears begin to flow.

He takes her hand and leads her towards the hall as he reports back to control on his radio:

'Katryna is unharmed but the suspect fled through the kitchen door . . . yes, get the road-blocks set up and send some dog-units over here . . .'

She walks beside the police officer, leaning her hand against the wall, brushing against her diploma from her make-up course.

'Give me a moment,' the officer says, and opens the front door to secure their exit.

Katryna bends down to put her trainers on as a cascade of blood sprays across the hall mirror. Then she hears the sharp crack of the gun and the echo from the house on the other side of the road.

The plain-clothes officer throws his arm out, manages to grab the coats and pulls them with him as he falls. He collapses on his back among the shoes. The hangers rattle as blood pulses from the bullet-hole in his black jacket.

'Hide,' he gasps. 'Go and hide again . . .'

Two further shots ring out and Katryna moves backwards. Someone is screaming like an animal outside. She stares at the wounded police officer, and at the blood seeping along the cracks in the tiled floor. A window pane shatters as another shot echoes through the neighbourhood.

Katryna runs at a crouch through the living room, slipping on the

Tabriz rug and hitting her shoulder against the wall, but she manages to keep her balance, carries on out into the passageway and opens one of the cleaning cupboard doors. The mop handle falls out, pulling the red bucket with it, and the strainer comes loose and clatters on to the floor. Katryna picks the mop up and tries to get it to stand up among the clothes. A jacket falls down and the thick hose of the vacuum cleaner pushes the other door open.

She hears two more shots, leaves the cupboard and carries on towards the kitchen. She sees the glass door and the darkness outside, opens the cellar door and starts to go down the steep staircase.

She's so frightened she can barely breathe, and can only think that this is an organised hate-based crime, that the racists have found them, that they're upset about Adam buying a new Jaguar.

She can hear police cars through the stone walls, and thinks that she can hide in the boiler room until the police have caught the intruder.

Her anxiety increases as she heads down into the darkness.

She clings on to the cool handrail, blinks and opens her eyes wide, but can hardly see a thing.

The air smells of stone, damp pipes and oil from the boiler.

She's treading carefully, but the steps still creak under her weight. Finally she reaches the tiled floor. She blinks and can make out the washing machine as a paler shape in the darkness next to the door with the rope around its handle. She turns round and moves in the opposite direction, past Adam's old pinball machine, and into the boiler room. She carefully closes the door behind her and hears a whining sound.

Katryna stands still with her fingers on the door handle, listening. The pipes are clicking faintly, but otherwise everything is quiet.

She moves further in, away from the door, thinking that she'll just sit here, it won't be long, not now that the police have arrived.

She hears the whimpering sound again. Very close to her.

She turns her head but can't see anything.

The whimpering becomes a weak wheezing sound.

It's coming from the safety valve of the hot-water tank.

Katryna feels her way forward and finds the paint-stained stepladder standing against the wall.

She unfolds it in silence and moves it to the wall beneath the window up by the ceiling.

Someone has stolen Lamassu, she thinks. The embroidered cloth with her protective deity, her protector, that's why this is happening.

She can't stay in the house, she never wants to come back here again. She twists the two catches of the window and is pushing the little window against the weeds when she feels a cold draught around her ankles.

Someone's coming up behind her, she's convinced of it.

Someone's got in through the cellar door, they've cut the rope holding it closed and are on their way inside.

It's impossible to open the window properly. She tries again, but it keeps hitting something. Panting for breath, she reaches out with her arm, through the weeds, and feels that the lawnmower is parked too close.

She tries to push it away with her hand, pushing even though she can feel the stepladder slide backwards beneath her. She turns the wheel of the lawnmower by hand and manages to roll it a few centimetres.

The window slides open and she starts to crawl out as the door to the boiler room bursts open and the light is switched on. The old starter switch makes the fluorescent tube flicker. Katryna tries to scramble out as the steps are yanked away from beneath her and clatter to the floor. Her legs thud against the wall, her knees sting, but she clings on to the frame and fights to pull herself up.

The first stab of the knife hits her back so hard that she hears the point scrape the concrete wall in front of her.

92

Adam Youssef is lying on his stomach on the paved path outside his home, with his hands cuffed behind his back. His thigh is throbbing, his black jeans are wet with blood, but the superficial gunshot wound doesn't really hurt. Blue lights from various vehicles are pulsing over the dark greenery of the garden in a peculiar rhythm.

A police officer presses his knee into Adam's shoulder blades and yells at him to be quiet while he explains the situation to the operational team.

'Katryna's still in there,' Adam pants.

The operational lead officer is in direct contact with the head of the Stockholm Rapid Response Unit, trying to coordinate their efforts. The first team is forcing the windows and doors, securing entry and letting the paramedics through.

The officer who has been shot is rolled out on a stretcher while staff at the Karolinska Hospital in Huddinge have been warned to prepare for immediate sedation and an operation.

Adam tries to pull free but is struck so hard across the kidneys that he loses his breath. He coughs, and feels the police officer pressing his knee against the back of his neck, grabbing his jacket and roaring at him to lie still.

'I'm a police officer, and—'

'Shut up!'

The second officer takes Adam's wallet, backs away slightly, and the gravel crunches beneath his shoes as he looks at Adam's police badge and ID.

'National Crime,' he confirms.

The police officer removes his knee from Adam's back and stands up, breathing hard. As the pressure is removed from his neck and lungs, Adam catches his breath and tries to roll over on to his side.

'You shot a plain-clothed police officer,' the officer says.

'He had my wife, I saw her with him, and thought—'

'He was the first officer on the scene and he was on his way out with her . . . everyone had received that information.'

'Just get her out!' Adam begs.

'What the hell are you two doing?' a woman shouts.

It's Margot. Adam sees her legs through the blackberry bushes by the road, as she walks through the gate and stops.

'He's a police officer,' she says, and takes several shallow breaths. 'It's his wife who—'

'He shot a colleague,' one of the officers says.

'It was an accident,' Adam says. 'I thought—'

'Don't say anything else,' Margot interrupts. 'Where's Katryna?'

'I don't know, I don't know anything . . . Margot—'

'I'm going in,' she says, and he watches her feet move along the path.

'Tell her I love her,' he whispers.

'Help him up,' Margot tells the two officers. 'And get those handcuffs off – put him in one of the cars for the time being.'

She starts to walk towards the house with both hands round her stomach.

A young man from the rapid response unit comes out through the front door with his helmet in his hand. He passes Margot and throws up right across the front steps, then carries on down the garden path with a glazed look on his face. He unfastens his bulletproof vest and lets it fall to the ground, emerges on to the street and throws up again between two parked patrol cars, then leans on the bonnet of one of the cars and spits.

The two officers take hold of Adam's arms, pull him up on to his feet and lead him away from the house. He feels blood trickling down his thigh from the gunshot wound. They lead him off to a patrol car and sit him in the back seat, but leave the handcuffs on.

Another ambulance passes the cordon and is waved forward by the police. Adam can hear the sharp clatter of a helicopter and looks towards the front door to see if Margot is coming out with Katryna.

When the fourth video was received at National Crime, the system spun into action instantly, the way that it should.

One of the technicians was a good friend of Adam Youssef. He recognised Katryna on the film and issued immediate emergency information on the National Crime intranet, then called Adam.

To save time and maintain tactical efficiency, a so-called 'special event' was declared, and the various divisions within the police coordinated their efforts as rapidly as possible.

The alarm was sounded on police radio covering the Southern and Western Police Districts, as well as the City Centre, Nacka and Södertörn.

The officer closest to Bultvägen 5 was a plain-clothes detective rather than a patrol car. He was on the scene just seven minutes after the video was received by the police.

93

It feels like an eternity before Adam sees Margot again. She's walking slowly, holding the handrail, then stops with her hand round her stomach. Her nose is pale and her forehead is shiny with sweat as she walks towards him out in the street.

'Get those fucking handcuffs off,' she says with barely suppressed anger to the police officers.

They hurry to free Adam. He massages his wrists and looks into her eyes, sees her dilated pupils and feels a wave of nausea rise in his stomach.

'What's going on?' he asks in a frightened voice.

She shakes her head, comes closer, glances quickly towards the house and then looks back at him again.

'Adam, I'm sorry, I can't tell you how sorry I am.'

'What for?' he asks stiffly, opening the car door.

'Sit down,' she says.

But he gets out of the car and stops in front of her, with a peculiar feeling of being completely weightless.

'Is it Katryna?' he asks. 'Just tell me. Is she hurt?'

'Katryna's dead.'

'I saw her in the doorway, I saw her . . .'

'Adam,' she pleads.

'Are you sure? Have you spoken to the paramedics?'

She hugs him, but he pulls free, takes a step back, and sees some heavy blackberries swaying on a thin branch.

'I'm so terribly sorry,' she says again.

'You're sure she's dead? I mean, the ambulance . . . what's the ambulance doing here if she's . . .?'

'Katryna will stay here until the forensic examination of the scene is complete.'

'Is she in the hall? Can you tell me where she is?'

'In the boiler room, she must have hidden in the boiler room.'

Adam looks at her and the pain in his thigh is suddenly throbbing, all-encompassing. He watches all the police officers leave the house and gather for a debriefing over by the command vehicle.

A flash of insight passes through his mind. His wife was almost safe, but he shot the police officer who was on his way out with her.

'I shot a colleague,' he says.

'Don't think about that now . . . you're sleeping at mine tonight, I'll call the boss.'

She tries to take hold of his arm but he turns away.

'I need to be alone . . . sorry, I . . .'

The helicopter is hovering a short distance away, over the sports ground, it looks like.

'Did they get the preacher?' he asks.

'Adam, we're going to get him, he's in the area, we're deploying everything we've got, absolutely everything.'

He nods a few times, then turns away again.

'Just give me a moment,' he whispers, takes a few steps and picks at the branch of a bush.

'You have to stay here,' Margot says.

Adam looks at her for a few seconds, then begins to wander slowly out into the garden. He's holding his face, pretending to try to absorb what she's said, but he knows he needs to see Katryna, because he doesn't believe them, it can't be true, it isn't true, Katryna has nothing to do with this.

Adam starts walking round the house. The green hose is lying in the unmown grass. A swarm of gnats is visible in the shimmering blue light. It gets darker when he reaches the back of the house.

Adam sees himself as a black silhouette in the red dome of the round barbeque. He goes round the corner and sees that the cellar door is open. The rope has been cut. He goes inside. The lights are all on down there.

He can hear people walking about upstairs. A forensics officer is laying out walking plates.

Adam takes another step in, and that's when he sees Katryna in the cold neon light of the boiler room. She's sitting leaning against the boiler, and there's blood everywhere, on her sweatpants, her vest, the floor. Her hair is tucked behind one ear, but most of her face is gone, hacked off. Dark blood glints across the whole of her ribcage, and her left hand appears to be squeezing the fingers of her right hand.

Adam staggers backwards, hears the sound of his own breathing, knocks over a packet of washing powder, stumbles over his own wellington boots, and emerges into the garden again.

He's gasping for breath, but can't get enough air into his lungs, and starts poking at his mouth.

Nothing is comprehensible any more.

The alarm was sounded half an hour ago, and now everything is irrevocable.

Adam turns to walk back and is just passing the compost heap when he hears a branch creak in the forest. An officer comes round the corner of the house and calls for him, but he carries on in amongst the trees, following the sound of someone moving in there.

Behind him the floodlights are switched on, flooding his home and garden with light. The trunks of the trees shine grey, as if they were covered by a layer of ash. As if he were in an underground forest.

Twenty metres in stands a man, looking at him. Their eyes meet between the gently glowing stems, and it takes Adam a few seconds to realise who the man in front of him is.

The psychiatrist, Erik Maria Bark.

It's like a lightning flash in his head when he realises everything. Awareness hits him like an axe striking a block of wood.

Adam reaches down and pulls the little pistol from his ankle. There's a rasping sound as the velcro comes loose. He feeds a bullet into the chamber, raises the pistol and fires.

The shot hits the top of a branch in front of Erik's face and is deflected, splinters fly up and he sees the psychiatrist flinch.

His hand is shaking, he tries to aim lower, the psychiatrist moves backwards and he fires again. The shot simply disappears, as dark branches sway between the two of them.

He sees the psychiatrist run, crouching down, then slide down a slope and vanish behind a thick tree trunk. Adam follows, but he can no longer see him. He runs straight into some fir branches. Police officers who have heard his shots come running from the garden and the entire edge of the forest is suddenly full of bright light.

'Put your gun down!' someone calls out. 'Adam, put your gun down!'
Adam turns round and raises his arms.

'The killer's still in the forest!' he gasps. 'It's the hypnotist, it's the
fucking hypnotist!'

94

Erik takes a deep breath and stares up at the night sky and dark tree-tops. He must have passed out after he fell. His back is hurting badly. He knows he scraped himself as he slid down the slope.

He stands up and reaches his hand out to the wet rock face. He can smell moss and ferns, and looks up to see the glow of bright lights flickering through the trees above.

He crouches down and pushes his way through the undergrowth, holding a branch out of the way and moving away from the slope.

The distant sound of dogs barking merges with the clattering noise of an approaching helicopter.

Erik followed the preacher down a narrow path, but it grew so dark as the trees became thicker that he lost track of him. He stood for a while and listened, but heard nothing more than the wind through the branches high above him. In the end he decided to go back to the car and wait there, when sirens from a number of emergency vehicles all seemed to converge somewhere on the road on the far side of the woodland.

He began to walk in that direction instead, thinking that Joona must have put the police on the right track, that they may even have caught the preacher.

The forest was overgrown and rocky, and it took him time to make his way through in the dark, but after a while he could make out flashing blue-grey lights between the trees, and suddenly he was standing in front of Adam Youssef from the National Criminal Investigation Department.

Adam looked me in the eyes and fired, Erik thinks as he runs down a slope. What's happened? What happened at the Zone after I left?

Loose stones slide under his feet and he almost falls, grabs a branch with his hand and cuts himself on something. He feels his palm grow wet with blood and stops, gasping, trying to calm his breathing as he hears the helicopter above the treetops again.

Do they think he's involved in the murders because he didn't tell the whole truth about knowing the victims?

Erik thinks about how he lied to the police, how he withheld Rocky's alibi and kept quiet about what Björn said under hypnosis.

The helicopter hovers above the forest, searching with spotlights, getting closer and closer. He needs to hide. Branches rustle, treetops sway, leaves come loose and swirl through the air.

He can feel the clattering of the rotors inside him. Erik presses against a tree, standing absolutely still as the branches lash around him.

This is completely mad, Erik thinks, feeling the whirling air tug at his clothes.

I was very nearly shot.

Dry earth and fallen pine needles fly up into his face.

The helicopter sweeps on, and the searchlight moves away through the forest, flickering through the tree trunks.

He's the person they're hunting.

In a few rays of light some twenty metres away he sees two heavily armed response unit officers with helmets, bulletproof vests and green assault rifles.

One of them turns in Erik's direction just as the light of the helicopter reaches him through the canopy of trees.

Adrenalin shoots through Erik's blood like an injection of ice.

A shot fires just as everything goes dark again. He see the flare of the barrel as the bullet slams into the tree trunk immediately above his head.

The sound of the shot echoes off the rocks.

The helicopter rises up and the clattering sound is deafening.

Erik rushes at a crouch across a clearing without looking back, sliding down on his backside, running through dense undergrowth, until he can see streetlights through the branches.

He carries on, approaching the road with caution. A car drives past and some distance away he can see a roadblock, spike strips, patrol cars and officers in black uniforms.

Erik hides behind some bushes, his back wet with sweat. The uniformed officers are close now. He can hear them talking into their radios, then they walk away, in the other direction, towards the command vehicle with its black windows.

The helicopter makes another circuit of the woodland. The sound echoes hard between the houses along the road. Erik slides down into the ditch and climbs up the other side, not looking at the police, and walks straight across the tarmac road. He hurries through two crooked gates next to a rusty turnstile, and follows a path leading to Västberga School's playing field. A red running track forms a huge ellipsis round a football pitch, and the floodlights on their tall poles are illuminated.

Erik's heart is beating so hard that it hurts his throat as he picks up one of the footballs by the fence behind the goal and walks over the touchline. He heads slowly across the pitch, in the middle of the lights, kicking the ball in front of him.

As he reaches the centre circle the helicopter flies over again. He doesn't look up, just keeps kicking the football ahead of him.

With every metre the distance between him and the police is growing. With the ball at his feet he makes his way across the whole playing field.

The helicopter is already a long way away when Erik kicks the ball into the goal, crosses the track, climbs over the gate and emerges on to a road where the traffic appears to be flowing perfectly normally. He passes Telefonplan underground station, and is still heading away from the police operation when Joona Linna calls him.

'Joona, what's going on?' Erik asks, trying to keep his voice steady. 'The police are hunting me with a helicopter, they've tried to shoot me. This is crazy, I haven't done anything, I was just following the preacher . . .'

'Hang on, Erik, just hold on . . . Where are you now? Are you safe?'

'I don't know, I'm walking along an empty street, past Telefonplan . . . I don't understand any of this.'

'You followed the preacher to Adam's home,' Joona says. 'His wife is the latest victim, she's dead.'

'No . . .' Erik gasps.

'They're all panicking,' Joona says darkly. 'They seem to think you're guilty of the murder because—'

'So talk to them!' Erik interrupts.

'You were seen near the house right after the murder.'

'Yes, but if I—'

Erik falls silent as he hears a car approaching. He ducks into a doorway and turns his back to the street.

'Can't I just hand myself in?' he asks once the car has gone.

'Not without a plan,' Joona replies.

'You don't trust the police?' Erik asks.

'They just tried to shoot you,' Joona says. 'And if that wasn't a mistake, then there are people in the force who are out for revenge.'

Erik runs his hands through his wet hair, struggling to understand all the improbable things that have happened over the past few days.

'What are my options?' he asks in the end. 'What do you think I should do?'

'If you can let me have a bit of time, I'll try to find out what's happening with the police operation,' Joona says. 'I'll find out what they're saying about you internally, and if there's a safe way for you to come in.'

'OK.'

'But you need to lie low,' Joona says.

'How do I do that? What do I do?'

'They've already got your car, you can't go home, you can't go to any of your friends. Ditch your phone after this conversation, because you know they can track it even when it's switched off. They're probably tracing it now, so we don't have much time.'

'I understand.'

Sweat is running down Erik's cheeks as he tries to listen to Joona's advice.

'Find a cash machine and take some money out, as much as you can, this is your only chance to do that . . . But before you withdraw the money you need to work out how to get to another part of town quickly, because they'll be ready if you make the slightest mistake.'

'OK.'

'Buy a used pay-as-you-go phone and call me so I've got the number,' Joona goes on. 'Don't contact anyone else, and go and sleep in a shelter that won't demand any ID.'

'After this, everyone's going to believe I'm guilty,' Erik says.

'Only until I find the preacher,' Joona replies.

'If I can get a chance to hypnotise Rocky, I know I could find out the sort of details that—'

'That's no longer possible,' Joona interrupts. 'He's back in custody.'

95

When Joona gets back to his old room early the next morning, Margot is sitting behind her desk wearing a T-shirt with the text 'Guys with trucks are not lesbians'. Her thick plait has almost come unravelled, she has dark rings under her eyes and deep lines around her mouth.

'I've been to an emergency meeting of senior officers,' she tells him, helping herself to a bag of sweets. 'The regional police chief, Carlos, Annika from the National Police Board. The preliminary investigation is now top priority, we're getting a lot more resources . . . A national alert has been issued, and they're preparing for a press conference tomorrow.'

'How's Adam?' Joona asks.

'I don't know, he's been relieved of duty, doesn't want to see a counsellor . . . he's got his family round him, but . . .'

'Terrible,' Joona says.

Joona hopes Erik has taken his advice to destroy his phone immediately after their conversation.

During the large police and emergency services operation at Sofa Zone in Högdalen they had to charter a bus to take all the people they'd apprehended to the custody unit in Huddinge while they waited for a decision from the prosecutor about arrests. The high number of dead and injured were assumed to be the victims of a bloody power-struggle in the criminal underworld.

One of the men taken into custody for possession of narcotics was Rocky Kyrklund. He had eleven capsules each containing 250 milligrams of 30 per cent heroin hidden in his clothes.

'We saw the murderer at the Zone. Erik followed him to Katryna,' Joona says, leaning forward.

'How do you know that?'

'Erik didn't do it,' Joona says.

'Joona,' Margot sighs. 'You can discuss this with me. I know the two of you are friends, but be careful when you see the others.'

'They need to know that he's innocent.'

'You don't want it to be Erik, but perhaps he's been deceiving you,' she says patiently.

'I saw a man in a yellow raincoat at the Zone, and remembered what Filip Cronstedt said about yellow oilskins . . . Erik followed him, and ended up at Adam's.'

'So how do you explain the fact that he knew all the victims, including Katryna?' Margot says, holding his gaze.

'When did he meet her?'

'She was with us one time when Adam and I were round at his,' she replies. 'And Susanna Kern worked at the Karolinska as a nurse, she was on a course where Erik was one of the lecturers . . . We've got security camera footage of him talking to her.'

Joona gestures with his hand as if to say that the information is irrelevant.

'So why would Erik be known as the preacher?' he asks.

'He's smart, he's tricked you . . . he can make Rocky remember anything he wants him to.'

'Why?'

'Joona, I don't know everything yet, but Erik has been close to the investigation, and has been hampering our progress . . . We've finally got a witness statement from Björn Kern and it's very clear that Erik didn't tell us that Susanna's body was posed with her hand over her ear.'

'Did he see that when he was hypnotised?'

'Erik knew the information about the ear would lead us to Rocky, and then to him, and—'

'That doesn't make sense, Margot.'

'And Erik visited Rocky at Karsudden a few days before I asked him to go.'

Joona's eyes turn cold as ice as he puts his hand on the folder.

'This isn't evidence,' he says. 'You know that, don't you?'

'It's enough to bring him into custody, and enough for a search warrant, enough for a national alert,' she replies stiffly.

'It sounds to me like he's been conducting his own investigations, and the rest is just coincidence.'

'He fits the perpetrator profile. He's divorced, single, has a history of substance abuse, and—'

'So have half the police force,' Joona interrupts.

'The murders are extremely voyeuristic . . . we know that Erik is obsessed with filming his patients, even under hypnosis, when they don't know anything about it.'

'That's just to stop him having to take notes.'

'But he's got thousands of hours in his archive, and . . . and a stalker is almost always slow, methodical . . . The investment in time is part of the ownership process, part of the quasi-relationship that develops.'

'Margot, I hear what you're saying, but could you at least entertain the possibility that Erik is innocent?' Joona asks.

'That's possible, certainly,' she replies honestly.

'In which case you also have to consider the possibility that we're losing sight of the real murderer, the one we're calling the preacher.'

She forces herself to look away from him and glances at the time.

'The meeting's about to start,' she says, getting to her feet.

'I can find the preacher if you want me to,' Joona says.

'We've already got him,' she replies.

'I need my gun, I need all the material, the reports from the crime scenes, the post-mortems.'

'I really shouldn't agree to that,' she says, opening the door.

'And can you arrange for me to see Rocky Kyrklund in prison?' Joona asks.

'You don't give up, do you?' she says with a smile.

They walk slowly along the corridor together. Margot stops Joona outside the meeting room.

'Bear in mind that the people waiting in here are Adam's colleagues,' she says with her fingers on the door handle. 'The tone of the meeting is likely to be pretty tough, they need to vent their anger. It's their way of showing their support for him, and the force as a whole.'

96

Joona follows Margot into the large meeting room. She makes a gesture that simultaneously say hello to everyone and tells them to remain seated.

'Before we start . . . I know emotions are running high at the moment, and we're a tolerant bunch, but I'd still like to encourage everyone to stick to a civilised tone,' she says. 'The preliminary investigation is entering a new phase, and will now be actively led by the prosecutor while we focus on making a quick arrest.'

She stops and catches her breath.

'But our bosses have asked me to bring in Joona Linna, seeing as he is the homicide detective with the best results . . . there's no contest, frankly, and . . .'

A few of the officers clap while others sit there staring at the table.

'Naturally he won't be officially involved in the preliminary investigation, but I hope he'll be able to give the rest of us mere mortals a few tips along the way,' Margot jokes, even though her eyes show no sign of amusement.

Joona takes a steps forward and looks at his former colleagues seated around the pale wooden table before speaking:

'Erik is no murderer.'

'What the fuck?' Petter mutters.

'Let's hear him out,' Margot says curtly.

'I appreciate that there's a lot of evidence pointing at Erik . . . and he should certainly be brought in for questioning, but seeing as I'm here to tell you what I think—'

'Joona, I just want to say that I've had a meeting with the prosecutor,' Benny says. 'Her opinion is that we have very compelling evidence.'

'The puzzle isn't finished just because three pieces fit together.'

'For fuck's sake, Erik was there,' Benny goes on, 'outside the house.

We found his car, he knows the victims, he's lied to the police, et cetera, et cetera.'

'I understand that you've already shot at him with live ammunition,' Joona says.

'He's regarded as extremely dangerous and probably armed,' Benny says.

'But it's all a mistake,' Joona says, pulling out a chair.

He sits down at the table and leans back in his chair, making it creak.

'We're going to bring Erik in,' Margot says. 'And he'll be remanded in custody and given a fair trial.'

'Try catching a will-o'-the-wisp,' Joona says quietly, thinking how the law is doomed never to achieve justice.

'What's he talking about?' Benny asks.

'The fact that you're directing your own fears against an innocent man, because—'

'We're not fucking afraid,' Petter interrupts.

'Calm down,' Margot says.

'I'm not going to sit here and listen to—'

'Petter,' she warns.

The room falls silent. Magdalena Ronander fills her glass of water and tries to catch Joona's eye.

'Joona, maybe you're thinking slightly differently because you're no longer a police officer,' she says. 'I don't mean anything negative, but that might be why we don't understand what you're saying.'

'I'm saying that you're letting the real murderer get away,' Joona replies.

'Right, that's enough of this bullshit,' Benny roars, slamming both hands down on the table.

'Is he drunk?' someone whispers.

'Joona doesn't give a shit about the force, and he doesn't give a shit about us,' Petter says in a loud voice. 'There's so much fucking talk about him, I don't get it. Look at him, he dropped his fucking gun, it was his fault Adam got shot, and now—'

'Maybe it would be best if you left,' Margot says, putting a hand on Joona's shoulder.

'And now he comes here and tries to tell us how to run an investigation,' Petter concludes.

'One more thing,' Joona says, standing up.

'Just shut up,' Petter snaps.

'Let him speak,' Magdalena says.

'I've seen this plenty of times,' Joona says. 'When family, friends or colleagues are directly affected, it's easy to start thinking of revenge.'

'Are you trying to say that we aren't going to act professionally?' Benny asks with a cold smile.

'I'm saying that there's a chance that Erik will contact me, and I'd like to be able to offer him safe passage,' Joona says seriously. 'So that he dares to turn himself in and have his innocence proven in court.'

'Of course,' Magdalena replies, looking at the others. 'That's right, isn't it?'

'But if it's true that you've already fired at him – how am I supposed to convince him to hand himself in?'

'Just tell him we guarantee his safety,' Benny says.

'And if that isn't enough?' Joona says.

'Lie better,' he grins.

'Joona, have you actually seen the pictures of Katryna?' Petter says agitatedly. 'I can't believe it's even her . . . What do I say to my wife? This is so fucking sick . . . I mean, think about Adam, think about what he's going through right now . . . I have to say, I personally don't give a shit what happens to your friend.'

'Everyone's upset,' Margot says. 'Obviously, we want to make it easier for him to hand himself in, and naturally, he'll get a fair trial—'

'Assuming he doesn't hang himself in his cell before then,' says a young officer who has been quiet up to now.

'That's enough,' Magdalena says.

'Or swallows some broken glass,' Benny mutters.

Joona pushes his chair back and nods towards the others.

'I'll be in touch when I've found the real killer,' he says, and leaves the room.

'He's totally fucking pathetic,' Petter mutters as his steps fade away down the corridor.

'Before we go on I want to say something,' Margot begins. 'Like you, I believe that Erik is the murderer, but if we all take a step back . . . Can we even entertain the possibility that we might be wrong, that Erik is actually innocent?'

'Aren't you supposed to be giving birth soon?' Benny asks sarcastically.

'I'll give birth when I'm done with this case,' she replies drily.

'Let's get to work,' Magdalena says.

'OK . . . This is how things stand at the moment,' Margot says. 'We've issued a national alert, but we know that Erik's got enough money to leave the country . . . We've started our searches, of both Erik's home and his place of work . . . We're trying to trace his mobile phone . . . his bank cards have been blocked, but he managed to withdraw a large amount last night . . . the area around the cash machine is being searched . . . We're watching five addresses, and . . .'

She tails off when there's a knock at the door. Anja Larsson enters the room. Without acknowledging the others she leans over and has a whispered conversation with Margot.

'OK,' Margot says after a while. 'It looks like we've managed to trace Erik's mobile. He's somewhere close to Växjö, in Småland. It looks like he's heading south.'

97

Erik is lying wrapped up in the grey cover he took from a parked motorbike. He wakes up, freezing. It's light now, and he realises he's underneath an amelanchier in a thicket of ornamental shrubs. He must have slept for three hours, and his body feels tight with cold. His whole body aches as he sits up and looks around. A dark bronze woman in old-fashioned clothes stares blindly at him from her plinth.

The sun is shining off the green leaves, sparkling in the cold.

Erik climbs over a red fence and crosses over to the shaded side of the street. He slowly warms up as he walks. He can't really believe everything that happened yesterday.

He was heading towards Aspudden on foot when he spoke to Joona, who told him to get rid of his phone. Erik ducked into a doorway, copied down the most important numbers in his contacts, then switched his phone off.

In front of a bike shop on Hägerstensvägen he found a bus with the word 'Smålandsbussen' on the side. A group of weary-looking youngsters in crumpled clothes was gathered on the pavement. Parents were helping to unload rucksacks and sleeping bags from the open baggage compartments.

Erik went inside the bus, pretending to look for something that had been left behind, and quickly pushed his mobile down between two seats.

He stepped out of the rear door, grabbed a cap from a case and tucked it inside his jacket, then carried on towards the underground station. He stopped at the cashpoint in front of the Nordea Bank. He didn't look up, but was aware of the security camera as he withdrew the maximum amount possible from his account. Then he walked back towards the bus again, and watched as the doors closed and it drove off.

Only a couple of youngsters were left on the pavement.

Erik pulled on the baseball cap as he hurried along Södertäljevägen, crossed the Liljeholmen Bridge, bought water and a large hamburger from the Zinkensgrillen kiosk, and headed into a back street where he stood in a doorway and ate. When he was done he carried on walking, steering clear of main streets with banks and traffic surveillance cameras, and just kept walking for as long as he could, until he eventually found himself in Vitabergsparken.

Erik runs his fingers through his hair to flatten it. His clothes are creased but not dirty enough to attract attention. He needs to stay hidden until he can talk to Joona. He daren't take any risks, even if the misunderstanding has hopefully been cleared up by now.

Erik starts to cross the street but stops abruptly between two parked cars when he happens to see a convenience store.

His stomach gurgles with unease.

Among the notification of lottery wins and adverts for the football pools, the flysheets of the evening tabloids scream: POLICE HUNT SWEDISH SERIAL KILLER.

He recognises himself from the pixelated photograph. In accordance with press ethics they have kept his identity hidden. It's only a matter of time, but for the moment his features are concealed by a mass of grainy squares.

The early edition of the other tabloid has no picture, but the headline covers the whole flysheet in capital letters:

NATIONAL ALARM – SWEDISH PSYCHIATRIST SOUGHT FOR FOUR MURDERS.

Under the headline the paper's contents are listed: victims, pictures, brutality, police.

He steps up on to the pavement and passes the shop as it gradually dawns on him the police really do believe that he murdered Katryna and the other women.

He's the man they're hunting.

Erik turns into a side street and his legs start to shake so badly that he has to slow down and eventually stop. He stands there, clutching a trembling hand to his mouth.

'Oh, God,' he whispers.

Everyone Erik knows will work out that he's the man being referred to when they read the articles. Right now they'll be calling each other, shocked, excited, disgusted.

Some of them will be full of schadenfreude, others will be sceptical. It feels like he's falling, but somehow he's still standing.

Benjamin will know it isn't true, Erik thinks, and starts walking again. But Madeleine will be frightened once his real identity starts to be blared out.

Through an open car window he catches fragments of a conversation in which he imagines he hears his own name mentioned.

Erik thinks that he's going to have to hand himself over to the justice system after all, so that he can defend himself.

This can't go on.

He pulls out a blister-pack containing four Mogadon pills, presses one into his hand, but changes his mind and throws the whole lot in a rubbish bin.

On Östgötagatan he finds a small shop selling second-hand mobile phones. While he's waiting to be served he listens to the news on the radio. A neutral voice explains coolly that the hunt for the suspected serial killer is now in its second day.

His stomach contracts as if he were about to be sick when he hears the voice say that an arrest warrant has been issued for a psychiatrist at the Karolinska Hospital on reasonable suspicion of having murdered four women in the Stockholm area.

The police are saying little otherwise, out of consideration for the ongoing investigation, but are hoping to receive further information from the public.

The man behind the counter, with the arm of his glasses held together by a piece of tape, asks how he can help, and Erik tries to smile as he explains that he'd like a pay-as-you-go mobile.

A senior police officer is explaining about the resources that have been deployed in the search, and how this has already given positive results.

Erik changes direction as soon as he leaves the shop. He switches streets a number of times, but is aiming to leave the centre of the city via Danvikstull.

He doesn't dare stop and take out the phone before he's passed the Tram Museum. He stands facing a yellow brick building and calls Joona Linna.

'Joona, this is impossible,' he says quickly. 'Have you seen the papers? I can't keep on hiding.'

'You have to give me more time.'

'No, I've made up my mind. I want you to arrest me and take me to the police.'

'I can't guarantee your safety.'

'I don't care,' he says.

'I've never seen the police so cut up, and not just Adam's colleagues. It's right across the board,' Joona says. 'It's one thing to risk your own life, you're aware of that when you enter operational service, but violence of this sort, directed at a police officer's wife . . .'

'You have to tell them I didn't do this, you—'

'I have, but they've linked you to each of the victims, and you were seen at the crime scene . . .'

'What do I do?' Erik whispers.

'Stay hidden until I find the preacher,' Joona replies. 'I'm going to talk to Rocky, he's in custody in Huddinge Prison.'

'I could hand myself over to one of the evening tabloids,' Erik says, aware of how desperate he sounds. 'I could tell my own story, my version, and then I'd have journalists with me when I went to the police.'

'Erik, even if that was possible, they're already talking about your suicide in custody, about you hanging yourself or swallowing a piece of glass before the trial . . . It's all a lot of talk, but I don't want you to take the risk right now.'

'I'll call Nelly, she knows me, she knows I can't have done this—'

'You can't do that. The police are watching her house . . . you need to find someone else you can stay hidden with, someone more distant, unexpected.'

Erik and Joona end the call. The cars are standing still, the bridge is being opened. Three sailing boats are on their way out to the Baltic.

98

Huddinge Prison is one of the largest secure facilities in the Swedish judicial system. Rocky Kyrklund is only suspected of basic narcotics offences and is therefore not subject to any particular restrictions, but he is regarded as a high escape risk.

The prison is a vast V-shaped, brown-brick building, with an entrance flanked by tall pillars. At the rear are two wings shaped like fans, each of whose top floors contain eight individual exercise areas.

Rocky is the only person who knows who the unclean preacher is. He's met him, spoken to him, and has seen him kill.

Joona has to hand over his keys and phone at the security check. They X-ray his shoes and jacket, and he is searched after passing through the metal detector. A black-and-white cocker spaniel circles him, sniffing for explosives and drugs.

The prison officer waiting for him at the door introduces himself as Arne Melander. As they head towards the lifts he tells Joona that he's a competitive angler, that he came third in the Swedish coarse fishing championships at the start of the summer, and that he's heading to the Fyris River at the weekend.

'I went for bottom fishing,' Arne explains, pressing the lift button. 'And used pink- and bronze-coloured maggots.'

'Sounds good,' Joona says seriously.

Arne smiles, his cheeks lift and grow rounder. He has a large grey beard and is wearing glasses and a dark-blue Nato sweater that's stretched tight across his big stomach.

His baton and alarm swing from his belt as they leave the lift and pass through the security doors. Joona waits quietly as the prison officer pulls his card through the reader and taps in the code.

They say hello to the duty officer, a white-haired man with a lazy eye and thin lips.

'We're running a bit late today,' the duty officer says. 'Kyrklund has just gone out for some air. But we can check if he wants to come back in.'

'Please do,' Joona says.

After the murder of prison officer Karen Gebreab the rules have been tightened, and no member of staff is allowed to be alone with any of their clients. The inmates are often desperate, in a state of upheaval after their crimes, the humiliation of their arrest, and the recognition of their failure in life.

Joona watches Arne Melander as he stands a little way off talking into a communications radio. He stares at the bare walls, the doors, the shiny linoleum floor and the coded locks.

Huddinge prison is evidently high security, totally enclosed, with reinforced doors and walls, entrance checks and camera surveillance. But the staff are only armed with batons.

Maybe they've got teargas or pepper spray, but no guns, Joona thinks.

A few years before Police Academy Joona was picked to join the paratroopers' newly formed special ops unit, where he was trained in military Krav Maga, with a particular focus on urban warfare and innovative weaponry.

He still finds himself automatically scanning for potential weapons each time he enters a room.

He's already spotted the stainless steel skirting boards and door-lintels in the prison.

The grooves on the heads of the screws have been planed off so they can't be removed with ordinary tools, but the boards have started to drop towards the floor with the passage of time. Maybe the food trolleys have caught on them, or perhaps the floor-cleaner.

Joona has noticed that some of the skirting boards could be nudged off with his foot. If you wrapped your hands in some cloth, you could pull the whole length of skirting board off, bend it twice, and in twenty seconds create a sort of noose that could be wrapped round an opponent's neck and tightened using the protruding lengths of metal.

Joona remembers the Dutch lieutenant, Rinus Advocaat, a sinuous man with a scarred face and dead eyes, who demonstrated that sort of weapon, and showed how to control your enemy's movements and basically decapitate him by tightening the noose.

'He's on his way,' Arne says amiably to Joona.

Rocky is walking behind two prison officers. He's wearing pale green prison overalls and sandals, and has a cigarette tucked behind his ear.

'Thanks for cutting short your time outside,' Joona says, walking towards him.

'I don't like cages much anyway,' Rocky says, and clears his throat. 'Why not?'

'Good question,' he replies, and shoots Joona an interested glance.

'You're booked into a monitored interview room, number eleven,' Arne tells Joona. 'So I'll be sitting on the other side of the glass.'

'I remember the crayfish pots when I was little, at night . . . It's around this time of year,' Rocky says.

They stop outside the door while Arne unlocks it.

'I used to shine my torch at the crayfish, and using just the beam I could force them into the pots,' Rocky goes on.

Interview room 11 is shabby, and contains a table, four chairs, and an internal phone to summon the prison staff.

The legs of the chairs are supposed to be unbreakable, but if you were to lay one of them on the floor, climb up on to the table and jump on to the curved back, the laminate would shatter and you could quickly fashion a shiv, a simple knife, out of it, Joona thinks.

'So the guard can see me through glass?' Rocky asks, nodding towards the dark window.

'It's just a security precaution.'

'But you're not frightened of me?' Rocky smiles.

'No,' Joona replies calmly.

The thickset priest sits down and his chair creaks beneath him.

'Have we met before?' he asks with a frown.

'At the Zone,' Joona says evenly.

'At the Zone,' Rocky repeats. 'Should I know where that is?'

'It was where the police arrested you.'

Rocky screws up his eyes and gazes into the distance.

'I don't remember any of that . . . They say I had a load of heroin on me, but how could I have afforded that?'

'You don't remember the Zone? Sofa Zone in Högdalen?'

Rocky purses his lips and shakes his head.

'An industrial unit with loads of sofas and armchairs, prostitutes, people openly dealing heavy drugs, guns . . .'

'Well, I've got a neurological injury from a car crash, I have trouble remembering things,' Rocky explains.

'I know.'

'But you want me to confess to the drugs offences?'

'I don't care about that,' Joona says, sitting down opposite him. 'You only have to say it wasn't your jacket, that you picked up a jacket you found on the floor.'

Neither of them speaks for a short while, and Rocky stretches out his long legs.

'So you want something else,' he says warily.

'You've mentioned a person you call the unclean preacher several times . . . I need your help to identify him.'

'Have I met this preacher?'

'Yes . . .'

'Is he a priest?'

'I don't know.'

Rocky scratches his beard and neck.

'I've no idea,' he says after a while.

'You described how he killed a woman called Natalia Kaliova, he chopped her arm off,' Joona goes on.

'A preacher . . .'

'He was the one who murdered Rebecka Hansson.'

'What the hell are you up to?' Rocky roars and stands up suddenly, toppling his chair behind him. 'I murdered Rebecka Hansson. Do you think I'm stupid or something?'

Rocky backs away, stumbles over the overturned chair and almost falls, throws his arm out and plants his large hand on the reinforced glass.

The prison officer comes in but Joona holds up a calming hand towards him as he sees several more guards running along the corridor.

'We don't believe you did it,' Joona says. 'Do you remember Erik Maria Bark?'

'The hypnotist?' Rocky says, licking his lips and brushing his hair back.

'He's found a woman who can give you an alibi.'

'And I'm supposed to believe that?'

'Her name is Olivia,' Joona says.

'Olivia Toreby,' Rocky says slowly.

'You started to remember under hypnosis . . . and everything suggests that you were convicted of a murder that the preacher committed.'

Rocky comes closer to him.

'But you don't know who this preacher is?' he asks.

'No,' Joona replies.

'Because everything is locked inside my mashed-up brain,' Rocky says hollowly.

'Would you agree to be hypnotised again?'

'Wouldn't you if you were in my position?' he asks, and sits down again.

'Yes,' Joona replies honestly.

Rocky opens his mouth to say something, but falls silent and puts his hand to his forehead. One of his eyes has started to quiver, the pupil seems to be vibrating, and he leans forward, holding on to the table and breathing hard.

'Bloody hell,' he says after a while, and looks up.

His forehead is shiny with sweat, and he gazes up at Joona and the prison officers that have entered the room with a look of dreamy bemusement.

99

Joona stops District Prosecutor Sara Nielsen in the middle of the steps outside the district court on Scheelegatan. Because he can't take Erik with him into the prison, he needs to persuade the prosecutor to release Rocky on bail in advance of his trial.

'I called you about Kyrklund,' he says, standing in front of her. 'He can't stay in prison.'

'That's for the district court to decide,' she replies.

'But I don't understand why,' Joona persists.

'Buy a book on Swedish law.'

A strand of blonde hair blows across Sara's face, and she brushes it aside with one finger and raises her eyebrows as Joona starts to speak.

'According to chapter twenty-four, paragraph twenty,' he says, 'a prosecutor can revoke the decision to remand a suspect in custody if that decision is no longer justified.'

'Bravo,' she smiles. 'But there's a clear risk that Kyrklund will evade the course of justice, and a tangible danger that he would commit further offences.'

'But we're only talking about minor narcotics offences, punishable by a year's imprisonment at most . . . and it's extremely doubtful that possession could even be proven.'

'You said it wasn't his jacket over the phone,' she says in a bright voice.

'And that the reason for holding him in custody in no way warrants this degree of intrusion into his life.'

'Suddenly it feels like I'm standing on the steps of the City Court holding fresh custody negotiations with a former police officer . . .'

'I can arrange for supervision,' Joona says, following her down the steps.

'It doesn't work like that, as you well know.'

'I understand that, but he's ill and needs constant medical attention,' Joona says.

She stops and lets her eyes roam over his face.

'If Kyrklund needs a doctor, the doctor can come to prison.'

'But if I were to say that this is a particular treatment that can't be carried out in prison . . .'

'Then I'd say you were lying.'

'I can get a medical certificate,' Joona persists.

'Go ahead, but I'm pressing charges next Tuesday.'

'I'll appeal.'

'Nice try,' she smiles, and starts walking again.

100

Joona is sitting on one of the rear pews in Adolf Fredrik Church. A girls' choir is rehearsing for a concert up at the front. The choir leader gives them the right note and the teenagers start to sing O *viridissima virga*.

Joona sinks into memories of the long, light nights in Nattavaara after Summa's death. Sunlight floods through the arched windows of the church, mixed with autumn leaves and stained glass.

The choir pauses after a few minutes, the girls take out their mobiles, gather in groups and walk through the aisles, chatting as they go.

The door to the porch opens and closes quickly. The churchwarden looks up from her book, then carries on reading.

Margot comes in with two heavy plastic bags in her hands. They hit the pew as she squeezes in next to Joona. Her stomach has swollen so much that it presses again the shelf for hymnbooks.

'I really am sorry,' Margot says in a half-whisper. 'I know you don't want to believe it, but take a look at this.'

With a sigh she lifts one of the bags on to her lap and pulls out a printout showing a fingerprint match. Joona quickly reads through the various parameters of the comparison, then checks the first-level details himself, and sees the similarities in the lines and patterns.

There are three perfectly defined fingerprints, and the match with Erik Maria Bark is one hundred per cent.

'Where were the prints found?' Joona asks.

'On the little porcelain deer's head that was in Susanna Kern's hand.'

Joona gazes out into the nave. The choir is gathering once more, the choir leader claps her hands to get their attention.

'You asked for evidence before,' Margot continues. 'These fingerprints are evidence, aren't they?'

'In a judicial sense,' he says in a low voice.

'The searches are still going on,' she says. 'We've found our serial killer.'

'Have you?'

Margot puts the bag containing material from the preliminary investigation on Joona's lap.

'I really wanted to believe you, and the idea of the preacher,' she says, leaning back and breathing hard.

'You should,' Joona replies.

'You met Rocky, I arranged for you to be able to question him,' she says, with a hint of impatience. 'You said you needed to do that before you could find this unclean preacher.'

'He doesn't remember anything now.'

'Because there isn't anything to remember,' she concludes.

The choir starts singing, and the girls' voices fill the church. Margot tries to make herself more comfortable and tucks her plait over her shoulder.

'You traced Erik to Småland,' Joona says.

'The rapid response team stormed a charter bus and found his phone tucked between two seats.'

'Oops,' Joona says drily.

'He hasn't put a foot wrong so far, he's staying out of the way like a professional,' she says. 'It's almost as if he's been given advice about what to do.'

'I agree,' Joona says.

'Has he contacted you?' Margot asks.

'No,' Joona replies simply.

He looks down at the other bag, still on the floor between them.

'Is that my pistol?'

'Yes,' she replies, pushing the bag towards him with her foot.

'Thanks,' Joona says, gazing down into it.

'If you carry on looking for the preacher, I have to remind you that you're not doing so on my orders,' Margot says, starting to squeeze out of the pew again. 'You haven't received any material from me, and we never met here – do you understand?'

'I'm going to find the murderer,' Joona says quietly.

'Fine, but we can't have any more contact . . .'

Joona pulls out his pistol, under cover of the pew, ejects the magazine in his lap, pulls the bolt back, checks the mechanism, trigger and hammer, then puts the safety catch back on and reinserts the magazine.

'Who the hell uses a Colt Combat?' Margot asks. 'I'd have backache within a week.'

Joona doesn't reply, just tucks the pistol into his shoulder holster and slips the spare magazine in his jacket pocket.

'When are you going to accept that Erik might be guilty?' she asks roughly.

'You'll see that I'm right,' he says, meeting her gaze with icy calmness.

101

Nelly Brandt is sitting at her computer, typing. Her neatly made-up face is blank with concentration as her blonde hair curls softly over her shoulders. She's wearing a beige suede skirt and a gold polo-necked sweater that sits tightly round her body.

When Joona comes in and says hello to her she doesn't answer, just stands up and goes over to the window and picks a deep pink flower from the bush outside.

'There you go,' she says, giving the flower to Joona. 'With my heart-felt thanks for the magnificent detective work—'

'I can understand that—'

'Hang on,' she interrupts. 'I need to pick another one.'

She reaches out and picks a second flower, and hands it to Joona.

'For the whole of the Swedish police force,' she says. 'Fucking impressive . . . No, I'm going to have to go out and dig up the whole bush . . . if you open the boot of your car, then—'

'Nelly, I know the police have got it wrong,' Joona says.

It's as if all the air goes out of her, she sits down at the desk and rests her head on her hands, tries to say something but can't get the words out.

'I'm still trying to find the real murderer,' Joona goes on. 'But I need someone who can take over where Erik left off.'

'I'd be happy to help,' she says, looking up at him.

'Can you hypnotise people?'

'No,' she laughs, taken aback. 'I thought . . . that's not my area, I actually find it a bit creepy.'

'Do you know anyone who could help me?'

She twists the engagement ring on her freckled finger a couple of times and tilts her head.

'Hypnosis is tricky,' she says bluntly. 'But there are a few people with a good reputation . . . Not that that's the same thing as being brilliant. It's like a generally applicable algorithm: the reputation of the best people in any field goes down to compensate for brilliance.'

'You mean there's no one as good as Erik?'

She laughs, flashing her white teeth.

'Nowhere near as good . . . even if he's not exactly doing much for his reputation right now.'

'Is there someone I could talk to?'

'Anna Palmer here is supposed to be pretty good. It depends what you're after. She hasn't got Erik's experience when it comes to psychological trauma and states of shock, of course.'

Nelly leads Joona along the corridor, but after a little while she slows down and asks him if she's in danger.

'I can't answer that,' Joona replies honestly.

'My husband's working late all week.'

'You should ask for police protection.'

'No, not police protection, this is all too much . . . It's just that we noticed that the lock at the back of the house was damaged yesterday.'

'Have you got someone you can go and stay with?'

'Yes, of course,' she says, blushing slightly.

'Do that, until this is over.'

'I'll think about it . . .'

102

Anna Palmer sees Joona in a small, book-lined room. There's a desk, and a narrow window overlooking the hospital grounds. She's a tall woman with short, lead-grey hair and visible veins beneath her eyes.

'I know someone who was in a car accident ten years ago,' Joona begins. 'He suffered fairly severe brain damage . . . This isn't my area, obviously, but the way it's been explained to me, he suffers from ongoing epileptic activity in the temporal lobes of both sides of his brain.'

'That can certainly happen,' she says, jotting down what he says.

'His big problem is his memory,' Joona goes on. 'Short and long-term . . . sometimes he remembers every detail of an event, sometimes he forgets that it ever took place . . . I'm hoping that hypnosis might help him break through the barriers.'

Anna Palmer lowers her notepad and folds her hands on the desk. Joona notices tiny red eczema scabs on her knuckles.

'I don't want to disappoint you,' she says in a weary tone of voice. 'But a lot of people have unrealistic expectations about what hypnosis can be used for.'

'It's very important for this person to remember,' Joona replies.

'Clinical hypnosis . . . is about making suggestions, as a sort of internal self-help . . . and it's nothing to do with revealing truths,' she explains apologetically.

'But this sort of brain injury doesn't mean that his memory has been erased. It's all there, it's just that the path to it is blocked . . . I mean, couldn't hypnosis help him to find a different path?'

'It would certainly be possible to get to that point, if you were very skilful,' she concedes, scratching the red marks on her hands. 'But what do you do when you get there? No one would be able to differentiate between his real memories and his imagination, seeing as his brain can't tell the difference.'

'Are you sure? I mean, we think we can tell the difference between memory and imagination, we're convinced that we can.'

'Because we store certain information together with an awareness that those are genuine memories – like a sort of code, an introductory note, a prefix.'

'So shouldn't that code still be in his brain?' Joona persists.

'But extracting that at the same time as his memories . . .' she says, shaking her head.

'Is there anyone who could do that?'

'No,' she replies, closing her notepad.

'Erik Maria Bark claims he can.'

'Erik is very good at . . . he's probably the best person in the world at putting patients into a state of deep hypnosis, but his research isn't evidence-based,' she says slowly, and there's a glint of something in her eyes.

'Do you believe what the papers have been saying about him?'

'I have no way of judging that . . . But he does have a leaning towards the perverse, the psychotic . . .'

She stops herself.

'Is this conversation actually about him?' she asks bluntly.

'No.'

'But it's not about a friend of yours, is it?'

'It never is . . . I'm a detective with the National Criminal Investigation Department, and I need to question a witness suffering from organic memory loss.'

The corners of Anna Palmer's mouth twitch.

'That would be unethical, seeing as anything said under hypnosis is the opposite of reliable, and has no place in a legal context,' she says curtly.

'This is about detective work, not—'

'I can promise you that no serious practitioner of clinical hypnosis would do this,' she says, raising her voice and looking him in the eye.

103

Erik walks across the bridge at Sickla, with his cap pulled down and his head lowered, then makes his way around the heights of Hammarbybacken, where Benjamin learned to ski, and heads into the forest.

It's practically impossible to move in Stockholm without getting caught on camera. There are speed cameras along the roads, cameras monitoring the boundary of the congestion-charging zone, traffic surveillance cameras at junctions, tunnels and bridges. There are security cameras in shops, trains, buses, ferries and taxis. Twenty-four hours a day, petrol stations, car parks, harbours, terminals, railway stations and platforms are monitored. Banks, department stores, shopping centres, plazas, pedestrianised streets, embassies, police stations, prisons, hospitals, fire stations are all watched.

Erik is extremely tired, and the blisters on the soles of his feet burst as he makes his way through the forest towards Björkhagen.

The sky is growing dark, and Erik feels his legs shake when he stops in the little park behind the house where Nestor, his former patient, lives.

Erik follows the path to a wooden door with a tarnished bronze letterbox. The colour of the building reminds him of wet foam-rubber.

There's a light on in the kitchen on the ground floor.

From here he can see right into Nestor's living room. Erik switches windows and sees Nestor sitting in an armchair.

There's no sign of anyone else in the flat.

Erik's hands are shaking and he feels as though he can't take another step as he rings the front door.

'Can I come in?' he asks as soon as Nestor opens the door.

'This is unexpected,' Nestor mutters. 'I'll p-put some coffee on.'

Nestor lets Erik in, closes and locks the door, then disappears inside the flat. Erik takes his shoes off with a sigh, hangs up his crumpled jacket, and smells his own sweat. His socks have stuck to his bleeding heels and his cold fingertips are itching in the heat of the hallway.

He knows that Nestor lives in the same flat he grew up in. The ceilings are low and the oak parquet floor is so old that the varnish has worn off. There are dog-shaped ornaments everywhere.

Erik walks through the living room. The single cushion on the sofa is threadbare and on the low table are a pair of glasses and a crossword, beside a large figurine of hunting dogs and dead pheasants.

In the kitchen Nestor is setting out cups and a plate of biscuits. There's a frying pan containing sausage and potatoes on the stove.

'You told me I could ask for a favour, anything at all,' Erik says, sitting down at the table.

'Yes,' Nestor says, nodding emphatically.

'Can I stay here for a few days?'

'Here?'

A sceptical, boyish smile flits across Nestor's face.

'What for?'

'I've had a bit of a row with my girlfriend,' Erik lies, leaning back.

'You've got a g-girlfriend?'

'Yes,' Erik replies.

Nestor pours coffee into their cups and says he has a spare room with a guest bed already made up.

'Could I have some of the food that's left over?'

'Of c-course, I'm sorry,' he says, switching the hotplate on.

'You don't have to warm it up for me,' Erik says.

'Don't you want . . .?'

'No, it's fine.'

Nestor scrapes the food on to a plate and puts it in front of Erik before sitting down opposite him.

'Have you thought any more about getting a dog?' Erik asks.

'I n-need to save up some money,' Nestor replies, lifting his coffee-spoon a few millimetres and surreptitiously looking at his reflection.

'Of course,' Erik says as he eats.

'I work over there at the ch-church,' Nestor says, gesturing towards the window.

'At the church?' Erik asks, feeling a shiver spread down his spine.

'Yes . . . well, not really,' Nestor smiles, holding one hand in front of his mouth. 'I w-work in the pet cemetery.'

'The pet cemetery . . .' Erik nods politely, looking at Nestor's slender hands and the yellowing polyester shirt under his pullover.

Erik finishes the food and drinks his coffee as he listens to Nestor telling him about the oldest cemetery for domestic pets in Sweden, over on Djurgården. It was established when the author August Blanche buried his dog there in the nineteenth century.

'I'm b-boring you,' Nestor says, getting to his feet.

'No, I'm tired, that's all,' Erik says.

Nestor goes over to the window and looks out. Black shapes are moving against the paler sky, trees and bushes blowing back and forth.

'It will soon be dark,' Nestor whispers to his reflection.

There are two greyhounds on the windowsill, next to a pot plant. Nestor touches their heads, out of sight of Erik.

'Can I use the bathroom?' Erik asks.

Nestor shows him through the living room, and points to an extra door behind a curtain.

'This is the old c-caretaker's flat, but I think of that d-door as an emergency exit,' he says.

The bathroom has tiles halfway up its walls, with a deep bathtub and a shower curtain with seahorses on it. Erik locks the door and takes his clothes off.

'The red toothbrush is Mother's,' Nestor calls through the door.

Erik stands on the mouldy shower mat in the scratched bathtub, showers and washes the wounds on his body. On top of the bathroom cabinet above the basin is an old light-bulb box. Some lipsticks and a mascara pen stick out from it.

When Erik emerges Nestor is standing in the hall waiting for him. His wrinkled face looks worried.

'I'd really like to t-talk about something . . . it's something that . . .' he begins.

'What is it?'

'I . . . what do I d-do if the new dog dies?'

'We can talk about that tomorrow.'

'I'll show you to the g-guestroom,' Nestor whispers, turning his face away.

They go back into the living room again, past the kitchen to a closed door that Erik hasn't noticed before because it's on the far side of a cupboard.

Above the bed in the spare room is a large poster of Björn Borg kissing the Wimbledon trophy. On the wall opposite is a shelf full of porcelain dogs.

There's an old corner cupboard painted in traditional folk-art style. The top door is decorated with a hand-painted motif: the ages of man, from cradle to grave. A man and woman stand side by side on a bridge where each step represents a decade. On the top step the pair stand tall as fifty-year-olds, but death lurks beneath the bridge in the form of a skeleton with a scythe in his hand.

'That's lovely,' Erik says, looking at Nestor, who is still standing in the living room.

'I sleep in . . . M-mother's room. I moved in there when . . .'

Nestor cranes his neck oddly, as if he wanted to look at someone standing behind him.

'Goodnight,' Erik says.

He takes hold of the door handle to close it, but Nestor puts his hand on the door and looks at him with anxious eyes.

'The r-rich need it, the poor already have it, but you f-fear it more than death,' Nestor whispers.

'I'm a bit too tired for riddles, Nestor.'

'The rich need it, the p-poor already have it, but you fear it more than death,' Nestor repeats, then licks his lips.

'I'll think about the answer,' Erik says, and closes the door. 'Well, goodnight.'

Erik sits down and stares at the hideous wallpaper with its repeated pattern that looks like ornate coats of arms, garlands, peacock feathers, and hundreds of eyes.

The roller-blind is already closed, and he switches the light off and detects a faint smell of lavender as he folds back the heavy covers and gets into bed.

He's so exhausted that all his thoughts drift away and lose their shape. He's just about to tumble over the boundary into sleep when he hears a small creaking sound in the room. Someone is trying to open the door quietly.

'What is it, Nestor?' Erik asks.

'A clue,' the soft voice says. 'I c-can give you a clue.'

'I'm very tired, and—'

'Priests think it's b-bigger than God Himself,' Nestor interrupts.

'Can you close the door, please?'

The handle clicks as Nestor lets go of it and pads away across the parquet in the living room.

Erik falls asleep, and in his dreams little Madeleine is standing by his bed, blowing on his face and whispering the answer to Nestor's riddle.

'Nothing,' she whispers, blowing on him. 'The rich need . . . nothing, the poor have nothing . . . And you fear nothing more than death.'

104

Erik is pulled from sleep by a breeze on his face. Someone is whispering quickly, but stops the moment he opens his eyes. The darkness is almost impenetrable, and it takes him a few seconds before he realises where he is.

The old horsehair mattress creaks when he rolls over.

Even if he was fast asleep, some part of him was alert, a force that yanked him from sleep.

Perhaps he just heard water running through the building's pipes, or the wind pressing against the window.

No one has been whispering in his room, everything is still and dark.

Erik wonders if this was where Nestor was sleeping when he slipped into psychosis, when the rattling of the pipes turned into voices, into the old woman brushing dandruff from her long grey hair who told him you shouldn't look your nearest and dearest in the eye when you kill them.

Erik knows it was all about the dog Nestor was forced to put down when he was a child, but he still used to shiver every time Nestor imitated the woman's creaking voice.

He thinks of the way Nestor used to sit with his hands clasped in his lap and his head lowered, a little smile would play on his lips and he would flush slightly as he dispensed advice on how to murder a child.

The old cupboard creaks and the shadows by the door are hard to interpret. He closes his stinging eyes and goes back to sleep, but wakes up again immediately when the door to the guestroom closes.

Erik thinks that he's going to have to tell Nestor to leave him alone when he's sleeping, that he doesn't have to keep checking on him, but he can't be bothered to get up now.

A car passes on the street outside, and its chill light finds its way past the roller-blind, slides across the patterned wallpaper and disappears.

Erik stares at the wall.

It looks like a trace of the light has been left on the wall once the car has gone. He thinks that there must be a weak lamp by the shelf that he hasn't seen before.

Erik blinks, stares at the motionless blue light, and realises that there's a peephole between the rooms.

The light is coming from the other bedroom, Erik thinks when everything suddenly goes dark.

Nestor is looking on to his room right now.

Erik lies absolutely still.

It's so quiet that he can hear himself swallow.

The blue light becomes visible again and he can hear intense whispering through the wall.

Erik quickly gets dressed in the darkness and moves closer to the light.

The point of light is between the two lower shelves of the bookcase. The little hole would be invisible if the porcelain animals were arranged differently.

It's positioned in the very darkest part of the pattern on the wallpaper, so small that he realises he's going to have to press his face to the wall and put his eye right next to the hole to be able to see anything.

He moves a porcelain puppy in a basket, leans his hands on the wall and carefully puts his head between the shelves, feeling the wood against his hair and the wallpaper touching the tip of his nose.

When he is right next to the hole he can see straight into the next room.

There's a mobile phone on the bedside table, the screen is lit up, illuminating the alarm clock and the oval pattern of the wallpaper. Erik manages to catch a glimpse of the neatly made bed and a framed photograph of a young child in a christening gown before the light from the phone goes out.

He hears rapid footsteps somewhere in the flat and tries to pull his head back, but his hair catches on a splinter in the wood. The porcelain figures tinkle ominously.

Erik puts his hand up and tries to free his hair as the door opens behind him.

He pulls his head out and hears the figurines on the shelf rattle. Nestor comes towards him and he backs away.

'I've called the p-police, I c-came back to tell you,' Nestor whispers. 'It's your t-turn to get h-help now, I've spoken to them several times, they're here now.'

'Nestor, you don't understand,' Erik says forlornly.

'No, no, you d-don't understand,' Nestor interrupts in a friendly voice, and switches on the lamp in the window. 'I said it's your t-turn to get medicine and—'

There's a sudden noise, like a stone hitting the window, the dark roller-blind quivers in the light from the lamp, and a cascade of glass falls down behind the blind and tinkles over the radiator.

Nestor lurches. He's been shot, right through his body with a high-velocity weapon. Blood sprays out of the exit hole in his shoulder.

He looks at the blood in surprise.

'They p-promised . . .'

He stumbles, falls on to his hip and looks up with a confused expression.

'G-get out through the extra door,' he hisses. 'Go down into the laundry room, straight through, and you'll be in the next building . . .'

He puts his knuckles on the floor as if to push himself up.

'Lie down,' Erik whispers. 'Just lie flat.'

'Run across the schoolyard, then follow the church wall t-to the forest and the pet cemetery.'

'Lie still,' Erik repeats, then runs at a crouch towards the door.

When he reaches the living room he hears Nestor's front door being forced open. There's a crash and splinters and pieces of metal from the lock clatter across the floor.

'Hide in the little r-red house,' Nestor gasps behind him.

Erik turns round and sees that Nestor has stood up to point. The glass in front of Björn Borg's smiling face explodes and the echo of a shot resounds between the buildings. Nestor is holding one hand against the side of his neck as a torrent of blood pulses out between his fingers.

Three of the flat's windows shatter, and distraction grenades explode, flashing with such ferocity that time seems to stand still.

Erik staggers backwards.

The silence is like a sandy beach. Slow waves roll in, then pull back with a crackle.

He feels his way through the living room, unable to see anything but the freeze-frame image of the bedroom with Nestor's silhouette against the window, and the drops of blood hanging in the air in front of the cupboard door with death hiding under a bridge.

Erik's hearing has been knocked out, but he feels further blasts as waves of pressure against his chest. He walks straight into the battered sofa, and feels his way along its back.

Then the shock lifts, his eyes are working again, and he makes his way round the table and magazine rack, but he's still as giddy as if he were very drunk.

Lights from guns sweep round the hall and kitchen.

His ears start to ring, but he still can't hear anything around him.

He locates the extra door behind the curtain, unlocks it and creeps out into the back stairwell. He almost trips over the first step but grabs hold of the handrail.

He makes his way downstairs on unsteady feet, then walks until he reaches a metal door, and finds himself in the laundry room. He feels his way along the wall until his fingers make contact with the light switch, turns the lights on and hurries past washing machines, trolleys and bins full of empty bottles as he tries to remember what Nestor said.

His head feels strangely detached, as if none of this really concerns him.

His temporary blindness lingers as silvery spots. Any light source stronger than five million candelas activates all the photocells in the eye, meaning that everything you see after being dazzled seems to happen slightly out of synch.

At the end of the long corridor is a door, and he runs up a narrow flight of steps and finds himself in a different stairwell.

Erik walks out into the cool night air. There are no emergency vehicles on this side of the block. Presumably the rapid response unit are some distance away.

Erik hurries through the little park. In the cold he can feel that one of his ears is wet. He touches his cheek and realises that he's bleeding. Without looking round he walks straight across Karlskronavägen and past a car park and some dirty recycling bins. Broken glass crunches beneath his feet.

The tarmacked schoolyard is empty. A beer can rolls in the wind, the basketball hoops on their posts have no nets.

High above a helicopter is approaching. The clatter of the rotors is audible across the rooftops, and Erik realises that his hearing is starting to come back.

He walks on, more slowly, gasping for breath, then creeps round the building and in amongst the trees. It's almost pitch-black here. Erik holds his hands out in front of his face to protect himself from branches, until he sees the low church wall.

Fear is beginning to catch up with him as he follows the wall through tall nettles.

Deep within the forest there's a sudden concentration of tiny graves, decorated by children. He sees headstones with dogs' collars hanging off them, graves with squeezy toys, drawings, photographs and flowers, homemade crosses or painted stones, burned-out candles and sooty lanterns.

105

It's past two o'clock in the morning, but Joona is standing in the middle of his room at the Hotel Hansson. The floor is covered with photographs from the crime scenes and post-mortems.

Because Erik's house is out of bounds for the duration of the search, the police have sent him to a hotel.

His jacket and pistol are lying on the untouched bed. He's had a Caesar salad in his room, the remains are under the shiny metal dome on the low coffee table.

As Joona reads the forensic experts' analyses of the crime scenes he compares them with the pictures, post-mortem reports and test results from the National Forensics Laboratory.

Rocky's nightmares were genuine memories, everything he said under hypnosis was true, the same murderer has returned – the unclean preacher has started killing again. After the murder of Rebecka Hansson the serial killer went into a long cooling-off period. He waited in a state of cold-storage until the next escalation began.

For a stalker, following someone is like a drug-addiction, it's impossible to stop, he has to get closer, make contact, give gifts, and as time passes develops a real relationship with them inside his own head. Outwardly he can exhibit submissive gratitude, but in actual fact he is extremely resentful and jealous.

The police have a list of almost seven hundred names who fit the basic outline of the perpetrator profile: bishops, pastors, priests and members of their families, deacons, churchwardens, caretakers, undertakers, preachers and faith healers.

Joona believes that the perpetrator is intentionally trying to make it look like Erik is guilty of the murders, but he can't find any connection between Erik and any of the men on the list.

What Joona is looking for now among the reports and analysis is something definite that will allow him to cross most of the names off the list.

There's nothing that stands out in the material, but perhaps different elements could be combined in an unexpected way. Joona tries separating the pieces of the puzzle and seeing if there are other ways of putting them together.

He walks across to the pictures of the deer's head and a tub of melted ice cream, and stops in front of the photograph of Sandra Lundgren's murder weapon. The stained knife was photographed where it was found, on the floor beside her dead body. The flash from the camera shimmers like a dark sun in the brown blood.

He reads that it is a chef's knife, with a stainless steel blade that's twenty centimetres long, and then examines Erixon's careful sketches attempting to reconstruct the brutal process of the attack from blood traces and spatter patterns.

The perpetrator has worn the same footwear each time: touring boots, size 43.

Joona tries to identify clues that have been missed, things that don't match the overall picture. He pores over picture after picture, and stops in front of a photograph with the number 311: a blue pottery fragment that resembles a bird's skull, with white bubbles along one edge, and a sharp point that's smooth as ice.

He leafs forward to the item in Erixon's report and reads that it was tucked between the cracks in Sandra's floor, and was only found when low-level light was shone across the floor. According to the laboratory analysis, the tiny, two-millimetre-long fragment consists of glass, iron, sand and chamotte clay.

Joona moves to the report from Adam Youssef's home. In spite of the gunfire, the murderer chose to go through with his plan, and according to the preliminary report Katryna was missing the false fingernails from both her hands.

The preacher takes trophies, then marks the places he's taken them from with the victim's hands, like a judgement in a trial.

At quarter past three Anja Larsson calls to say that she has just been informed about an imminent operation. The police have received a tip-off that is regarded as highly credible. A man claims that Erik is sleeping in the spare room in his flat. Erik had been his psychiatrist some years ago.

'The man has been told to leave the flat.'

'Who's leading the operation?' Joona asks.

'Daniel Frick.'

'He's one of Adam's best friends.'

'I understand what you're saying,' Anja says. 'But I don't think there's anything to worry about, because this operation is still being led by the National Response Unit.'

Joona goes over to the window and looks down at the hire car he's left parked on the pavement rather than in the hotel's garage. It's a gun-metal grey Porsche with six cylinders and 560 horsepower.

'Where's the flat?'

'Because everyone knows that I'm loyal to you, Margot has decided that I should be kept outside the current investigation . . . and she's got a point, because if I knew the address I'd tell you.'

Anja doesn't know where the operation is going to take place, but she's worked out that it must be somewhere south of Stockholm. She says the response unit has been given permission to use pump-action shotguns, assault rifles, repeaters and PSG 90 sniper rifles.

After the call Joona stands and gazes at the floor of the hotel room. Hundreds of pictures, lined up in rows, from wall to wall, with the floor lamp reflecting off the glossy surface of the photographs.

He carries on reading Erixon's crime scene analysis, but his mind keeps wandering to Erik and the impending operation.

Joona walks to the other side of the room, looks at a picture of a fragment of yellow fibre, then reads a lab report about a piece of trampled leaf left on the kitchen floor in Maria Carlsson's home. It turned out to be a fragment of stinging nettle.

He looks at the enlargement on the photograph. The tiny piece of leaf fills the whole sheet of paper, like a spiky green tongue. The hairs look like crystal needles, or fragile pipettes.

Dawn comes and the sky in the east grows paler. Narrow streaks of sunlight filter past chimneys and gables, over the roofs and copper ornaments of Vasastan.

The operation must be over by now, Joona thinks, and calls Erik on his new phone.

He tries a second time, but gets no answer.

Even though it's only half past five in the morning, he decides to call Margot. He has to know if they've caught Erik, but can't ask straight out about the operation because he doesn't want to get Anja in trouble.

'Have you managed to arrest an innocent suspect yet, then?'

'Joona, I'm asleep . . .'

'I know, but what's going on?'

'What's going on? You're not actually allowed to ask, but a former patient of Erik's called and said that Erik was in his flat,' she replies in a tired voice.

'Can I have a name?'

'Confidential, I can't talk to you, I told you that.'

'Just say if it's something I ought to know about.'

'The patient told the police he'd left Erik alone in the flat . . . The National Response Unit went in, saw an armed man and shot live ammunition . . . it turned out that the person in the window was the patient, who had returned to the flat.'

'And Erik wasn't there?'

He can hear her trying to sit up in bed.

'We don't even know if he'd been there at all, and the patient's on an operating table right now and can't be interviewed or—'

'What if he's the preacher?' Joona interrupts.

'Erik's guilty . . . But maybe the patient knows where he is. We'll question him as soon as we can.'

'You should station armed guards at the hospital.'

'Joona, we've found blood in Erik's car, it might not mean anything, but it's been sent for analysis.'

'Have you looked for a set of yellow rain-clothes in the patient's flat?'

'We didn't find anything special,' she replies.

'Are there stinging nettles outside the flat?'

'No, I don't think so,' she says in a bemused tone.

106

Joona sits down on a chair for the first time in several hours and reads more about the killer's steps in Sandra Lundgren's flat, looks at the sketches and thinks that there's something unusually agitated and frenetic about the murders. They're planned, but they aren't rational.

Joona compares this with the post-mortem reports' description of theatrical aggression, but can't help thinking that the degree of controlled preparation is actually a disguise, and that the aggression itself is the perpetrator's natural state.

He is about to make a note to investigate the medical history of Erik's former patient when his phone rings.

'Joona, it's me,' Erik whispers. 'They tried to kill me. I was hiding out at Nestor's, he's an old patient of mine, the police must have thought it was me they could see in the window. They shot him twice, it was like an execution. I didn't think the police in Sweden could do something like that, it's completely insane.'

'Are you somewhere safe now?'

'Yes, I think so . . . You know, he only came back to tell me what he'd done, to say that the police had promised not to hurt me, and then they shot him through the window.'

'Has it occurred to you that he could be the preacher?'

'He isn't,' Erik replies instantly.

'What was his problem when he was—'

'Joona, that doesn't matter, I just want a trial, I don't care if they convict me, I can't stay—'

'Erik, I don't think I'm being monitored, but don't tell me where you are,' Joona interrupts. 'I only want to know how long you can stay hidden where you are.'

The phone crackles as Erik moves.

'I don't know, twenty-four hours, maybe,' he whispers. 'There's a tap here, but nothing to eat.'

'Are you likely to be found?'

'There's probably not much risk of that,' Erik replies, then falls silent.

'Erik?'

'I don't understand how I could have ended up in this situation,' he says quietly. 'Everything I've done has only made things worse.'

'I'm going to find the preacher,' Joona says.

'It's too late for that, it's too late for everything now, I just want to give myself up without being killed!'

Joona can hear Erik's agitated breathing down the phone.

'If we manage to hand you over and keep you alive in prison, these crimes carry a life sentence,' Joona says.

'But I don't think I'd be convicted – I can hypnotise Rocky before the trial.'

'They'd never let you do that.'

'No, maybe not, but . . .'

'I went to see Rocky,' Joona says. 'He's in Huddinge Prison for possession of drugs, he remembered you, but nothing about the Zone or the preacher.'

'It's hopeless,' Erik says.

Joona leans against the window and feels the cool glass against his forehead. Down in the street a taxi stops outside the hotel. The driver's face is grey with tiredness as he walks round the car to take the luggage out.

Joona glances down at his hire-car, watches the taxi drive off, and when he looks up again he's made up his mind.

'I'll try to find a way of getting Rocky out today . . . and then we'll meet up so you can hypnotise him,' he says.

'Is that your plan?' Erik asks.

'You said you could unearth specific details about the preacher if you were able to hypnotise Rocky again.'

'Yes, I can, I'm pretty sure of that.'

'In that case I'll be able to find the real killer while you stay in hiding.'

'I just want to hand myself in and—'

'You'll be found guilty if it goes to trial.'

'That's ridiculous, I just happened to be nearby when—'

'It's not just that,' Joona interrupts. 'Your fingerprints were on an object found in Susanna Kern's hand.'

'What object?' Erik asks in astonishment.

'Part of a porcelain animal.'

'I don't get it, that doesn't mean anything to me.'

'But the fingerprint match is one hundred per cent.'

Joona hears Erik walk up and down, it sounds as though he's walking across a wooden floor.

'So everything points at me,' he says in a low voice.

'Have you got a picture of Nestor?'

Erik tells him how to log into the medical records of the Psychology Clinic before they end the call. Joona puts his pistol and jacket on, then goes down to reception to get a printout of Nestor's picture before leaving the hotel room again.

He walks past his hire-car and turns into the much narrower Frejgatan.

Outside one of the doorways stands an old Volvo, the sort with no ignition lock. Joona looks round quickly. The street is completely deserted. He takes a step back, then kicks in the rear side-window.

The alarm of a car further down the street goes off.

Joona opens the front door from the inside, moves the seat back, pulls his screwdriver out of his pocket, prises off the cover around the ignition and loosens the panels on the steering column. He leans over and inserts the screwdriver into the upper part of the column, and carefully breaks the steering lock.

Quickly he pulls on a pair of gloves, gets in the driving seat, loosens the red cables on the ignition cylinder and peels back their plastic covering. As soon as he twists the ends together music starts to play on the radio and the inside light comes on. He shuts the door, pulls out the brown wires and puts them together, and the engine starts.

The streets aren't yet full of cars as he drives out to Huddinge. A plastic rosary hangs off the rear-view mirror. There are already lorries on the road, but the commuters are still drinking coffee in their homes.

In Huddinge he drives past the imposing prison building and carries on south, pulls on to a track leading into the forest, turns the car round, parks, then starts walking back towards Stockholm.

107

Joona Linna gets out of the taxi on Surbrunnsgatan, pays and walks across the street to his grey hire-car. The engine starts with a gentle hum, he leans back in the leather seat and pulls away from the kerb.

When he reaches Huddinge Prison he parks right in front of the entrance, next to a metal fence, and calls Erik's number.

'How are you getting on?' he asks.

'OK, but I'm starting to get hungry.'

'I've changed my SIM-card, so you can tell me where you are now.'

'Behind St Mark's Church, outside the wall. There's a pet cemetery in the woods. I'm hiding in a red wooden shed.'

'That's fairly close to the police raid on Nestor's flat, isn't it?'

'Yes, I heard the ambulance last night,' Erik says quietly.

'I'll bring Rocky out to you an hour from now,' Joona says, glancing up at the imposing edifice of the prison.

He puts his pistol and mobile in the glove-compartment, leaves the key in the ignition and then gets out of the car and walks in through the tall pillars.

He buys three sandwiches at the kiosk, asks for a bag, and then goes over to say why he's there.

After going through the usual security procedures Joona is shown inside the prison. The same prison officer as before is standing waiting for him.

Joona notes that Arne has a telescopic baton from Bonowi. It's made of sprung steel, and designed to hit the muscles in the upper arms and thighs.

His name-badge sits slightly crookedly on his pilled Nato sweater. His handcuffs are dangling from his belt at the base of his broad back.

In the lift Arne takes off his glasses and polishes them on his sweater.

'How's the fishing?' Joona asks.

'I'm heading to Älvkarleby with my brother-in-law later this autumn.'

The interview room is one of the monitored rooms, in which one wall consists of a pane of glass, making it possible for people in the next room to observe everything going on inside.

Joona sits down on a chair and waits with both hands resting on the tabletop until he hears voices approaching along the corridor.

'He's called the naked chef because he was naked when he started,' the duty officer is saying as the door opens and Rocky is led into the room.

'No,' Arne says, 'that's not right . . .'

'My wife and I saw Jamie Oliver at the book fair in Gothenburg fifteen years ago. He was completely naked. Stood there making spaghetti alle vongole.'

'My shoulders hurt,' Rocky sighs.

'Just keep quiet,' Arne says, pushing him down on to a chair.

'Give me a scribble and he's all yours,' the duty officer says as they leave the room.

108

Rocky looks paler today, and has dark patches under his eyes – he's probably suffering from withdrawal. Arne Melander sits in the adjoining room watching them, but he can't hear what they are saying. The soundproof glass wall is intended to protect the confidentiality of conversations between defence lawyers and their clients, but also to allow the police to question suspects without the contents of their conversations leaking out.

'They say they can keep me locked up in this fucking place for six months,' Rocky says in a gruff voice, rubbing under his nose.

'You've talked about a preacher,' Joona says, in a final attempt to avoid putting his plan into action.

'I have problems with my memory after—'

'I know,' Joona interrupts. 'But try to remember the preacher, you saw him kill a woman called Tina.'

'That's possible,' Rocky says, his eyes narrowing.

'He chopped off her arm with a machete. Do you remember that?'

'I don't remember anything,' Rocky whispers.

'Do you know someone called Nestor?'

'I don't think so.'

'Look at this picture,' Joona says, handing him the printout.

Rocky studies Nestor's thin face carefully, then nods.

'He was in Karsudden, I think . . .'

'Did you know him?'

'I don't know, there were different sections.'

'Are you prepared to meet Erik Maria Bark and let yourself be hypnotised?'

'OK,' Rocky says with a shrug.

'The problem is that the prosecutor is refusing to let you out,' Joona says slowly.

'Erik can always come and hypnotise me here.'

'That isn't possible, because the police think Erik carried out the murders.'

'Erik?'

'But he's as innocent as you were.'

'Vanitas vanitatum,' Rocky says with a broad smile.

'Erik found Olivia, who . . .'

'I know, I know, I go down on my knees and thank him every evening . . . But what do you expect me to do about it?'

'We're leaving together, you and me,' Joona replies calmly. 'I'll take one of the guards hostage and all you have to do is come along with me.'

'Hostage?'

'We'll be out in seven minutes, long before the police get here.'

Rocky looks at Joona, then at Arne sitting behind the glass.

'I'll do it if I can have my wraps back,' Rocky says, leaning back and stretching his legs.

'What sort of heroin was it?' Joona asks.

'White, from Nimroz . . . but Kandahar would do fine.'

'I'll sort it,' Joona says, taking a flattened roll of duct tape from his pocket.

With his eyes half-closed, Rocky watches the former police officer wrap the heavy-duty tape round his hands.

'I'm sure you know what you're doing,' Rocky says.

'Bring the bag of sandwiches,' Joona says, pressing the button on the intercom to indicate that the meeting is over.

A few moments later Arne opens the door and lets Joona out into the corridor. The idea is for him to lead Joona out of the prison, then take Rocky back to his cell.

While the prison officer locks Rocky inside the interview room, Joona goes over to the other door where the bottom of the skirting board has come loose. He leans down. Slips his fingers into the gap and pulls upwards. The screws spring free from the concrete wall along with their brown plastic rawlplugs.

'You can't do that!' Arne exclaims.

Crumbs of cement rain down on the floor as Joona yanks up the skirting board. The top screws are stuck and Joona jerks hard, twisting the metal until there's a bang as the last screws come loose.

'Are you listening?' Arne says, drawing his baton. 'I'm talking to you.'

Joona takes no notice of him. He holds the skirting board out in front of him, stamps down hard with his foot, bends down and turns it, then stamps again.

'What the hell are you doing?' Arne asks with a nervous smile, coming closer.

'I'm sorry,' Joona says simply.

He knows what sort of training Arne Melander has received, and that he's going to approach with his left hand outstretched, trying to hold him off while he attempts to strike Joona on the thighs and upper arms with sweeping movements of the baton.

Joona moves towards him with long strides, knocks his arm away and then lands his elbow in the heavy man's chest, making him stagger back. His knees give way but he puts out a hand to support himself and manages to sit down on the floor.

Joona stumbles forward from the momentum of the blow, but stays on his feet and snatches the prison officer's alarm from him before he has time to react. He cuts his lower arm as he puts the bent part of the skirting board around Arne's neck, then pulls the handcuffs from his belt and attaches one cuff to the point where the ends of the skirting board intersect.

'Stand up and let Rocky out,' he says.

Arne coughs and turns round heavily, crawls to the wall and leans against it as he gets to his feet.

'Unlock the door.'

Arne's hands are free, but Joona is steering him from behind with the protruding ends of the skirting board. His neck is trapped in the noose-like bend, the sharp edges of the metal pressing against his neck.

'Don't do this,' Arne pants.

Sweat is running down his face and his hands are shaking as he unlocks the door of the interview room. Rocky comes out, picks up the baton and presses it on the floor to make it contract again.

'Arne, if you help us we'll be out in four minutes and then I'll let you go,' Joona says.

The prison officer limps ahead of Joona, and keeps trying to slip his fingers under the metal noose.

'Use your passcard and type in the code,' Joona says, steering him towards the lift.

As they travel down through the building Arne holds one hand against the mirror and keeps looking up at the camera in the hope that someone will see him.

The metal has already cut through one layer of the duct-tape around Joona's hands.

When they emerge into the lobby it takes just a matter of seconds before the rest of the prison staff realise what's going on. Like a pressure wave, the atmosphere goes from relaxed to intense. Some sort of silent alarm has evidently been activated, a light is flashing beneath one desk, and prison officers who had been sitting talking moments before hurry to their feet. Chairs scrape the floor, papers fall to the ground.

'Let us through!' Joona calls, steering Arne towards the exit.

Seven guards are approaching anxiously from the corridor, they're clearly having trouble reading the situation, and Joona tells Rocky to watch his back.

Rocky extends the baton again and walks backwards behind Joona towards the airlock.

The officer who was sitting in the security command centre hurries over. His task now is to slow things down and delay the escape for as long as possible.

'I can't let you out,' he says. 'But if you give yourselves up, then—'

'Look at your colleague,' Joona interrupts.

Arne whimpers as Joona pulls the ends of the metal outwards. The noose tightens around his neck and blood starts to trickle down his dark sweater. He tries to hold the metal back with his hands, but stands no chance.

'Stop!' the security officer yells. 'For God's sake, stop!'

Arne stumbles sideways, into a display of information for visitors, sending brochures falling to the ground around him.

'I'll let him go when we get outside,' Joona says.

'OK, everyone move back,' the security officer says. 'Let them through, let them go.'

They pass through the bleeping metal detector. Prison officers and other staff get out of the way. One officer is recording everything on his mobile phone.

'Forward,' Joona says.

Arne whimpers quietly as they approach the exit.

'Oh, God,' he whispers, holding his left arm.

A dog is barking frantically on the other side of the security airlock, as guards rush outside the glass doors to get into formation.

'Let them through!' the security officer calls, following them out through the airlock. 'I'll come with you, make sure you get out.'

He pulls out his card, taps in the code and opens the door.

'Who the hell are you, really?' he gasps, looking at Joona Linna.

Outside the prison the sun is shining, the sky is a radiant blue above them as they walk across the paved entrance area towards Joona's grey Porsche.

Joona walks round the vehicle and pushes Arne to the ground, and apologises as he fastens the other handcuff to the metal fence behind the car. The security officer stands and watches them as the prison guards mill about inside the glass doors only a dozen metres away from them.

Joona gets in quickly and starts the car.

Before Rocky has time to close the door he drives over the kerb, down the grass slope, past the cement blocks and out on to the road, where he accelerates hard towards the forest where the old Volvo is waiting.

109

Nestor was taken to the Karolinska University Hospital in Huddinge, where a team operated on him and managed to stop the bleeding. Nestor was lucky, his condition is already stable, and he's been moved from the Intensive Care Unit.

Margot has put two uniformed officers outside the post-operative care unit.

Nestor is conscious again, but in a state of severe shock. He's being given extra oxygen through a tube in his nose, and the saturation of his blood is under constant monitoring. A pleural drain has been inserted above his diaphragm, and bubbly blood is running out through the tube.

Nelly has spoken to Nestor's consultant and has suggested a low-level sedative out of consideration for his medical history.

Nestor cries the whole time Margot tries to explain the chain of events from the police's point of view, up to the storming of his flat.

'But Erik wasn't there – so where was he?' she asks.

'I d-don't know,' Nestor sobs.

'Why did you call and say that . . .'

'Nestor, you have to understand that none of what happened is your fault, it was just an accident,' Nelly says, holding his hand.

'Has Erik been in touch with you at all?' Margot asks.

'I d-don't know,' he repeats, staring past her.

'Of course you know.'

'I d-don't want to talk to you,' he says quietly, and turns his face away.

'What line of work are you in?' Margot asks, taking a ham sandwich out of her large bag.

'I'm retired . . . but I d-do a bit of gardening work . . .'

'Where?'

'For the council . . . d-different places,' he says.

'Do you have a lot of trouble with weeds?' Margot asks.

'Not really,' he says, looking curious.

'Stinging nettles?'

'No,' he says, picking at a tube.

'Nestor,' Nelly says gently. 'You've probably worked out that Erik and I are good friends . . . and like you I think it would be best for him to hand himself in to the police.'

Tears well up in Nestor's eyes again, and Margot goes over to the window so she doesn't have to watch him cry.

'I'm riddled with b-bullets,' he says in a loud voice, and puts his hand on top of the bandage covering the wound in his chest.

'It was a terrible accident,' Nelly says.

'God wants to k-kill me,' he says, pulling the oxygen tube from his nose.

'Why do you think that?'

'I can't bear it,' he whimpers.

'You know . . . the Jews say that a righteous man can fall seven times and get up again, but the ungodly stumble when calamity strikes . . . and you're going to get up.'

'Am I r-righteous?'

'How should I know?' she smiles.

'That's what you m-meant, isn't it?'

Nelly can see that the oxygenation of his blood is falling, and reattaches the tube to his nose.

'Erik saved me and I just wanted to save him,' he whispers.

'Yesterday, you mean?' she asks tentatively.

'He c-came to me and I gave him food and l-lodging,' he says, and coughs lightly. 'They p-promised not to hurt him.'

'How did he look when he came to you?'

'He had an ugly c-cap on, and his hand was bleeding. He was d-dirty and unshaven, and had scratches on his face.'

'And you just wanted to help him,' Nelly says.

'Yes,' he nods.

Margot is standing by the window eating her sandwich, but can still hear Nestor's careful answers. His description of Erik fits someone who ran off through a forest and has been sleeping rough.

'Do you know where Erik is now?' she asks slowly, turning round.

'No.'

Margot meets Nelly's gaze, then leaves the room to set a large-scale police operation in motion.

'I'm starting to get t-tired,' he says.

'It's a bit early for the medicine to take effect.'

'Are you Erik's g-girlfriend?' Nestor asks, looking at her.

'What did Erik say before he left?' Nelly asks, but can't help smiling. 'Do you think he's planning to give himself up?'

'You m-mustn't be angry with Erik.'

'I'm not.'

'My mother says he's b-bad, but . . . she c-can just shut up, I think . . .'

'Get some rest, now.'

'He's the nicest m-man you could get,' Nestor goes on.

'I think so too,' she smiles, and pats his hand.

'We meet sometimes . . . but you c-can't see me,' Nestor says. 'You can't hear me, and you c-can't smell me. I was b-born before you and I'll be waiting for you when you die. I can embrace you, b-but you can't hold on to me . . .'

'Darkness,' she replies.

'Good,' Nestor nods. 'If a man carried my b-burden, he . . . he would . . .'

Nestor closes his eyes and gasps for breath.

'I'm going to go home now,' Nelly says quietly, and carefully gets up from the edge of the bed.

When she leaves the post-operative care unit she notices that the police officers are no longer guarding the door.

110

The bell in St Mark's Church is ringing under an open sky. The wheel turns, pulling the great bell with it. The heavy clapper hits the metal and the peal reaches across the wall of the churchyard, in amongst the trees, all the way to the buried animals.

The dirty single pane of glass in the window of the shed where Erik is hiding rattles. The red shack in the pet cemetery consists of thin timber walls and a stained chipboard floor. Presumably there would once have been a plastic mat on the floor. The shed may have been used by local cemetery workers before everything was streamlined. In recent years only Nestor has been here, as the solitary but conscientious guardian of the animals' last resting place.

On one wall there is a cold-water tap above a large zinc trough.

Erik has moved five sacks of compost and lined them up on the floor to form a bed.

He's lying on his side listening to the church bell. The smell of earth around him is pervasive, as if he was already lying in his grave.

Who can understand their own fate? he thinks, watching the morning light shine in through the grey curtain and wander slowly across the sacks of grass seed and grit, spades and shovels, then down across the floor to an axe with a rusty blade.

His gaze lingers on the axe, staring at the blunt edge with its deep indentations, and thinks that Nestor must use it to chop off roots when he's digging graves.

He turns on his bed, trying to get more comfortable. He spent the first few hours curled up in the corner behind the sacks, he'd cut his thigh on a sharp branch, had a ringing sound in his ears, felt nauseous and was shaking all over.

The ambulance siren died away, the helicopter disappeared, and silence enveloped the little shed.

After a few hours he began to feel a bit safer, dared to stand up, and went over to the tap, where he drank some cold water and washed his face. The water splashed up on to a plastic sleeve that had been pinned to the wall. The drips ran down a price list from the Association of Stockholm Pet Cemeteries, on to the discoloured chipboard.

He called Joona and told him what had happened, aware of how incoherent and repetitive he sounded, and realised that he was in shock. He lay back down on the sacks, but couldn't sleep, his heart was beating far too fast.

His ear has stopped bleeding now, but is still humming, as though he were hearing everything through a piece of thin fabric. Gradually the jagged, dazzling halo of light fades and he closes his eyes.

He thinks about Jackie and Madeleine and hears children's voices in the distance. He creeps over to the window. They're probably playing in the woods behind the school.

Erik has no idea what he'd do if they come over here. His face could be on the front pages of all the papers today. A wave of anxiety washes through him, leaving him feeling utterly chilled.

Spiders' webs rustle when he slides the curtain aside a few more centimetres.

The pet cemetery is a beautiful place, lots of grass and deciduous trees. A small path leads away from the church and over a wooden bridge, lined by tall stinging nettles.

On one grave a number of round stones form a cross, and a child has made a lantern out of a jam-jar, with red hearts painted round the outside. The candle is just visible beneath the rainwater and fallen seeds.

Erik thinks about his conversation with Joona again. He knows he can find his way into Rocky's memories if he gets the chance. He's already hypnotised him, but he wasn't looking for the preacher then.

But how long can he stay here? He's hungry, and sooner or later someone is going to find him. He's far too close to the school, the church, and Nestor's flat.

He swallows hard, gently touches the wound on his leg, and tries again to work out how his fingerprints could have ended up in Susanna Kern's home. There has to be a simple explanation, but Joona seems to think that they're dealing with an attempt to make him look guilty of the murders.

The thought is so ridiculous that he can't take it seriously.

There has to be a rational explanation.

I'm not afraid of a trial, Erik thinks. The truth will come out, if I can just have a chance to defend myself.

He has to hand himself in.

Erik thinks he could seek refuge in the church, he could ask the priest for communion, for God's forgiveness, anything at all, as long as he gets shelter.

The police can't shoot me in a church, he thinks.

He's so tired that tears come to his eyes at the thought of giving himself up and putting his fate in someone else's hands.

He decides to creep out and see if the church is open, but then he hears someone crossing the little wooden bridge that leads to the pet cemetery.

Erik ducks down quickly and goes and sits in the corner where he hid to start with. Someone is walking along the path, groaning oddly to himself. There's a tinkling sound, as though whoever it is had kicked over the homemade lantern on the grave.

The footsteps stop and everything goes silent. Perhaps he's putting flowers on a dog's grave? Perhaps he's listening for sounds inside the shed.

Erik sits in the corner thinking about the dog that Nestor was forced to drown. In his mind's eye he sees the flailing legs, the animal's attempts to swim as the sack filled with water.

The man outside spits noisily and carries on walking. Erik hears him come closer, walking through the dead bushes, their thin branches snapping under his shoes.

He's right outside the shed now, Erik thinks, looking around for a weapon, glancing at the spade, then the axe with the short handle and blunt blade.

Something starts trickling down the wall of the shed, splashing the tall grass. The man outside is urinating, slurring to himself as he does so.

'You do your best,' a deep voice mutters. 'You come home, nice and quiet, but . . . nothing's good enough any more . . .'

The man lurches over to the window and peers in. The grass scrapes and his shadow falls across the wall with the spades and shovels. Erik presses himself against the wall next to the window, clearly hearing the man's breathing, first with his mouth open, then through tight nostrils.

'Honest work,' he mutters, and carries on through the low-growing blueberry bushes.

Erik thinks that he's going to have to wait for the drunk to disappear before going to the church and handing himself in.

He tries again to imagine that Nestor is the killer, but he can't honestly believe that Nestor is driven by a compulsion to turn himself into the arbiter of life or death.

The sun goes behind a cloud and the grey curtain loses its transparency again.

On a shelf stands a dusty thermos flask, with a plastic bag tucked between it and the wall, a little grey urn and a painted plaster bulldog.

Erik just has time to see Nestor's shaving mirror quiver on the wall, sending a glint of a reflection across the floor, before the door of the shed swings open.

111

Erik scrambles backwards and a green folding chair clatters over onto the floor. The opening door hits the wall then bounces back and hits a very large shoulder. Dust is swirling round the bulky figure, who's panting as he makes his way into the shed. Rocky Kyrklund coughs and hits his head on the dangling light bulb. He's dressed in prison-issue clothing, his face is sweaty and his hair is hanging pale and grey around his big head.

Joona comes in right behind him, shuts the door and stops the swaying bulb with his hand.

'Viihtyisä,' Joona says.

Erik tries to say something, but he can barely breathe. When the door flew open he got so scared that his cheeks felt like they were burning.

Rocky mutters something to himself, picks up the folding chair and sits down. He's out of breath as he glances round the little room.

'You came,' Erik says in a weak voice.

'We made our way through the forest from Nacka gård,' Joona says, taking three cheese and salad baguettes out of a bag.

They eat in silence. Rocky is sweating from withdrawal, and breathing hard between mouthfuls. When he's finished he goes over and drinks some water from the tap.

'It's more expensive to bury people,' he says, gesturing towards the price list.

Drops of water glisten in his beard. Shadows dance behind the curtain.

'I think we're fairly safe here,' Joona says, removing the last of the duct tape from his hands. 'The operation has already been downgraded. Externally they're claiming that they received inaccurate information, because Nestor wanted to commit suicide.'

'But he is still alive, isn't he?'

'Yes,' Joona replies, meeting Erik's gaze.

His blond hair is sticking up, and his eyes have regained the chilly blue of an October sky.

Erik chews the last of the bread.

'If this doesn't work, I thought I'd hand myself over inside the church,' he says, trying to keep his voice steady.

'Good,' Joona replies quietly.

'They can't shoot me inside a church,' he adds.

'No, they can't,' Joona replies, even though they both know it isn't true.

Rocky is standing by the price list smoking, muttering to himself and picking the little plastic caps off the tops of the drawing pins.

'I'm ready to start,' Erik tells him, crumpling the wrapper of his sandwich into a ball.

'Sure,' Rocky nods, and sits down on the chair.

Erik looks at him, his dilated pupils, the colour of his face, listens to his breathing.

'You've marched through the woods, your body is still working hard,' he says.

'Maybe it won't work, then?' Rocky asks, stubbing his cigarette out with his foot.

'I'd like to start with some relaxation . . . the fact that the brain is active is no problem, you're not supposed to be asleep, after all . . . all we want to do is gather all that activity and focus . . .'

'OK,' Rocky says, leaning back.

'Sit comfortably,' Erik goes on. 'You can change position as much as you like during the hypnosis, you don't need to worry about that, but each time you move you'll sink deeper into a state of relaxation.'

Joona and Erik know that this is their chance, the opportunity they've been waiting for.

They don't need much, just a name, a location, or some other definite detail.

If they can only come up with one defined parameter, the pattern that's already emerged will refine itself to an arrow pointing straight at the preacher.

Erik can't force the process, and needs to take his time leading Rocky into a very deep trance in order to reach the most inaccessible memories.

'Rest your hands on your lap,' Erik goes on in a quiet voice.

'Clench them tight, then relax, feel how heavy they are, feel them sink, they're being pulled down towards your thighs, your wrists are feeling soft . . .'

Erik concentrates on not letting his need for a result show in his voice, as he slowly works his way through the whole of Rocky's body, watching as his shoulders gradually relax. He talks for a while about his neck, about how heavy his head feels, and taking deep breaths, as he almost imperceptibly approaches the moment of induction.

In a monotone voice he describes a wide, sandy beach, with gentle waves rolling in and out of the shore, as the white sand shimmers like porcelain.

'You're walking along the edge of the water, towards a headland,' Erik says. 'The wet sand feels solid under your feet, it's easy to walk on, warm waves lap around your legs, grains of sand swirl round . . .'

He describes the tiny, ridged seashells and the coral rolling in the bubbling surf of the waves.

Rocky is slumped on the creaking folding chair, his jaw has relaxed and his eyelids look heavy.

'All you're doing is listening to my voice and you feel fine, everything is nice and safe . . .'

Joona is standing next to the window looking out at the pet cemetery. His jacket is open and the butt of his pistol shimmers red against his chest.

'In a little while I'm going to count backwards from two hundred, and with each number you're going to sink deeper and deeper into relaxation. And when I tell you to open your eyes, you're going to open your eyes and remember every detail from the first time you met the man you call the preacher,' Erik says.

Rocky remains still, with his lower lip drooping slightly and his huge hands on his thighs. He looks like he's asleep, dreaming.

Erik counts down in a deep, soporific voice, his eyes monitoring Rocky's breathing, the movement of his bulging stomach.

Parallel to the actual hypnosis process, Erik sees himself sink through murky water. It's so dark with mud that he can barely see Rocky in front of him, as air bubbles rise from his beard and his hair sways in the current.

Erik breaks the sequence of numbers, skips a few, but keeps counting down at an imperceptibly slowing rate.

He knows he needs to find precise memories.

The water gets even darker the deeper he goes. The current is stronger, pulling at his clothes from the side. The whole time, Rocky looks like he's undergoing grotesque metamorphoses in the tugging, muddy water, as if his face were made from loose sacking.

'Eighteen, seventeen . . . thirteen, twelve . . . soon you're going to open your eyes,' Erik says, and watches Rocky's slow breathing. 'There's nothing to worry about here, nothing dangerous . . .'

112

Rocky has entered such a deep trance that his heart rate is lower than during deep sleep, his breathing is like that of a hibernating animal, but at the same time parts of the brain can be activated to a state of extreme focus.

It's very nearly time to make him turn his attention to the preacher, and try to explain what he's seen, try to dig out the crystal-clear memories that are lying preserved, right next to dreams and deliriums.

Rocky's head is lolling forward and his dirty hair is scattered with pine needles after the hike through the forest.

'Four, three, two, one, and now you open your eyes and remember exactly where you first met the unclean preacher . . .'

Through the streaming brown water Erik sees Rocky shake his head, but in reality he is sitting on the chair with his eyes open and trying to moisten his lips with his tongue.

His stomach is moving in time with his slow breathing, his chin lifts and his eyes stare straight through time and matter.

Erik thinks that he needs to repeat his words and include a subtle command to get him to start talking.

'As soon as you feel ready, you can . . . *tell me what you see.*'

Rocky licks his cracked lips.

'The grass is white . . . crunching underfoot,' he says slowly. 'A black veil flutters from the top of the staff . . . and small snowflakes are drifting to the ground . . .'

He starts muttering something Erik can't make out.

'Listen to my voice and tell me what you remember,' he reminds him.

Rocky's forehead is wet with sweat, he stretches out one leg and the chair creaks under his weight.

'The light is the colour of chalk,' he says quietly. 'Falling through the windows in the deep alcoves . . . Against a gold-leaf ceiling hangs the defeated saviour . . . together with the other criminals.'

'You're inside a church now?'

Deep down in the fast-flowing, dirty water, Rocky nods in response. His eyes are open wide and his hair is floating to the right of his head.

'Which church is it?' Erik asks.

He can hear his own voice tremble, and tries to force himself to be calm, to find a tranquillity within the hypnotic resonance.

'The preacher's church.'

'What's it called?' Erik asks, feeling his heart start to beat faster.

Rocky's mouth moves slightly, but the only sound that comes out is a few clicks from his lips. Erik leans forward over his shoulder and hears the slow exhalation, the voice coming from deep in his throat.

'Sköld-inge,' he says groggily.

'Sköldinge Church,' Erik repeats.

Rocky nods, leans his head back and forms a soundless word with his lips. Erik exchanges a quick glance with Joona. They've got what they need. He ought to bring Rocky out of his deep trance now, but can't help asking another question.

'Is the unclean preacher there?'

Rocky smiles sleepily and raises a weary hand as if to point at the tools on the wall of the little shed.

'Can you see him?' Erik persists.

'In the church,' Rocky whispers as his head lolls forward again.

Over by the streaked window Joona is starting to look stressed. Perhaps some visitors have arrived in the pet cemetery.

'Tell me what you can see,' Erik says.

Rocky trembles, and a drop of sweat falls from the tip of his nose.

'I see the old priest . . . With rouge over the stubble on his drooping cheeks . . . the lipstick, and his stupid expression, morose and silent . . .'

'Go on.'

'Ossa . . . ipsius in pace . . .'

Rocky whispers to himself, his face twitches and he shifts uneasily on the creaking folding chair. Flakes of green paint fall on to the chipboard floor. Joona moves backwards and silently draws his pistol.

'Do you know what his name is?' Erik asks. 'Say what his name is, loud enough for me to hear.'

'The ugly old priest . . . with his scrawny arms, covered in tracks from all the fucking junk he's injected over the years,' Rocky says, and his head jerks to one side. 'Cloudy from bleeding under the skin and wrecked veins, but now he's wearing his snow-white surplice, no one's seen anything, no one knows what's going on . . . his sister and daughter by his side, his closest colleagues . . .'

'Are there other priests in the church?'

'The pews are full of priests, row after row after row . . .'

Even though Joona is very quietly telling him to bring the hypnosis to an end, Erik urges Rocky to go deeper.

'Down to a place where there are only real memories . . . I'm going to count down from ten . . . and when I get to zero, you'll be in Sköldinge Church, and . . .'

Rocky stands up, his head jerks, his eyes roll backwards and he collapses over the chair. He hits the floor, his head striking the bags of compost, and his feet twitch spasmodically. His body arches, as if he's trying to do the crab. His top slides up and he's gurgling gutturally with pain as his mouth gradually stretches open and his neck pulls back. His spine creaks. Erik hurries over and moves tools and equipment out of his reach.

The floor thuds as Rocky rolls on to his side, and a moment later his epileptic attack switches to chronic cramps. Erik kneels down and holds both hands under Rocky's big head to stop him hurting himself.

His legs are kicking and jerking hard, crashing his heels down on the floor. Joona is holding his gun close to his body and looking at Erik with icy grey eyes.

'You need to find a new hiding place,' he says. 'I saw police officers in the woods by the school, they've probably had another tip-off, otherwise they wouldn't be here again. They'll be bringing in dogs if they haven't already done so, and searching with helicopters.'

Rocky's attack is fading, but he's still breathing fast and one of his legs jerks a few more times.

Erik rolls him gently on to his side. Rocky blinks. He's soaked with sweat as he lets out a tired cough.

'You had an epileptic fit while you were hypnotised,' Erik explains.

'God,' he sighs.

'Erik, you have to go, get as far away as you can, and hide,' Joona says again.

113

Erik quickly drinks some water, wipes his mouth, opens the door cautiously and looks out at the pet cemetery, then leaves the shed. Without looking back, he walks along the path between the trees and the little graves. When he reaches the forest he starts to walk faster. He gets to a wider path and runs for a while.

He can hear dogs barking over towards the school. Erik leaves the path and heads into denser forest instead. He forces his way through pine thickets, scratching his cheek and one eyelid and making them sting. He crouches down and makes his way through the trees, through spiders' webs and over glossy fungi and mushrooms.

He's so out of breath now that his body is dripping with sweat. The ground slopes down steeply in front of him. The barking is getting closer and he can hear police officers shouting instructions to their dogs.

Erik gets a stitch and presses his hand hard against his side, and carries on running through the forest, which has suddenly opened up. He can see reeds and bulrushes between the trees, and just has time to detect an acrid smell of marshes and fermentation before one foot sinks into the wet moss. He can hear the sound of a helicopter further away over the treetops.

Erik hurries forward but the ground feels like it's rocking, water rises around his feet, up over his ankles, and he realises he can't keep going across the bog. He needs to turn back, but sinks deeper and almost falls. He leans one hand against a tree trunk. The cool moisture is rising out of the ground, and there's a sucking sound as the wet moss lets go of his foot. He has to crawl back, getting his knees wet and cold. He eventually reaches firm ground and starts running.

A dragonfly flashes past, and he sees a white deer's skull lying next to a rotten log.

He jumps across a furrow full of deep, brown water, with a layer of black leaves at the bottom. Without looking back he runs into the forest once more. Twigs snap under his feet and after a while he can't run any further, and walks as fast as he can instead. He holds larger branches aside with his hands and lowers his head to protect himself from twigs.

The dog patrol is closer now, their barks echoing tinnily like thunder.

They've picked up his scent, soon they'll have caught up with him.

A strong impulse to just lie flat on his stomach and give up, hand himself over to the police overwhelms him. Imagine, this could all be over, he could be warm again, allowed to rest and start to focus on what's happened, and whoever has done this to him.

I'm going to give up now, he thinks, and stops, his heart pounding. There are no hiding places in the forest.

Then he remembers Nestor getting shot straight through his chest.

The calls are drawing nearer, a hunting team surrounding their prey.

Erik goes cold inside.

He has to try to reach the buildings by the ski slope, carry on round the bog in a wide arc, then find his way out through the forest.

He sets off running again, dodging between the trunks, through dense undergrowth. Twigs scratch at his face, arms and legs.

The dogs are barking frantically behind him.

He's so out of breath that his throat feels raw, and he knows he has no chance of outrunning the dogs if they've been set loose.

Dry pine cones crunch beneath his feet. Flowering heather brushes his legs. The ground is sloping up now, and the lactic acid in his muscles makes his calves feel tight and heavy.

A tall rock face covered in sphagnum moss and lichen rises up between the trees. He keeps running and starts to climb, forcing himself upwards when the moss starts to slip beneath him and he begins to slide and ends up scraping his hands to stop himself.

When he's finally at the top he lies down, flat out. His heart pounds against the rock beneath him. He wipes the sweat from his eyes and sees the ochre-coloured housing blocks in Björkhagen above the trees. A crow caws and shuffles clumsily at the top of a fir. Below him, not far away, on the edge of the marsh, he can see the police officers circling round with their dogs straining at their leads. The police are talking into their radios and shouting to each other, and pointing out across the bog. Suddenly one of the dogs signals that it's picked up a scent. It turns back into the forest, following his trail through the trees. Its leash stretches tight and the dog starts barking loudly.

Erik shuffles backwards and hears the helicopter approaching. He crouches down and starts to run, aware that he has to put some distance between him and the dog-patrol. His legs tremble with the exertion as he runs sideways down the slope, into denser forest again. He follows a path and emerges on to a running track covered with damp bark chippings. A woman in a pink tracksuit is standing still, stretching her muscles, and he hesitates briefly before running past her. Her neck and chest are sweaty. She has a distant look on her face and he sees that she's listening to music on her headphones. Just as he passes her she looks up at him. Her face stiffens and she looks away a little too quickly. He realises that she's recognised him, and sees her start to move in the opposite direction out of the corner of his eye.

He carries on round the next bend and stops in front of a map of the nature reserve. A red dot at the bottom marks Sickla Park, where he is now. He looks along the route of the Sörmland Trail, at the running tracks, marshes, watercourses and lakes, then decides to carry on down towards the water at Sicklasjön.

Erik takes long strides across a patch of tall blueberries, then runs straight into the pathless forest.

Dog patrols are approaching from several directions now. He forces his way through a thicket and catches his jacket on a branch. Erik can feel himself starting to panic, tears the cloth loose, and stumbles out into a clearing. He's so out of breath that he bends double for a few moments, spits, then carries on through the trees.

114

Erik runs past a fallen tree and carries on through the forest as he hears the barking of the dogs echo between the tree trunks.

After half a kilometre or so he reaches a stream. The bottom is covered with red stone, and the water shimmers brown with iron.

Erik steps into the ice-cold water and wades along the stream, hoping the dogs will lose his scent for a few minutes.

He wishes he could phone Jackie to tell her that he's innocent. He can't bear the thought of her believing that he's a murderer. The media and social networking sites must be full of exaggerated accusations, details from his life, things from long ago that are now being dragged up as proof of his guilt.

Erik tries to wade faster but slips on a stone, falls and hits his knee on the bottom, and lets out a gasp. Cold and pain shoot up through his bones, up into his spine and neck.

He stands up and tries to run. The stones slide and slip beneath his feet, his clothes are heavy and the water foams up around him.

He reaches a bend. The banks are steeper here, the water-channel narrower and faster ahead of him.

The trees lean over the water and he has to bend down beneath their branches. He carries on wading as the stream passes through thicker forest. He can no longer hear the dogs, just the water lapping around his legs.

He makes his way round another bend and decides to get out of the stream. Dripping with water, Erik scrambles out of the water and hurries through the forest on squelching shoes. Exhaustion and his clinging clothes mean that he keeps stumbling.

Up ahead he can see the shimmering water of the long, thin Sicklasjön. He sinks down behind a large rock, pushing past the narrow trunks of a clump of rowan trees, panting so hard that his chest hurts.

This is hopeless, he thinks.

It's over, I haven't got anywhere to go.

He has loads of acquaintances, people he socialises with, colleagues of many years' standing, a few good friends, but no one he can call right now.

He's pretty sure that Simone would be willing to help, but she's probably being watched. And Benjamin would do whatever he could, he knows that, but Erik would rather die than put his son in any danger.

There are only a few people he knows he could call.

Joona, Nelly, and maybe Jackie.

If Jackie has gone to see her sister, perhaps he could borrow her flat – assuming she doesn't believe what the papers have been saying.

Erik looks at his phone. It's only got 4 per cent of its battery charge left. He doesn't want to put Nelly at risk, but he calls her number anyway.

If her phone's being monitored then that's that, but if he's going to stand any chance at all he has to take the risk. He's completely surrounded out here, he has no other option.

The sound of the helicopter clatters in the distance, then all he can hear is the wind in the treetops. His phone crackles and he hears the ringing tone, and then there's a click.

'Nelly,' she answers in a calm voice.

'It's me,' he says. 'Can you talk?'

'I don't know, I think so,' she says. 'If this counts as talking . . .'

'Nelly, listen, I don't want to cause any trouble, but I need help.'

'What's going on, really?' she asks.

'I didn't do the things they're saying about me, I've got no idea what this is all about.'

'Erik, I know, I know you're innocent,' she says. 'But can't you just hand yourself in to the police? Say you surrender, I'll support you, be a witness, anything.'

'They'll shoot me the moment they catch sight of me. You've no idea what—'

'I understand how you feel,' she interrupts. 'But doesn't it just get even worse the longer you wait? The police are everywhere—'

'Nelly—'

'They've taken your computer, they've packed your whole office into boxes, they're outside our house in Bromma, they're at the Karolinska, and—'

'Nelly, I need to stay in hiding for a while, there are no other options, but I want you to know that I'll understand if you can't help me.'

'I love adventures,' she says sarcastically.

'Please, Nelly . . . there's no one else I can ask.'

He can hear the dogs barking again. Closer now.

'I can't get involved,' she says quietly. 'You can see that, it would cause problems for Martin, but . . .'

'Sorry I asked,' Erik says, feeling black hopelessness fill his heart.

'But I've got an old place,' Nelly goes on. 'Have I ever told you about Solbacken, it used to belong to Dad's parents?'

'How do I get there?'

'Erik, I'm probably not much good at car chases, I haven't got the balls, but I can go and . . . I don't know, I can rent a car at Statoil or something . . .'

'You'd do that for me?' he asks.

'Tell me you love me,' she replies cheerfully.

'I love you.'

'Where shall we meet?'

'Do you know the bathing beach at Sickla strand? Erik asks.

'No, but I'm sure I can find it.'

'There's a school or nursery right next to the beach – wait there until I show up.'

He hears the dogs again, as their barking echoes through the trees.

Erik crouches down and runs through the dense undergrowth at the edge of the water, and pulls off his shoes and heavy trousers. He bundles his clothes up and hides in the bushes as a helicopter passes low overhead.

His pursuers are getting closer, the dogs sound eager and are barking excitedly.

Dressed in just his underpants and vest he wades out into Sicklasjön. The chill stabs at his feet and legs.

He can hears sirens from emergency vehicles from several directions, carried across the water and through the trees.

Erik sees blue lights flashing over on Ältavägen, on the bridge across the inlet leading to Järlasjön. There are at least three police cars. The vehicles' lights reflect off the metal struts of the bridge and across the crowns of the trees on both shores.

The helicopter roars over the treetops again and he sinks quickly into the water. He holds his breath, but can clearly feel the change in the current as the helicopter passes. The water of the lake forms small waves radiating out in rapid circles.

He carries on, further out, slipping down amongst the water lilies, between their long stalks and the slimy bottom of the lake. There he lets the bundle of clothes containing his phone fill with bubbling water and sink.

In the other direction, beyond the dam, he can see that the bridge over the Sickla Channel has been blocked off. There are police cars everywhere. The tall fibreglass railings shimmer like huge plates of blue light. A helicopter is hovering above the ski slope.

Erik starts to swim, taking big strokes, feeling the cold against his lips and the smell of seawater. It can't be many hundred metres to the other side. Two jetties reach out into the water in front of the housing blocks erected by Atlas Copco after the war to house their guest-workers.

115

Erik swims, keeping his head low and trying not to disturb the surface of the lake too much. He's already more than one hundred metres out. The water merely laps quietly as he takes his broad strokes, but thunders in his ears when he's underwater.

He raises his head enough to be able to look ahead. Drops of water sparkle on his eyelashes as he sees the two jetties before they disappear behind the swell. The current is pulling him a long way off to one side.

High above the nature reserve the helicopter is clattering, but he can no longer hear any dogs.

Erik swims, thinking about how he lied nine years ago, and stole Rocky's whole life from him – and didn't spare him a thought until now.

He slows down, and treads water as he sees that he's just fifty metres from the two protruding jetties. A few children in bathing costumes are running about on the damp wood. There are people sitting with picnic baskets, blankets and folding chairs in the late summer warmth.

A motorboat appears to be approaching from the channel.

Erik swims towards the shore, beyond the beach. At the far end gnarled weeping willows hang over the water. The tips of their bright green branches trail in the undulating water.

The motorboat skims silently towards him, its prow striking the waves as the boat slows down.

Erik takes aim for the trees, fills his lungs with air, then dives below the surface.

He swims underwater with powerful strokes, feeling the coolness of the water against his face and eyes, its taste in his mouth, and the muffled sound as his ears fill.

The dappled daylight shimmers on the bubbles rising from his arms.

Beneath the water the motorboat makes a metallic buzzing sound.

Erik's shoulders are straining from the effort. It's further to the shore than he thought. The water below him is completely black, but the surface looks like molten tin.

His lungs feel tight. He has to breathe soon. The buzzing sound of the motorboat gets louder.

He keeps swimming, but is getting closer to the surface, has no energy left, needs oxygen.

Shimmering bubbles drift around him.

He kicks out with his legs and feels his diaphragm tighten, cramping in an effort to force his lungs to breathe in some air.

The water gets lighter, full of swirling sand. He can make out the bottom beneath him, rough blocks of stone and coarse sand. He takes one last stroke with his arms, then pulls himself forward across the stones with his hands.

Erik breaks the surface, gasps for breath, coughs, puts his hand over his mouth, coughs again and spits out a mouthful of slime. He's rocking with the swell from the boat. His vision goes dark and he gasps and wipes the water from his face with trembling hands.

He makes his way up on to the rocks on unsteady legs, then collapses. His whole body shakes as he sits behind the curtain of branches. The police boat is moving along the lake, but its engine is no longer audible.

Even if Nelly manages to leave her house and hire a car, it will be a while before she gets here. It makes sense to wait beneath the trees and dry off a bit before he makes his way to the meeting point.

The sound of shouting, laughing children fades away as if in fog. In the distance the sirens are howling, and the helicopter goes on circling above the nature reserve on the other side of the lake.

After half an hour or so Erik leaves his hiding place, climbs up the rocks, crosses the footpath and steps behind a large hazel bush. The ground in the shade beneath the branches is littered with toilet paper. He moves on towards the rust-red exterior of Sickla recreation centre.

Suddenly the sound of a siren echoes loudly between the walls, and he stops abruptly, his heart pounding. People are sitting at an outdoor café a short distance away, eating and drinking, quite unconcerned. The vehicle disappears and Erik carries on walking. He's just thinking that he needs to wait on the other side of the building, hidden by the bushes, when he catches sight of Nelly. She's wearing a green floral-print dress, and her blonde hair is tied up with a scarf of the same colour.

On the other side of the street is a black jeep. Nelly shades her face with one hand as she looks down towards the water.

Erik walks across the grass and steps across some low bushes, and is just emerging on to the pavement when Nelly catches sight of him. Her lips part as though she were suddenly frightened. Erik looks round for traffic, then walks straight across the road in his wet underpants. Nelly looks him quickly up and down, then lifts her chin as if they were about to have a perfectly ordinary discussion about patients.

'Original, but quite sexy,' she smiles, quickly opening the back door. 'Get under the blanket.'

He huddles down on the floor behind the seat and pulls the red rug over himself. The sun-heated car smells of plastic and leather.

Erik hears Nelly get in the driver's seat and close the door. She starts the engine and pulls away to the left, bumping off the kerb and then speeding up, and he slides back towards the seat.

'We know Rocky was wrongly convicted of the murder of Rebecka Hansson, but—'

'Not now, Nelly,' he interrupts.

'But do we know he's innocent of these new murders? I mean . . . What if he's started copying the murder he was convicted of . . . just to put the blame on you?'

'It's not him, I hypnotised him, he saw the preacher and . . .'

'But couldn't he just have divided himself into different characters? So that he's the unclean preacher when commits the murders?'

Nelly falls silent and inserts a disc into the CD player. The car fills with Johnny Cash's heavy voice: *Wanted man in California, wanted man in Buffalo, wanted man in Kansas City, wanted man in Ohio . . . wanted man in Mississippi, wanted man in ol' Cheyenne. Wherever you might look tonight, you might see this wanted man.*

Erik lies there with the blanket on top of him, smelling the sand on the mats on the floor, and can't help smiling at the fact that Nelly is trying to be funny at a time like this.

116

Rocky is asleep on the passenger seat next to Joona. His big head lolls to the side when the road bends. The landscape is sparsely populated and desolate, almost abandoned.

Joona is driving fast, thinking about the text message Lumi sent him earlier today. She wrote that she loves Paris, but misses their conversations up in Nattavaara.

Just beyond Flen the road and railway come together on two narrow strips of land. A long goods train thunders past next to the car, closer and closer. The brown trucks reflect off the water. The road and rails converge at an arrowhead, the train passes beneath them and then appears alongside again before dark pine forest comes between them.

The forest gradually grows thinner, and the landscape flattens into huge fields. Combine harvesters roll across the fields in clouds of dust, cutting off the stalks and separating wheat from chaff.

Sköldinge is on route 55, not far from Katrineholm. Joona turns off to the right and sees a few red houses through the trees, then the sandy-coloured church with its pointed spire, rising from the plain.

Sköldinge Church.

An ordinary Swedish church out in the countryside, dating back to the twelfth century, surrounded by rune stones.

The gravel crunches beneath the tyres as he pulls over and stops in front of the parish house.

Maybe they have found the serial killer now. The preacher from Rocky's nightmarish memories. The old priest with rouged cheeks and arms full of needle tracks.

The church door is closed and the windows dark.

Joona pulls his Colt Combat from its holster and notices that the tape is dirty and has started to peel off. He usually wraps sports tape round the lower part of the butt so that his hand doesn't slip if he finds himself in a drawn-out firefight.

He pulls out the magazine and checks that it's full, presses it back in and feeds a bullet into the chamber even though he can't really believe that the unclean preacher is just waiting for them inside the church.

Nothing is that simple.

The path has been raked, and the churchyard is well tended. The sun is filtering through the leaves of a huge oak.

The preacher is an extremely dangerous man, a serial killer who never rushes, who takes his time, who watches and plans, down to the last detail, until something else takes over and he turns into a wild animal.

His weakness is his arrogance, his narcissistic hunger.

Joona glances towards the church, then across the fields. He has two extra magazines of ordinary parabellum bullets in one pocket, and one magazine of fully jacketed ammunition in the other.

Even if the preacher isn't here, he thinks, even if he's never been here, this is the end of the road.

If he can't find something here that can convince Margot, then it's over, Erik will be found guilty even though he's innocent, just like Rocky was found guilty years ago of murdering Rebecka Hansson.

And the serial killer will go free.

Today is the day everything gets decided. Erik can't keep on running, he's got nowhere left to go, the hunters will drive him out of the forest.

And he himself has broken an inmate out of jail, used violence against a prison officer, threatened his life.

Disa would have said he was just under-stimulated, that he needs to get back to work. It's too late for that now, but he had no choice, in which case the consequences are irrelevant.

When Joona opens the door Rocky wakes up and looks at him with narrow, sleepy eyes.

'Wait here,' Joona says, and leaves the car.

Rocky gets out and spits on the ground, leans against the roof of the car and draws a line in the dirt with his hand.

'Do you recognise where we are?' Joona asks.

'No,' Rocky says, looking up at the church. 'But that doesn't mean anything.'

'I want you to wait in the car,' Joona repeats. 'I don't think the serial killer's here, but it could still be a dangerous situation.'

'I don't give a shit,' Rocky says bluntly.

He follows Joona between the graves. The air is fresh, as if it had just been raining. They pass a man in jeans and a T-shirt standing outside the porch, smoking and talking on his mobile.

The transition from bright sunlight leaves them almost completely blind when they walk into the darkness of the porch.

Joona moves quickly to one side, ready to draw his pistol.

He blinks and waits for his eyes to adapt before going in amongst the pews beneath the organ loft. Huge pillars hold up the roof and ornate frescos.

There's a knocking sound, and a shadow flits across the walls.

There's someone sitting in one of the front pews.

Joona stops Rocky, draws his gun and holds it hidden beside his hip.

A bird hits the window. It looks like a jackdaw that's got caught in a piece of twine, and keeps hitting the window when it tries to fly off.

The door to the sacristy is ajar. On the wall is a hazy cross in a circle.

Joona slowly approaches the huddled figure from behind, and sees a wrinkled hand holding on to the back of the pew in front.

The bird hits the window again. The shrunken figure slowly turns its head towards the sound.

It's an elderly Chinese woman.

Joona carries on past her, still concealing his gun, and looks at her from the side. Her face is downcast, impassive.

Beside the medieval font Mary sits like a child. Her wide, wooden dress falls in heavy folds around her feet.

At the centre of the altarpiece Christ hangs on the cross against a sky of gold, just as Rocky described it under hypnosis.

This was where he first met the unclean preacher, when the entire church was full of priests.

Now he's back.

Rocky has stopped in the darkened doorway beneath the organ loft. The instrument's pipes stick up above him like a row of quill pens.

He's standing still, irresolute. Like an apostate, he doesn't look up at the altar, and just stares down at his big, empty hands.

The Chinese woman stands up and walks out.

Joona knocks on the door of the sacristy, nudges the door open slightly and peers into the gloom. A set of vestments is hanging ready, but the room looks empty.

Joona steps aside and looks into the gap between the hinges, sees the uneven stone wall, like billowing fabric.

He opens the door further and walks in, his pistol at his chest. He quickly looks round at the liturgical textiles. High above, pale daylight filters in through a deep alcove.

Joona crosses the floor to the toilet and opens the door, but there's no one there. There's a wristwatch on the shelf above the hand-basin.

He raises his pistol and opens the door to the wardrobe. Chasubles, cassocks and stoles hang side by side, different colours for different seasons of the religious calendar. Joona quickly pushes the clothes aside and looks towards the back of the wardrobe.

There's something on the floor in one corner. A pile of magazines about sports cars.

Joona returns to the nave and walks past Rocky, who has sat down in one of the pews, and goes outside, where he asks the man by the door where the priest is.

'That's me,' the man smiles, dropping his cigarette in the empty coffee mug by his feet.

'I mean the other priest,' Joona explains.

'There's only me here,' he says.

Joona has already looked at his arms, they're free of injection scars.

'When were you ordained?'

'I was ordained as a curate in Katrineholm, and four years ago I was appointed as the priest here,' the man replies amiably.

'Who was here before you?'

'That was Rickard Magnusson . . . and before him, Erland Lodin and Peter Leer Jacobson, Mikael Friis and . . . I can't remember.'

The man has cut his hand, there's a grubby plaster across his palm.

'This probably sounds like a strange question,' Joona says. 'But when would a church be full of priests . . . in the pews, like the congregation?'

'When a priest is ordained, but that would be in a cathedral,' the priest replies helpfully, picking his mug up off the ground.

'But here?' Joona persists. 'Has this church ever been full of priests?'

'That would be for a priest's funeral . . . but that's up to the family to decide, it depends who gets invited . . . there are no special rules for priests.'

'Have you buried priests here?'

The man looks out across the headstones, the narrow paths and neatly trimmed bushes.

'I know that Peter Leer Jacobson is buried here in the churchyard,' he says quietly.

They go inside the porch, and the young priest's arms get goose-bumps from the coolness of the stone.

'When did he die?' Joona asks.

'Long before I got here. Fifteen years ago, maybe, I don't know.'

'Is there a record of who was here when he was buried?'

The man shakes his head and thinks for a moment.

'No record, but his sister would know, she still lives in the widows' home owned by the parish . . . He was a widower, and looked after her . . .'

Joona goes back inside the dimly lit church. Rocky is standing smoking beneath the medieval triumphal cross above the rood screen. Jesus and his entire emaciated body is dotted with red wounds, like an old heroin addict.

'What does "*Ossa ipsius in pace*" mean?' Joona asks.

'Why do you want to know?'

'You said it under hypnosis.'

'It means "his bones are at peace",' Rocky says in a rough voice.

'You were describing a dead priest – that's why he was wearing make-up.'

They walk quickly under the arch towards the door as Joona thinks about Rocky's description of a funeral service with an open coffin. The deceased priest was made-up and dressed in a white cassock, but he wasn't the unclean preacher. The funeral was simply the first time Rocky met him.

117

Beneath an ornate wrought-iron arch bearing the name 'Fridhem', a flight of stone steps leads up to the parish home for clergymen's widows, where Peter Leer Jacobson's older sister Ellinor was given permission to stay on after his death. Together with a younger woman from the Sköldinge village, she runs a café with a small exhibition about the village, and what life was like in bygone times for priests and their families.

Fridhem consists of three red cottages with white window frames and gables, open shutters and old-fashioned tiles on the roofs. The houses sit on three sides of a neat patch of lawn, with café tables beneath the weeping birch trees.

The two men enter the café and pass through a cramped room lined with framed black-and-white photographs. Joona glances along the pictures of buildings, teams of workers, priests' families. Three glass cabinets contain mourning jewellery made of jet, letters, inventories and hymnbooks.

Inside the pleasant café Joona buys two cups of coffee and a plate of biscuits from an elderly women in a flowery apron. She looks nervously at Rocky, who doesn't smile back when she tells them that the price includes a refill.

'Excuse me,' Joona says. 'But you must be Ellinor? Peter Leer Jacobson's sister?'

The woman gives him a quizzical nod. When Joona explains that they've just spoken to the new priest, who said so many nice things about her brother, her clear blue eyes fill with tears.

'Peter was very, very popular,' she says in a tremulous voice, then tries to catch her breath.

'You must have been very proud of him,' Joona smiles.

'Yes, I was.'

In a rather touching gesture, she pulls her hands together over her stomach in an effort to calm down.

'There's something I was wondering,' Joona goes on. 'Did your brother have a particular colleague, someone he worked closely with?'

'Yes . . . that would have been the rural dean in Katrineholm . . . and the vicars of Floda and Stora Malm . . . And I know he spent a lot of time in Lerbo Church towards the end.'

'Did they see each other privately as well?'

'My brother was a fine man,' she says. 'An honourable man, very well liked . . .'

Ellinor looks around the empty room, then walks round the counter and shows Joona a framed newspaper cutting from the King and Queen's visit to Strängnäs.

'Peter was chaplain at the jubilee service in the cathedral,' she says in a proud voice. 'The bishop thanked him afterwards, and—'

'Show her your arms,' Joona tells Rocky.

Without changing his expression at all, Rocky rolls up the sleeves of his top.

'My brother was the orator at the diocesan meeting in Härnösand, and he—'

The old woman trails off when she sees Rocky's ravaged arms, uneven and stained from hundreds of injection scars, dark with veins that have disintegrated from the ascorbic acid he's used to dissolve the heroin.

'He's a priest too,' Joona says without taking his eyes off her. 'Anyone can get trapped.'

Ellinor's wrinkled face turns pale and motionless. She sits down on the wooden bench with her hand over her mouth.

'My brother changed after the accident . . . when his wife passed away,' she says in a quiet voice. 'Grief destroyed him, he withdrew from everyone . . . thought someone was following him, that everyone was spying on him.'

'When was this?'

'Sixteen years ago . . .'

'What did your brother use to inject himself with?'

She looks at him with exhausted eyes.

'On the boxes it said Morphine Epidural . . .'

The woman shakes her head and her old hands flutter restlessly over her apron.

'I didn't know anything . . . he was all alone in the end, not even his daughter could stand it, she looked after him for as long as she could, but now I understand why she couldn't go on.'

'But he was still able to conduct services, do his job?'

She raises her bloodshot eyes towards Joona.

'Oh yes, he conducted his services, no one noticed anything, not even me, because we no longer spent any time together . . . but I used to go to the morning service, and . . . Everyone said his sermons were stronger than ever . . . even though he himself was growing weaker.'

Rocky mutters something and walks away from them. They watch him through the window as he emerges on to the lawn and goes and sits down at a table under the weeping birch.

'How did you find out?' Joona asks.

'I was the one who found him,' the old woman replies. 'I was the one who took care of the body.'

'Was it an overdose?'

'I don't know, he'd missed the morning service, so I went into the rectory . . . There was a terrible stench in there . . . I found him in the cellar . . . he had been dead for three days, naked and filthy, covered in scabs . . . he was lying in the cage like an animal.'

'He was lying in a cage?'

She nods and wipes her nose.

'All he had was a mattress and a can of water,' she whispers.

'Didn't you think it was odd that he was in a cage?'

The old woman shakes her head.

'It had been locked from the inside . . . I've always thought that he tried to lock himself in to escape the drugs.'

A younger woman in a similar apron comes out and stands behind the counter when some more customers arrive.

'Could one of your brother's colleagues have helped him write his sermons?' Joona asks.

'I don't know.'

'He probably had a computer, could I take a look at it?'

'He had one in the office, but he wrote his sermons by hand.'

'Have you kept them?'

Ellinor slowly stands up from the bench.

'I took care of his estate,' she says. 'I cleaned out the rectory so

that there wouldn't be any gossip . . . but he'd got rid of everything
. . . There were no photographs, no letters or sermons . . . I couldn't
even find his diaries, he'd always kept a diary . . . He used to keep
them locked up in his bureau, but it was empty.'

'Could they be anywhere else?'

She stands still and her mouth moves silently until the words
come.

'I've only got one diary left . . . It was hidden in the drinks cabinet,
they usually have a secret compartment at the back, where gentlemen
could keep their saucy French postcards.'

'What did it say in the diary?' Joona says.

She smiles and shakes her head.

'I would never read it, you don't do that sort of thing . . .'

'Of course not,' he replies.

'But many years ago Peter used to get his diaries out at Christmas
and read about Mother and Father, and about ideas for sermons . . .
he wrote very well.'

The door to the café opens once more and a draught sweeps through
the cosy room, spreading the smell of fresh coffee.

'Do you have the diary here?' Joona asks.

'It's in the exhibition,' she says. 'We call it a museum, but it's really
just a few things we found here.'

He goes with her to the exhibition. An enlarged photograph from
1850 shows three thin women in black dresses in front of the home
for widows. The buildings look almost black. The picture was taken
early one spring, the trees are bare and there's still snow in the furrows
of the field.

Beneath the picture is a short caption about the priest who had
Fridhem built so that his wife wouldn't have to marry the next priest
if he died before her.

Next to the earrings and necklace of polished jade lies a rusty key
and a small colour photograph showing the funeral of Peter Leer
Jacobson. A man dressed in black is acting as marshal of ceremonies,
holding the black veil. The bishop, and the priest's daughter and sister
are standing by the coffin with their faces lowered.

They walk past pictures of the mine at Kantorp, women and children
sorting the ore in bright sunshine, Sköldinge workhouse, and the
opening of the railway station. One black-and-white photograph of

the church has been hand-tinted, so that the sky is pastel blue, the vegetation looks tropical, and the wooden construction of the new steeple shines like polished bronze.

'Here's the diary,' Ellinor says, stopping in front of a glass cabinet containing an array of objects.

118

On top of a linen cloth lies a rusty hairgrip, a pocket watch, a white hymnbook bearing the name 'Anna' in gold writing, a page of old church accounts, Luther's *Small Catechism* and the priest's diary, with a lilac strap round its stained leather binding.

The old woman looks at Joona with frightened eyes as she opens the case and removes the diary. On the front page, in ornate handwriting, are the words 'Peter Leer Jacobson, priest, volume XXIV'.

'I don't think it's right to read other people's diaries,' she says with a hint of anxiety in her voice.

'No,' Joona says, and opens the book.

He sees at once that it's old: the first entry is dated almost twenty years ago.

'We don't have the right to—'

'I have to,' Joona interrupts.

He leafs through, staring at the handwriting in the hope of finding something about the person who wrote Peter's sermons.

The administration of the parish has become more onerous, the guidelines stricter. I fear that finances will come to govern my church more and more. ~~Why not start selling indulgences again [Sic!].~~

Today is the fifth Sunday after Epiphany, and the liturgical colours are getting darker again. The theme is 'Sowing and Reaping'. I don't like the warning in Paul's Letter to the Galatians about not mocking God. 'For whatsoever a man soweth, that shall he also reap.' But sometimes you haven't sown, yet must still reap. I can't say that to my congregation – they want to hear about the riches of heaven.

Joona looks up and sees the old woman leave the room with her hands hanging by her sides.

I met the pasty-faced contract priest in Lerbo for a private conversation. He was probably expecting me to talk about my drinking. He's young, but his faith is so strong that it makes me feel bad. I decided not to visit him again.

My daughter is growing up now. The other day I watched her without her knowing. She was sitting in front of the mirror, she had her hair just like Anna's, and was smiling to herself.

Today is the fifth Sunday after Easter. The theme for the sermon is 'Growing in Faith'. I think about Grandmother and Grandfather who went to Guinea before they moved to the farm in Roslagen. In my congregation there is no place for missionary work, and that makes me wonder.

Joona sits down on one of the old chairs beneath the photographs. He leafs through the book, reading about the duties of the liturgical year, Christmas carols, summer services at some mill or other. He goes back through it again, looking for any further mention of the priest in Lerbo, and finds himself in the middle of Easter.

The Gospels turn their attention to the empty grave, but around the dinner table we talked about the Old Testament text describing the last plague to strike Egypt. My daughter said that God loves blood, and referred to one of Easter's biblical texts: 'And the blood shall be to you for a token upon the houses where you are: and when I see the blood I will pass over you.'

My wife and I haven't shared a bedroom for a year now. I usually stay up late, and I snore like a mechanical digger (according to her). But we often sneak in to each other at night. Sometimes I go with Anna to her bedroom in the evening just to watch her get ready. I've always liked watching her take off her jewellery at night, pressing the little studs back on to her earrings and putting them in the case next to each other. Anna is quietly attentive to detail. She doesn't reach behind her back when she takes her bra off, but slips the straps over her shoulders, slides the bra down to her waist and turns it round before unfastening it.

When I sat on her bed last night watching her plait her hair ready for bed, I thought I could see a face at the dark window. I got up and

went over, but I couldn't see anything, so I went out on to the veranda,
then into the garden, but everything was quiet and I looked up at the
starry sky instead.

Joona looks out of the window and sees that Rocky is still sitting
under the tree, with his eyes closed and legs outstretched. He carries
on reading.

~~*I saw the pasty-faced priest from Lerbo in the supermarket yesterday, but*~~
~~*didn't have to say hello.*~~

Fourth Sunday in Lent.
So we have reached the midpoint of Lent. Headache, sat up late
drinking wine, reading and writing.

Today we think about 'the bread of Life'. The holy days of Easter are
almost upon us, and the heavy fist of existence presses us to the ground.

Joona leafs forward, glancing at the pages about Trinity Sunday and
the transition to the gentler half of the church calendar, before stopping
abruptly and reading:

It has happened, terrible, impossible. I shall write about it here, and beg
God for forgiveness, then I shall never mention it again. My hand is
shaking as I write this, two days later:
Like old Lot I was tricked into breaking the Lord's commandment,
but I am writing to understand my role in this, my share of the guilt.
It got rather late, and I drank more wine than I could handle, more
that I usually do, and I was drunk when I went to bed and fell asleep.

In hindsight I think I was aware on some level that it wasn't Anna
who crept into my bed in the darkness, she smelled like Anna, she was
wearing my wife's jewellery and nightshirt, but she was scared, her body
was trembling as I lay on top of her.

She didn't whisper at all, she didn't sigh like Anna, she was breathing
as if to resist giving in to pain.

I tried to turn on the lamp, I was still so drunk that it fell to the floor, I stood up, staggered, followed the wall with my hand and turned on the main light.

In my bed sat my daughter. She was wearing make-up and smiling, even though she was scared.

I roared, I shouted, and rushed over and tore Anna's earrings from her ears, I rubbed her face on the bloodstained sheet, I dragged her down the stairs and out into the snow, I slipped and fell, got up again and shoved her away.

She was freezing, and her ears were bleeding, but she was still smiling.

I shall be punished, I must be punished, I should have seen this coming. Isolation and blossoming, her creeping, spying, always fiddling with Anna's jewellery and make-up.

Joona stops reading, looks at the rusty key and the black earrings in the case, and at the text about having to take on the last priest's wife. He leaves the exhibition with the diary in his hand, passing the picture of the skinny widows. Out in the café Ellinor is putting small coffee cups on saucers on the shelf behind the counter. The porcelain tinkles gently as she stacks it. A lethargic fly has flown in through the open doors and is now bouncing against the window as it tries to get out.

Ellinor turns round when she hears Joona come in. It's clear from her face that she regrets mentioning her brother's diary.

'Can I ask how Peter's wife died?'

'I don't know,' she says curtly and carries on stacking cups and saucers.

'You said you were friends, you and Anna.'

The old woman's chin trembles.

'I think you should leave now,' she says.

'I can't,' Joona replies.

'I thought you were interested in Peter's sermons, that's why I . . .'

She shakes her head, picks up a tray containing coffee and two pastries, and starts to walk towards the door.

Joona follows her, holding the door for her and waiting as she takes the tray over to the customers in the garden.

'I don't want to talk about it,' she says weakly.

'It wasn't an accident?' he asks sharply.

Her face becomes completely helpless and she looks like she's about to cry.

'I don't want to,' she pleads. 'Don't you understand? It's too late . . .'

She lowers her face and sobs quietly to herself.

The other woman comes in and puts her hands on Ellinor's shaking shoulders. The other customers get up and change tables.

'I'm a police officer,' Joona says. 'I can find this out, but—'

'Please, leave now,' the other woman says, hugging Ellinor.

'It was just an accident,' the old priest's sister says.

'I don't want to upset you,' Joona goes on. 'But I need to know what happened, and I need to know now.'

'It was a car accident,' Ellinor whimpers. 'It was pouring with rain . . . they drove straight into the church wall, the car buckled and crushed Anna, she hit her face so badly that . . .'

She sits down unsteadily at one of the tables and stares ahead of her.

'Go on,' Joona says gently.

The woman looks up at him, wipes the tears from her eyes and nods.

'We saw it from the rectory . . . My brother ran out, down the road . . . and I followed him through the rain, and saw their daughter fighting to get her out, she was using the car-jack . . . kept hitting it against the car . . . and I just screamed and ran off through the thicket of willow . . .'

The woman's voice cracks, and she opens and closes her mouth a couple of times before she goes on:

'There was broken glass and wreckage from the car everywhere, and there was a smell of petrol and hot metal . . . Their daughter had given up, she was just standing there waiting for her father to get there . . . I can still remember the look of shock in her eyes, and her peculiar smile . . .'

Ellinor raises her hands and looks down at her palms.

'Dear God,' she whispers, 'the girl had just got home from Klockhammar School and there she was, standing there in her yellow raincoat looking at her mother. Anna's face was crushed beyond recognition, there was blood everywhere, all over . . .'

Her voice fails her again and she swallows, then continues slowly.

'Memory is a strange thing,' she says. 'I know I heard a very high voice as I got closer through the rain, it was like a child talking . . . And then it started to burn, I saw a blue bubble enclose Anna, and the next moment I was lying in the wet grass in the ditch and the flames were spiralling around the whole car. The birch-tree alongside caught fire, and I—'

'Who was driving?'

'I don't want to talk about it . . .'

'The daughter,' Joona says. 'What's her name?'

'Nelly,' the old woman replies, looking up at him with exhaustion etched on her face.

119

Joona tries to call Erik as he walks between the café tables towards Rocky.

His phone is switched off.

He dials Margot Silverman's private number but there's no answer, so he calls his former boss at the National Criminal Investigation Department, Carlos Eliasson, instead and leaves a short voicemail.

Rocky is still sitting in the shade under the weeping birch, picking biscuit crumbs from his stomach. He's taken his shoes and socks off and is wriggling his toes on the grass.

'We have to go,' Joona says when he reaches him.

'Did you find the answers to your questions?'

Joona carries on past Rocky and hurries down the steps towards the car park. He's thinking that Peter didn't keep volume twenty-four of his diary in the bureau with the others because its content was too shameful. And because of that, Nelly missed it when she destroyed the rest of them.

Towards the end of the diary Peter describes how his daughter was sent to an old-fashioned girls' boarding school.

Joona stops in front of the stolen car and thinks that Nelly was fourteen when she started at Klockhammar School outside Örebro. She was at boarding school for six years. It's possible that she didn't see her parents at all during that time, but never let go of her fixation on her father.

The feeling of loving and being rejected, of giving everything and having everything taken from you, led to her developing a serious personality disorder.

She studied her mother, tried to be like her, to take her place.

Rocky has got his shoes back on but is holding his socks in his hand as he comes down to the car park and opens the door.

'Is the unclean preacher a woman?' Joona asks.

'I don't think so,' Rocky replies, looking him in the eye.

'Do you remember Nelly Brandt?'

'No,' he says, getting in the passenger seat.

Joona removes the plastic covering the ignition cylinder, twines the red wires together, removes the tape from the brown starter wires and touches the ends together, causing a spark as the engine bursts into life.

'I don't know how much you remember from being hypnotised,' Joona says as he drives. 'But you talked about the first time you saw the unclean preacher . . . You met her at a funeral here in Sköldinge, but the person you described was the priest in the coffin, her father, Peter . . .'

Rocky doesn't answer, just stares blankly through the windscreen as their speed increases along the narrow road through the fields and forest.

Joona thinks that the mother went to fetch her grown-up daughter from Klockhammar School and let her drive back.

Her mother was sitting next to her, maybe took her seat belt off when they turned off the main road and drove up to the church.

Nelly probably saw her father in the windows of the rectory as she suddenly put her foot down and drove straight into the wall.

Perhaps her mother wasn't dead, just badly hurt and trapped in the wreckage.

In which case what Ellinor saw through the rain makes sense, Nelly fetched the car-jack from the boot and beat her mother in the face until she was dead.

Perhaps she set light to the car in front of her father's eyes.

But after her mother's death Nelly looked after him, isolated him from the world around him, keeping him to herself, and becoming everything for him.

Her father lived another two years. Nelly kept him locked up and helpless, keeping him in a cage and making him dependent on morphine.

She would let him out on Sundays and gave him sermons that she had written for the morning service.

He was broken, a wreck, an addict.

Joona thinks that they may have had fragments of normal life, it isn't unusual that people who are held captive for a long period of time are allowed short periods of normal life with their captor. Perhaps they ate dinner together, sat on the sofa, watched particular television programmes.

In the end he worked out how to lock his cage from the inside, and slept on the mattress.

It's possible that he died of an overdose, unless he just got ill.

A large number of priests attended the funeral, some of them sitting in the pews while others assisted with the ceremony.

One of those priests was Rocky Kyrklund from the parish of Salem.

They've just driven past Flen, and a lake is shimmering silver and blue to the right of the car as Joona takes out his phone, brings up a list of staff at the Karolinska Institute and finds a photograph of Nelly.

'Look at this picture,' he says.

Rocky takes the phone, holds the screen away from the daylight and then gasps for breath.

'Stop!' he roars. 'Stop the car!'

He opens the door as they're speeding along, but it hits a railing and bounces back, and glass from the broken window flies into the car. The door is hanging loose, scraping along the tarmac. Joona pulls over to the verge and comes to a halt with two wheels up on the grass.

A lorry blows its horn angrily behind them and passes so close that the ground shakes.

Rocky walks out into the field beside the road, striding past the plastic-wrapped bales of hay lying scattered across the ground, stops, and holds his face in his hands.

120

Joona sits there with the engine running, picks his phone off the floor and tries to call Erik again. Rocky stands in the field with his face turned up towards the sky for a long while before returning to the car. He yanks the broken door off, tosses it in the ditch and gets back in his seat.

'I remember her,' he says without looking at Joona. 'She had her head shaved, pale as candle-wax, she went to Klockhammar School . . . After the funeral I had sex with her on the floor of the hall in the rectory . . . it didn't mean anything, we'd been talking and drinking coffee, and I was in no hurry to get home.'

Joona says nothing, aware that even though the photograph triggered Rocky's memory, the flood of information is finite. He could lose touch with his past again at any moment.

'I remember it all,' Rocky says dreamily. 'She came looking for me in Salem, came to the services . . . She was just there, as part of my life, without me really realising how it had happened . . .'

He drifts off in thought and pokes a cigarette out of the packet with trembling hands. His rough grey hair is frizzy and his thick eyebrows have tightened across the top of his nose.

'I'm a priest,' he says eventually. 'But I'm also a man . . . I do things I might not always be proud of. I'm not boyfriend material, I'm clear about that, I've never been faithful or . . .'

He falls silent again as if the strength of his memories has taken his breath away.

'Sometimes I slept with her, sometimes she had to wait, I never promised her anything, I didn't want her fucking sermons . . . I remember, it was always about me watching out for promiscuous women . . . "Her house is the way to hell" . . .'

The car shakes as a bus drives past, and Joona sees Rocky gaze out across the field and lake at the little cluster of trees in the distance.

'When I told her I was fed up with her, she disappeared,' he goes on. 'But I understood that she was still creeping around outside the rectory . . . I opened the door and shouted into the darkness, telling her to leave me the fuck alone.'

He stops talking again and Joona waits in silence so as not to pull Rocky out of his fragile reminiscences.

'The following evening she came to the church with twenty capsules of white heroin and it all started again . . . it went fucking fast,' he says, looking gloomily at Joona. 'I was hooked as good as instantly. We shared needles, she followed me everywhere, talking about God, preaching, sank into squalor with me, wanted to be with me, wanted to be part of me.' He shakes his head and rubs his face.

'We hung out at the Zone, I didn't care about all her preaching . . . it was mostly extreme interpretations of the Bible, proof that we should get married . . . a whole worldview in which a jealous God proved her right.'

A trace of pain flashes in his eyes as he looks darkly at Joona.

'I was drugged and stupid,' he says. 'I told her I loved Natalia. It wasn't true, but I still said it.'

All the energy goes out of him and his chin sinks to his chest.

'Natalia had such beautiful hands,' he says, then falls silent.

His face is suddenly very pale and he looks out at the fields. His forehead is shiny with sweat, and a drop falls from his nose on to his chest.

'You were talking about Natalia,' Joona says after a while.

'What?'

Rocky looks at him uncomprehendingly, leans out of the car and spits on the grass. A car pulling a trailer full of chopped wood drives past.

'Nelly showed pictures of the people she was planning to kill,' Joona goes on. 'But Natalia had to die in front of you . . .'

Rocky shakes his head.

'All I know is that God lost me somewhere along the way, and didn't bother to go back and look,' he mutters hoarsely.

Joona doesn't say anything more. He takes his phone out and calls Erik's number again, but still can't get through.

He calls Margot but gives up after ten rings.

Now he knows who the preacher is, but he can't prove anything, and he's got nothing to give the police. There's a chance that Margot might listen to him, but he may well have gone too far when he broke Rocky out of jail.

Joona tries to understand why Nelly has been stalking Erik. They're only colleagues, and Nelly is married to Martin Brandt. It must have been going on for years, and it isn't going to end well.

121

Grit flies up behind them as they set off again. The car fills with a thunderous, jolting wind.

As Joona pushes the car as hard as it will go, he tries to get a picture of the serial killer clear in his mind. After they had sex following her father's funeral, Nelly transferred her affections to Rocky. She stalked him, followed him, made herself part of his life, tried to control him with drugs, and killed the women who threatened their union. She created an impossible life for Rocky by making sure he was the main suspect for the murder of Rebecka Hansson. In the end she kept him in a cage, was supplying him with heroin and thought she owned him completely, when he managed to escape. He stole a car in Finsta and crashed on his way to Arlanda. The accident left him with serious brain damage, he lost all appeal to her and ended up being sentenced to secure psychiatric care.

Maybe Nelly caught sight of Erik when he was called in as an expert witness during Rocky Kyrklund's trial.

Joona shudders at the thought that Nelly probably started stalking Erik as long ago as that, slowly and systematically getting closer to him.

She studied and got her qualifications, got a job at the same place as him, married Martin and supported Erik during his separation from Simone.

After the divorce her assumption of ownership grew stronger, and she started to keep watch on him, couldn't bear any sign of competition, and became pathologically jealous. She probably wanted him to choose her of his own accord, that he would have eyes for no one but her, but when that didn't happen something snapped inside her and she had to act in order to stop herself falling apart.

When Erik embarked on an affair with Maria Carlsson, she probably thought everything would be fine if she could just get rid of her rival.

A stalker always develops a relationship with their victim in their imagination, a relationship that they convince themselves is real and reciprocated.

In her head Nelly may have believed that she was married to Erik, and when she saw him betraying her with Maria Carlsson, attracted by Sandra Lundgren, flirting with Susanna Kern and maybe just smiling at Katryna Youssef, a vicious beast woke up.

Joona turns off towards Malmköping, stops in the car park outside Lindholm's Floor and Building Services and switches to a better car.

They're driving along the E20 motorway at 190 kilometres an hour when Margot calls from her private phone.

'There's a warrant out for your arrest, did you know that?' she asks.

'I know, but . . .'

'You're going to end up in prison for this,' she cuts him off.

'It was worth it,' he replies quietly.

A few seconds of silence follow.

'Now I realise why you're a better detective than me,' Margot says in a subdued voice.

Joona overtakes a black Corvette on the inside and pulls out again just in time to overtake an articulated lorry with a mustard-yellow trailer.

'Our forensics team have found strands of Erik's hair in Sandra Lundgren's bath, we've already got his fingerprints on the deer's head, he's connected to all the victims, he's got thousands of hours of video-recordings in his basement, and—'

'It's too much,' Joona says.

'And the analysis of the blood in Erik's car showed that it was Susanna Kern's . . . and now it's getting too much even for me,' she says heavily.

'Good,' Joona says.

'Erik's a doctor . . . this doesn't make sense, because all four murders show clear signs of forensic awareness . . . And someone like that doesn't end up with blood in their own car . . . Someone left those traces of blood on the back seat to frame him.'

'You've met the real killer,' Joona says.

'Is it Nestor?'

'It's Nelly Brandt . . . she's the preacher.'

'You sound sure,' Margot says.

'It's Erik she's after, he's the one she's been stalking, the victims are just rivals in her own head.'

'If you're certain about this, I'll get an operation organised at once,' Margot says. 'We'll hit her home and workplace at the same time.'

Joona drives on towards Stockholm as he thinks of how Nelly has stalked Erik for years, mapping the lives of any women he showed an interest in, trying to understand what they had that she couldn't offer. She saw them flashing their jewellery, their painted lips, beautiful nails, and wanted to take that away from them, punish them, and then emphasise their bare ears or ugly hands.

But when that wasn't enough she tried to take the whole world away from him. Like Artemis with her hounds, she organised a hunt, Joona thinks. She's a skilful huntress, she isolates her prey, wounds it, and harries it towards capture until there's only one way out.

Her intention was for Erik to realise that everything pointed at him, and go on the run before the police caught him. Everyone would shun him, until in the end he turned to the only person who was still prepared to let him in.

If he hasn't been caught by the police by now, he must have sought protection from Nelly.

122

Jackie is feeling restless. She goes out into the kitchen and thinks about getting something to eat, even though she isn't really hungry.

Maybe she should just have a quiet sit down and drink a cup of tea.

She feels across the worktop with her hand, along the tiles, past the big mortar, and finds the pot of tealeaves with the little glass knob.

Her hands stop.

She feels her way back to the stone mortar.

The heavy pestle isn't resting in the bowl like it usually is.

Jackie runs her fingers across the whole worktop but can't find it, and thinks that she'll have to ask Maddy about it once things between them have calmed down a bit.

She stifles a yawn and fills the kettle with water.

During the days following her row with Erik, Maddy kept saying that Erik was sad and that he'd never want to come back to them now. Maddy tried to explain that she forgets loads of things, and embarked on a long description of how she'd forgotten keys and notes and football boots.

Jackie has tried to explain that she isn't angry any more, that it isn't anyone's fault when things don't work out between two grown-ups. But then the media witch-hunt started.

Jackie hasn't told her daughter why she's keeping her home from school. She's postponed all her lessons with her pupils and has cancelled all her work as an organist.

To help the days pass and to stop herself thinking so much, she's been spending all her waking hours at the piano, practising scales and finger exercises until she feels ill and her elbows hurt so much that she has to take painkillers.

Obviously she hasn't told her daughter what they're saying about Erik on the news.

She'd never be able to understand it.

Jackie can't understand it herself.

She doesn't listen to the television any more, can't bear to hear the speculation, the wallowing in pain and grief.

Maddy has stopped talking about Erik now, but she's still very subdued. She's been watching children's programmes for younger children, and Jackie has a feeling she's gone back to sucking her thumb.

Jackie feels a lump of anxiety in her stomach when she thinks about how she lost patience with Maddy when she didn't want to play the piano today. She told her she was acting like a baby, and Maddy started to cry and shouted back that she was never going to help with anything ever again.

Now she's hiding in her wardrobe, with blankets, pillows and stuffed toys, and she doesn't answer when Jackie tries to talk to her.

I have to show her that she doesn't have to be perfect, Jackie thinks. That I love her no matter what, that it's unconditional.

She walks along the cool hallway into the living room, which is flooded with sunlight from the windows. The light feels like streaks of hot water, and she knows the piano is going to feel as warm as a large animal.

Out in the street some sort of engineering work is going on, she can feel the muffled vibration of large machines beneath her bare feet, and she can hear the old windowpanes rattle in their frames.

In the middle of the parquet floor she feels something sticky beneath her heel. Maddy must have spilled some juice. There's a fusty smell in the room, a smell of nettles and damp soil.

An itchy, electric sense of danger flares up inside her, and she feels a shiver run up her spine to her neck.

It's hardly surprising that she's shaken up after everything that's happened, the things that are being said about Erik are terrible, she thinks as she wonders if she just heard something from the window facing the courtyard.

She listens, and walks closer to the glass. Everything is quiet, but someone could easily be standing there looking at her when the curtains are open.

She moves cautiously towards the window and puts her hand out to touch the glass.

She closes the curtains, the hooks jangle on the rails, and then everything is quiet again, apart from the gentle sound of the curtains swaying against the wall.

Jackie goes over to the piano, sits down on the stool, lifts the lid of the keyboard, settles more comfortably, lowers her hands and feels something lying across the keys.

It's a piece of fabric.

She picks it up and feels it. It's a cloth or scarf of some sort.

Maddy must have put it there.

It's a piece of intricate embroidery. She follows the pattern of the stitches with her fingertips.

It seems to be some sort of animal, with four legs, and wings or feathers on its back, and a man's head with a curly beard.

She stands up slowly as her whole body goes cold, as if she had just fallen straight through broken ice.

There's someone in the room.

She felt it a moment ago, just now.

The parquet floor creaks behind her back under the weight of an adult body.

A feeling of absolute danger makes the world shrink to a compact point in which she is utterly alone with her terror.

'Erik?' she says without turning round.

Something rustles slowly and the vibration from the floor makes the empty fruit-bowl on the table rattle.

'Is that you, Erik?' she asks as calmly as she can. 'You can't just turn up here like this . . .'

She turns round and hears the sound of unfamiliar breathing, shallow and agitated.

Jackie moves slowly towards the door.

He stays where he is, but there's a sort of squeaking sound, as if he were wearing plastic clothes, or rubber.

'We can talk through everything,' she says, with obvious fear in her voice. 'I overreacted, I know I did, I wanted to call you . . .'

He doesn't answer, just shifts his weight from one foot to the other. The floor creaks beneath him.

'I'm not cross any more, I think about you all the time . . . it's going to be fine,' she says weakly.

She moves into the passageway leading to the hall, thinking that she has to get out, that she has to lure Erik out of the flat, away from Maddy.

'Let's go and sit in the kitchen – Maddy hasn't come home yet,' she lies.

There's a sudden thudding sound on the floor, he's rushing towards her and she holds up a hand to stop him.

Something strikes her raised arm. The pestle glances off her elbow and she staggers backwards.

The adrenalin rushing through her veins means that she doesn't even notice the pain in her arm.

Jackie backs away, holding her injured arm up, turns and walks into the wall, hits her knees against the little table, grabs the glass bowl that Maddy usually uses for popcorn, and strikes out hard. She hits him and drops the bowl. He falls forward into her and Jackie hits her back against the bookcase.

Jackie can feel his rain-clothes against her body. She pushes him away with both hands and smells his bitter breath on her face.

Books crash to the floor.

It isn't Erik, she thinks.

That isn't his smell.

She runs, with her hand against the wall, into the hall and reaches the front door, and starts to turn the lock with shaking hands.

Heavy footsteps approach from behind.

She opens the door, but something jangles and the door bounces back.

The safety chain, she forgot the safety chain.

She pulls the door shut, fumbles with the chain but she's shaking too much and can't unfasten it.

The person who wants to kill her is coming closer, making a little purring sound in their throat.

Jackie pushes the twisted chain sideways with her fingers and suddenly it comes loose, she opens the door and tumbles out into the stairwell. She almost falls, but manages to reach her neighbour's door and bangs on it with the palm of her hand.

'Open the door!' Jackie screams.

She feels movement behind her, turns round and puts her arms up in front of her face to shield it from the blow.

Jackie falls against her neighbour's door, blood runs down her cheek and she lets out a deep gasp as the next blow knocks her head sideways.

A bitter flower blossoms and fills her mouth and nostrils, a warm flower with petals like thin feathers.

123

From where he's lying, Erik can't hear anything except the sound of the engine, the monotonous thrum of the tyres on the tarmac, and Nelly's inadvertent little sighs as she concentrates on the traffic.

After Sickla strand, she drove for twenty minutes around central Stockholm, with lots of traffic lights, turns and changes of lane. Then she stopped and got out of the car, and was gone for a long time. Erik lay there completely covered by the blanket, occasionally shifting position very carefully, waiting. He fell asleep in the heat of the car, but woke up abruptly to the sound of voices right outside the car.

It sounded like two men quietly discussing something with each other. He tried to hear what they were saying, he thought they sounded like police, but wasn't sure.

He lay motionless with the heavy blanket over his back, trying to breathe carefully. The whole of his right side went numb, but he didn't dare change position until long after the voices had gone.

After another forty minutes or so Nelly came back. He heard her open the back of the car and lift some heavy luggage in with a groan. The car rocked, and then she got into the driver's seat. She started the engine and Igor Stravinsky's *Symphony of Psalms* filled the car.

When they emerged on to the motorway he dared to lift the blanket from his face. Nelly's voice sounded cheerful when she called out to him over the music, saying she must be mad to be doing this, but that she went through a serious punk phase when she was sixteen and still wanted revenge on the cops and all the other fascist bastards.

They've been driving for over an hour when she slows down, pressing Erik against the back of the driver's seat in front of him.

The large vehicle turns sharply into an uneven track. Small stones clatter against the underside of the chassis. She slows down even more, and Erik hears branches scraping against the roof and windows. The car rocks over lumps and potholes before coming to a halt. There's a click as the handbrake is applied on, then silence.

The driver's door opens and when the cool air carrying a hint of diesel reaches him, he finally dares to sit up on the back seat. Dazed, he looks out across overgrown ruins and sees a white sky, leafy treetops and large fields that have been left fallow.

They're deep in the countryside. Grasshoppers are chirruping in the tall grass. Nelly stands and looks at him with shining eyes. Her floral green dress is creased around her thighs, and strands of her blonde hair have escaped from the scarf round her head. One of her cheeks seems to be blushing oddly, as if she's had a knock. Everything is so quiet and there's so little wind that Erik can hear the charms on her bracelet jangle as she adjusts the glittery bag on her shoulder.

He pushes the door open and climbs out carefully on to the grass. His vest has dried, and his whole body aches.

Nelly has parked in an overgrown courtyard. A yellow two-storey house stands in the middle of the ruins of some sort of factory. A tall brick chimney rises from a sooty oven. The buildings are surrounded by weeds, and through the tall grass he can make out the remains of a huge grid of railway sleepers.

'Come on, let's go inside,' Nelly says, licking her lips.

'Is this Solbacken?' Erik asks in surprise.

'Nice, isn't it?' she says, and giggles.

Broken glass shimmers in the courtyard, and there are bricks and soot-blackened sheets of corrugated tin lying in the tall grass. The foundations of some of the buildings have collapsed in on their cellars, and the shafts look like empty pools with weeds growing at the bottom, and brick arches leading to underground tunnels.

An old washing machine stands in a clump of young elms, along with a few dirty plastic chairs and a couple of tractor tyres.

'Now I want to show you the house, I love it,' she says, tucking her hand under his arm with a contented smile.

The whole of the main house is surrounded by dark green stinging nettles. The gutter has come loose and is resting on the roof of the veranda.

'It's really nice inside,' she says, trying to pull him along.

The ground sways and he feels suddenly sick, and he finds himself staring at a pool of brown water with a sheen of oil on its surface.

'How are you feeling?' Nelly asks with an anxious smile.

'It's hard getting a grip on everything . . . that fact that I'm here now,' he replies.

'Let's go inside,' she says, walking backwards towards the house without taking her eyes off him.

'I hypnotised Rocky this morning,' Erik tells her. 'He remembered the person who murdered Rebecka Hansson, he said the name of the church where they met.'

'We'll have to try to tip the police off about that,' she says.

'I don't know . . . everything's—'

'Come on, let's go in,' she interrupts, and sets off towards the house.

'I haven't had any time to think, I've just been running,' he says as he follows her across the yard.

'Of course,' she replies in a distant voice.

A crow hops away and flaps up over the roof. The cable of a television aerial hangs down the front of the building into the weeds. Drifts of wet leaves lie beside an old drum of diesel with a grubby Shell logo on the side.

'I need to find a way of handing myself in,' Erik says.

He follows her up a green path that has been trodden through the tall nettles.

'They shot Nestor in front of me, I can't believe it,' he goes on.

'I know.'

'They thought he was me, and they shot him through the window, using snipers, it was like an execution . . .'

'You can tell me everything when we get inside,' Nelly says with a little frown of impatience between her eyebrows.

Resting against the wall among the nettles is a snow-shovel with a broken handle. The paint of the veranda is hanging off in large strips, and one of the windows is broken. There's a piece of plywood covering the hole instead of glass.

'Now you're here, anyway,' Nelly says. 'You can feel safe. I mean, I'm happy for you to stay as long as you like.'

'Maybe you could contact a defence lawyer once everything's calmed down?' Erik suggests.

She nods and licks her lips again, then tucks a lock of hair behind her scarf.

'Hurry up,' she says.

'What is it?' he asks.

'Nothing,' she says quickly. 'I just . . . you know . . . all this talk about everyone hunting you. And sometimes the neighbours call round when they see I'm here.'

Erik glances along the narrow track at the edge of the field. There are no other houses in sight, just overgrown fields and a strip of forest.

'Come on,' she repeats with a tense smile, and takes his arm again. 'You need something to drink, and some warm clothes.'

'Yes,' he agrees and follows her along the path through the nettles.

'And I'll make something nice to eat.'

They go up the steps to the little veranda. There are grimy bags of rubbish leaning against the outside wall, next to a plastic tub filled with bottles and rainwater. Nelly turns the key in the lock, opens the front door and walks into the hall ahead of him. There's a click but nothing more when she tries to turn the light on.

'Need to check the fuse-box,' she giggles.

A set of blue overalls covered in oil-stains is suspended from a hanger beside a silver-coloured padded jacket. In the shoe-rack are a pair of worn wooden clogs and some rough boots with black stains on them. Above a small sofa hangs an embroidered sampler with a biblical quotation: *For love is strong as death, Song of Solomon* 8:6.

A sweet smell of raw chicken and overripe fruit hangs in the air.

'It's an old house,' she says softly.

'Yes,' he says, thinking that he'd really prefer to get away from here.

Nelly stands and looks at him with a smile, so close that he can see that her face-powder has settled in rings around her eyes.

'Do you want a shower before we eat?' she asks without taking her eyes off him.

'Do I look like I need one?' he jokes.

'You're the best judge of how unclean you are,' she replies seriously, and her bright eyes shine like glass.

'Nelly, I'm incredibly grateful for everything you've—'

'Anyway, here's the kitchen,' she interrupts.

As she pushes at the heavy door beside the sofa Erik hears a creaking metallic sound.

The noise rises a couple of notes, then stops abruptly.

He follows her hesitantly into the gloomy kitchen. A stench of rotten food hits him. Weak light filters through the closed venetian blinds. It's hard to see anything. Nelly has gone in and is turning the tap on.

Erik stands inside the door and feels a shiver run down his spine. The whole kitchen is full of rusty tools and engine parts, blocks of firewood, crumpled plastic bags, shoes and pans of old food.

'Nelly, what's happened here?'

'What do you mean?' she says lightly as she fills a glass with water for him.

'The whole kitchen,' he says.

She follows his gaze to the worktop and closed blinds. Three dark paraffin lamps are sticking up from an open kitchen drawer.

'We must have had a break-in,' she says, holding out the glass.

He walks in and barely reaches her when the kitchen door shuts behind him with a loud slam.

Erik spins round with his heart pounding in his chest. The powerful spring of an oversized self-closing mechanism is singing metallically.

'God, that gave me a fright,' he sighs.

'Sorry,' Nelly says, unconcerned.

124

Nelly switches on a torch and puts it down haphazardly on the worktop. The light shines at the layers of cobwebs on the venetian blinds.

Erik stands still and tries to take in what he's seeing. A large fly buzzes around the kitchen and lands on the door to the cellar. From one door-post hangs an iron bar that seems to function as a barrier across the door.

'A woman that feareth the Lord, she shall be praised,' Nelly whispers.

'Nelly, I don't really understand what all this is about.'

There are two knives lying on the floor next to a rolled-up rag-rug, the gearbox of a car and a dirty hymnbook.

'You're home,' she says with a smile.

'Thanks, but I—'

'There's the door,' she points.

'There's the door?' he repeats, uncomprehendingly.

'It's better if you go down on your own,' she says, holding out the glass of water.

'Down where?' Erik asks.

'Now don't argue,' she giggles.

'You think I ought to hide in the cellar?'

She nods eagerly.

'Isn't that a bit over the top? I don't think—'

'Be quiet!' she yells, and throws the glass of water at him.

The glass hits the wall behind him, falls to the floor and shatters. He feels the water splash his legs and feet.

'What are you doing?'

'Sorry, I'm just a bit stressed,' she says, rubbing her forehead.

He nods and walks over to the door to the hall and pulls the handle, but the powerful spring-loaded mechanism has locked the door. There's no key in the hole. Adrenalin floods his body as he hears her approach from behind. He yanks at the door but it doesn't move a millimetre.

'I just want you to do as I say,' Nelly explains.

'Well, I'm not thinking of going down into some fucking—'

Erik can't understand what's happening, but something hits him hard across the back and all the air goes out of him as his forehead hits the door. He stumbles sideways. It feels like he's got cramp in his left shoulder, then realises that warm liquid is running down his back.

He looks down and sees splashes of blood in the filth on the linoleum floor, turns to face Nelly and realises that she has hit him with a lump of wood, which is now lying on the floor by her feet.

'Sorry, Erik,' she all but laughs. 'I didn't mean . . .'

'Nelly?' he gasps. 'You hurt me.'

'Yes, I know, it's not easy, but I'm helping you. Nothing to worry about,' she says.

'I didn't do what they're saying about me,' he tries to explain.

'Didn't you?'

He moves sideways then turns back towards Nelly again, and sees that she's picked up a heavy crowbar from the worktop.

'Don't you understand . . .? I'm innocent!'

Erik backs away and bumps into the table, on top of which is a full washing-up bowl. The dirty water slops over the side and splashes on to the floor.

Nelly moves quickly towards him and strikes. He blocks the blow with his lower arm, it hurts so much he almost passes out, and he stumbles backwards into the pale blue door of the pantry.

She swings again but misses his head. Splinters fly from the edge of the door. He lurches to the side and manages to knock over a tray of empty jam-jars. They roll across the worktop and fall to the floor, scattering shards of broken glass.

'Nelly, stop it!' he gasps.

His arm is probably broken, he's having to support it with his other hand.

Nelly has a look of intense concentration on her face as she pursues him. He throws his head back and she turns her body and strikes again. The crowbar misses his face and brushes past the tip of his nose. The back of his head hits an open cupboard door. He tries to get away but puts his foot down on a piece of broken glass just as she lashes out again.

He blocks the powerful blow with his broken arm and shrieks with pain. His vision goes black for a moment and his legs give way. Erik falls to his knees. He stares at the filthy floor and the blood running down his injured arm.

'Stop, just stop,' he pleads, and tries to get up, but the next blow hits him on the temple.

His head is knocked sideways. Everything goes quiet inside him, as though he had simply come to a stop.

He fumbles for support with his hand.

His field of vision contracts to a narrow tunnel, he sees the kitchen shrink as Nelly leans forward and smiles at him.

Erik tries to stand up. He realises he must have trodden on more glass, because he feels the pain like a distant itch, far away, under his foot, down in the ground somewhere.

He falls backwards, rolls on to his side, and lies there panting with his cheek against the floor.

'Oh, God . . .'

'And the just, upright man is laughed to scorn,' she mutters. 'But ask now the beasts . . .'

Through his limited field of vision he sees Nelly open the door to the cellar and stick a wedge under it with her foot.

He smells her perfume as she bends over, takes hold of him under his arms and drags him across the floor. He's completely powerless, his feet just hang limp, leaving a trail of blood across the floor.

'Don't do it,' Erik pants.

She pulls him towards the staircase, he tries to cling on to a cupboard but can't hold on. Blood is trickling over his cheek and down his throat and neck. He tries to grab hold of the door frame but is too weak to resist.

Nelly walks backwards down the stairs, dragging him into the darkness. His feet fall heavily with each step.

He can barely see anything, just feels the pain shooting from his arm with each step down. Far above he can make out the glow of the torch. Then he loses consciousness.

125

When Erik opens his eyes in the darkness he notices the stench of old excrement and far gone decay. His right arm is excruciatingly painful and his head is throbbing with pain.

He can't see anything, and a scorching wave of panic crumbles his thoughts, scattering them across the flaring darkness. He can't understand what's happened, and his entire body feels tense, wary, ready for flight.

All he really feels like doing is calling for help, but he forces himself to lie still and listen. The room is completely silent.

Occasionally he hears a vague rumbling sound, like wind in a chimney.

He carefully touches his wounded arm and discovers that it's been wrapped in paper.

Erik's heart begins to beat faster.

This is madness, he thinks.

Nelly hit me, seriously hurt me, my arm is probably broken.

When he tries to roll over, he can feel dried blood sticking his hair and cheek to the mattress.

He raises his head and gasps with dizziness. His temple pounds as he forces himself up onto his knees.

The effort makes Erik breathe hard through his nose, and he tries to listen again but can't hear any movement, no sound of breathing apart from his own.

He stares out into the darkness, blinks, but his eyes don't get used to it.

Unless I've gone blind, this room is entirely devoid of light, he thinks.

Now he remembers being dragged down a steep flight of steps into a cellar before he passed out.

He holds his injured arm tightly to his body as he stands up, but before he manages to straighten up he hits his head on something.

There's a faint rattle of metal.

Crouching, he creeps forward with his hand outstretched, but only walks two steps before he reaches some bars.

Something wet pops beneath one of his feet.

Erik tries to feel his way forward, following the mesh, and reaches a corner.

It's a cage.

His heart thuds in his chest and he feels panic rising once more, his pulse thunders in his ears and it feels like he can't breathe.

He begins to understand. Everything that has happened to him slides apart, piece by piece, forming clear, isolated events – as if illuminated by ice-cold light.

Erik keeps moving round, trampling on something that feels like a blanket. He feels along the mesh with his good hand, running his fingers along the thick bars, investigating the corners. They've been welded together. With his fingers he can feel the lumpy joints where the bars have been welded to the mesh on the floor and roof of the cage.

Nelly, he thinks.

Nelly has done all of it.

Somehow she's the person known as the unclean preacher. A serial killer, a stalker.

Erik stands on the mattress and finds the hatch with his fingers. There's a dull rattle as he pushes it, and the cage sways around him.

He sticks his fingers out and feels the large padlock, twists and tries to pull it, but it soon becomes obvious that the lock can't be forced, not even if he had a sturdy crowbar.

Erik kneels down again and tries to breathe calmly. He leans on his left hand and closes his eyes in the darkness, when a sound makes him start. The door up in the kitchen is opening.

Steps creak on the staircase and a patch of light grows steadily larger.

Someone is coming down, holding a torch.

He leans forward and sees the green dress around Nelly's legs.

The beam from the torch veers across the steps and wall, where a large patch of plaster has fallen off. The handrail is loose and pulls some more mortar off when she leans on it.

Erik feels like he's going to be sick.

She killed Maria Carlsson, Sandra Lundgren, Susanna Kern and

Katryna Youssef – completely innocent women that he happened to come into contact with.

How can he possibly understand that Nelly did that? That she sat astride them and hacked at their faces and throats with a knife, long after they were dead?

She's reached the bottom now. The light sweeps past him and he sees that the cage is made of welded reinforcing mesh. He's surrounded by rust-brown iron rods in a close grid-pattern. The heavy lock is made of brushed steel, sealing a hatch made of a double layer of mesh with welded hooks.

Shadows slide across the walls of the cellar as she stops and looks at him.

Her face is flushed with excitement and she's panting for breath. Erik sees that his left hand is brown with rust from the mesh. His vest is torn, hanging in shreds around his waist.

'Don't be frightened,' Nelly says, pulling an office chair towards the cage. 'I know, right now you're trying to work out how it all fits together, but there's no rush.'

Without taking her eyes off him, she puts the torch down on an old kitchen table. Erik sees it light up the wall by the stairs, and is able to make out the rest of the room in its indirect light.

Beside him is an old mattress. The striped fabric is stained with dark patches in the middle, as if someone had lain there for a long time.

In the other corner is a faded plastic bucket full of murky water, next to a china plate with a washed-out floral pattern and a network of fine cracks.

This must have been the cage Rocky spoke about.

He was here for seven months before he managed to escape.

He got out of the cage and stole a car in Finsta, only to crash and end up getting sentenced for Rebecka's murder.

In the shadows outside the cage Erik can see dead rats and a bundle of wooden sticks with sooty ends.

Nelly's black bag is under the table.

Erik brushes his hair from his eyes, thinking that he has to talk to her, to make himself something more than just a victim for her.

'Nelly,' he says weakly. 'What am I doing here?'

'I'm protecting you,' she says.

He coughs and thinks that he needs to speak in his usual voice, has to sound like her colleague at the Karolinska, not sound afraid, dehumanised.

'Why do you think I need protecting?'

'Loads of reasons,' she whispers with a smile.

Some of her blonde hair has slipped out from her headscarf, and her thin dress has dark sweat stains under the arms and across her chest.

She says she's protecting me, he thinks. Nelly believes that she's protecting me for loads of reasons.

She hasn't brought me here to kill me.

Rocky sat in this cage, and wasn't tortured or mutilated, but possibly chastised and beaten.

Spiders' webs full of flies and woodlice sway from the mesh down by the floor. He looks at the dark opening at the other end of the cage. The faint breeze across the floor is coming from the passageway.

He needs to think.

She was the person who set the police on him. She knew he would run, but that he wouldn't have anywhere to go, and that sooner or later he'd turn to her of his own volition.

He was the one who called her, begged to come out here.

That was what she wanted, there was nothing coincidental about it, it all fits too well.

She must have been preparing this for several years, she was probably watching him before she even started work at the Karolinska Hospital.

She's been stalking him.

She's been close to him for so long that she could predict every movement he would make, she's been able to manipulate all the evidence to make him look guilty.

Erik sees a spider slowly crawl across a dead rat. He thinks that his life has fallen apart and that he may well be stuck here until he dies.

Because no one knows where he is.

Joona is looking in the wrong place. Sköldinge Church is just a confused muddle of memories in Rocky's brain.

His family and friends and the rest of the world will remember him as a serial killer who vanished without trace.

I've got to escape, Erik thinks. Even if the police catch me and a court sentences me to life imprisonment.

126

Nelly leans forward and looks at him with an expression he can't read. Her pale eyes are like shining porcelain globes.

'Nelly, you and I are both rational individuals,' Erik says, aware of the quiver of fear in his voice. 'We respect each other . . . and I understand that you didn't mean to hurt me as badly as you did.'

'It's just such a pain when you don't do what I say,' she sighs.

'I know it feels like a pain, but it's like that for everyone, it's part of life.'

'OK, fine,' she says blankly.

She whispers something to herself and moves an object on the kitchen table. Sand falls on to a dusty sheet of glass, a small picture that's leaning against the wall. It's a framed contract of cooperation between Emmaboda Glassworks, Saint-Gobain, and Solbacken Glassworks.

'My arm's hurting badly, and my . . .'

'Are you saying you need to go to hospital now?' she asks derisively.

'Yes, I need to get my arm X-rayed, and—'

'I dare say you'll be fine,' she interrupts.

'Not with an epidural hematoma,' he says, touching the wound to his temple. 'I could have arterial bleeding, here, between the dura mater and the inside of my skull.'

She looks at him in astonishment, then laughs.

'Bloody hell, that really is pathetic!'

'I mean . . . I'm just saying that if I'm going to be happy here, you're going to have to look after me, make sure I'm OK . . .'

'I am, you've got everything you need.'

Erik thinks that someone who's capable of what Nelly has done has an insatiable emotional hunger, she's desperately needy and can switch from devoted love to impassioned hatred in an instant.

'Nelly,' he asks tentatively, 'how long are you thinking of keeping me locked up?'

She smiles at the floor, embarrassed, glances at her nails, then gives him an indulgent look.

'Initially you'll plead and maybe threaten me,' she says. 'You'll promise all sorts of things . . . and soon you'll try to manipulate me in different ways by saying you're not planning to escape, that you only want to help me sweep the stairs.'

She adjusts her dress and looks at him in silence. After a while she crosses her legs and moves a little, so that the light from the torch brushes her cheek.

'Nelly, I'm grateful to you for letting me stay here, but I don't like the cellar, I don't know why, that's just the way it is,' Erik says, but gets no response.

He looks at her and tries to remember how they first met.

She must have been somewhere in the vicinity when he was conducting his examination of Rocky, and then she applied for a job in his department.

How had she got it?

The head of personnel had committed suicide. That was just after she started.

Nelly was funny and easy-going, talkative, in a charming, self-deprecating way.

He went through a tough time when he got divorced from Simone. Particularly at night, all those long, sleepless hours. Nelly persuaded him to go back to using pills. She gave him Valium, Rohypnol, Sobril, Citodon – all the old pills he'd managed to kick several years before.

They drank and took their pills together, made fun of it. Now he can't understand what he was thinking. They'd kissed, then ended up in bed together. She insisted on putting on a nightie that Simone had left behind, and he tried not to show how uncomfortable that made him feel.

Now he remembers something that happened very recently. It had been an unusually difficult day, one of his patients had been sectioned and put in a straitjacket, and he had spent hours with the relatives listening to their recriminations. Afterwards he was tired and it was so late that he decided to stay at the clinic and sleep on his bunk.

Nelly was there too, working overtime. She gave him a Rohypnol and then made them drinks out of medical spirit and Schweppes Russchian.

He must have taken too many drugs or drunk too much, because he'd slid rapidly into deep sleep.

He knows he slept for a long time, and very deeply, and that Nelly helped him get undressed before she went home.

But he dreamed that someone was kissing him, licking his closed lips and making him hold a cold glass ball, pressing it into his limp hand.

Through his drugged dream Nelly came back to him. Her tongue was pierced and she took his penis in her mouth. Then he dreamed that a deer came into his office, the same way Nelly had, and walked past his bunk to stand behind the floor lamp, raising its head and looking at him with bashful eyes.

Erik couldn't sleep in the dream. Light filtered through his eyelashes and he could see Nelly. She was on her knees, pressing a cold, hard object into his hand. It was a small, brown, porcelain deer's head.

Now she's sitting there silently watching him with an impassive expression. As if she were waiting for his slow recuperation.

After a while she takes some neatly folded clothes out of a plastic bin-bag and puts them on her lap.

'Are those clothes for me?'

'Yes, sorry,' she says, rolling them up and passing them to him through the mesh.

'Thanks.'

He unfolds a pair of dirty jeans with muddy stains on the knees, and a washed-out T-shirt with the words Saab 39 Gripen printed across the chest. The clothes smell of sweat and damp, but Erik pulls off his tattered vest and gets changed very gingerly.

'You've got a sweet little tummy,' she says, and giggles.

'Yes, haven't I?' he says quietly.

With a coquettish gesture she raises her chin and loosens the scarf covering her hair. Her blonde hair is stiff with blood. He forces himself to look her in the eye, not look away even though his heartbeat is speeding up with fear.

'Nelly, we're together,' he says, swallowing hard. 'We've always been together . . . but I've been waiting, because I thought you were with Martin.'

'With Martin? But . . . you mustn't think that meant anything,' she says, blushing.

'The two of you seemed happy.'

Her mouth turns serious and her lips tremble.

'It's just you and me,' she says. 'It's always been us . . .'

He's having trouble breathing, but tries to sound natural when he speaks.

'I didn't know if you regretted what happened, that time —'

'Never,' she whispers.

'Me neither, I know I've done some silly things, but only because I felt abandoned.'

'But —'

'Because I've always felt we had a unique connection, Nelly. We always have had, the whole time.'

She wipes tears from her eyes and looks away. She rubs her nose with a trembling finger.

'I didn't mean to hurt you,' she says quietly.

'I wouldn't say no to a couple of Morfin Medas,' he says in a lighter tone.

'OK.' She nods quickly, wipes her face, then gets up and leaves.

127

As soon as Nelly reaches the kitchen and closes the door behind her, and puts the heavy bar across it, Erik begins yanking at the mesh. He pulls as hard as he can, and manages to bend it a couple of millimetres, but realises that it will never give way.

He kicks at it with his bare soles, feels the metal burn into the arches of his feet, and hears nothing but a solid thud from the cage. He shifts round desperately and tugs at the corner, seeking a weak point in the construction, pushes up at the roof, but there are no gaps anywhere, no loose welding joints. Then he lies down on his stomach, stretches out with his left hand until he can reach one of the wooden sticks with his fingertips. He rolls it closer until he's able to get a grip on it and pull it into the cage. He moves to the other side of the cage, holds the stick out and can just reach the strap of Nelly's Gucci handbag. Carefully he raises the stick, making the bag slide closer to him. He pants with pain whenever he has to put any pressure on his injured arm. It feel likes an eternity before he drags the bag over to the mesh. With shaking hands he hunts around for the keys to the padlock among Nelly's gold-plated lipstick holders, travel hairspray and powder. In a side pocket he finds her mobile phone. Because he can only use one arm he puts the phone on the floor, leans over it and dials the SOS Alarm number.

'SOS 112, what's the nature of the emergency?' a calm voice says.

'Please listen . . . you need to try to trace this phone,' Erik says in as loud a voice as he dare use. 'I've been locked up in a cellar by a serial killer, you've got to come and—'

'The reception's very bad,' the voice interrupts. 'Can you move somewhere—'

'The murderer's name is Nelly Brandt, and I'm in the cellar of a yellow house on the way to Rimbo.'

'I can't hear anything now . . . Did you say you were in danger?'

'This is serious, you've got to come,' Erik explains, glancing quickly towards the staircase. 'I'm in a yellow house on the way to Rimbo, there are fields all around and I saw ruined buildings on the site, an old factory with a tall chimney, and—'

The door to the kitchen rattles and Erik ends the call with trembling fingers, drops the phone on the floor but manages to pick it up and slip it back inside the bag. He hears Nelly coming down the steep steps and pushes the handbag back towards the table with the stick. It almost topples over and he has to nudge its lower side with the end of the stick. He stretches out as far as he can to slide the bag back in place.

She's almost down now.

Erik pulls the stick back and hides it under the mattress, and notices a faint trail through the dirt on the floor.

Nelly reaches the floor of the cellar. She's holding a broad-bladed kitchen knife in her hand. Her face is sweaty, and she brushes her blood-streaked hair back and looks at her bag on the table.

'You were gone a long time,' he says, leaning back against the mesh.

'The kitchen's a bit of a mess,' she explains.

'But you've got some morphine?'

'To the hungry soul, every bitter thing is sweet,' she mutters, and puts the white pill on the end of the knife-blade.

She smiles blankly and reaches it towards the mesh.

'Open wide,' she says distantly.

With his heart pounding Erik leans his face towards the rusty mesh, opens his mouth and sees the point of the knife come closer.

It's trembling, and he hears Nelly's breathing quicken as she puts the tip of the knife in his open mouth.

He feels the underside of the cold blade against his tongue before carefully closing his lips around the knife.

She pulls it out again and the blade hits the side of the mesh with a clang.

Erik pretends to swallow the pill, but tucks it between his cheek and his back teeth. A bitter taste spreads through his mouth as his saliva dissolves the outer layer. He daren't swallow the pill. It doesn't matter how much pain he's in, he can't risk becoming drowsy and sleepy.

'You've got new earrings,' he says, sitting back on the mattress.

She smiles briefly with her eyes on the hand holding the knife.

'But I haven't been good enough,' she says quietly.

'Nelly, if only I'd known that you were waiting for me . . .'

'I stood in the garden and saw you looking at Katryna,' she whispers. 'Men like beautiful fingernails, I know that, but my hands have always been strange, there's nothing I can—'

'You've got lovely hands, I think they're lovely. They're—'

'Lovelier than she is now, anyway,' Nelly interrupts. 'That just leaves your little teacher . . . I've seen you together, I've seen her slippery mouth and—'

'There's no one but you,' he says, trying to keep his voice steady.

'But I haven't got any children, I haven't got a little girl,' she whispers.

'What are you talking about?' Erik asks, and feels his body go utterly cold.

'Probably best not to take fire into your bosom, unless you want—'

'Nelly, I don't care about them,' he says. 'I've only got eyes for you.'

She lunges quickly with the knife. He jerks his head back and the knife hits the mesh where his face was a moment ago.

She's panting and looking at him with disappointment, and he knows he's gone too far, that she knows he wasn't telling the truth.

'What you're saying,' she gasps. 'I don't know, it's a bit like seeking death by chasing the wind.'

'What do you mean? I'm not seeking death, Nelly.'

'It isn't your fault,' she mutters, and scratches her neck with the knife-blade. 'I don't blame you.'

She takes a few steps back and the shadows close around her pale face, painting big, black holes where her eyes should be, and drawing dark shapes across her neck.

'But you'll see what mortality looks like, Erik,' she says, and turns towards the stairs.

'Don't do anything silly now,' Erik calls to her.

She stops and turns round. Sweat has run down her cheeks and her make-up has almost come off now.

'I really can't accept that you're going to carry on thinking about her,' Nelly says in a steady voice. 'If you are going to think about her, then it should be a face without eyes and lips.'

'No, Nelly!' Erik shouts, watching her disappear up the narrow staircase.

He sinks down on to the floor, spits out the half-dissolved pill in his hand, and puts the loose remains in one pocket of his jeans.

128

Margot knows it's pretty unlikely that Nelly Brandt is either at her home in Bromma or at work at the Karolinska. Even so, she can't help feeling a deep anxiety in her body as she sits in her car further down the road and watches the National Task Force spreading out around the white modernist villa in Bromma.

If she disregards the black-clad and heavily armed police officers, the entire area is dreamily peaceful, like one of many childhood evenings.

Margot is following the operation on the radio, and the tension inside her is almost unbearable. She can't help imagining the silence being shattered by screams and discharged weapons.

Her radio crackles as the head of the operation, Roger Storm, reports directly to her.

'She's not here,' he says.

'Have they looked everywhere?' she asks. 'Basement, attic, garden?'

'She's not here.'

'And her husband?'

'Sitting watching the diving on television.'

'What does he say?'

'I got straight to the point, but he says he's sure Nelly isn't involved . . . they've read all about Erik and he says Nelly is just as shocked as him.'

'OK, I don't give a shit about that right now, as long as he can tell us wherever the fuck she is,' Margot says, looking over towards the house.

'They haven't got anywhere else – he's got no idea,' Roger replies.

'Is the response team finished?'

'They're on their way out.'

'Then I'm coming in,' Margot says, and opens the car door.

The moment she stands up she feels a dull ache at the small of her back. She realises immediately what it means, but still carries on, and slowly makes her way up to the wide-open front door.

'I'll give birth when I'm done with this case,' she tells the officer standing at the door.

The hall is large, but cosy and welcoming. A Carl Larsson painting hangs opposite the door. The response unit are on their way out, helmets in hand, their automatic rifles swinging from their straps.

In the gloom of the living room, a rather plump man is sitting in an armchair. He's loosened his tie and undone his top button, and there's a microwaved meal on a tray on the coffee table. He looks shocked, keeps rubbing his thighs and looking in bewilderment at the police officer who is talking to him.

'It's a big house,' he's explaining. 'It's enough for us . . . And in the winter we usually go to the Caribbean and—'

'Your extended family – don't they have houses?' Margot interrupts.

'I'm the only one who lives in Sweden,' he replies.

'But if your wife was to borrow a house to go to – where would that be?'

'I'm sorry, I've got no idea, I . . .'

Margot leaves him and heads upstairs, looks round, then goes into a bedroom and takes out her phone.

'Nelly Brandt isn't at home, and she isn't at the Karolinska,' she says as soon as Joona answers.

'Does she have any connection with any other properties?' Joona Linna asks.

'We've checked all the registries,' Margot replies, gasping as the next contraction hits. 'They don't own any other houses, they've got no summer cottage, no land.'

'Where did she live before?'

Margot takes out the printout of information she requested the moment she last spoke to Joona.

'According to the population registry, she lived at Sköldinge rectory until ten years ago . . . then there's a gap of four years before she shows up here.'

'She lived with Rocky Kyrklund in his rectory,' Joona says.

'We've got people there, but these days it's sheltered housing for—'

'I know, I know.'

'Obviously she could have rented a flat second- or third-hand.'

'In the diary there are references to a farm in Roslagen,' Joona says.

'There's no farm, nothing she's got any connection to. Her family has never owned any land, and she's the last of her line.'

'But Rocky escaped from her and stole a car in Finsta. We don't know how far he walked on foot first—'

'There must be a thousand farms around Norrtälje,' Margot interrupts.

'Check all her paperwork. I mean, if she's renting a farm from someone else, she may have paid electricity bills that don't have her name on them, things like that.'

'We should be getting a decision about an official search warrant in a couple of hours.'

'Start looking, and carry on until someone stops you,' he says.

'OK, where do I begin?'

'If you think the husband's telling the truth, you'll need to look among her personal things.'

'I'm upstairs . . . They've got separate bedrooms,' she says, walking into an airy room with dove-blue wallpaper.

'We can keep talking while you search . . . Tell me exactly what you're looking at.'

'The bed is made and she's got a few books on the bedside table, looks like psychology books.'

'Check the drawers.'

Margot opens the two drawers in the bedside table and tells him that there are no documents there.

'They're practically empty . . . a pack of Mogadon, throat sweets and hand cream,' she says.

'Ordinary hand cream?'

'Clarins.'

She puts her hand in the drawer and finds a little plastic tub.

'A tub of dietary supplements.'

'What sort?'

'Iron . . . iron hydroxide.'

'Why do people take that? Do you?' Joona asks.

'I eat enough meat for five people instead,' Margot says and closes the drawers.

'Is there a wardrobe?'

'I'm on my way into her walk-in wardrobe,' she says, walking in between the rows of clothes.

'What's in there?'

'Dresses, skirts, suits, blouses . . . don't think I'm envious, but it's all Burberry, Ralph Lauren, Prada . . .'

She falls silent as she stares at one wall.

'What's happening?' Joona asks.

'Her shoes . . . I might have to have a little cry after all.'

'Carry on.'

'Joona, I just want to say . . . I've done a lot of research, I've studied all the major cases of obsessive stalking, from John Hinckley to Mona Wallén-Hjerpe . . . and no one comes anywhere close to the level of Nelly's fixation . . . she's the worst stalker ever.'

'I know.'

'Where do I look now?'

'Poke about at the back,' Joona replies. 'Look behind shelves, under boxes, you need to find something.'

They end the call and Margot looks everywhere, leaning against the wall and crawling right to the back, but she finds absolutely nothing. Just as she walks back into the bedroom she sees Roger Storm reach the top of the stairs. His face is sweaty and he looks at her with his eyes wide open as he comes towards her. Margot sighs and presses her clenched hand against the small of her back to suppress the next contraction.

'What is it?' she asks in a subdued voice.

'We've received another film,' he says.

129

The sun has gone down and Rocky has just woken up beside Joona, the streetlamps are coming on and they are approaching Södertälje when Margot calls back.

'We've received a new video,' she says in an anguished voice. 'Presumably it's someone Erik knows, or has at least—'

'Describe the film.'

'Nelly is already inside the victim's home when she begins filming . . . The woman seems injured, she's sitting curled up in a corner . . . and at the end, at the end of the film there's a small foot . . . It's dark, but it looks like there's a child lying on the floor.'

'Go on.'

'It's a perfectly ordinary bloody room, old walls and uneven wallpaper . . . there might be a big chimney outside the window, but Forensics aren't done yet.'

'Go on.'

'I'm watching the video on an iPad right now . . . the woman has short black hair, she's thin, and I don't know . . . she's bleeding, she's almost unconscious and she's moving her hands as if she can't see anything, or—'

'Listen,' Joona interrupts. 'Her name is Jackie Federer and she lives at Lill-Jans plan.'

'I'll send the rapid response unit,' she says, and ends the call.

Joona doesn't have time to explain that she may well no longer be in her flat, because Nelly will want to kill Jackie in front of Erik's eyes, just as she killed her mother in front of her father, and Natalia in front of Rocky.

They drive past a minibus parked at the side of the road with a puncture. A bearded man in shorts and with sunburned legs is putting out a warning triangle.

'You talked about a cage, about being locked in a cage,' Joona says to Rocky.

'When was that?'

'Nelly had you locked up somewhere.'

'I don't think so,' he replies, staring out at the road.

'Do you know where that might have been?'

'No.'

'You escaped and stole a car near Norrtälje.'

'I thought you were the one who goes around stealing cars,' he mutters.

'Think . . . It was a farm, there may have been a chimney . . .'

Rocky sits there watching the landscape flash by, and as they pass the junction for Salem he lets out a deep sigh. He rubs his face and beard with his big hands, then looks back at the road again.

'Nelly Brandt murdered Rebecka Hansson,' he says slowly.

'Yes.'

'God came back to look for me after all,' he says, crumpling an empty cigarette packet.

'It looks like it,' Joona replies gently.

'Maybe I'll be punished for escaping and for having heroin in my pockets . . . but after that I can go back to being a priest.'

'You've already been wrongly convicted, you won't be sentenced again,' Joona says.

'Can you stop here?' Rocky says calmly. 'I need to take a look at my church.'

Joona pulls over to the verge and lets him out. The big priest closes the car door, knocks on the roof, and then sets off in the direction of the turning for Salem.

130

When he was allocating work earlier that day, Ramon Sjölin, commanding officer of the Norrtälje Police, decided that Olle and George Broman could take one of the patrol cars.

They're father and son, and don't often partner each other. Their colleagues joked that at last Olle, the father, would get a lesson in proper police work.

Olle loves his colleagues' banter, and is immensely proud of his son, who is a head taller than him.

As usual the day passed peacefully, and towards evening they drove out to Vallby industrial estate, seeing as there had been several reports of break-ins there in the past six months. But everything was calm and they didn't call in, and carried on towards Rimbo after a wee-break.

Olle's back is hurting, and he tilts the seat back a bit further, looks at the time, and is about to say they'll give it half hour then head back to the station when a call from the regional communications centre comes in.

SOS 112 received a phone call thirty minutes ago.

A man called from a phone with very bad reception.

The operator could barely hear anything, but analysis of the recording of the short conversation suggested that the man needed help, and described a location involving a ruined factory somewhere in the vicinity of Rimbo.

They had been able to identify the place as the house that had been built after the big fire at Solbacken Glassworks.

'We're on our way back to the station,' Olle mutters.

'You haven't got time to take this first?' the operator asks.

'OK, we'll take it,' he replies.

Large drops of rain are falling on the roof of the car. Olle shivers and closes his window, managing to squash a brimstone butterfly.

'Suspected domestic down in Gemlinge,' he tells his son.

George turns the car round and heads south, past large farms that open up the landscape in the middle of the black forests.

'Mum reckons you don't eat enough vegetables, she was going to make carrot lasagne,' Olle says. 'But I forgot to buy the carrots, so we're having beef patties instead.'

'Sounds good,' George grins.

The fields are completely dark now. One wing of the butterfly falls down the inside of the window and drifts on the warm air from the vent.

They stop talking when they turn off and start heading along the narrow track. The deep potholes make the suspension creak, and branches scrape the roof and sides of the car.

'For God's sake, this place is derelict,' George says.

The car's headlights open up a tunnel through the darkness and make the swirling moths and the tall grass at the side of the track shine like brass.

'What's the difference between a cheese?' Olle asks, absurdly.

'I don't know, Dad,' George says, without taking his eyes off the track.

'There are holes in the cheese, but no cheese in the holes.'

'Brilliant,' his son sighs, and drums his hands on the wheel.

They turn into a large yard and see a huge chimney etched against the night sky. The tyres roll slowly over crunching gravel. Olle leans closer to the windscreen, breathing through his nose.

'Dark,' George mutters, turning the wheel.

The headlights sweep across bushes and rusting machine parts when they are suddenly reflected back at them.

'A number plate,' Olle says.

They drive closer and see a car with its boot open parked in the yard among the ruins of the glassworks.

The two men look towards the yellow house. It's surrounded by tall stinging nettles, and the windows are black.

'Do you want to wait and see if they carry out a television?' Olle asks quietly.

George turns the wheel to the left and lines the car up so that the headlights are pointing straight at the veranda before putting the hand-brake on.

'But the call was about a suspected domestic,' he says, and opens his door. 'I'll go and take a look.'

'Not on your own,' his dad says.

The two police officers are wearing light protective vests under the jackets of their uniforms, and on their belts they're carrying their service pistols, extra magazines, batons, handcuffs, torches and radios.

Their thin shadows stretch out over the ground, reaching all the way to the house across the nettles.

George has pulled out his torch, and suddenly imagines he's seen something move behind the broken glass of the ruins.

'What is it?' Olle asks.

'Nothing,' George replies with a dry mouth.

The leaves rustle in the darkness, and then they hear a strange noise, like someone crying out in anguish from within the forest.

'Bloody deer, scaring people like that!' Olle says.

George shines his torch at a deep shaft between some collapsed brick walls. There are fragments of glass scattered among the weeds.

'What is this place?' George whispers.

'Just stick to the path.'

The flat disc of the torch moves over the dirty windows of the house. The glass is so filthy that it reflects no more than a grey shimmer.

They wade through the tall nettles and George makes a joke about the garden being greener than his dad's.

One pane in the veranda has been nailed over with plywood, and there's a rusty scythe leaning against the wall.

'The row was probably about whose turn it was to do the cleaning,' Olle says quietly.

131

Through the mesh of his cage, Erik watches as Jackie takes a cautious step backwards. She's frightened and confused, trying to grasp the situation without succumbing to panic. Nelly must have had her locked up somewhere in the house before she forced her down the stairs.

Erik doesn't know what Nelly is thinking of doing, but he can see her exultant fury as she stands and stares at Jackie with her chin jutting out.

He daren't plead with her – anything he says will only make her jealous. Thoughts chase through his head in an attempt to find something that could break through her wounded rage.

Jackie makes a clicking sound with her tongue and takes a step forward. She walks straight into the beam from the torch and stops for a moment as she feels the slight warmth.

Now Erik can see how badly injured she is, dark blood shining on her temple, and there are bruises on her face and a tear in her bottom lip. Her shadow fills the whole wall. Off to one side, just in front of her, Nelly wipes the sweat from her right hand onto her dress and picks up the knife from the table.

Jackie hears the movement and backs up until she reaches the brick wall. Erik sees her run her hand across it, feeling for any deviations with her fingers, something to help her orientate herself.

'What have I done?' Jackie asks in a frightened voice.

Erik looks down, waits a few seconds, then looks at Nelly instead, but she has already noticed him looking at Jackie. Her mouth is so tense that the sinews in her neck are visible.

She wipes the tears from her cheeks and the knife twitches in her right hand as she approaches Jackie.

Erik sees that Jackie can sense Nelly's presence. She doesn't want to show how afraid she is, but the movement of her chest betrays the shallowness of her breathing. He can see that she instinctively wants to duck down, but is forcing herself to stand up straight.

Nelly moves slowly sideways and grit crunches beneath her shoes.

Jackie tilts her head slightly towards the sound. Blood has congealed across her ear, temple and cheek.

Nelly holds the knife out towards Jackie and looks at her through narrow eyes. The point of the blade moves in front of the blind face and a weak reflection trembles on the ceiling. Jackie raises a hand and the knife glides out of the way, but returns at once and slowly lifts the collar of her blouse.

'Nelly, she's blind,' Erik says, struggling to remain calm. 'I don't see the point—'

Nelly jabs the point of the knife between her breasts. Jackie whimpers and touches the superficial injury with one hand. Her fingertips get covered with blood and an expression of unadorned fear and confusion fills her pale face.

'Look at her now,' Nelly says. 'Look at her. Look!'

Jackie feels along the wall with her fingertips, walks straight into the table and almost falls, stumbling over a brick and taking a long stride to stop herself going down.

'Very elegant,' Nelly giggles, and brushes the bloody hair from her face.

Jackie backs away and Erik hears her breathing, like a wounded animal's.

Nelly circles round her and she moves to face the sound, holding her hands up the whole time to protect herself, and trying to get her bearings in the room.

She walks into the table again and Nelly creeps behind her and jabs the knife into her back.

Erik forces himself not to scream.

Jackie groans with pain, takes a step forward, stumbles and hits one knee on the floor. She gets up quickly as blood runs down her clothes, down one leg, and takes a few fumbling steps with her hands in front of her.

'Erik, why are you doing this?' Jackie asks in a tremulous voice.

'Why are you doing this?' Nelly mocks.

'Erik?' she gasps, turning round.

'It's over between us,' Erik says harshly. 'Don't imagine that—'

'Don't talk to her!' Nelly shrieks at him. 'I don't give a shit about anything now, I'm not going to let the two of you—'

'Nelly, I only want to be with you, no one else,' Erik interrupts. 'I only want to look at you, at your face, and—'

'Do you hear that?' Nelly screams at Jackie. 'What's wrong with you? He doesn't want some fucking blind bitch. Got that? He doesn't want you.'

Jackie says nothing, she just sinks to her knees, shielding her face and head with her arms and hands.

'Nelly, that's enough now,' Erik says, no longer able to keep his voice steady. 'She understands, she's no threat to us, she—'

'Get up, he says that's enough, he wants to look at you . . . Show your face . . . your pretty little face.'

'Nelly, please—'

'Get up!'

Jackie slowly gets to her feet and Nelly lunges with full force, but the blade misses her neck. The knife slides over her shoulder, right next to her throat. Jackie screams and falls backwards. Nelly jabs again but hits nothing but thin air. She catches the blade on a shelf on the wall and some tins of food topple over and fall to the floor.

'Nelly, stop it, you've got to stop!' Erik cries, tearing at the mesh.

Jackie shoves her with both hands and Nelly staggers backwards, falls across the wooden sticks and drops the knife.

'Bray a fool in a mortar among wheat with a pestle,' Nelly whimpers in a high voice as she sweeps her hands across the floor.

She grabs hold of one of the tins, gets to her feet and hits Jackie with it, hard in her stomach, left breast and collarbone. Jackie screams and manages to knock the tin from Nelly's hand, rolls over on to her side and tries to get to her feet.

Gasping, Nelly looks around at the dark shadows in the room, and finds her knife on the floor by the wall.

'Now I'm going to take her face,' Nelly mutters in a voice that sounds like she's got a mouth full of saliva.

Jackie is on her knees with her face unprotected; blood pours down her back. She's found a small screwdriver, and gets unsteadily to her feet, panting for air.

Nelly wipes the sweat from her eyes, her green dress is smeared with dark stains. Jackie turns away from her and finds the stairs.

Nelly smiles at Erik, then goes after Jackie. She raises the knife and stabs, but the blade misses and lands wrong, cutting a wound between Jackie's neck and shoulder.

Jackie falls forward onto both knees, hits her forehead on the first step and collapses.

Nelly staggers back with the knife in her hand, and blows the hair from her eyes when a bell suddenly rings.

With the knife trembling in her hand, Nelly glares up at the stairs with a look of indecision on her face. The bell rings again and she says something to herself, goes quickly past Jackie and up the stairs, then closes and locks the door behind her.

132

The two police officers wait on the veranda, but they can't hear anything. Just the wind in the trees and the chirruping of insects in the weeds.

'What's the difference between a ham sandwich with gherkins . . . and an old man with a cigarette in his arse?' Olle asks, ringing the bell again.

'I don't know,' George says.

'OK, I'll ask someone else to buy the sandwiches tomorrow.'

'Dad . . . really . . .'

Olle laughs and shines his torch at the peeling door with its rusty handle. George knocks hard on the window next to them, then steps aside.

'Let's go in,' Olle says, gesturing to his son to back away down the steps as he takes hold of the door handle.

He's about to open it when a warm glow appears. The grey hall window suddenly looks welcoming. The door is opened by an elegant woman with a headscarf round her hair and a paraffin lamp in her hand. She's in the process of buttoning a yellow raincoat over her chest, and looks at the two police officers with bemused surprise.

'God, I thought it was the electrician – we've got a power cut,' she says. 'What's happened?'

'We received an emergency call from here,' Olle replies.

'What for?' she says, looking at them.

'Is everything OK?' George asks.

'Yes . . . I think so,' she says anxiously. 'What sort of emergency?'

The steps creak as George takes a step closer. The woman smells strongly of sweat and there's a splash of something on her neck.

Without knowing why, he turns round and shines the torch out into the darkness along the front of the house.

'It was a man who called – is there anyone else in the house?'

'Only Erik . . . Did he call you? My husband has Alzheimer's . . .'

'We'd like to talk to him,' Olle says.

'Can't you do that tomorrow? He's just had his Donepezil.'

She raises her hand to brush the hair from her forehead. Her fingernails are black, as if she's been digging in the earth.

'It won't take long,' Olle says, taking a step inside.

'I'd rather you didn't,' she says.

The two police officers look into the hall. The wallpaper is brown and a homemade rag-rug covers the worn linoleum floor. On the wall is a framed biblical quotation, and a few outdoor clothes are hanging neatly on hangers. George watches his father go into the hall, shivers and glances back at the car. Insects have been drawn to the strong headlights and are swirling like captives in their beam.

'I'm afraid we're going to have to speak to your husband,' Olle says.

'Do we have to?' his son asks quietly.

'We received an emergency call,' Olle tells the woman. 'I'm sorry . . . but this is how it works, we have to come in.'

'It won't take long,' George says.

They wipe their shoes carefully on the doormat. A curl of flypaper hangs in the same corner of the hall as the ceiling light. There are hundreds of flies covering the sticky paper, like black fur.

'Can you just hold this?' the woman says, passing the paraffin lamp to Olle.

The light from the lamp flickers across the walls. George waits behind his dad as the woman pushes the door to the dark kitchen open with both hands. A creak of metal echoes through the hall. George hears her talking about her husband's illness as she walks into the darkness of the kitchen. The stench emerging through the open door hits them. Olle coughs and follows the woman, holding the lamp in his hand.

The yellow light plays over the chaos in the kitchen. There's broken glass, saucepans and old tools everywhere. The filthy floor is smeared with fresh blood and the drips are splattered high up the cupboard doors.

Olle turns back to his son, who's right behind him, when the door suddenly shuts with immense force. It hits George square in the face and he's thrown backwards, hitting his head on the hall floor.

Olle simply stares at the door, sees the huge spring, then looks at his son's foot sticking out between the door and the post.

When he turns round the woman is holding a long-handled axe over her shoulder, and before he has time to move she strikes. The blade enters his neck, from above and off to the side. The blow sends him reeling sideways and he sees his own blood spatter the woman's raincoat. He gets jerked off balance as she pulls the axe free and takes a step forward to stop himself falling.

She calmly takes the paraffin lamp from his hand and sets it on the worktop before lifting the heavy axe over her shoulder again.

Olle wants to shout to his son but he has no voice, he's on the point of losing consciousness, black clouds are billowing up in his field of vision. He puts one hand to his neck and feels blood running down inside his shirt as he tries to draw his pistol, but there's no strength left in his fingers.

The woman strikes again and everything goes black.

Out in the hall George opens his eyes and looks around. He's lying on his back, and his forehead is bleeding.

'What the hell just happened?' he gasps.

He feels his nose and bleeding forehead with trembling hands.

'Dad?' he says, noticing that his foot is stuck in the door.

His ankle feels broken, but strangely enough it doesn't hurt. He pulls, and realises he hasn't got any feeling in his toes.

Confused, he looks up at the ceiling and sees the spiral of flypaper swaying above him. He hears thuds from inside the kitchen and pushes himself up on to his elbows, but can't see anything through the crack in the door.

He fumbles and manages to pull his torch from his belt, and points it into the kitchen. His dad is lying on the floor with his mouth open, staring at him.

Suddenly his head rolls over a few times when the woman shoves it aside with her foot. It rolls and spins on the bloody linoleum floor.

George is seized by utter panic, lets out a loud scream, drops the torch and tries to move backwards, kicking at the door with his free foot, but it's like he's caught in a man-trap. He fumbles for his pistol but can't manage to pull it out. He needs to take his glove off first, and puts his hand to his mouth to use his teeth, when the door suddenly opens and he's free.

Panting, he shuffles backwards and hits his back against a small desk, and a bowl of coins falls to the floor, scattering money around him.

He manages to get his glove off and pulls his pistol from its holster as the woman in the yellow raincoat comes out into the hall. She raises the axe above her head, striking the lamp and bringing the coil of flypaper down. The heavy blade hits his chest with terrible force, cutting straight through the thin protective vest and his ribcage, down into his heart.

133

Erik stretches out through the mesh of the cage to reach Jackie, but she's too far away from him, his fingertips flail at the air behind her back. Without knowing if she can hear him, he keeps talking to her the whole time, saying she needs to get up and make her way out through the tunnel.

Nelly has already been gone several minutes.

At first he didn't even know if Jackie was alive, she just lay slumped on the floor without moving, but when he lay on the floor against the mesh of the cage he could hear her breathing.

'Jackie?' he says again.

He knows she'd be dead now if the doorbell hadn't rung. In spite of the silence, he knows it's the police, it must be the police, they did hear his phone call.

As long as they realise how serious it is, he thinks. As long as they've sent enough officers.

He picks the stick up from the ground, reaches out with it and gently pokes Jackie with the blunt end.

'Jackie?'

She slowly moves one leg, turns her face and coughs weakly.

Once again Erik explains what's happened, what Nelly has done, how he got the blame, but that Joona knows the truth.

She lifts one hand tiredly to the superficial wound on her neck.

Erik has no idea how much she understands of what he's saying, but he repeats that she needs to get away, that she needs to hurry.

'You need to fight now, you won't survive otherwise,' he says.

She doesn't have long, he's been listening for pistol shots, for voices, but can't hear anything.

'Jackie, try to stand up now,' he pleads.

Finally she sits up. Blood is running from her eyebrow, down over her cheek, and she's gasping for breath.

'Can you hear me?' he says again. 'Do you understand what I'm saying? You need to run, Jackie. Can you stand up?'

He says nothing about calling the police, doesn't want to give her false hope. She needs to get away, because he doesn't trust the police not to fall for Nelly's lies.

Jackie stands up, groans and spits blood on the floor. She lurches forward but stays on her feet.

'You need to get away from here before she comes back,' he repeats.

Jackie stumbles towards his voice, breathing heavily, with her arms outstretched.

'Go in the other direction,' he says. 'You have to get out of the ruins and away across the fields.'

She makes her way carefully past the tins on the floor and reaches the cage with her hands.

'I'm locked in a cage,' he says.

'Everyone's saying you killed four women,' she whispers.

'It was Nelly . . . You don't have to believe me, as long as you get away from here . . .'

'I knew you didn't do it,' she says.

He strokes the fingers clinging to the cage, she leans forward and rests her forehead on the rusty metal.

'You've got to keep going a bit longer,' he says, stroking her cheek. 'Turn round, so that I can take a look. You've been wounded . . . Jackie, you're seriously hurt, you need to get to a hospital. Hurry up and—'

'Maddy's still at home,' she whimpers. 'Thank God, she was hiding in her wardrobe when—'

'She'll be fine,' Erik says. 'She'll be fine.'

'I don't understand any of this,' Jackie whispers, and her face crumples with anxiety.

'How does it feel when you breathe?' Erik asks. 'Try to cough . . . You'll be OK, your pleural cavity is probably damaged, but you were lucky, Jackie. Listen, there's a little torch on the table, you can feel its warmth, you'll know where it is.'

She wipes her mouth, nods and tries to pull herself together.

'Can you fetch it? There's nothing between you and—'

He breaks off when he hears a loud thud from upstairs. It's the kitchen door slamming shut, thanks to the powerful spring.

'What was that?' she whispers, her lips quivering.

'Hurry up, you can walk straight towards the torch, there's nothing on the floor between you and the table.'

She turns and walks towards the tiny source of heat, feels across the tabletop, picks up the torch and returns to Erik with it.

'Do you know where the opening to the tunnel is?' he asks.

'More or less,' she whispers.

'It's fairly narrow, it's a small brick opening, no door,' he explains as he hears someone scream up above. 'You need to run away, get as far away as you possibly can . . . Take this stick, you can use it to feel your way.'

She looks as if she's about to break down. Her face is drained of colour, her lips already white with the shock to her circulation.

'Erik, it won't work—'

'Nelly will kill you when she comes back . . . Listen, there's a passageway . . . I don't know what it looks like further along, it could be blocked, but you have to try to get out . . . the whole area is surrounded by ruins, and you'll . . . you'll be able to—'

'I can't,' she whimpers, twisting her head back and forth in an anxious, repetitive pattern.

'Please, just listen to me . . . When you reach the cellar with no ceiling, you'll have to climb up to reach ground level . . .'

'What are you going to do?' she whispers.

'I can't get out, Nelly's got the key round her neck.'

'But . . . how am I going to find my way?'

'In the darkness, the blind man is king,' he says simply.

Her faces trembles as she turns round and starts to walk, feeling the ground in front of her with the stick.

He holds the torch up and tries to guide her. The angled light makes the shadows stretch and shrink.

'There's a load of roof tiles on the floor ahead of you,' he says. 'Move a little to your right and you'll be heading straight for the opening.'

Then the pair of them hear the bar being lifted from the cellar door, as it jolts and scrapes back against the wall.

'Hold your hand out now,' Erik whispers. 'You'll be able to feel the wall on your left . . . just follow that . . .'

Jackie walks into something that clatters, a tin of paint rolls away, and Erik sees her shrink with fear.

'Don't stop,' he hisses. 'You have to get home to Maddy.'

The door above them opens, closes, and clicks, but there's no sound of footsteps on the stairs.

Jackie has reached the opening now, and Erik watches her carry on into the passage, holding one hand against the wall and sweeping the ground ahead of her with the stick.

Erik points the torch at the floor and sees Nelly come down the stairs and step out into the middle of the cellar. Her yellow oilskin is smeared with blood and she's clutching a smaller kitchen knife in her hand.

Her eyes are staring straight at him.

He doesn't know how much she has time to see before he switches the torch off. Everything goes completely dark, as if someone had swept the whole world away from them.

'Nelly, they'll send more police officers,' he says, holding his injured arm with his hand. 'Do you understand? It's over now . . .'

'It's never over,' she replies, and stands quite still a metre or so away from him, just breathing.

There's a clattering sound from the tunnel. Nelly giggles and walks across the floor. Erik hears her hit the stack of tiles, go round them and carry on through the darkness towards the tunnel.

134

Jackie is heading along a narrow passageway as fast as she can. Her right hand is feeling its way along the wall, and she's moving the stick to and fro in front of her.

She needs to get as far away as she can, try to find a way out and then keep going until she finds help.

Fear is washing over her, it's almost like being burned, and she manages to kick a bottle lying on the floor that she missed with her stick. It tinkles as it rolls away across the rough floor.

Her fingertips slip across the bricks and crumbling mortar, she notes that she's passing a seventh vertical indentation in the wall. She keeps count automatically because it makes things easier if she has to find her way back.

Jackie is having difficulty breathing, the pain in her back flares up like a beacon with every step she takes. Warm blood is still trickling from the wound, down between her buttocks and along her legs.

She isn't sure if Erik was telling the truth when he said she wasn't seriously hurt, or if he was only trying to calm her down so that she would dare to escape.

She coughs and feels a cramping pain from her injured lung, just below her shoulder-blade.

Her stick isn't quite quick enough.

Her shin hits some sort of apparatus with sharp tin corners and dangling cables. She has to clamber over the machine and her legs are trembling with effort and fear. She has no way of knowing how long the passageway is, but she has a feeling that she's inside a system of tunnels and cellars.

She's walking a little too fast the whole time, and knows there's a serious risk that she's going to trip over.

She passes a room on her left, it's there as a gap in the acoustics.

Jackie decided to stop counting the indentations, she needs to concentrate on finding a way out.

'Nelly's coming!' Erik calls from the basement room behind her. 'She's on her way now!'

His voice sounds frightened, weakened by the long tunnel, but she hears him and understands his warning.

Nelly's coming after her.

Jackie tries to move faster, makes her way round an armchair and carries on along the wall, her fingers brushing a number of shelves. Something rattles behind her and she almost cries out in fear.

It's getting harder and harder to breathe. Jackie holds her hand over her mouth and tries to cough quietly as she presses ahead. Mid-stride, her face hits something. An open cupboard door. It slams shut, and there's a tinkling sound of glass objects rattling on shelves.

Memories of the violence she has been subjected to flash past: the feeling of a sharp knife-blade being yanked out with a sigh, and the constricting pain in her back.

Her breathlessness feels like a weight, she knows she's breathing too hard, but it still doesn't feel like she's getting enough oxygen.

She moves the stick quickly and lets the other hand brush over bricks and joints, past a thick cable, along bare brick again, then some old window frames that are stacked against the wall.

She's trying to read the space the whole time.

Whenever she hears an opening, she stops for a few seconds and listens, to check if it's another passageway or just an enclosed room.

She keeps moving along the main passageway, seeing as the weak draught across the floor seems to be coming from up ahead.

A protruding bolts tears the skin of her knuckles, and now she can hear her pursuer behind her.

Nelly shouts something to her, but Jackie can't make out the words.

The voice makes panic bubble up inside her and the hand holding the stick is sweating.

She trips over a brick, loses her balance and starts to fall. She throws her arm out, puts her hand through some thick spiders' webs and hits the wall hard. Her back shrieks with pain, cutting through her like a javelin with the sudden contortion, and she can taste blood in her mouth.

A crash from the tunnel behind her makes her ears ring. It sounded like the cupboard full of glass objects falling over. She hears a load of glass break, shattering and scattering across the floor.

Jackie wipes her sweaty hand on her legs, takes a firm grip of the stick and carries on as fast as she can. The fingertips of her right hand have gone numb from the rough brick wall.

She can hear footsteps behind her – much faster than her own.

Jackie turns into a side-passage in panic.

Her heart is pounding.

This isn't going to work, she thinks. Nelly knows her way round these tunnels, this is her territory.

Jackie forces herself to go on. The passageway is narrower than the last one. She stumbles over some old fabric and feels something catch round her foot and drag along behind her.

'Jackie?' Nelly shouts. 'Jackie!'

She tries not to cough, feels herself pass a hole in the wall fairly close to the roof, and hears air streaming through it as something grabs at her clothes. It's holding on to her blouse, pulling her backwards. She flails her arms in panic, and hears the fabric tear. She's stuck, and is trying to pull free when she hears Nelly once more.

She must have followed her into the side-passage.

Jackie pulls at her blouse and turns round, puts her hand under her left arm and feels a thick pipe. She walked into a pipe that's somehow hanging from the roof, it's got caught in her clothes and she has to back up several metres to free herself.

Nelly is close now, mortar is crunching under her boots and her clothes rustle as she moves.

Breathing through her nose, Jackie carries on along the passageway, then she hears Nelly let out a whimper – she too has walked into the dangling pipe.

A metallic clang echoes off the walls.

Jackie hurries on and emerges into a large room with a slower echo.

There's a smell of stagnant water in the air, like an old aquarium. Jackie keeps moving, and almost immediately bumps into something and drops her stick.

She's breathing far too quickly, she bends over and feels a large trough filled with dusty soil, twigs and pieces of bark. The pain in her back almost makes her topple forwards, but she goes on searching beside the trough, feeling tentatively across old bottles, spiders' webs and twigs.

She hears Nelly call out to her, she's nearer again.

Jackie gives up looking for the stick, she'll have to go on without it. With her arms outstretched she feels her way past a series of alcoves with brick walls dividing them.

She stops in front of a large object that's blocking the whole room. It's a long, steel washbasin. She feels along it to one end, and has just made her way round it when she hears Nelly's footsteps behind her.

Jackie clicks her tongue loudly, the way she has learned to. The room around her reflects the sound as vague echoes that her brain turns into a three-dimensional map. She clicks again, but is far too scared for it to work well; she doesn't have time to listen properly, can't get any real sense of the room.

Panting for breath, she moves on. Her whole body is shaking and she doesn't know how to stop it. She turns her head and clicks again, and suddenly becomes aware of an opening off to her left.

Jackie reaches the wall with her hands, follows it until she finds the opening, and once again feels the coolness of air from outside.

It's a narrow passageway, its floor covered with loose grit and what smells like the charred remains of wood and plastic. One foot treads straight through a windowpane lying on the ground, and it shatters with a loud crash. She knows she's cut her foot, but stumbles on across the floor. As she reaches out to the wall her fingers dislodge crumbs of dry mortar, and then she hears Nelly stand on the glass.

She's right behind her.

Jackie breaks into a run, with one hand against the wall and the other stretched out in front of her. She runs into a wooden trestle and falls over it, lands on her left shoulder and groans with pain. She tries to crawl but something hits the floor right beside her. It sounds like a plastic pipe, or a broom-handle.

Jackie crawls forward and hits her head on the wall. She manages to get up onto her feet again, stumbles across some fallen bricks, and leans against the wall.

135

Jackie isn't entirely sure of the direction of the passageway. She turns and follows the wall backwards for a metre or so, listens, but can no longer hear Nelly. Her own breathing is so laboured that she has to hold one hand over her mouth in an effort to stay quiet.

Something rustles in front of her, down on the floor, moving slowly.

It's only a rat.

Jackie stands completely still, breathing through her nose. She has no idea how to find her way out. Terror is preventing her from thinking, she's too stressed to be able to interpret her surroundings correctly.

A short distance away from her something creaks. It sounds like a heavy door, or even an old mangle. She desperately wants to hide, curl up on the floor with her arms over her head, but she forces herself to go on.

Her feet crunch on stones, charred pieces of wood and drifts of sand and grit. The walls have collapsed in places, completely blocking the corridor, and she has to clamber over the heaps. Stones roll down the slope behind her, and fragments of glass break into smaller pieces.

Jackie hears air rushing through a small gap higher up, and keeps crawling, leaning on her hands. A broken plank scrapes her thigh and her feet slide across bricks and mortar.

There's a rustling sound behind her and she climbs faster until she hits her head on the roof. She can feel the breeze on her face, but can't locate the opening. She fumbles desperately in front of her with her hands, trying to push through stones tangled in metal wire, sweeping aside loose mortar, and then she finds the narrow gap. Jackie puts her fingers through a piece of chicken-wire and pulls. She manages to loosen a large stone, digs the hole a bit larger, and cuts her palm. She shuffles forward and tries to crawl through. Groaning, she manages to push one arm and her head through, stones tumble away on the other side of the hole and she forces her way through, kicking with her legs and panicking that she's going to get stuck.

Jackie fumbles in front of her with her hand, trying to get a grip on anything to help her pull herself through the hole. She can't hear Nelly behind her, has no idea if she's scrambling up the heap of rumble with her knife raised.

Jackie feels a piece of tape with her hand and starts to pull herself through as she pushes as hard as she can with her legs. Chicken-wire and stones scratch her back, but she makes it out. Taking a load of grit with her, she shuffles down the other side, catches her foot on the edge of the hole, pulls, then pushes her foot back, angles it differently and finally it comes loose.

Jackie slides down the heap of rubble and reaches a floor. Without having any idea of where she is, she walks forward with her hands outstretched until she finds a wall, and begins to follow that instead.

The bricks are colder here, and she realises she must be getting closer to a way out. She turns a corner and finds herself in a larger room. The ceiling is much higher here, noises rise and spread out, like a gentle sea.

Jackie stops and rests for a moment, trying to catch her breath. She leans forward on her knees, her whole body shaking with exhaustion and shock.

She has to go on, she thinks. Has to find a way out.

With bleeding fingers she feels along the wall with her hand, then hears a metal door open with a creak some way off to the right.

Jackie crouches down and hopes she's hidden behind something. She tries to breathe silently but her heart is pounding hard in her chest.

Nelly must have gone a different way, she thinks. Nelly knows the layout of the rooms, where the passageways lead.

The knife-wound is hurting much more now, it feels oddly stiff and she's having trouble breathing. She can't help letting out a quiet cough, and feels warm blood trickle down her back.

Still crouching, she moves slowly forward, and hits something that scrapes metallically. She lowers her hands and feels that it's a spade.

'Jackie,' Nelly calls.

She stands up cautiously and carries on along the wall, clicks her tongue and realises that there's an opening ahead on her left.

'Jackie?'

The echo of Nelly's voice hits the wall on the other side. Jackie stops to listen. All of a sudden she's sure: Nelly shouted in the wrong direction.

She can't see me, Jackie thinks.

It's so dark in here that she can't see me.

Nelly's blind.

Moving slowly now, Jackie bends over, picks up a small stone and throws it away from her. It hits a wall, bounces on to the floor and hits something.

She stands still and hears Nelly move towards the sound.

Jackie returns to the spade and carefully picks it up. The blade scrapes the ground and Nelly stops, panting for breath.

'I can hear you!' Nelly says, with laughter in her voice.

Jackie moves closer and can smell her perfume. Step by step she puts her feet down on the floor and listens to the gentle crunch of the gravel.

Nelly moves backwards and walks into a bucket, which falls over with a clatter.

She can't see me, but I can see her, Jackie thinks as she gets closer, listening to Nelly's strained breathing and the smell of sweat through her perfume.

Jackie can clearly sense Nelly's billowing presence, hear the movement of the knife through the air, and sense the movement of her feet as she backs away another couple of steps.

She knows I'm here, but she can't see me, Jackie thinks again. She squeezes the handle of the spade, cautiously adjusts her grip, clicks with her tongue, and knows at once where the wall is, and where Nelly is standing.

Nelly is panting and stabbing quickly in different directions. The knife hits nothing but air and she stops.

She listens, her anxiety audible in her breathing.

Jackie approaches silently, feeling the heat radiating from Nelly's body. She follows the movements of the knife, then takes a step forward and strikes hard with the spade.

The heavy blade hits Nelly on the cheek with a short clang. Her head jerks sideways and she collapses onto her hip.

She roars with pain.

Jackie walks round her, listening to every movement, every breath.

Nelly is whimpering to herself and tries to stand up. Jackie strikes again, but the spade passes close to Nelly's head, the metal merely pushing through her hair.

Nelly gets to her feet and jabs with the knife. The point cuts into Jackie's lower arm. She backs away instinctively and walks into the bucket that Nelly hit earlier, then steps quickly to the side with her heart thudding. Her arm is stinging with pain from the cut, and blood is dripping down into her hand. Adrenalin is coursing through her, making the hairs on her arms stand up and she shakes the blood from her hand, wipes it on her skirt, and takes a fresh grip on the spade.

She approaches as silently as she can. She can hear Nelly crouching down and jabbing with the knife, and can feel the dampness of her exhaled breath. Without a sound, Jackie circles her, then changes direction and strikes with all the strength she can muster. The blow is ferocious. The spade hits the back of Nelly's head. Jackie hears her sigh and fall forward, without putting her hands out to break her fall.

She hits out again, and strikes Nelly across the head with a wet sound, and after that she doesn't hear anything.

Jackie backs away, panting. Her hands are shaking and she listens, but can't hear the sound of breathing. She approaches warily, pokes at Nelly with the spade, but her body is limp.

Jackie waits, hearing her own pulse thump in her ears. Then she jabs hard with the point of the spade, but there's no reaction.

Jackie is breathing fitfully, and anguish washes over her. Her stomach churns. She puts the spade down and moves closer to Nelly, her legs shaking beneath her. The steaming warmth of the body rises up towards her. Carefully she leans over until she can feel Nelly's back with her fingers. She's wearing a raincoat, the rough fabric squeaks beneath her fingers.

Erik said she had the key round her neck.

Jackie feels tentatively up her back to her neck, and feels that Nelly's hair is wet with warm blood.

Her fingers fumble clumsily inside Nelly's collar, feeling along her sticky neck until she finds a chain and tugs at it, but it won't come loose.

She needs to roll Nelly on to her back. She's heavy, and Jackie has to use both hands, and push with one leg.

The body rolls over and Jackie ends up sitting astride it. With her fingers shaking, she undoes the first button at the neck of the raincoat, but stops when she hears a squelching sound, as if Nelly were moistening her mouth.

Jackie undoes another button, and thinks she can hear little clicks, as though Nelly were blinking her dry eyelids.

Fear pulses through her head and she tears Nelly's dress open at the neck, grabs hold of the key on the chain, and starts to pull it over her bloody head.

136

Joona has been following the signs to Rimbo, but he leaves road 280 at Väsby and is heading towards Finsta when Margot calls to tell him that Jackie and her daughter aren't in the flat at Lill-Jans plan. All the evidence suggests they've been abducted; there are traces of blood on the floor, all the way out into the stairwell. The door to the wardrobe has been smashed and on the wall inside the child had written 'the lady talks funny'.

Joona repeats several times that they have to find the house near Finsta, that's where she's taken Jackie and Madeleine. Erik is probably already there in his cage, or will be very shortly.

'Find the house – that's the only thing that matters right now,' Joona says before they end the call.

He's passed plenty of farms in the darkness along the way, and has seen agricultural premises and sawmills with chimneys of varying sizes.

He's driving fast along the black road, not letting himself think that it might be too late, that time has already run out.

He has to fit the pieces of the puzzle together.

There are always questions to ask, answers still to find.

Nelly keeps repeating herself the whole time, returning to old patterns, he thinks.

There has to be a farm in Roslagen that Nelly somehow has access to.

The farm didn't belong to her family, but her grandfather may have managed it, Joona reasons. He was also a priest, and the Swedish Church owns a great deal of land and forest, and a large number of properties.

As he drives, Joona tries to think through the case again and consider everything he had read and seen long before he knew that Nelly was the person Rocky called the unclean preacher.

Everyone makes mistakes.

He needs to find something that can connect a farm in Roslagen with the video featuring Jackie.

Joona thinks about the yellow raincoat, the narcotic substances, the collection of trophies, and the way she clearly marked the places she took them from on the bodies, then about her completely ignorant husband out in Bromma, her expensive clothes, hand cream, the jar of nutritional supplements, and then he picks up his phone and calls Nils Åhlén.

'You've climbed up onto a very precarious branch,' Åhlén says. 'That escape from prison wasn't exactly—'

'It was necessary,' Joona interrupts.

'And now you want to ask me something,' Åhlén says, and clears his throat.

'Nelly takes iron pills,' Joona says.

'Maybe she suffers from anaemia,' Åhlén replies.

'How do you get anaemia?'

'A thousand different ways . . . everything from cancer and kidney disease to pregnancy and menstruation.'

'But Nelly takes iron hydroxide.'

'Do you mean iron oxide-hydroxide?'

'She's got speckled hands,' Joona says.

'Freckles?'

'Blacker . . . proper pigment change, and—'

'Arsenic poisoning,' Åhlén interrupts. 'Iron oxide-hydroxide is used as an antidote to arsenic . . . and if she's got dry, speckled hands, then . . .'

Joona stops listening when he finds himself thinking about one of the photographs he left on the floor of his hotel room.

A picture of a two-millimetre-long splinter that looks like a blue bird's skull.

The fragment had been found on Sandra Lundgren's floor. It looked ceramic, but actually consisted of glass, iron, sand and chamotte clay.

He drives past a big red barn, and thinks that the little bird's skull was a tiny shard of slag, a by-product of glass production.

'Glass,' he whispers.

The ground around old glassworks is often contaminated with arsenic. They used to use great quantities of the poisonous semi-metal as a refining agent, to prevent bubbles and to homogenise the glass.

'A glassworks,' Joona says out loud. 'They're at a glassworks.'

'That could fit,' Nils Åhlén says, as if he had been following Joona's internal thought process.

'Are you sitting at your computer?'

'Yes.'

'Search for an old glassworks in the vicinity of Finsta.'

Joona is driving along beside a lake that shimmers in the darkness behind the trees and bushes as he hears Nils Åhlén hum while he taps at his keyboard.

'No . . . all I'm getting is one that burned down in 1976, Solbacken glassworks in Rimbo, used to make sheet glass and mirrors . . . the land is owned by the Swedish Church, and—'

'Send the address and coordinates to my phone,' Joona interrupts. 'And call Margot Silverman.'

Joona brakes sharply and turns hard right, locking the wheels. He puts the car into reverse, throwing up a shower of grit, veers backwards into the road, changes gear and puts his foot down again.

137

Gasping with pain, Erik pokes the copper pipe through the roof of the cage, uses one bar as a pivot and tries to prise the next one up. The lever is still a bit too short, even though he hangs off the end with the whole of his weight. There's a crash as the pipe slides out. Erik falls to the floor, hitting his good arm against the mesh.

Breathing hard, he gets up and switches the torch on, and sees that he's managed to bend the metal another few centimetres.

He listens out for noises from the tunnels, but he hasn't heard anything since Nelly chased after Jackie.

Erik has scanned the cellar with the torch, but hasn't been able to find a better tool than the length of copper pipe he managed to drag towards the cage.

The welded joints of the cage are all solid and carefully made, but with the help of the pipe he's succeeded in bending one of the bars in the roof to the point where he's starting to believe it might be possible to break it. It could take hours, days, even, but it isn't completely impossible.

He pushes the pipe through the mesh in the roof, then stops.

Shuffling steps are approaching along the passageway. Erik pulls the pipe back and hides it under the mattress, picks up the torch and listens. There's someone there, he heard right, there are footsteps approaching.

He switches the light off and thinks that he has to play along, no matter what happens. He hasn't got a choice, it would be far too easy for Nelly to kill him in the cage.

He waits in total silence, listening to the crunching footsteps and the sound of breathing in the room outside the cage.

'Erik?' Jackie whispers.

'You have to get away from here,' Erik whispers quickly.

He switches the torch on and sees that Jackie is standing a metre away from him. Her face is dirty and bloody, she's gasping for breath and seems to be in a very bad way.

'Nelly's dead,' Jackie says. 'I killed her.'

'Are you hurt?'

She doesn't answer, takes a couple of steps towards him, reaches the mesh and sticks her hand in. He strokes her fingers and shines the light up at her to look at her injuries.

'Can you manage to get out and fetch help?' he asks, stroking the hair from her blood-streaked face.

'I've got the key,' she says, and coughs weakly.

She leans against the cage, pulls the chain over her head and gives him the key.

'I killed her,' she gasps, and sinks to the floor. 'I killed another human being . . .'

'It was self-defence,' Erik says.

'I don't know,' she whispers, and her face dissolves into tears. 'It's impossible to know . . .'

Erik reaches his hand out beside the hatch, puts the key into the padlock, turns its and hears the click as the loop slides out of the casing.

He climbs out with the torch in his hand, and hugs Jackie on the floor. Her breathing is erratic and shallow.

'Let me look at the wound to your back,' he whispers.

'Don't worry about that,' she says. 'I need to get home to Maddy, just give me a few moments . . .'

Erik shines the torch at the peeling walls, the table and shelf.

'I think the door to the kitchen is locked, but I'll go up and check,' he says.

'OK,' Jackie nods, and makes another attempt to stand up.

'Stay where you are,' Erik says, and heads up the steep steps.

On the brown, anti-slip linoleum there are bloody boot-prints. He gets up to the heavy metal door, jerks the handle down and pulls and pushes the door, but it's locked.

He yanks the handle and looks round with the torch to see if the key's on a hook anywhere, but can't find anything and goes back down to Jackie. She's managed to rise from the floor, leaning on the mesh of the cage with one hand.

'The door's locked,' Erik confirms. 'We'll have to get out through the tunnels.'

'OK,' she replies in a quiet voice.

'I think she killed the police officers who came,' he says. 'They will come and find us, but we have no idea how long that's going to take, and you need to get to hospital straight away.'

'We walk,' she pants.

'You can do it,' Erik says, putting her hand on his shoulder. 'I've got a torch, I can see where we're going.'

He leads her into the passageway, round an armchair and a small padded footstool. Some old window frames are leaning against the wall and dusty light bulbs sit in yellowed sockets.

They cross another passageway with steep steps leading downwards, and pass a toppled cupboard, treading carefully across the broken glass.

In the light of the torch and with Erik's help, getting through is straightforward, and they emerge into a large room with long tin wash-basins, rows of taps, and cubicles with crumbling plaster.

On the ceiling there are empty strip lights with no coverings. The cables are just hanging down. A large trough full of soil stands in the middle of the floor. Rust has eaten through the green metal of the trough, and the stick that Jackie used to guide herself is lying on the floor beside it.

They carry on through the room into a corridor lined with dented clothes lockers. There's a water-pipe attached to the ceiling, but one end has come loose and is hanging down like a spear, curving under its own weight.

Erik shines the torch along the narrow passageway. The walls have collapsed and parts of the ceiling have fallen in, the passage is full of bricks, grit and wood, all the way up to the ceiling.

Erik opens a door and they carry on along a different tunnel, turn right, go through a rounded arch and are suddenly out in the fresh air.

They're standing in a large room, and a sharp wind is blowing. The roof has gone, and the tall chimney is visible against the dark sky. The light of the torch shimmers off a huge metal extractor hood. The tiled floor is dirty and cracked.

Tall weeds are growing through an aluminium ladder lying on the ground in front of a huge oven. Erik barely has any strength left in his injured arm, but he manages to lift the ladder and pull it free of the weeds. He shoves some fallen bricks and gravel aside with his foot and props the ladder up against the wall.

He helps Jackie to climb up, and follows right behind her. She slips and he drops the torch when he catches her. It clatters down between the rungs, hits the ground and goes out abruptly.

The pain in his arm is throbbing as though it's trapped in a piece of machinery by the time they emerge into the tall grass growing around the ruins. Jackie is leaning hard against Erik as they make their way through thistles and low bushes. An empty police car is parked up, its headlights shining straight at the yellow house. They walk past it, across the rough yard and out onto the track, away from the house.

138

Joona is driving as fast as he can on the poor roads. Margot has organised a police operation, but he can't risk them getting there too late. The Norrtälje Police haven't been able to get any response from their patrol car in the area.

The headlights sweep across the field as he swerves onto the narrow gravel track through the forest. The tyres slide across the loose surface, unable to get any grip, but he steers into the skid and manages to overcome it. He puts his foot down again and the car thunders along the uneven track.

Two deer run across ahead of him and he brakes and sees them leap through the light and disappear among the trees.

The car judders, slowing almost to a halt as it hits a deep puddle, throwing up a cascade of water on both sides.

Joona pulls out of a bend and accelerates again. The white light stretches out along the straight track by the side of the field, forming a glowing tunnel through the darkness.

Now he can see the tall chimney of the glassworks between the trees, like a black obelisk against the lead-grey sky.

Far ahead at the very limits of the beam of the headlights he sees two figures. They're standing in the road, in a motionless embrace.

It's Erik and Jackie, he's almost certain of that.

A stone strikes the undercarriage and the light disappears from the road for a few seconds.

Branches lash the windscreen and it's hard to see their faces, unsteady in the wavering light.

Up ahead near the ruined buildings he can see empty cisterns and heaps of crushed glass.

A deep pothole in the road forces Joona to slow down and swerve. There's a bang, and the light of the headlamps lurches high above the two figures.

And then he sees the light reflect off something yellow at the side of the road.

Nelly.

She's standing not far behind Erik and Jackie. Her raincoat catches the light from the headlamps. She's moving forward with her face lowered, across a shimmering green layer of crushed glass.

Joona blows his horn, changes gear and puts his foot down. Grit flies up beneath the underside of the car. The car lurches and the glove compartment opens, scattering its contents across the seat. He veers off the side of the track and tall weeds lash the windscreen.

Joona blows his horn as Nelly gets closer to the pair from behind. She's striding purposefully through the nettles and undergrowth.

Erik squints towards the car, he looks relieved as he waves.

Joona blows his horn again and again, loses sight of them for a moment, rounds a slight bend and sees that Nelly is holding a knife in her hand.

She steps across the ditch and now she's right behind them, crouching down and staying in their shadow.

Still blowing his horn, Joona speeds up along the track, and the engine roars. In the shaky light of the headlamps he sees Nelly walk right up to Jackie and stick the knife into her.

A heavy branch smashes one of the headlights and the ruins to the right of the car disappear in sudden darkness.

In the weakened light Joona sees Jackie collapse on the rough track. Erik is still holding her hand.

Some branches are swaying by the side of the road, but Nelly has vanished.

Joona brakes hard, the tyres smoke as they slide across the loose grit, he swerves and the windscreen smashes, sending glass swirling into the car and hitting his face. Branches and grass lash the body of the car as it slides to a halt with two wheels in the ditch.

Joona clambers out onto the bonnet of the unsteady car, jumps down onto the track and runs over to Erik, who's kneeling down next to Jackie.

'I didn't see anything,' he says, tugging Jackie's blouse open and touching the knife to see how deep it goes. 'It could have hit one of her kidneys, we need an ambulance as soon as—'

'Where's Maddy?' Joona interrupts.

'At home in the flat, we've got to call—'

'She's not in the flat,' Joona says. 'Nelly snatched her along with Jackie.'

'Dear God,' Erik whispers, looking up at him.

'Could she be inside the house?'

'There's a cage in the basement, and loads of tunnels that . . .'

Jackie is gasping for breath and Erik can feel her pulse getting weaker. He glances quickly towards the house, brushes his fringe from his face and sees something yellow glint in one of the windows on the upper floor.

'There's a light in the window,' he points. 'They must be . . .'

He breaks off when Jackie's pulse disappears completely, and puts his ear to her chest. Her heart has stopped, all he can hear is a muffled sound from deep within her.

'Get an air ambulance!' he yells. 'Her heart's stopped, it's urgent, it's desperately urgent!'

So as not to have to pull the knife out, Erik leaves her on her side. He begins chest compressions, no longer aware of the pain in his arm as he counts thirty quick compressions, then blows into her lungs twice before resuming the compressions again, hearing Joona give the address and coordinates to the emergency services operator.

'Make sure Jackie survives – I'll get her daughter,' Joona says, and sets off running towards the house.

139

Joona runs across the yard and draws his pistol. The headlights of the police car are still shining towards the car with the open boot, as well as straight at the yellow house. A smell of fire suddenly fills the still night air. He pushes through the tall nettles and sees white smoke billowing like steam from the weeds around the foundations of the building.

He jumps up on to the veranda, raises his gun, opens the front door and sees the dead police officer on the floor.

His torso is dark with blood, his face turned aside.

Joona aims his pistol at the next door as he steps over the body, leans down and picks up the cracked torch from the floor and shines it into the kitchen.

In the dwindling light he can see a scene of horrific brutality. The floor is covered with blood and the other policeman's head is lying a metre away from his body. He never even managed to pull his pistol from its holster. Blood has splashed the glass of an unlit paraffin lamp standing on a chair. There's a roaring sound from deep down in the basement, and a thin veil of grey smoke slips across the ceiling and envelops an old smoke alarm.

Joona hurries through the chaotic kitchen and through another door. He carries on past a living room and into a narrow passageway with an open staircase leading to the next floor. Sooty smoke is rolling beneath the ceiling like a murky river.

A paraffin lamp explodes from the heat in the next room, and pale blue flames take hold of the walls and ceiling. Parts of the burning floor collapse into the basement and sparks and smoke swirl up.

He can feel the rising heat in his face as he carries on up the stairs. The wallpaper is alight and the fire is curling around the floor of the upper storey.

Joona realises that Nelly is burning the little that implicates her as the perpetrator. If Jackie doesn't survive and the house is gone, all that will be left is the evidence against Erik.

The light from the torch turns yellow as it grows even weaker.

He reaches the upper floor, aims the pistol in front of him and makes his way into a girl's room. The pink, rose-patterned wallpaper is covered with photographs of Erik. A lot have been taken surreptitiously, but some are portraits, and others seems to have come from professional journals and photograph albums.

On a shelf in the darkness stands a collection of things she's stolen from Erik. Wine glasses, books, deodorant, and the wooden elephant from Malaysia. A brown corduroy jacket is draped over a blue shirt on a wooden hanger.

There's a hissing sound from deep below the floor under his feet. He hears the fire sucking up more oxygen and can feel the air getting harder to breathe.

The torch goes out and he shakes it and gets back a weak, unsteady beam.

Joona carries on and sees that Nelly has arranged her trophies from the victims in front of a mirror on a dressing-table.

It doesn't amount to much, just some bottles of nail-varnish, a lipstick from H&M and a red bra. On a pink plate lies the metal tongue-stud in the shape of Saturn, a hairclip and Susanna Kern's earrings, some false fingernails and a pearl necklace that's blackened with blood.

The torch goes out and Joona puts it down carefully on the floor.

He approaches the door to a bedroom with a sloping roof, moves slightly to one side and suddenly catches sight of Madeleine in the murky light.

She's lying on the floor next to a bed, in the middle of the room. Her mouth is covered with tape, and there's a pool of blood under her head.

Joona thinks that the little girl is the trophy Nelly took from Jackie.

She's breathing, but seems to be unconscious.

He can't see any sign of Nelly, but the door beside the bed is sticky with blood around its handle.

The room is rapidly filling with pale smoke, and Joona is aware that time is running out.

He glances quickly at the little girl, then aims his gun to the right and hurries forward.

The heavy axe comes towards him from the left. Joona has misread the room and sees the movement too late. He just manages to pull his head back, and the blade swings past his face and embeds itself deep in the wall.

The air fills with dust and plaster.

Nelly tries to yank the axe free, but Joona hits her from below across the face with the butt of his pistol.

Her head flies back and saliva sprays from her mouth. She lands crookedly on her back and the floor seems to rock beneath her as black smoke billows from the gaps between the floorboards.

Joona stumbles backwards from the force of his own blow, and knocks over a chair holding some plastic hangers.

Nelly sits up and is suddenly beside Madeleine. Joona can't understand how it happened in less than a second.

The bed has moved.

Then he realises that he's been looking at a large mirror. The reflection made him think that Maddy was in the middle of the room, at a safe distance.

The fire crackles and hisses as it absorbs oxygen.

Holding his pistol by his side, Joona tries to get a grip on the room again. Large fragments of mirrored glass are leaning against the walls and furniture, throwing the perspective and making the room look very different.

Nelly's nose is bleeding, she's pulled the girl towards her and is clutching her tight. Smoke is swirling around them and Joona can't see if she's armed.

'Let the girl go,' Joona calls, moving cautiously closer.

Above the closed door to his left oily black smoke is filtering into the room. Pictures of Erik on the floor are curling up in the heat from below.

'Will you let the girl go?' Joona repeats.

'Yes,' she replies softly, but carries on holding her in her arms.

Madeleine opens her tired eyes and Nelly kisses her on the head.

'Nelly, we have to get out . . . all of us. Do you understand?'

She nods weakly and looks into his eyes.

The door ahead of Joona flares up in a bright blue glow, and is suddenly surrounded by billowing flames that lap at the ceiling, leaving black marks behind them. The room beneath them is roaring and the entire house is creaking, as if great rocks were rubbing against each other.

'Can you help me?' she asks, without taking her eyes off him.

'Yes, I can,' he replies, trying to see what she's hiding by her hip.

She smiles at him oddly, almost devotedly, as if she were suddenly full of reassuring certainty.

Sparks and sooty smuts are drifting upwards on the hot-air currents and the cooler air is being sucked down towards the floor, closer to the fire. The dirty curtains in front of the window flare up as the flames coil around the fabric.

'What does the fire say?' she mutters, getting to her feet.

With unthinking harshness she pulls Madeleine up from the floor by her hair. The girl is frightened, there are tears running down her cheeks.

'Nelly,' Joona says again. 'We have to get out. I'll help you, but I—'

With a crash a large panel of the wall to the next room collapses on to the floor between them, plasterboard, torn wallpaper and wooden laths, all enveloped in black smoke. Tiny glowing sparks flicker in the grey fog above their heads.

'But I won't let you hurt the girl,' he finishes his sentence.

In one of the mirrors Joona sees that Nelly has pulled out a knife. She's holding Madeleine by the hair with her other hand, pulling it so hard that the girl is having to stand on tiptoe.

The floor is vibrating beneath their feet.

Heat is flooding in from the side now, and the collapsed door frame catches fire. Black smoke fills the room and the flames climb greedily towards the ceiling.

'Drop the knife – you don't have to do this,' Joona cries, aiming his pistol towards the shape behind the flames.

He tries to move sideways, but can only just make out the yellow oilskin through the smoke and fire.

'It's never enough,' a very high child's voice says.

Joona's thoughts switch in a fraction of a second. At first he thinks it's Madeleine speaking, then the realisation that her mouth is taped shut makes him squeeze the trigger of his pistol instead.

He fires through the flames three times.

The bullets hit Nelly in the middle of her chest, and in the mirror off to one side behind her Joona sees blood spurt out between her shoulder blades. The large mirror collapses beneath her and shatters on the floor.

Madeleine is standing perfectly still, with her hand on the wound to her neck. Blood is running between her fingers, but she's alive.

Nelly's high-pitched voice has been a foreboding of death every time.

Joona rushes over to the girl, kicks the knife from Nelly's hand even though he knows she's dead, picks Madeleine up and backs away through the smoke.

Nelly is lying on her back among the fragments of broken mirror, her mouth open. She's lost one of her boots and her foot is twitching in her filthy nylon stocking.

A plastic bottle topples over and paraffin splashes out across the floorboards, there's a hiss and then the fire leaps up through the floor.

They're hit by a wave of heat. Joona stumbles backwards with the girl, just making it through the doorway as the floor of the bedroom gives way under Nelly's weight.

She's sucked down and vanishes into a shaft of raging flame.

Joona's trouser leg catches fire as he shuffles backwards with the girl in his arms.

The flames are reaching up with a howl all the way from the cellar, striking the bedroom ceiling. Burning pieces of the lamp fall in a cloud of swirling sparks. The windowsill is ablaze and the glass shatters with a bang.

Joona pulls Madeleine with him further into the girl's bedroom. The walls covered with pictures of Erik are on fire.

'I'm going to take this off,' Joona says, and pulls the tape from her mouth. 'Did that hurt?'

'No,' she whispers.

A tall cupboard collapses through the floor of the bedroom and disappears into the shrieking inferno.

'Let's try to get out,' he says, wrapping his leather jacket around her. 'The smoke's dangerous, so I want you to breathe through the lining. Can you do that?'

She nods, and he picks her up and starts to carry her down the stairs. The glow from the fire is flickering across the walls. Sparks are drifting up between the steps. From somewhere deep in the basement there's a screech of twisting metal.

The fire is climbing the wall then pulling back, leaving sooty traces across the wallpaper.

Joona breathes hot air into his lungs and begins to cough.

There's a crash in the room beneath them as the heat blows out all the windows at the same time. Glass rains down onto the floor and air streams in, making the flames leap up towards the ceiling with a roar.

The burning lampshade spins on its cable.

The girl coughs and Joona shouts to her to keep breathing through the lining of his jacket.

In the living room below the bedroom the walls are burning from floor to ceiling. The heat forces him towards the television room. Parts of the ceiling are collapsing and the girl screams as burning dust rains down on them.

Joona coughs again and puts his hand down on the hot floor to steady himself. His lungs are burning, and smoke-poisoning is making him dizzy and tired. He knows he doesn't have many seconds left, so holds his breath and gets to his feet again. With the girl in his arms he takes a few faltering steps forward, then carries on through the thick smoke in the next room.

His eyes are streaming and he's having trouble seeing. The sofa catches alight and sparks swirl up into his face on the hot wind.

There's a thunderous roar behind their backs, like a lashing sail, and the fire throws itself at them.

He steps over a smoking bundle of carpets and shoves the door open.

The kitchen is ablaze, and burning sections of the ceiling are crashing down. An explosion sends splinters of glass and fire across the room.

Joona's lungs are straining and burning, he'll have to breathe soon, his heart is pounding desperately.

The end of one of the roof beams comes loose and falls like a heavy pendulum, crushing the kitchen table and embedding itself deep in the floor.

The linoleum floor is bubbling and the walls are rippling with fire.

A bucket of water is boiling.

The powerful spring mechanism has contorted out of shape, bending the door back on one hinge.

Joona steps over the dead police officer's body. The hall is full of flames. The heat and howling roar wrap themselves around him and the child. He knows he needs oxygen desperately, but forces himself to fight the urge to take a breath.

Surrounded by fire, he fights his way forward and kicks the burning front door open. It comes loose from its hinges and crashes down the front steps.

Joona emerges on to the veranda with the girl in his arms. His face is black with soot and his clothes are burning. Police and paramedics rush towards them with fire-extinguishers and blankets.

Margot Silverman is forced to take a step back from the heat and lets out a gasp as a powerful contraction hits her, then feels her waters break and run down between her thighs.

The clattering downdraught from the helicopter's rotor-blades sends rubbish and dust flying in a wide circle.

Erik is holding Maddy's hand as the helicopter takes off. She's lying strapped to a stretcher next to Jackie, and smiles up at him before closing her eyes.

They rise unsteadily into the air, and Erik sees Joona lying on all fours on the ground, coughing. He's surrounded by police officers and paramedics. Margot is trying to resist as she is led away to a waiting ambulance.

The yellow glow of the burning house and the pulsating blue lights of the emergency vehicles fill the yard.

Joona slowly gets up, takes his pistol from its holster and throws it on the ground, then holds out both hands so he can be cuffed.

The helicopter turns, tilts forward and picks up speed.

Erik watches as the whole house collapses into the flames, and the smoke curls up into the sky like a black umbilical cord. The shadow of the tall chimney stretches jerkily across the ruins and neglected fields.

epilogue

Erik Maria Bark is sitting in his sheepskin armchair, looking out at the white October sky through the tall windows. Detective Superintendent Margot Silverman is walking up and down across the polished oak floor, holding her baby daughter at her breast.

Erik and Rocky Kyrklund have both been cleared of suspicion of any involvement in the murders. Without apologising for anything, Margot is outlining the key points of the long reconstruction of events she has been working on since September.

Nelly probably began stalking Erik at the time of Rocky Kyrklund's trial. She transferred her fixation to him, just as she had transferred her fixation to Rocky at her father's funeral.

It turned out that Nelly once registered for a medical degree in the USA, but there's no sign of any qualifications, employment history or specialist training. She probably taught herself everything on her own. Her house in Bromma contained hundreds of books about neurology, psychological trauma and disaster psychiatry.

There was nothing to suggest that her husband had any idea about her double life. She spied on Erik in secret, slowly getting closer to him and building up a collection of pictures of him in the house at the burned-out glassworks. After Erik's divorce, she began to imagine that she and Erik were actually married.

Erik closes his eyes and hears gentle piano music through the walls as he listens to Margot's voice.

In Nelly's case, obsessive fixation syndrome was linked to a narcissistic personality disorder that led to her trying to resemble Erik, to become everything for him. And the more she felt she owned him, the more she needed to watch and control him.

She wanted him to see her, to love and desire her. Her need was insatiable, until in the end she was like a fire, growing and growing until everything was consumed.

Nelly was deeply marked by her religious upbringing, by the constant presence of the church and her father's sermons. She had studied the Old Testament closely, and its jealous God convinced her that everything she felt was right.

She spied on the women she thought Erik was attracted to, and became fixated on their individual attributes. Driven by pathological jealousy, she filmed them to unmask their supposedly coquettish behaviour before stripping them of their beauty and attractiveness.

It isn't easy to see how her jealousy was aroused, or how she selected her victims. The evidence suggests that each murder only served to accelerate the process. When there was no way back, she turned her hostility against Erik; she was like a rabid animal, prepared to attack anything and everything.

The build-up of stress led her to think that the police investigation was going too slowly, so she started to leave more clues. Tormented by jealousy, she murdered her rivals and at the same time set a trap for Erik, one that would end up leading him to her.

Nelly had killed her mother in front of her father, she had killed the woman Rocky claimed he loved in front of him, and she had been planning to kill Jackie in front of Erik.

She would have taken Madeleine as a trophy, leaving Jackie without a face, with her hand over her womb to illustrate her particular crime.

Margot falls silent, carefully moves her baby up towards her shoulder and strokes her back until she burps.

When Margot has left the house, Erik walks towards the gently rippling piano music and opens the double doors to the living room. The grand piano is standing in the middle of the floor, and appears to be playing itself. Only when he walks round the oversized instrument can he see the look of concentration on Madeleine's face as her fingers dart across the keys.

Erik sits down quietly next to Jackie on the sofa and after a while she leans her head on his shoulder.

The paramedics managed to stabilise Jackie's heart with a defibrillator before she was put in the helicopter. She was given emergency sedation, and underwent a seven-hour operation in the University Hospital in Uppsala.

For Erik everything feels like he's woken up from a long nightmare, and, as Jackie laces her fingers between his, all he feels is a deep gratitude that they're alive and that Cupid had another arrow in his quiver for him.

Madeleine lets the final notes fade before stopping the strings, then waits for silence to spread through the room before looking up and smiling at them.

Erik stands up and applauds, and doesn't stop until Madeleine starts to adjust the stool. He walks over and sits down, changes the sheet-music, closes his eyes for a few seconds, then begins to play his étude.

On Friday, 24 October the protracted main hearing in Stockholm District Court comes to an end. The presiding judge and the three lay judges regard it as proven beyond reasonable doubt that Joona Linna is guilty of a number of serious crimes in connection to the jailbreak at Huddinge Prison.

The verdict should have been expected in spite of the extenuating circumstances, but when the sentence is pronounced Erik gets to his feet. Jackie and Madeleine stand up beside him, followed by Nils Åhlén, Margot Silverman and Saga Bauer.

Joona remains seated next to his defence lawyer, his head lowered, as the judge reads out the unanimous verdict.

'The court finds Joona Linna guilty of violence against a public official, aggravated criminal damage, assisting a felon to escape from custody, alleging a public office, and aggravated theft . . . The defendant is sentenced to four years in prison.'

22016

791·43

X

Shakespeare and the Film